FIRE, FURY & CHAOS

STRINGS OF FATE: **BOOK THREE**

MELISSA J. KINCAID

LOTS OF LOVE CREATIONS

Also by Melissa J Kincaid

The Strings of Fate series:
Love, Blood & Fury
Magic, Midnight & Starlight
Fire, Fury & Chaos
After The Fury

Content Warning:
This instalment of the *Strings of Fate* series is intended for New Adult
to Adult audiences. It includes coarse language, scenes of violence and
murder, implications towards genocide, kidnapping, torture, physical and
emotional abuse (some towards a child/teenager), thoughts of suicide and
death, as well as sexual themes and detailed sex scenes.

Fire, Fury & Chaos

STRINGS OF FATE BOOK THREE

MELISSA J. KINCAID

Fire, Fury and Chaos
A Strings of Fate Novel: Book Three
By Melissa J. Kincaid

ISBN (Paperback): 9780645054866
ISBN (Hardback): 9780645054880
ISBN (eBook): 9780645054873
ISBN (Special Edition Paperback): 9781764048644

Published by Lots of Love Creations.

Edited by Carolyn Gilpin.

This novel is entirely a work of fiction. The names, characters and incidents portrayed in it are the work of the author's imagination. Any resemblance to actual persons, living or dead, events or localities is entirely coincidental.

Commissioned art by @kalynne_art (Kalynne Pratt) consisting of characters Ariiaya, Elijah, Lorch, Celadine, Ghila and Queen Ariiaya.

Cover design, map and illustrations by Melissa J Kincaid.

To you, my dear reader, for sticking with me until the end.
I am more grateful than you could ever know!

THE LAND of FYTHNAR
AYRITH
BORDER TOWN
WEST COURT
SCHOOL OF FATE
THE SLITHER
COLKIRK
THE WASTES
LILIDALE
THE IVORY PLAINS
MIRFIELD
FJOLL
SOUTH COURT
ERSTONIA

THE DRAGON'S TEETH
NORTH COURT
BONEMIRE
VIRIDYA
THE
IRE DEPTHS
AMBERBOURNE
EAST COURT
TRADER'S BAY
EVERGRAVE
THE COVE
SKAALD

Pronunciation Guide

Main Characters

Ariiaya Trillia:	Arr – ee – aya	Trill – ee – ah
Elijah Wolfe:	Ee – lie – jah	Wolf
Lorch Kruel:	Lor – k	Crew – el
Krepth Hallier:	Kre – p – th	Hal – ee – er
Nemesis Rion:	Ne – meh – sis	Ree – on
Tikkani Alinar:	Tik – an – i	
Emerson Alinar:	Em – er – son	
Quinn:	K – win	
Valdis:	Val – dis	
Lynnera:	Lin – era	
Sybell:	Si – bell	
Ghila:	Gill – ah	
Klotho:	Clo – tho	
Etropos:	E – tro – poss	
Lakhesis:	La – kes – is	
Iniq:	Ee – neek	
Lucada (Luc):	Luck	
Celadine Clover:	Cell – a – deen	Clo – ver
Valerie Gray:	Va – ler – ee	Gr – ay
Lyda Wild:	Lid – ah	Wi – ld
Roarke Serling:	Row – ark	Ser – ling
Aellan Trillia:	Ay – lan	Trill – ee – ah

Court Families, Creatures and Towns

Freya:	Frey – ah	
Jero:	Jer – row	
Thogan:	Tho – gan	
Kadec Brolikian:	Kad – ek	Bro – li – kee – ann
Tyverus:	Tie – ver – us	
Hannera:	Han – eera	
Brohem:	Bro – hem	
Eliverus:	Ee – lie – ver – us	
Ouroboros:	Oo – ruh – bo – ruhs	
Kryvern:	Cry – vern	
Fythnar:	Fi – th – nar	
Viridya:	Vir – id – ee – ya	
Ayrith:	Air – ith	
Sapphine	Saf – een	

CHAPTER ONE

ARIIAYA

Ariiaya Trillia stood firm in the silence that followed her departure from the western shore, her insides a riot of enmity and anguish, guilt and rage. Her thoughts returned to the circumstances that had led to their current location, which was now safely aboard a boat heading back to Ayrith, the spring city in the west, an hour after finding Elijah on the outskirts of Border Town.

Lorch's face shadowed with distrust and disgust.

Blood.

Colleen's severed head hitting the earth.

Blood.

Soldiers obliterated into red dust.

Blood.

A woman standing over Elijah's hunched form, her face a twist of sick delight.

His scream as it split the air.

It hadn't taken her long to find him, despite the turmoil of the army's withdrawal, and the memory would haunt her like a spiteful ghost. Elijah had risen to his feet much more slowly than normal, and as he turned to face her, she realised something wasn't right. His face was the same as the one she knew so well, but there was something devastatingly different about him. Blood speckled the fine hairs of his beard and lashes, tendrils of black hair hung over drawn brows that framed eyes of deep quicksilver mist.

His eyes. That was the difference. Devoid of recognition; blank and filled with haze.

She worried that he was no longer the man she'd fallen in love with.

With one command from the woman behind him, his weapon was drawn, and he was upon her with unrelenting force – confirming those fears.

Elijah wasn't in control, because this male was trying to *kill* her.

"Elijah, stop, please…"

She had pleaded with him as he rained blows down upon her, all to the chorus of a woman's claps of delight. She had quickly noted the woman's features while attempting to block the strikes, trying to figure out who she was. She had black hair that was tinged chocolate in the afternoon light, trimmed and angled to her jawline in uneven, choppy waves. Her skin was pale with little dimples on her cheeks that were painfully familiar.

Then there were her eyes, storm clouds with flecks of darker grey near the pupils like pebbles in a crystal-clear lakebed. She would have thought her stunningly beautiful, if it were not for the madness emanating from her in dark, acrid tendrils. Arii had almost choked as her suspicions on the woman's identity began to manifest.

Arii's sharp eyes had noticed a glint of something around the Fae woman's neck – an amulet hooked on a chain of black links, seemingly fashioned from darkness itself, carved into a serpent devouring its own tail. As if sensing her gaze, the woman's pale hand had lifted to clutch the trinket protectively, before hissing dismissively; *"Kill her and make it quick. I do not wish to keep* him *waiting."*

Her perusal had cost her. That was when Elijah's elbow cut through her distracted defences and slammed into her nose, shocking her with a hideous *crack*.

If Nem hadn't blocked the charge of his sword and slammed him back with a burst of magic, Arii knew he would not have hesitated in delivering the killing blow.

She had thrown all she had into their fight, and if not for Nem and Krepth's well timed intervention, she would have been fatally bested.

She was not foolish enough to believe it otherwise. The relentlessness that he had shown in their fight had left her previous training sessions with him in the dust. He'd been holding back before, and she'd always suspected it.

Now, she *knew* it.

There had been none of his previous hesitation this time.

Pain still buzzed behind Arii's nose now, which Elijah had so easily broken, and she was sure she had a fracture in her eyebrow somewhere, the blossom of pain thrumming behind her eyes and temples. Nem had almost fully healed her injuries before Arii had insisted that she stop, wanting some of the pain to remain as a punishment for not staying and fighting for him. She should have stayed and fought.

But she had let him go.

She'd let them *both* go.

She'd abandoned them with hardly a fight. Lorch remained in the acidic clutches of his hateful father, while Elijah had been left to a fate pulled by the strings of another.

The thought stung like rope ripped from her grasp, a heated ache that left her feeling raw.

She considered throwing herself over the edge of the ship and returning to Elijah several times on the way back to the spring palace. But somehow, a semblance of sense remained stubbornly fixed in the back of her mind.

Water stroked the sides of the boat, its rhythmic rocking doing nothing to sooth her turbulent insides. Rain pelted their cloaks in fat droplets, soaking through to the skin and making Arii's mood darken to borderline rancid. In the distance the western island of Fythnar grew larger, a monolith littered with a rainbow of spring shades, visible even through the rainy mist.

"Arii," said Nem softly, appearing quietly beside her, eyes worried. "What happened?"

"I'll tell you what happened," glowered Krepth, "Exactly what we thought would happen, plus a shitload more. King Pain-in-the-

Arse golden boy showed up with a battalion of undead. He attempted to use Elijah's adoptive mother as leverage in seizing him without a fight, but when he refused, the bastard killed her. I've never seen Elijah lose control like that…" the Shifter paused, leaning forward and staring down at his dirty hands, water pooling on his palms. "He annihilated the majority of Lorch's battalion to literal bloody dust with hardly a thought…"

Arii did not need to look to know her friend's fingers and hands were speckled with the blood of their enemies.

Nem's worry marched along their life bond like a trail of ants, yet Arii could not find her voice. It had all happened so quickly.

Elijah was no doubt on his way to the hands of the enemy… and they had chosen to run rather than stay and fight. Fight whoever possessed him. Fight until she got through to him. What she felt inside was nearing anxious torture, a feeling she had not felt since the eve of Elijah's challenge in the Permafrost Arena.

"I know this isn't what you want to hear right now but leaving Elijah behind was the right thing to do," began Nem.

Arii raised her head slowly, rain droplets clinging to her lashes, voice portraying her inner numbness. "You're right, I don't want to hear that right now."

Krepth shook his head as he stood and made his way to the ferryman to fix up payment.

Nem raised her palms as she tried to placate her friend. "Contrary to your fear and anger about what happened, you know Elijah better than any of us. You know he will fight this with everything he has–"

Arii's voice was like a snap. "You don't understand… Elijah is *gone*."

"Is he? Are you certain of that?"

No, no she wasn't. Not truly.

Arii knew that she was stubborn, and so was her heart, it seemed. But despite what she witnessed – the way his face had been voided of all recognition – she felt something deep in her soul, a little ember that stoked whenever he was around. That little ember had not gone out, and she hoped beyond hope that it meant that the Elijah she loved was still inside the vessel that the mysterious woman occupied with tainted magic. There was no other explanation as to what was responsible, and that magic was *powerful*.

She wrenched her gaze to the looming shoreline, hardly noticing that the rain had stopped and the clouds were drifting lazily away. By the time they alighted upon the shores of Ayrith, the sky was a sickeningly cheerful shade of blue – a complete and utter contrast to Arii's feelings.

Waiting for them on the docks was the reddish figure of a man with arms crossed over his chest and an expression that was anything but sunshine.

Roarke Serling asked, "Prince Eliverus… where is he?"

"Obviously not with us," seethed Arii.

Nem gently – and a bit forcefully – led her past the soldier and towards the stone steps leading to the castle. Arii did not fight her.

Kadec's personal guard had probably been sent to gauge their condition before allowing them back to the castle. Behind her, Arii could hear Krepth suggesting they could offer an explanation once they were out of their sodden clothing and in the Prince's meeting room with a stiff drink.

The place was as lush as it had been when they first arrived here, dense clusters of tulips and roses rimming the cobblestone road, setting their route in pink, white and blue. Arii's fingers unconsciously picked at the skin around her soiled fingers in a habit she still couldn't seem to shake. Instead of causing a fuss – which on the inside Arii was itching to do – she remained pliant, following her best friend towards the tall castle doors.

Inside though, she could feel a storm churning.

Hell hath no fury like an enraged assassin. And she was edging eagerly towards violence.

However, the fire of anger fizzled to embers shortly after. As she entered the meeting chambers, one face in particular whipped towards her. Tikkani stormed forward, eyes glossy with unshed tears.

Her hand snapped across Arii's cheek, leaving behind a stunning sting.

The entire room fell silent, the murmurings of her friends dying away to watch as the young elf bristled.

"How could you?" Tikkani said, voice wavering.

Shocked, Arii pressed a hand to her cheek. Before she could speak, Tikkani continued, Quinn hovering behind her, as if thinking he may have to rip the elf from danger.

"How could you go and not tell us? You may be a Fae, Arii, but that doesn't mean you are invincible. You can't just go and risk your life without backup. We didn't follow you halfway across Fythnar to just be left behind." Tikkani swallowed, before whispering, "Not only are we your friends, but we are also your family."

Before Arii could respond, Tikkani embraced her in a fierce hug. "You *scared* us, Arii!"

Arii's eyelids fluttered closed as she returned the embrace. "I'm sorry, Tikkani."

She was right. They were her family. It had been so long since she had such a thing, and she was severely unpractised.

Tikkani leaned back, her face a mask of seriousness. Her golden eyes saw through Arii in that moment, saw through the defences she could no longer keep erected behind a wall of rage and fire. She couldn't blame the elf's anger; she would have felt the same if her friends had done something just as reckless. The elf gazed over Arii's shoulder at the people behind her. Arii could see the dawning in Tikkani's eyes at the absence of a particular tall, stone-solid presence.

Tikkani held her at arm's length, "Don't worry, Elijah will get just as stern a talking to when we get him back."

Arii forced a weak smile, awkward but seemingly enough for the elf. They turned to join the group gathered at a long table, the dark-skinned Prince at the head. Prince Kadec kept his expression schooled, but Arii could see questions shining in his bright eyes.

Questions she wasn't sure she was prepared to answer yet.

The Prince stood, placing his hands on the tabletop, the tail of his hair falling over his shoulder as he said, "Tell me what happened to Prince Herington."

KREPTH

Hummingbirds streaked upon the wisps of a spring breeze, the hum of their wings like bees in Krepth's ears. They dipped in and out of the thatches of honeysuckle flowers adorning both sides of the balcony on which he stood. The Shifter's eyes drifted over the radiant city of spring below, painted in a backdrop of blue sky and lazy white clouds that kissed the endless sea on the horizon. The air tasted of salt and smelled of roses, a picture-perfect day, yet within him rumbled storm clouds of disquiet.

He had been standing sentry to the meeting now taking place in the rooms behind him. He had to give the Prince of Spring credit – the man knew how to throw together a meeting just as well as a party. Despite short notice, the table in the centre of the room was piled high with fresh fruits and silver platters of vegetables in bite-sized pieces. There was bread and cheese, along with a huge golden-roasted boar and a steamed crayfish, shell glistening with melted butter.

Though it all looked and smelled divine, Krepth couldn't help but think it was over the top.

So much effort and it remained untouched, betraying the sombre mood.

Krepth entered the room, silently despite the marble floor. Like the animal his soul adopted, he moved like a prowling wolf, the tips of his cloak swishing at his heels. There was a shiver of tension in the air, a mixture of each of his friends' worries. His gaze glided to the silver-haired female by the closest wall, for it was her feelings that he was attuned to the most, second to those of Arii. He had no siblings, but he and the violet-eyed female considered each other as such.

Her wounds were his, and he'd be damned before he'd allow

anyone to hurt her, including the future king of Fythnar. Rage made his fingers itch, as if claws may just erupt from the tips, brought on by the memory of Arii being slammed almost to a pulp under the hands of the man who was meant to one day rule the realm.

On the outside, Krepth remained the picture of composure he was known for.

Nearby, Nemesis stood like a statue, but her eyes flickered with emotion.

"We have to plan now for a new course of action to protect this land in the war to come, one that cannot solely rely on the return of its king. We must prepare ourselves for a battle that will now be heavily tilted in the enemies' favour, now that we are without our strongest asset." Kadec's manner was wiped of any jest.

A tense silence followed, broken only by birds chirping merrily from beyond the wide-open doors of the balcony. Krepth eyed the others, gauging their reactions. Quinn rolled an apple from hand to hand along the table where he sat, mop of hair hanging over his earth-coloured eyes. His jaw was forward in an uncharacteristic display of unease, his eyes fixated on the rolling fruit. Nearby, Tikkani paced, worrying an index finger between her teeth, her gaze traveling between Arii and the Prince as the events of the past morning settled in. Her twin Emerson sat at the table, upturned eyes narrowed, his fiancé Luc hovering at his shoulder, sunlight dancing across the Shifter's dark skin.

A few paces away stood the stranger, Nocturne, his bicoloured eyes skipping back and forth, expression assessing, his voice silent.

Kadec turned to Arii. "If what you believe is true, and his abductor *is* his sister, then we need to learn more about who she is and what kind of magic she possesses. We also must prepare ourselves for the very likely possibility that we may see Eliverus on the opposite side of the battlefield."

Arii had divulged her thoughts to Krepth and Nem before the meeting, telling them her suspicions as to the wraith's identity. Despite her obvious discomfort and anger, she had repeated the story to the room.

Hearing it a second time did not help to convince Krepth that the Herington princess was still alive, let alone on the side of the enemy. Krepth wasn't wholly convinced about the woman's identity, but he did believe Arii knew Elijah best, and if she spied tells that hinted at shared blood, then he would indulge her.

Krepth did not need to look at Arii to know how Kadec's words would strike, for he could sense the anger shivering from her in waves. He pre-empted her reaction fast enough to throw out a hand as she jolted from her seat, halting her mere inches from the Prince of the West.

"That's it? Are we to continue on as if Elijah never existed?" Her chin slanted, eyes narrowing at the barrier in the form of Krepth's arm, which he was now very afraid of losing. Arii shoved the limb away, before slamming a fist upon the table and exclaiming, "We have to go and find him!"

Kadec's attention was unmoving as he stared her down – unflinching and wholly Fae in that moment. There was a stillness to his form that reminded Krepth of a snake – poised and prepared to strike. Despite his normally cheerful demeanour, he was a figure of authority right now. Serious and emotionless.

Krepth could see a pinch in the corner of his mouth, though, betraying the unease the Prince felt. He was no more inclined than anyone else to go to war without Elijah.

"We're out of time," was Kadec's reply, earning him a feral hiss from Arii.

By the window, Nemesis shifted.

Arii's chair screeched back and toppled as she spun, anger getting the better of her. Nem met her in the middle of the room, predicting her movements through their life bond. Nem's voice was low, but not low enough that Krepth could not hear. "We will find him, calm yourself."

The silver-haired Fae cast her heavy gaze on the Prince, her hands holding firm on Arii's biceps as she quaked. Krepth felt the rage shift to his chest.

"Arii and I will go in search of Elijah." Nem announced.

Before Krepth could interject, Kadec replied, "I cannot allow it."

"Why?" whispered Emerson nearby.

If the elf's speaking out of turn fazed him, Kadec did not let it show. If anything, the man's moss-green eyes softened slightly, as if sensing the tension was becoming too much. "Ariiaya Trillia saw firsthand the wicked force that Valdis has amassed in Bonemire." There was almost a pleading edge to his words as he graced his eyes on Arii once more. "You have a knowledge of the beings he has under his control that will prove invaluable to our armies. We need you here, training our troops, preparing them for the fight ahead. And that will most certainly extend to the armies of our Southern and Eastern brethren too."

Krepth hated to admit it, but Kadec had a point. Arii had an intimate knowledge of the creatures they were to face, and knowledge like that was invaluable in the war to come.

But he could also admit that one of their biggest advantages had been the power Elijah wielded. Krepth had once despised the man, believing him partly responsible for the steady decline of their land, and for the abduction of Krepth's mother. But, after a time, he had come to respect him. Was that because of how many times he had saved their asses? Perhaps. But he had come to realise that it was ultimately because of how he treated Arii. Not much escaped Krepth's notice. He saw the way Elijah looked at Ariiaya, like she was a spring to a man lost in a blistering hot desert. There was some hesitation there, too, a healthy amount of respect, like he was watching a wild animal. Krepth noticed how Arii changed when she thought no one was looking, too. There was depth to her violet eyes that had always been there, but devoid of any kind of light. Now, those depths were filled with fire and stars.

She loved him.

Krepth could not remain angry any longer. He wanted to find his mother, rescue her, and that desire was greater than any other. But he knew that she would not want him to blame others for her fate, nor retain anger in his heart. She would want him to act, and that was what he planned to do. He would have already, but the Shifter was not stupid – he had no chance finding her on his own. He needed his friends.

He needed Elijah back, just as much as everyone else.

"Your affection… your loyalty to Eliverus is admirable, Ariiaya." Kadec sighed, passing his palm over the smooth wood of the dark mahogany table, as if using it to ground himself in the moment. He traced his gaze along them all, before dropping his attention to his hands. Krepth spied lines upon his dark skin which had not been obvious before, scars perhaps. Before he could wonder on them further, Kadec's hands turned into fists and he said, "I can see how much you all care for him. I too hope that he is not beyond saving, but we do not have time to hunt him down."

Nearby, Nocturne cleared his throat and approached the table, straightening his already perfectly pressed lapels. The stranger from another realm had helped them previously, but Krepth still didn't fully trust him, or his abilities. That magic was new, foreign, mysterious, and like a dog set in its ways, Krepth found himself adverse to accepting that, too.

"Let me escort Miss Trillia to the library. I'm sure being surrounded by the soothing vanilla and oak tang of old books and the sombre flicker of the candelabras, she will find some solace from her anger," Noct said.

At Arii's pointed stare, he added, "Women love books, right?"

A hint of violence ticked at the corner of Arii's eye.

Krepth kept the laugh creeping up his throat firmly caged behind his lips.

"That guy clearly has a death wish, and for his final breath to be in a library," whispered Quinn, causing Krepth's lips to tip up instead. The young Shifter had remained unusually quiet up until that point, and his elven partner, Tikkani, remained even quieter. Their friends had felt disappointed in being left behind when they'd gone to back up Elijah, but Krepth was thankful that they hadn't been there. He'd gotten used to their company.

Kadec nodded in answer to Noct, who glanced warily at Arii, as if viewing a lioness let loose from its cage.

Krepth couldn't hold back his grin anymore.

Good luck, mate.

The Prince continued. "I do not make this decision for any other reason than for the good of Fythnar. Ferrys to the mainland will be temporarily put on hold, until preparations are complete – or we receive word from Freya and the twin Princes that their forces are ready to move upon Viridya."

Did he seriously mean to strand them here? Keep them against their will, like prisoners?

Krepth's eyes focused on the back of Arii's head, observing the rigid set of her shoulders.

She would not remain here, he knew that.

Everyone knew that.

Question was, how much fury would she unleash upon Kadec's guards on her way out?

"Will Freya even come? Elijah was apprehended before he could complete the final trial." Nemesis said, obviously trying to deflect the topic, her voice tight. Their gazes met briefly, and his heart twinged when she was first to glance away.

Kadec's tone held no waver as he replied, "She will come."

The incessant chirping of birds filled the tense space again, their shrill cries almost becoming too much before Arii slowly turned, her eyes narrowed to slits. Her lips trembled back from her teeth, and just when Krepth thought she would spew fire, the Fae female simply said; "Fine, I'll train your troops, and I'll tell you everything I know about what I saw in Bonemire." She levelled a look at Noct and added,"and I will go to the library, after I scrub the blood from my hair."

Krepth blew out a breath, and he swore the others did too.

"Thank you, Ariiaya," responded Kadec, the lines either side of his eyes softening with relief as he turned to speak with his commander.

Whatever he had to say to the man in silver armour was lost upon Krepth's ears, his sole focus cast upon Arii as she stalked from the room.

Kadec dismissed the meeting a few moments later, exiting the room with his guards, leaving their little band of motley travellers with the untouched spread of food.

What a waste.

Nemesis threw Krepth a brief look, one which he replied with a small nod, before she too slipped from the room. Things were… strange between them, but when it came to their friend, all tension had to be pressed aside.

"Should we follow them?" whispered Tikkani, worrying her bottom lip between her teeth, approaching Krepth, closely followed by Quinn, Emerson and Luc.

"What Arii needs is a hot shower and a few moments alone to gather her thoughts. She isn't used to a support network, nor accepting comfort from one, but that does not mean she doesn't need it." Krepth blew a strand of raven black hair from his eyes, seeing the worried looks on his friends' faces. He forced a confident smile – one which he did not feel quite reached his eyes. "Give her some space. When she's ready, we will dredge up a plan to find Elijah. I know we all agree that Ariiaya can't do this alone."

CHAPTER TWO

ELIJAH

He was fire, he was fury, and he was chaos.

Elijah's insides were a tornado of fury and grief that he could not control. It was as if he were within a lucid dream, the sides of his vision blurring, sounds muted to a droning hum. His heart was shards of glass within his chest, flashes of memory assaulting his mind from all sides.

Lorch's emotionless, bottomless blue eyes as he gave the order for Elijah's mother Colleen's execution.

Arii's scream of rage and fear.

Colleen beheaded and dead on the forest floor.

His magic obliterating lives as if they were nothing.

Blood, so much blood.

Prince Kadec's cryptic warning, *"Those who are most likely to betray you will wear a face you know."*

Then his sister's storm-cloud eyes piercing the haze as she loomed above him, her face ghostly-pale as she slowly smiled, showing a flash of fangs.

"Hello, brother."

Something in the strangeness yet familiarity of her voice had him shocked long enough for the wicked talons of her telekinesis to take hold, grasping his brain in an unforgiving vice.

Then his movements were no longer his own.

He moved as if something else controlled him, what thoughts he had failing to meet his limbs, which came down upon Ariiaya without a hint of hesitation – and he begged it to end, but his cries fell upon deaf ears. Elijah was pressed against a thin pane of glass, seeing his body's intent but unable to stop it. Tears threatened his vision as he slammed his fists against the barrier that had pushed him back to a spectator behind his eyes, the slap of his palms and the blaring of his cries echoing uselessly. Steel swung through the air, intent on slicing skin and breaking bone – but his magic could not rise beyond a shiver of static.

His body was like a marionette guided by poisoned strings of a master puppeteer, one who had claws in his conscious mind, digging in so deep that darkness threatened to pull him into unconsciousness.

He saw the desperation, the pleading in Arii's eyes as his body continued to attack.

Stop.

He could see her mouth repeating his name over and over, even as his sword came within inches of her face as she skidded back.

Stop!

Still his weapon flew, tearing cloth and parting flesh. He did not feel the speckles of blood that hit the exposed skin of his arms, could not feel the rain as it began to fall in a fine mist from above. He could hardly hear the ominous boom of thunder in the distance, in time with his own raging heart.

He was going to kill her.

And he could not stop.

He was not in control of his actions any longer.

She was.

His sister.

Her laugh enveloped him, pressing away all other sound, snaking across his skin and making him shiver. Within the slowly receding consciousness of his mind, hands grasped his shoulders, and with a final cry, Elijah was wrenched back into darkness.

It had taken some time for him to awaken, for the black cloud to lift, and when he did, Elijah was faced with stale, tense air. Before him stood a figure. He spied black, thick heeled boots, before trailing his sight up to the wearer's once-familiar face. How could it be that his dead sister stood but a few feet from him now? She was not as he remembered her, of course, for the last time he saw her she was just a child – as was he. Her eyes, once wide and curious, were now narrowed and glazed in a pale face of devastating beauty.

Weight pinched at his wrists, causing his gaze to shoot down to his arms.

Shackles.

Elijah lifted his head, anger rising like hot lava as he jerked against his bonds. "What have you done? Where am I?"

Ghila's eyes narrowed, her lips hitching in a sly smirk. "Do you not remember your old childhood bedroom, Eliverus? Or… shall I call you Elijah now?"

Bedroom?

Elijah cast his gaze around the room. He had not even noticed the transition from black mist to a dull version of a medium-sized, lavish room back in castle Viridya. It was not any room he had been in recently, but it was far more luxurious than any he had lodged in during recent memory. A bed took up main residence of the space, dressed in linens of royal blue and silver, the frame carved from deep, rich oak. A nearby fireplace cast golden light across two short bookcases topped with hand carved toys and an array of books. A chest of drawers was set beside a cleared sitting area by the window. The small table and chairs were pushed aside to accommodate an easel, propped before windows draped with thick black curtains stitched with silver filigree. Beyond the windows, Elijah could see a pitch-black night speckled with stars. This place had been a cosy sanctuary once upon a time, a place where he could escape to paint and read.

He swallowed, hard.

This was his bedroom, exactly as he last saw it twenty years ago.

His voice was shaky as he whispered, "How?"

The air reverberated, and suddenly his sister crouched before him, her head cocking to the side like an owl inspecting a mouse. The action was more birdlike than Fae, her gaze assessing yet fleeting, as though she could not hold her attention long enough to make direct contact with his eyes. She followed his gaze to the easel, then drew back to him with a little huff. "I always wondered why you chose the smallest room. You had second choice after Brohem, and you could have chosen a far bigger one." A brief pause. "But you settled for perhaps the smallest and simplest."

At his silence, she finally met his eyes, flashing a glint of canines as she grinned, rising to her feet, arms crossing her chest, "How is it that we are here, you ask? Well, let us say that it is *you* who chose to place your conscious mind in this place. Most people retreat to a memory of comfort and familiarity when their mind is taken over. You fought relatively well, but it was for naught." Clucking her tongue, she turned to move a few steps away, before adding, "Pity, I expected more of a fight."

Elijah blanched, the shackles pinching his wrists. "What?"

"Good Goddess brother, I would have thought after so long you would have learned a far better vocabulary than simply *what*."

"How is this possible? I thought you were… dead." Try as he might, Elijah could not mask the hitch of awe mixed with grief that sullied his tone, made his words wobble. So much had happened over the span of the last few months, and of all challenges that could possibly have risen during his journey, *this* was the most unexpected.

She was before him again in a snap, her fingers grasping his chin, long, uneven nails digging into his skin like claws. Ghila's top lip hitched, and he saw shadows dancing in the depths of her grey eyes, her voice a low hiss. Her words pierced deep into his heart as she enunciated them slowly, evenly, hauntingly.

"I was *never* dead."

Before he could speak again, she tore away before spinning back to face him, teeth bared like a threatened animal. "I hoped and prayed that you would come find me, but instead you remained with *them*. All warm and fed in the castle where our family's blood had once painted the golden walls." Her eyes rolled, and her lips snapped shut as her head cocked – as if listening to a voice no one else could hear. "They were right… always right…"

Pain flared in Elijah's chest as he watched her. He didn't have to look long to notice that his sister had changed; none of the kind and gentle person he once knew remained. Familiar yet completely different. Ghila twitched a hand to her neck, fingers seeking something there.

He reached for his magic, but the pool was behind a wall of mist, just visible yet unable to be touched.

"I thought you were dead." Elijah whispered, unable to bring forth anything else in that moment.

"*Liar!*"

He flinched at her sudden outburst, attention shooting to the amulet now clutched so tightly in her fist that her knuckles bleached white. As quickly as her anger had risen though, it was gone, the shadow passing so quickly from her grey eyes that Elijah was surprised she hadn't suffered whiplash. With a resigned sigh and a skip, Ghila made her way towards the easel.

Elijah had been too distracted to notice the drape of cloth over the canvas.

She pinched a corner of the fabric, passing her thumb over it, and when she spoke, her tone held none of the fire from mere moments ago. Her voice was almost… different in a way that Elijah could not quite pinpoint, as if another person occupied her in that moment.

"Lies, lies, all that surrounds us is lies like dust upon stagnant air. But I will be the one to wrench open the window, allowing the crows in. They peck and prod at the windows, wanting to feast."

Elijah suddenly tasted metal and sugar.

Magic. Wrong, strange, different… yet familiar magic.

Madness swirled in the air – within this dream… reality… whatever this was, and she was speaking in riddles.

With a yank, the cloth fell away, revealing an oval-shaped mirror framed with rusted gold.

"Come closer, brother."

Slowly, he did. There wasn't anywhere else to go. The bindings that chafed his wrists had faded on whisps of smoke, leaving his skin raw and bloody. The pain was quickly made an afterthought as he approached, for what he saw within the mirror pressed away all thoughts of the present.

Instead of his mirror image peering back at him, he saw Ariiaya, her eyes wide and her lips moving soundlessly. She knelt on the blood-splattered earth, holding a blade across her front – which warred with one clenched in his own two hands. He was seeing a scene that involved himself and the woman he loved, watching like a spectator over his own shoulder, disjointed and strange.

Helpless.

Even though his thoughts were sluggish to rise, Elijah knew this was a reflection of the events that had just passed. When his body in the reflection thrust forward, elbow snapping and connecting with Arii's nose, Elijah had had enough.

"Stop! Stop it!"

Ghila toyed with an uneven curl of raven hair, tucking it behind her pointed ear. "But watching your smart-mouthed little girlfriend get the arse-kicking she so deserves is just too good to pass up."

"What in the Gods' name are you talking about?" His eyes darted back to the mirror, a wash of relief dousing him as the figures of Nemesis and Krepth appeared, grasping Arii's arms, pulling her reluctant form away in retreat.

Skimming a nail over the filigree border of the mirror, Ghila sighed and pressed a cheek to the cool metal, eyeing Elijah with a look teetering upon boredom. "I tried to get to you through her first. Her mind was *far* too easy to enter – like drifting straight through an open doorway. But remaining there was a challenge. She is by far the most stubborn thing I have ever encountered," a small grin, "and the most pretty. But…" another long sigh, "attempting to mould her mind was like playing with hot clay straight from the earth. No matter the design, it would still be made of dirt."

At Elijah's silence and expression, Ghila perked up, "She didn't tell you, did she?"

"She may have failed to mention it, but a lot was happening—"

Ghila's tone lifted, a singsong, almost childlike note entering her voice as she cut him off, "Naughty little bee, hogging the hive and withholding the honey!"

The sudden change in her again struck Elijah as incredibly bizarre. It was almost as if multiple voices resided within the shell of her form. He was afraid, truly afraid to know what had happened to his little sister all those years ago. While he'd been raised by Colleen, she'd been elsewhere, and something told him that wherever that was had not been good.

Pain entered Elijah's heart at the thought of his adoptive mother, like a fissure sundering his heart. A dark cloud rested on his thoughts. What was the point of having so much power if he was unable to save those that meant the most to him? Rather than a blessing, he felt his magic was a curse, and had thought this far too often of late.

Now, he was stuck in his own mind with the sister he believed to have been dead.

Her intentions were murky, and Elijah's gut feeling was that those intentions were far from good.

Though she had him in a vice, he did not wish to hurt her, no matter how desperate he was to return to his friends. To understand how to leave this place, without harming her, Elijah decided that fear and confusion would have to be pressed aside, and he would need to learn what made his estranged sister tick.

If that involved dredging up demons, hers and his own, so be it.

He eyed the scene in the mirror, the thinning forest and peeks of ocean view signalling that his body – and hers – were on the move. The forest had not thickened, nor could he spy the gravel roads that lead towards Viridya, leading him to believe they were heading southwest towards the ocean, and not the golden castle. Could it be that she wasn't in league with Valdis?

Ghila watched the moving picture, her expression rapt and eyes wide. Elijah swallowed in an attempt to clear his parched throat before speaking gently.

"Where are you taking me?"

Her head snapped to the side, gaze locking with his, features lighting up with a smile while her laugh hinted at madness. "They like to think they have me under control, but their foresight is not as it once was. They will do anything to retain what was theirs, weaving strings and deciding fates. But it will be *me* who delivers true justice."

The dull ache of a migraine bloomed behind his eyes as he tried to keep up with his sister's mad ramblings.

"Ghila, please, let my mind go."

He stepped forward, placing a tentative hand upon her shoulder. They both flinched, but not before he felt bones beneath her assassin's leathers. She was slight, almost frail, smaller than the other female Fae, like Ariiaya or Nem.

Then he almost gasped as her words registered.

Foresight. Strings. *Fate.*

Ghila was taking him to the School of Fate.

As far as he knew, one of the sisters, Klotho, was in league with Valdis, helping him fill his Nexus Crystals with magic, allowing him to wield bodies for his army of the dead. He wondered why Ghila did not just take him straight to Viridya – they weren't far from the golden castle, merely a few hours' ride. Would the sisters not just turn him over to Valdis anyway? Or why not just kill him? Eliminate the threat he posed to Lorch's reign?

Elijah's mind was a tornado of thought, but over the riot he heard Ghila utter, "Like a good little bird, I will return to my nest. Soon, but not yet. My talons need sharpening, and *then* we will see if Gods can fall."

Did she mean to… take down the Sisters of Fate? But why?

"You can stop this before you make a big mistake," he protested, eying the liquid shake of the mirror over Ghila's shoulder. She quirked her head to one side, smiling at him with childlike delight.

"Mistake?" She chuckled deeply, fingering the gilded frame of the mirror again. "The only mistake is that they did not cast away my bonds sooner. A mistake is expecting loyalty when none was given at the start."

Suddenly the image in the mirror changed, and Elijah spied mountains, the terrain flattening out to sparse trees and dirt. The Dragon's Teeth Mountains loomed in the background like monoliths, their peaks so high that low-lying clouds shielded their tips. He'd missed the moment that Ghila had altered their course, a split-second decision to start heading north. Confusion made him lean closer, close enough that he could hear the little, shallow breaths of his sister. Before he could voice that confusion, Ghila spoke, her voice far breathier than before.

"One does not challenge fate with blunt blades. As I said before, this little birdie's talons need sharpening, and you – my dear brother – will be my whetstone."

She was buying time, with no clear destination in mind. Frustration rose quickly within him, and Elijah stepped back from the mirror. "Why not just kill me, Ghila? Or better yet, *talk* to me." He blew out a breath, closing his eyes and willing his anger to lessen. He prided himself in his ability to quickly stem his anger and remain level-headed, but that was proving extremely difficult when they were *inside* his head. He tried again, eyes drifting open, fists loosening at his sides. "Please, tell me what you went through. Maybe then I can help you."

"Help me?" Ghila frowned, squinting as if the words made no sense to her. Elijah allowed for silence, watching the cogs turn in her expression as she thought over his words. Then, her smile was back, spreading widely across her beautiful face until he could see her fangs. When she began to laugh, Elijah felt his earlier headache stretch behind his eyes.

She was mad.

"The only thing that helps us now is to sate the thirst that drives us. We do not need *saving*, what we need is *revenge*."

There it was again. His sister spoke as if she were not alone within her own skin. He had noticed it a few times within the short space since his abduction, and it further spiked his need to find out what had happened to her, and in turn, how to escape this nightmare.

"Revenge? Upon whom?" Elijah tested, the hair on the nape of his neck rising in trepidation.

Ghila tipped her chin up, eyes shimmering in the firelight. "There are many, but let us start with one… upon you, my dear *brother*."

She spat the word like a viper spitting acid.

Revenge. Upon *him*.

She answered his unspoken question with a small chuckle, "You left us to die, now we *rise*."

The kind of madness he saw festering within her was unlike anything he'd ever seen, not even the madmen apprehended in the castle dungeons had showed such lunacy, and Elijah was sure he had seen his fair share of oddities during his time as the king's bodyguard. While interrogating prisoners, Elijah found that showing compassion, even just a grain of it, would sometimes yield results without violence. But the quickest and more sure-fire way to get the information you needed was with brutality.

Brutality – wrenching the truth from someone's mouth whether they were innocent or not. Elijah was no stranger to brutality, but he wouldn't hurt her; he wouldn't hurt his sister. He couldn't.

As if his thoughts sparked something alight, the nearby mirror began to waver and ripple, the dark glass warping slowly into a scene. His sister made a sound of delight, swirling on the tips of her toes until she was by his side, fingers digging deep into his arm as she clutched at him. "Oh, oh how exciting! Can you see that? I thought I would need to do a little digging to dredge up your memories, but look!"

Elijah felt sick as the mirror reflected the insides of a dark and dirty dungeon, the scene and his sister's words curdling in his stomach like spoiled milk. Ghila quickly let him go, and he heard her make a slight sound of distaste, as if the brief contact made her uncomfortable.

Thoughts of that quickly dissipated though, because his attention was solely fixated on the scene revealed in the mirror.

Elijah stared, for what he saw haunted his nightmares regularly.

Moonlight sheared through the bars of a dungeon window, casting silver light over Elijah's black boots. At his feet knelt a boy, not much older than sixteen, his arms behind his back, hair hanging in wet strands over his forehead. His shoulders shook, breath heaving from his parted lips as a line of blood dripped from his nose to the stone floor.

Though he was watching the scene as if from the outside, he vividly remembered the terrible smell that clung to such a depressing place. Mildew from the damp, soil from countless boots trudged through, shit from the dungeon's residents, and copper from the blood of those held and tortured here.

The Elijah in the mirror readied his fist, cracking his knuckles before striking, connecting with the boy's face and throwing him to the floor with such force that the boy's teeth clacked together. His voice echoed about the tiny room, low and dangerous, his face concealed in the darkness of his hood.

"Speak. Who hired you? Who hired you to poison the King?"

No. Not this memory.

He did not need to glance at his sister to know that she was grinning.

The boy spat on the floor, groaning pathetically. "I didn't know it was poison! Honest to the Goddess! Please, please listen. Please don't kill me!"

Elijah flexed his fingers as someone stepped from the shadows behind. Valdis stalked into a patch of moonlight; his copper hair tipped quicksilver as the light tore across his scarred face.

"You have been in service to the King as a squire since you could talk. Years of service, years of care under our good graces with a warm bed and food in your belly, and *this* is how you repay us?" Valdis growled, yanking a knife from his belt as he paused behind the boy, eying him as if he were a sewer rat.

Elijah knew this boy, and he had indeed served the Kruel family for years, faithfully. Why he would attempt to poison the King was beyond him, but it seemed extremely out of character. Something in his gut said that the boy told the truth, he had simply been the unknowing carrier of a fate orchestrated by another, not a collaborator.

"I didn't do it knowingly. Please…" the boy wailed, voice simmering to a pathetic whisper.

Elijah studied the spots of blood upon his fist as Valdis shifted, the tips of his boots entering his peripheral vision from under his hood. The man handed over a dagger, grip first, blade forged of pure gold.

"There have been whispers… whispers of a resistance, here, in our own city."

Elijah palmed the knife, watching the moonlight glint off its blade. A resistance. Elijah had heard the whispers, too. With every monarchy, there would always be those who would challenge their rule. It was impossible to please everybody in life, he knew that, but there were still those loyal to the late king and queen – those who did not fear magic but wished to see its return. The Elijah in the memory was not the same as the one peering into the mirror now – for his past self had feared what he knew of the history of the Fae. He had believed they were tyrants with too much power, trusting the stories told to him.

Now, though, Elijah was much better educated. Yes, there were things in the past that he knew had been terrible, Fae with no respect for the humans who lived with and served them. It only made him want to do better, *be* better than those before him.

"End this, Wolfe. The boy is proving useless to us. The poison's origins are being narrowed down by our best team of apothecaries."

Elijah's stomach knotted painfully, yet on the outside he remained as still as stone.

This was just a boy… he couldn't have knowingly tried to kill the King.

No mercy would be given, Elijah knew that. To let the boy go free, after the spectacle at the King's birthday in front of a throne room full of courtiers, would set a bad example.

Perhaps if Valdis were to leave the room, he could speak with the boy, try the tact of compassion rather than using his fists – as he knew was more Valdis' style. Perhaps he could throw the boy in the back of a carriage headed to Trader's Bay with a fistful of coins and make him board the next ship, never to return.

Valdis hovered by the cell door, his presence a heaviness at Elijah's back.

He would not depart until life blood was shed.

A threat upon the King equalled a threat upon Fythnar, and no matter how Elijah felt, his duty first and foremost was to Lorch. He knew that.

So, his words were an utterance, devoid of emotion, a whisper of white smoke in the chilly cell air.

"As you wish."

Beyond the mirror, Elijah fell to his knees, his heart cracking to the sounds of the boy's bleating cries for mercy as they reverberated around the room. Within him he cried for mercy too, the pain in his head spearing to his heart.

And he suffered, like he did most nights, within the nightmare of his past. He suffered for what felt like hours – when it had been mere minutes.

Until those cries abruptly stopped.

His sister's words echoed around him, like the wings of a hovering crow.

"The only thing that helps us now is to sate the thirst that drives us."

Elijah heaved, expelling bile onto the dream's marble floor.

"We do not need saving, what we need is revenge."

Ghila's smiling voice cut the air like a blade as she whispered, "Time to quench the thirst."

CHAPTER THREE

SYBELL

The air smelled of sea and sulphur as waves boomed through the old castle like crashes of thunder. Sybell wondered if she would ever get used to the sound, the smells, the glares of suspicious eyes as she prepared for another day of unbiased arse-kicking by fate.

Her mouth pressed in a line, she twined a length of cloth around her knuckles as her reluctant mentor entered the courtyard. A Fae woman with auburn blonde hair cut almost to her skull on one side of her head while the rest swept over the opposite shoulder to curtain half of her austere face. Sybell spied tattoos on her skin, thick yet elegant patterns curling up from her collarbone to fade into her clipped hairline. Southern, most definitely southern – if the thick accent that turned her speech into a snarl was any indication.

Sybell had to decipher the orders she barked most of the time, and she was pretty sure the woman liked her no better now that when she had entered the school's walls a week ago. Sybell still did not know her name, for the woman had not deemed her worthy enough of that gift. Her face was cast in a permanent frown as the salt air wavered her locks, which somehow remained perfect even as they circled one another. Despite the woman's harsh exterior, Sybell saw a rugged beauty there.

One she could appreciate if her arse wasn't handed to her every time they met in the ring.

And Gods, the Fury did not hold back.

Sybell being human did not protect her from the Fae's unnatural strength, nor did it earn her leniency in any area of her vigorous 'training'.

In the week which had followed her self-forced enlistment to the school of assassins, Sybell had felt her agitation growing like a weed. She had learned nothing but the sting of a backhand and the hurt of uninterested, belittling glares. None of the women took her seriously, nor did they see her worthy of proper assassin training. The only thing she had learned so far was to cover her fists in cloth, lest her skin split and open every time she managed to strike target.

A slight commotion nearby drew Sybell's attention as a small group of females garbed in travelling leathers mounted their horses. They weren't the first party to leave the castle in the last few days, and she wondered if they were another group charged with finding Ariiaya and Elijah, or if they were on their way to Viridya to join with Valdis' forces, although the groups returned every time. The last time they had come back with a limp body bundled in a cloak, bright red hair peeking from the wrappings. She pieced together that Devina had not returned and drew the conclusion that the woman had been slain. She wasn't sure how she felt about it, the woman wasn't pleasant. She didn't believe she deserved death though.

Curiosity continued to eat at her insides, a burning desire for further knowledge growing all the hotter in her veins. She had not seen her brother in weeks, and she often found herself wondering if he still lived.

Gods, she hoped he still lived.

Sibling spats aside, she missed his lopsided smile and blithe attitude.

Her stomach knotted with those thoughts, but they did not plague her for long. Sybell was jolted violently from her reverie with the deliverance of a fist to the side of her face, throwing her to the mossy cobblestones. Pain rocketed through her skull, singing to the extra pains in her hands and knees as they connected with the floor.

"Focus, *dunga*. You 'ave the concentration of a skraag beetle!" called her mentor, shaking out her hand and baring her teeth.

Sybell leapt to her feet, not caring that the term spoken in the woman's native tongue was most likely an insult. She jerked her stinging chin in the direction of the group. "Where are they going?"

"Not for you to know," the woman retorted, throwing another fist.

Sybell only just managed to duck, planting her feet and throwing up her arms to block the next barrage of strikes. Her weak forearms screamed in pain, but she held. Barely.

"I have knowledge! Use me, I could help," she cried, calling upon the small amount of combat knowledge that she possessed from her short time with Ariiaya, sliding a foot to the left and swiftly unsheathing her training sword. Sybell struck, stabbing the dull weapon at the woman's guts.

Her opponent spun; the movement oddly elegant in comparison to her gruff demeanour.

Frustration winded Sybell, causing her anger to rise. Anger was good, though, for it dredged energy from what little, untrained stores she had. She grabbed hold and yanked upon it with all her might.

Her mentor barked a laugh, canines flashing in the dull light. "Help? What could a *princess* possibly do to help?"

Her condescension brought forth a cry from Sybell's lips as she swung her sword. Their training sessions sometimes drew a few onlookers, mostly Fury assassins hoping for some light entertainment. But most days, between breaking fast and the afternoon, she could feel the eyes of her mother nearby, halting to observe with sadness and worry. Her golden locks were pulled into a messy bun on her head, her skin appearing washed out against her plain white robes. She seemed thinner… the worry over her son affecting her physically. Instead of casting them out, the Sisters had agreed to take in Sybell's mother and father, putting them to work in the kitchens and stables.

Sybell was relieved because she wasn't sure she could have lasted this week without them nearby. Most of their interactions had been fleeting, but they were safe, and that was what mattered most to her. This was in no way an ideal life for them, she knew that. So, she vowed to make sure this arrangement was temporary, for herself and for them.

She came here to learn how to fight, hold her own, and protect herself. The fact that the assassins still considered her a fragile little princess made her blood boil, but with it came a resolve to change their minds. She knew it wouldn't happen within a week, and time was of the essence. Who knew how long Valdis would keep her brother alive?

Lynnera's stifled gasp tore Sybell's attention for one split second, enough for her mentor to spin behind her, Sybell's own training sword pressed heavily against her neck.

"Yield," drawled the woman, voice heavy with wariness and perhaps boredom.

Sybell hissed through clenched teeth, her eyes locked on her mother, who stared back. "No."

"You are the most stubborn girl I have ever trained." Suddenly Sybell's breathing eased, and she sucked in a breath as the Fury added, "That is good."

Sybell swiped the back of her hand over her lips, wincing at the sting there. Hmm, that was certainly going to turn into a fat lip shortly. "Your accent, it's peculiar, can't say I hear the like in these parts very often. Southern, am I correct?"

The Fury stood, arms across her chest, eyes narrowed. Sybell hadn't even seen her return her weapon to the racks. Gods, she wasn't sure she could ever get used to the unnatural swiftness of the Fae.

"Matters not, where we began, *dunga*. Focus on your training, and perhaps even *you* can alter your fate."

It wasn't lost on Sybell how hypocritical they assassin's words were. If history mattered not, then why did she keep calling her princess?

And what in blazes was a *dunga*?

Sybell shot to her feet, agitation sending her hands balling to fists at her sides. "Why do you keep calling me that?"

"What?" The woman blinked as if suddenly perplexed.

"That word! An insult, I have no doubt. Are you so childish that you can't insult me in a way that I can understand?"

Nearby, Lynnera pressed a palm to her forehead, uttering an exasperated curse. This wasn't new, her mother often cursed when she thought no one was listening, almost silently chiding the universe for the daughter who threw all training of decorum out the castle window. She shuffled away, not wanting to witness the war of words, and possibly fists, that were about to erupt in the training circle.

Others lingered, hoping for a fight. This place wasn't short of excitement lately, with the looming threat of war; Sybell's arrival; and now the news that the heir to the north had been taken captive by a Mind Wielder. Opinions were divided amongst those in the school, some unsure if the true heir would bring any semblance of hope or change to the continent, or if the immense power he wielded would just land them all in the same predicament as they were now. Shunned, looked upon like monsters, used as swords for hire, forfeiting their lives in service to fate.

One thing they all could agree on was that Sybell shared blood with the fake boy king, and as far as anyone knew, the necromancer and usurper to the throne, too. That painted a huge target of acid hate on her back, a target she was determined would not cause her to falter in pursuit of her end goals.

She had to prove herself, she knew that, but the woman before her was not making that easy. Sybell stormed towards her and felt a tiny pinprick of satisfaction when she saw her swallow. She jabbed a finger into the centre of the woman's leather-bound chest. "Insult me like you truly mean it, southern-blood!"

Up this close, Sybell could see a twitch forming on the corner of her mentor's eye, her irises the colour of a lake frozen over with ice. Her cheekbones were prominent, housing her cool stare, a touch of colour rising to the surface of her pale skin. She had thicker lashes than Sybell had realised, and her lips were slightly pursed, fuller on the lower, in a scowl. They weren't so dissimilar in height, although the Fae had an inch on her, to which the woman usually used to her full advantage.

But now, she remained still, unnaturally so, in that strange Fae way that Sybell was growing accustomed to. So, she adopted the same stillness, boots planted as the Fae's cool stare slowly coasted over her face. There was a swift shimmer in her eyes, and Sybell did not need the instincts of a Fae to notice the very subtle change take over the woman.

Slowly, she began to smile. Her lips stretched, on the border between smile and grimace, as if unused to doing so. Fangs hinted in her smile, and Sybell found herself staring at her mouth, their bodies closer than she initially intended.

"*Dunga*, it means 'little lion' or 'cub', whichever you call an infant feline born of strong blood but not yet proven themself a lioness grown."

Sybell bristled, taking a step away, all too aware of the fire that had spread to unmentionable areas at the low timbre of the woman's voice and the intensity of her grey stare. Strong blood… a lioness cub, well, she wasn't sure whether to still feel insulted, or rather lightly flattered.

"Tora."

Sybell blinked dumbly.

The Fae sighed, head tilting towards a new commotion nearby as she repeated, "Tora, 'tis my name. That is all for today, little cub."

"Just Tora?" Sybell shot back, oddly moved by the gift of the surly woman's name without a fight to get it. She wasn't sure why she asked, but their brief closeness had perhaps piqued her interest in learning more.

"Just Tora," Tora replied, turning away.

Tora.

It suited her, and Sybell found that she was fine not knowing her surname, if she had one at all. Just Tora.

Footsteps clapped on stone nearby, yanking Sybell's attention. She moved to stand beside Tora, watching as three hooded figures escorted by leather-clad assassins passed beneath the portcullis to congregate in the bailey, where their training area was located. One by one they removed their hoods, red, white and black windswept hair dancing around incredibly beautiful faces. There was a weight on the air upon their entry, and Sybell found herself stiffening as three sets of otherworldly golden eyes landed upon her.

Sybell couldn't help it, she stepped forward, "Have you any news from Viridya?"

Have you any news of my brother, she thought.

An awkward silence stretched as the women accompanying the sisters gathered their small amount of traveling supplies. The one with red hair, Etropos, was the first to answer. "You are settling in nicely, princess," she said, gesturing at the bruise purpling on Sybell's cheek. Sybell touched her fingertips to her skin, wincing.

"Matters of Viridya no longer concern you," drawled the black-haired Fate, Klotho, her face set in a harsh glare. "You forfeited any involvement when you asked to be taken in as a Fury. Your sisters, this place, they are what matters most to you now."

Sybell seethed quietly. She was now coming to understand why Ariiaya had been so unattached, so emotionless. Their methods were archaic, unreasonable, blinding. Perhaps separating themselves from the other factions of the land had worked years ago to make their jobs as assassins easier, more formidable, more mysterious.

But times were changing, and they now needed to choose a side.

"Separating yourselves from what is happening in Viridya will only lead you all to death," Sybell snapped.

Tora drew in a breath beside her, and in that split second, Sybell knew she'd crossed a line.

Klotho slowly turned, her brows inching towards her hairline.

"You speak out of turn, fledgling."

The sister seemed… surprised, and a little curious. Sybell expected rage at her insolence, a backhand perhaps.

Instead, Klotho glared down her nose as the other two Fates sidled beside her, watching expectantly.

Knowingly.

Of course, they knew she'd speak up. Of course, they knew she wouldn't keep her mouth shut.

They were the Fates, seers employed by the Gods to know every string in the Tapestry, probably even her own. It crossed her mind suddenly that these women, with their golden eyes and timeless faces, probably knew exactly how her fate was to play out. Had they tugged her string from the tapestry, too? Had they poised it, readied it for cutting, awaiting the moment she made a wrong decision, a wrong move?

Sybell reined in her flaring temper, let it flow down to her toes as she exhaled a shaky breath. She needed to calm herself, organise her words and actions, or her plan to return and save her brother was going to fail. She drew upon the extensive lessons she'd been put through, the long days of learning how to speak, act and *think* like a princess.

She may have forfeited that duty, but she was still royal by blood.

"You have far too much power for it to just… go to waste," she began, casting her eyes over their silent faces. Lakhesis, with hair straight as strung silver, watched without emotion, her chin dipping into a subtle nod. Etropos, the fiery red-head, tilted her head, a small smile forming on her lips.

"The Gods, they guide you. They gave you their power. I don't think they'd be thrilled for that gift to be wasted if the world they left you was to plunge into darkness."

There was a moment of quiet, with just the sound of the briny wind howling between the crumbling stones and over the walls. The assassins who had gathered to watch stood like statues, the salty air thick with their amassing tension.

Suddenly, Etropos clapped, announcing, "Playtime is over, sisters. You all have work to return to!"

Like the turn of tide, their audience snapped into action as Etropos turned.

Something passed over the sisters' collective faces, something Sybell couldn't quite read. There was a long pause, one that would have been severely awkward had the assassins gathered to watch not begun to dissipate. The movement around them alleviated the severity of Klotho's stare. Gods, no wonder they called her the mean one.

"You'd do well to keep training, princess." Klotho finally said, her words doused in a tone that held secrets. Perhaps the sister truly did know something about her future. She blinked in surprise as she watched their backs drift from the area.

Despite having not really gotten anywhere, Sybell took the gentle dismissal as progress.

That… had been easy. Too easy, perhaps?

"Back to training, *dunga*," said Tora, heading for the training racks.

Sybell rolled her shoulders, letting loose the pressure she'd held there. She swore she heard a fine ripple of a sigh in her mentor's voice, like she too was letting go of some left-over tension.

"Thought we were done," Sybell mumbled.

Tora was silent, twirling two training batons so quickly that they were a blur.

Fine… she'd continue training, continue pretending that a world of shit wasn't stirring in a castle of gold to the east. She'd strengthen her muscles, and try not to die, all the while listening for anything new that could aid her in returning to Viridya. She knew she couldn't rescue her brother alone. She'd need to adjust her plan, use her wits and perhaps her stubbornness to convince the Fates to take a side.

Perhaps then she'd have a chance to make a difference.

She'd save her brother, even if it was the last thing she did.

ARIIAYA

The week passed lazily, the days drawing out at a snail's pace. The ache of Elijah's absence clawed at Arii's insides, taking little bites like bothersome ants. Her aggravation slipped behind a cool mask of indifference as she oversaw battalions of men and women in shining, russet armour, offering her small amount of knowledge about what they would face in the war against the North.

After the meeting a week ago, she'd shut herself in her room, deciding not to go to the library with Noct. The man had tried to coax her through the muffle of her door, but when his efforts failed, he left her with a promise to find her later.

She'd then avoided him all week, not up to absorbing any of his smoothly accented words or attempts at comfort. She'd avoided all of her friends and was relieved they knew her well enough to allow her space. But it wouldn't last, she knew that.

So far she had kept to Prince Kadec's terms, helping train his army, taking the place where Elijah would have been, but her mind wasn't fully fixed on her task. It churned with plans of her imminent escape, and how she'd kill his sister, and then rescue him. She took on a detached mentality, separating herself from her emotions, locking them in a box. Smooth, practiced… deadly.

Ghila Herington would regret taking away Elijah's will. She'd regret taking him from *her*.

The warmth of the spring air leached sweat from her skin, dark brown strands clinging to her jaw and neck like worms. There was a hint of humidity that she wasn't used to, and the stickiness further soured her already terrible mood. When the sky began to dull to deep greys, golds and blues of the afternoon, Arii stalked from the bustle of soldiers cleaning up for the day, craving time alone.

She finally headed to the library, taking a seat at a window facing west over the ocean.

Had it been any other day, the envelope of leather and paper of the library surrounding her would have provided her comfort. Solace. But not today, it seemed. Today the library felt like a cage, the many tomes encroaching upon her like speechless spectators, the floor to ceiling bookshelves and their potted greenery bringing forth a sense of claustrophobia.

As hard as she tried to lock the box holding her emotions, Arii could not shake the fearful restlessness that mixed with her anger, quivering and overflowing like a boiling kettle with a rattling lid. She chewed her fingers, picking at the scabbing skin around her nails, tasting blood. The questions – despite the quiet air of the library – continued to riot in her mind, as loud as an angry crowd.

She supposed the fact that Ghila lived was not exactly impossible – Elijah had survived the attack on his family, so his younger sister had a chance to defy her fate too. But what truly perplexed Arii was the fact that Ghila hadn't seemed to be on their side. Whatever she had done to Elijah had caused pain, and then taken away his free will. Arii was certain that what she had witnessed was something unexplored in their lore, something rare, something *forbidden*.

Mind magic.

To take away someone's free will and take control of their mind and body was the biggest breach of all that was natural – apart from bringing back the dead, of course.

Mind magic wasn't a subject that was thoroughly explored in Fae schools, mostly because it was rare, and also because those who had displayed the ability were executed upon discovery. Fae law saw Mind Wielders as one of the biggest threats to their way of life, and there was naught a slither of mercy for those caught.

There was a difference between Kadec's magic and that of a Mind Wielder, though. Kadec's magic was simply projections – placing something behind one's eyes to make them see scenes of a different reality.

He'd explained this to her when she'd described what she'd seen in Elijah's eyes, and the way he'd fought her. Even Kadec was not able to take control of someone's body and prise them from their own consciousness. During the ball, he had not seized possession of Elijah's body, but had only forced him to witness projections of scenes in his mind. And he had needed the help of a magic muting elixir to even access Elijah's mind at all. Elijah had been like a statue, unmoving while under the spell.

Ghila had torn her way into Elijah's mind, taking advantage of his grief. That was Kadec's guess, anyway.

Arii shivered, remembering how easily the wraith had slid into her mind. She was grateful that Ghila hadn't chosen to take over her body and get to Elijah that way. Perhaps it had been the distance between them? Maybe sharing one's blood made that kind of magic easier. It was somewhat comforting to know there was that limitation.

What did Ghila want with Elijah, anyway? When it came to a family reunion, Arii was expecting tears of joy, embraces of happiness… not taking a lost sibling hostage and causing him to attack his friends.

Arii sighed deeply. Of course the Herington line would consist of one of the most powerful Fae of their time, *and* a freaking Mind Wielder.

She wondered if their eldest brother, Brohem, had somehow survived, and was about to make an entrance too. She wouldn't close her mind to the possibility.

Arii perched on the edge of the cushioned settee, her knees bouncing restlessly as she glared at an open tome on the oak coffee table before her, a dark knot in the timber staring back at her like a beady, unblinking eye. The meeting with Kadec had left a sour taste in her mouth, the acidity remaining a week later. She had expected much more from him, seeing as he had just literally sworn his alliance to Elijah. She had expected a pledge to retrieve him. Instead, he had simply said; *"We cannot tangle with fate, Ariiaya. Things will work out in time, Elijah is the most capable being I know. He will fight this and return."*

Unbeknownst to Kadec, though, Arii was all about tangling with fate.

Arii knew she should have more faith in Elijah, but she couldn't stem the feeling of responsibility. It squeezed around her lungs, making every single breath near impossible.

Never before had she felt like this.

It was debilitating.

Thoughts create weakness, and feelings cause blindness.

A tiny part of her had to admit that, in this moment, she almost agreed with the Sisters of Fate.

This sense of hopelessness was nearly crippling.

"What did that book do to deserve such a glare of death?"

Arii jumped at the voice, "Fuck!"

"For a Fae, you are *very* easy to sneak up on," said Nocturne, leaning against the curve of wrought iron handrails that spiralled up to the second story of the library. The man's black suit was, as usual, immaculate, his black and blonde hair swept back from his intelligent, bicoloured eyes. Candlelight graced the angled features of his face, casting him half in shadow. His head tilted slightly, keen gaze assessing.

"Caught me uncharacteristically off guard…" she murmured, calming her restless legs and shooting him a *very* characteristic glare. "What do you want?"

Noct was silent for all but a moment, before pushing from the stairs and taking a seat across from her. Honestly, she'd expected Krepth or Nem to find her first. His presence still unnerved her, but she was getting used to the otherworldly stranger.

"I'm sorry about the Prince."

Arii bristled, "Why would you be sorry? If anything, I thought you'd be overjoyed by one less obstacle in your pursuit of my affections."

He grinned, and Arii glared, adding "I don't do affection, by the way."

Noct waved a long-fingered hand, "I gave up pursuing you ages ago."

She blinked, taken aback. "What?"

"It's obvious that your heart lies with the Prince, and I'm a man with an abundance of worlds and plenty of time to trapeze between them. There are plenty of fish in the sea for a realm hopper like me, especially when that sea is endless."

Arii suppressed a dramatic eye roll, and Noct took her silence as shock, adding, "Don't worry, little Fae, you won't suffer anymore unwanted advances from me. Besides, I like my women a little more… emotionally stable."

Arii blinked, before her expression turned to stone. "I am not emotionally unstable. You'll find I care for little, actually."

Noct leaned forward, a slow grin widening his face. "You may have built a fortress of stone around your heart, but I can see the cracks in your mortar." His grin fell, replaced with a look far more serious, one that made him seem suddenly much older… wiser. "You care no less than the plants care for rain, or the sun cares for the day. Perhaps your heart once had teeth, but now you love with the same fury with which you fight. Ferociously, and without mercy. If anyone can bring him back, it is you."

She hadn't even spoke Elijah's name, yet he was at the forefront of her mind… *always* at the forefront. She hadn't known Nocturne for long, yet he seemed to know her far better than she would have liked. She tried to not let that feeling manifest much further.

"You've gleaned all that from a few weeks of knowing me?" she asked, but an odd feeling of appreciation warmed in her chest at his words.

Noct's smile returned, and for once the tilt of his handsome lips carried none of the sass they normally did. "Much can be learned in a short time if you're observant enough."

There was a small pause, an oddly companionable silence that flowed into Nocturne's next words.

"This world isn't my own, obviously, but even though this one is thoroughly different to where I come from, there are details which carry across all worlds. For example, the laws of magic and their limitations are somewhat the same. With magic, there is always a loophole – not all is set in stone. There will be a way to free Eliverus from his captor. But, it will require effort, and a bit of travel off the beaten path."

Arii perked up and straightened in her seat. Finally, the man appeared to be useful, rather than just being observant. "Oh?" she inquired.

Noct linked his fingers together and cracked his knuckles. "But first, allow me to give you a lesson."

A long, drawn-out groan ripped from Arii as she slid down the settee's backrest.

Noct continued, ignoring her childish spat, "How much do you know of alternate worlds and how they are connected?"

"Honestly, until you showed up and threw me through an interdimensional void hole, I had no idea other worlds or... realms even existed." She threw an arm over her eyes. She decided she didn't have the mental strength for him today.

Noct stood and moved to a nearby bookshelf, skimming his fingers across the spines before halting on one about flora and fauna. He examined it as he returned to his seat. Even though she was acting like a pre-pubescent, slumped on the settee, he continued unfazed, halting on a page and turning it to face her. There was a printed image of a tree, inked with a thick base and many branching limbs.

"Imagine a tree, like this one." He tapped the picture, then ran a fingertip from the base and up along the limbs. "Now, imagine each limb is a world, and any branches running off those limbs as alternate realities of that world."

"Why do I feel this is about to get complicated," Arii murmured, peeking underneath her arm.

Noct continued as if she hadn't spoken, "All worlds are ultimately connected to the base of the tree," His finger circled the bottom of the illustration. "All connected in one way or another. The base is how we travel from one world to another, using it as a conduit, and no world is truly disconnected from the others. All worlds span from the mother tree – as it were, and with that comes similarities. All worlds have magic in some shape or form, some stronger than others. And all worlds have the same basic physics that pertain to that magic."

"Ph... Physics?" Arii echoed.

Noct's face blanked into a look almost like boredom. "Right, I keep forgetting that this is one of the more... primitive worlds."

"Primitive?" she echoed again, arm flopping against her chest, blinking.

"It's strange, actually. Fythnar has highlighting features, I suppose – a castle made entirely of gold, beautiful architecture that probably has not changed in centuries, formidable magic that, until recent history, was balanced and abundant. But then you lack basic advancements that I'm surprised haven't been discovered yet – such as electricity."

Arii sat straight, leaning forward on her knees, brows knitting. "Sure, we have electricity, the skies fill with storms, sometimes there are bolts that rain down–"

"Not *that* kind of electricity, I mean the kind harnessed to power the lightbulbs in your homes."

"Lightbulbs?"

"An alternative to lighting candles. Candles are an exceptional fire hazard, by the way. Pretty sure I saw an oil lamp or two downstairs, so I'm glad to see at least one of your courts is spending time on alternatives."

Suddenly, Arii had the thought that Nocturne, despite his look of high intelligence, suffered from a quickly moving attention span, and not in a good way. "What have candles got to do with trees?"

"Kindling…" The man blinked, realising he had become side-tracked, shaking his head. "I guess electricity is a lesson for another day. Anyway, as I was saying, all worlds share similarities. What I'm trying to get at is that I think there is something in my world that may also be in yours. A higher power, something that could heavily sway the war in favour of the good and may also assist in getting Elijah back."

"Now you're talking sense," Arii said, canines pinching her bottom lip in a slow smile, before promptly falling away. "You've held out on telling me this all week, why?"

"Here I thought *you* were avoiding *me*."

She had, she'd been avoiding everyone, but that was irrelevant to her now as her fingers began to curl into claws against her thighs.

Her displeasure must have shown on her face, too, because she could see the second Noct realised that he was in pouncing distance of a predator… one who had been causing others to tread eggshells for fear of inciting her barely-veiled anger all week. Noct's brows drew, and his bicoloured eyes wavered, his breath halting. "I had to do a little research first. To see if my theory had merit before I gave it to you. I didn't want to present you with false hope."

Somewhat placated, Arii nodded for him to continue, crossing her ankles and leaning back in her seat.

Noct put the book down and leaned back, digging in a pocket before pulling out a small, leather-bound pocketbook. He flipped to a page, holding it for her to see. Arii leaned forward, examining the crude drawing of charcoal, jolting back swiftly when the image registered.

A serpentine body curled into a figure eight, jaws devouring its own tail.

"You've seen this symbol before?" Noct observed, his voice smooth.

She found her voice swiftly, reaching for the book. Noct tilted back, keeping the book just out of her reach.

Odd.

"The Wraith, the woman who abducted Elijah… she had a pendant around her neck that looked just like that."

Noct's expression turned probing yet guarded. "Did she now?"

"What does it mean?" Arii slid forward, perched precariously upon a spike of flaring adrenaline.

"That is the symbol of the Ouroboros."

Arii waited for him to continue, feeling a flick of frustration at how slowly he slid the book back into his pocket.

"The Ouroboros is the symbol of eternal life, but also a symbol of immense power. Often it is depicted as a serpent without legs or wings, more like a snake, but in other worlds it is also depicted as a dragon. In yet other worlds it is depicted as animals such as a wolf or phoenix."

"Phoenix?"

"Ah, yes, you don't have those here. Another lesson for another time." His gaze was holding, as cunning as a fox. "The Ouroboros is an incredibly powerful symbol, and if you're successful in obtaining it, I have no doubt you will have an exceptional advantage in the war to come."

This was a lot to take in. Not only the existence of many alternate worlds and realities, but the fact that there was a new lead of hope when she was beginning to have none.

She could kiss him for this slither of hope.

Well, almost.

"Every world has objects of power, and the Ouroboros is one which doesn't have a permanent home."

"And this Ouroboros exists in your world, too?"

Noct clucked his tongue, and Arii could tell that he was holding something back. Then he spoke, rubbing at the nape of his neck, "Yes, it originates from my world, but I happen to know that it currently resides here in yours."

She was suddenly on her feet, earning her a wide-eyed blink from Noct. When he did not follow, she swished a hand. "Well, take me to it."

"Hold on, little Fae, it's not that simple."

Her stare was deadpan, "Why not?"

Noct sighed, long and hard, then finally stood, "It is only found if it wishes to be found."

"Oh, for fuck's sake."

"I can direct you to where I believe you can begin looking. But, honestly, you're not going to like it," said Noct.

Arii lifted her arms, "Can you not just... portal us to where this Ouroboros is hiding? Because it's hiding, right?"

"Yeess..." Noct drew out the word as Arii ground her teeth. "It is hiding, because if Valdis were to find it, it would not end well for you. Or for my world... or for any of the worlds for that matter."

She pinched the bridge of her nose. "Okay, where do we start?"

"I know someone who can tell us more. Gather your merry band of travellers, and make sure they can all swim. We are headed to the underwater city of Sapphine."

CHAPTER FOUR

ELIJAH

Everything was red.

Elijah's vision darted over translucent scenes of a battle, plate-armoured soldiers clashing with far less-protected people, all through a veil of crimson as it set the world on fire. Adrenaline made his pulse beat like a drum in his ears as the world solidified, the cover of his hood doing nothing to mute the sounds of screams.

This was a memory, one that often repeated when he tried to sleep at night. It was the largest scale of conflict within the city walls that he'd witnessed, the first proper battle since he'd joined the ranks of the Red Guard. This was where he'd proven himself worthy of being the King's bodyguard, where he'd lost a part of his humanity, a moment that set him upon a path he'd later regret.

Though the episodes of violence were the ones to visit him at night, this memory unspooled from the beginning, and even though Elijah knew where this was headed, he was unable to stop the scene from playing.

The people they faced were average town citizens – or so he'd thought. Their attire shouted poverty, all dirty rags and common weaves, until he spied clean vests and near new cloaks. The range of people had strings of doubt curling through his mind. It was not just those who lived harshly – who he couldn't blame for their discontent – but people who resided in the middle classes of their court, people who he assumed were content with their lives.

But these people were far from content, and the words within their shouts and jeers soon became clear in his ears.

'Let us in! Let us speak with the King!'

'He cannot continue to sit back while our people die!'

'Usurpers and a false boy king, a careless menace allowing disease and death to spread!'

Nearby, Commander Hawke stood, his hair sporting far less grey than the last time Elijah had seen him. His eyes were less creased with lines, his back ramrod straight, a hand resting on the pommel of his sword. He spoke to a man who headed the protest, his hand raised in a placating gesture. The words were becoming more heated, the man's demeanour more aggressive.

Elijah held the line along with a small contingent of soldiers at the castle gates, their faces creased in scowls as the crowd began to gather and thicken, their cries rising louder. He, as well as the others in his battalion, had noticed the tightening of security of late, as well as the thickening of the army ranks. Elijah wasn't ignorant to what was happening within their borders. He'd heard of the devastating power of magic, of the destruction it caused. He also knew of the culling that was happening to those who were found wielding it, and their fate should they be male.

'End the death, end the suffering!'

He remembered tilting his head, casting his eyes up to the wall of the golden castle, where he saw the swift flash of sunlight glancing off polished metal. Lorch was up there, staring down at the commotion, his father a permanent fixture beside him.

The rising of voices, some from his own contingent, attempting to placate the rising tension, brought his attention back. Elijah understood their grief – but he also couldn't help the scowl that turned his lips downward. The number of reports steadily flowing in told him that the Fae – or what little remained – were beginning to fight back in the form of protests scattered throughout the north, which were quickly turning from peaceful to violent. Guards were being targeted while doing their duty, their attackers using not only crudely made weapons, but magic too. Magic had been outlawed since the royal family's deaths, for he, as well as the entire court's human population, had been told of the unpredictable side effects of powerful magic. There had been rumours that those who couldn't contain the power ultimately were driven mad – reports alluding to this fact within recent history.

Elijah, though, could not shake the feeling that something was wrong. It was a nagging feeling deep in his gut, an anxiousness he could not explain, a shadow that had always been, ever since he could remember.

He understood why the Fae population protested, why they were angry – families were being torn apart; lives severed because of something that a few of these people had been born with. But did they not see that magic was chaos? Magic was destruction? Magic was death?

The Elijah within this dream believed this... believed what he'd been told.

Beyond the memory though, Elijah begged himself to see sense, to trust those instincts inside him that he'd previously ignored. History could not be manipulated though, so his cries did nothing. All he could do was helplessly witness his past.

Around them, cries of anger and challenge mingled into a song of quickly growing violence.

'Freedom! Freedom to the Fae!'

With that shout, hell broke loose. A man surged from the crowd, arm snapping back before tossing a bottle-shaped projectile at the castle wall, directly at the space where Lorch and his father stood. There was a cry of warning, before a loud smash and a *boom*, bodies scattering with an explosion that shook through the floor.

Glass and liquid rained down on them like spitfire, and Elijah ducked his head as flames singed his cloak and plate armour, the bitter scent of burning alcohol causing him to cough. A flash of a dagger had him reeling back, something singing in his blood to move move *move*, as he ducked and dashed around his attacker – a woman dressed in flour-stained overalls, her teeth bared with her words. "I didn't want to fight! None of us wish to fight!"

All semblance of a peaceful protest was shattered as the people fell upon the soldiers.

The woman's arms jabbed without rhyme or reason, her attacks sporadic and untrained. Her attire told Elijah that she was a baker, an average citizen who had joined the melee perhaps with the hope of making a difference.

Or perhaps she hadn't had a choice at all.

Like a gate slammed wide, the soldiers no longer held back, clashing with the citizens in an attempt to press them back and protect the castle.

"If you do not wish to fight," he ducked another haphazard strike, bringing his sword up to deflect a blow. "Then don't!"

The woman laughed, the sound devoid of humour. "Sometimes we must do what is wrong, to make things right."

Elijah brought his sword up again, deflecting her blow before pushing her back. The woman wobbled, unsteady on her feet, her eyes skittering left then right – perhaps taking in the state of the others around her. There was fear written on her face, despite the determination of her words.

"We will fight until we are free. We will fight until *he* is dead. We will fight until there is nothing left."

He.

She spoke of Lorch, of the boy who'd picked Elijah up from the mud, who had welcomed him into the castle and become his friend when Elijah had next to nothing else. He hadn't even had his memories, an awkward, unapproachable servant boy, yet that hadn't deterred Lorch.

The woman turned, throwing herself wildly at another soldier nearby. There was no structure to their progression, their lack of any formal training apparent as her unguarded back was bared to attack.

Something stayed Elijah's hand, though, he was not one to stab someone in the back. Whether it was moral or because he sensed something else arising, he hadn't time to think on it.

The conflict around him was escalating to a fever pitch, and until this moment the soldiers of the battalion had held back from being first to draw blood, despite the aggression of the crowd, and the draw of palm weapons and liquid bombs. Something sizzled along Elijah's skin, and it was not from the leftover plumes of fire.

The feeling was something altogether different.

Attention swayed to the left, the taste of something sweet rolling across the back of his tongue, Elijah caught the rising of hands, followed by a flash of blue.

A soldier who faced a man at Elijah's flank suddenly jerked, his body turning rigid, his sword dropping from his grasp. His head snapped back so fiercely that his helmet flew off, his arms as straight as fence posts as he began to scream. Blue light erupted from his eyes, his ears and his mouth, as if he were being lit from within.

The conjurer – a young man with straight, cherry blonde hair and delicately pointed ears, his face twisted in a snarl – kept his hands lifted, palms glowing blue, as the magic continued to boil the soldier from within.

The mass around them seemed to stop, just for a split second, breath held in transfixed horror as the soldier's screams ceased, and his body began to fall.

When it hit the cobblestones, he was nothing but a shell, an eyeless, gaping husk trailing smoke.

The sounds that proceeded this dulled to a muted medley, as Elijah stared down at the burned remains of a man who had been breathing mere moments ago. Something shimmered on the skin that had been left unburned, a film of magic that reminded Elijah of tiny diamonds.

He froze, transfixed, shocked, skin tingling and breaths shearing his throat.

What he saw, what he smelled, what he *felt* in retaliation to the use of magic – it scared him, it shook him to his core.

But most of all, it *called* to him, an unwanted curiosity shivering in the wake of the fear.

Elijah stared at the corpse, at the burnt-out eyes, the singed armour, the gaping mouth, for what felt like an eternity. The soldier, Randall, had been the same age as Elijah, a man who spoke a lot and smiled often, even during the harshest of training drills. A man who was becoming a friend.

Now, because of magic, he would never see another drill again, never be able to climb the ranks and serve his King.

Screams yanked the world back into sharp focus.

Someone was swearing, cursing with such vehemence that Elijah flinched.

"No! No magic! Fucking hell, Jaxion! This has gone too far!" A man yelled, hands flailing with anger, one side of his face smeared with ash.

The magic wielder, Jaxion, bared his teeth. "When will you stop thinking a protest is going to change things, Garth? The time for words is over. It's time to take back what is ours!"

Their words turned muffled as Elijah tuned them out, the sound of buzzing filling his ears as his fists clamped harder on his weapon.

All Elijah could see was the sightless, charred husk of Randall behind his eyes, burned into his eyelids as if he'd stared too long at the sun. He could hear Commander Hawke's shouts – orders to detain. To stop the battle as quickly as possible before innocent townspeople were hurt, or more destruction were to befall the homes and structures around them.

But how could they detain such power?

Magic was pain, magic was chaos, magic was *power*.

It couldn't be allowed to return; it couldn't be allowed to spread. If this could happen to one person in a few breathless moments, what would happen if it was allowed to rise unchallenged? Countless lives could be lost because of it.

This was what they'd been fighting against. This was why families were being separated, why the Fae were being suppressed.

Flares of blue and purple magic strobed, and another two soldiers began to writhe and fall, eyes burned out, skin shimmering blue.

The order changed from detain to eliminate as more soldiers fell.

Elijah's sword struck, impaling one of the Fae in the guts as his war cry mixed with the one of anguish that Elijah let loose from the safety behind the mirror. As a spectator, watching this memory unfold, he remembered the change in him in this moment, like a chord snapping. These people, with their fear, their aggression and passion, they were *his* people, but the Elijah within the memory did not know this yet.

Elijah watched the memory, watched as his past self fulfilled orders to eliminate, his insides now a riot of emotion, threatening to drown him. Those actions were that of someone who had been fed a concoction of untruths and inflated, fear riddled stories.

That was no longer him.

He continued to watch, body fixed, his sister's manic laughter in his ears.

Watched as he became a killer, and then shortly after, the King's bodyguard.

That is no longer me.

The hood that would conceal his identity from then on was lifted, his face disappearing into shadow, save for the downturn of his lips and the angle of his chin. The brand-new sword and black armour became a second skin, a layer between him and all that he was about to do in the name of the King.

"If we are to train together, we need to have trust. You need to trust me enough to see your face, Elijah."

His thoughts strayed to her. The skim of her fingers as they pulled back the hood of his cloak, his eyes meeting ones like purple fire. The trust in them as he gazed down at her, battered and bruised during their rescue in Bonemire. Her lips on his scars, unfazed by their vulgarity, her own skin a litter of scarred stories. Her touch, strong yet at times hesitant. Her words, barbed yet brimming with truth.

When she'd removed his hood for the first time in the library, she'd not only exposed his face, but perhaps peeled back the first layer of his defences too, and had been grounding and empowering him ever since.

"Show me a night where the future doesn't matter, Elijah."

Her lips on his, her hand in his hair, her wide, beautiful purple eyes blazing with *fire*.

Ariiaya.

Elijah recalled standing on the threshold of her rooms in Ayrith, faced with her look of clear pain. She'd tried to distance herself from him, but the pull they'd both felt was too strong to ignore. It was thoughts of her... always her, who pulled him back from the depths of darkness. Even now, when the sounds of battle faded to a background hum, he let those memories take hold.

"Tell me to go, tell me to stop, because if you don't, I fear I'll never be able to."

His hands in her hair, his lips on hers, his ice warring with her fire.

"Enough," came his sister's voice, and he was suddenly set free from the mirror's hold, the connection severing so violently that he stumbled back.

Elijah watched as Ariiaya's face faded from the mirror, its surface dying to rippling black.

Ghila pinched her chin, brows raised. "Interesting. The others weren't able to change the course of their memories. Your mind is proving stronger than I anticipated."

He motioned to the mirror, not allowing his breathlessness to show. "You see that I had no memories, and little control over my actions–"

"You knew exactly what you were doing, brother." Ghila snarled. "You served *them* instead of finding me!"

"I had no knowledge that the royal family was even mine. I didn't even know my true name!"

Why did she not understand him?

"Matters not now, I'm curious to see more of your betrayal... to me... to their memory... to our *kind*."

Drawing upon some of his past self, Elijah crossed his arms over his chest and let his displeasure show as a severe scowl.

"Enough, Ghila. You've proved your point. If you wish to delve any further, perhaps you should focus on my time after I left the Kruel family's employ. You'll see that I have changed."

A light laugh echoed around his old bedroom. "But that is nowhere near as fun!"

Elijah's jaw clenched, and he subtly reached again for the magic he felt hovering like a slumbering beast below his skin.

It remained asleep.

"Save your strength for our next game, big brother. You're going to need it."

Could she feel his attempt to grasp his magic?

Ghila gestured to the mirror, grey eyes wide, as another memory began to play. "Look!"

Of their own accord, his eyes drew to the mirror once more.

And Elijah began to hate himself anew.

SYBELL

The bath was scalding, and Sybell savoured the burn.

The tub was stained, the white porcelain marred from the saltwater in marks that wouldn't ever clean away. Dirt bobbed on the water's surface and she watched, submerged to her chin as steam plastered golden strands of hair to her face. The heat of the water was not friendly to the split skin of her palms, nor the scrapes on her knees and elbows, but it leeched a little of the tension from her muscles.

There was a knock at the door, and she sighed. "I know, time's up. Give me a moment," she called, before removing herself from the bath, pink and steaming.

Morning light penetrated the windows and cracks between the castle's crumbling mortar as Sybell donned brown leggings and a loose cream tunic, cinching a belt at her waist before roughly tugging her wild locks into a messy tail. She passed a miffed-looking pink-haired Fury in the hall, the one no doubt waiting for her turn in the tub. There were only two available to the students in the entire school, the other facilities of the bathroom limited to stalls with buckets and rags, like commoners. Not elite assassins.

She missed having her own bathroom.

Sybell ignored the female as the sound of water refilling the tub followed in her wake.

The tub was spelled to empty then refill anew for the next person to use.

Sybell wasn't sure she'd ever get used to such casual magic.

She had to admit, she'd been hesitant at first, fearful of the magic as she watched the tub fill of its own accord. She had wanted to ask it to not be so hot but speaking to a bathtub felt preposterous.

When she'd submerged in the heat, finally sure the castle was not about to harm her, she'd let herself relax for a few minutes before reflecting on thoughts that had emerged during her time here.

Why had the Fates and their assassins never risen up against those conducting the move against the Fae? They were powerful. They had influence from the Gods. They were meant to intervene when there were atrocities afoot and deliver justice… right?

Why had they allowed things to escalate as they had?

Now, as she moved down the stone hallway, her boots clapping the grimy floor, her curiosity boiled anew. She needed answers, and who better than the Fates themselves?

The door to their chambers was closed, and as she drew near, another set of footfalls met her ears.

"You cannot enter," growled Tora, cutting her off, arms crossing over her chest.

Sybell rebounded, throwing the Fury a glare. "Tora, now is not the time to test my patience. Let me through."

Tora lifted a brow. "You want an audience with the Fates?"

"Yes."

"Earn it."

Sybell bit her tongue. "Gods damn it, why are all Fae so infuriating?!"

There was amusement in the female's icy eyes.

"I only want to speak to them for a few minutes. Please, Tora."

The warrior was silent, eyes assessing Sybell's casual garb, noting she was unarmed. After a breath, Tora's arms fell to her sides. "You pose no threat, I suppose. Fine, but I will accompany you."

Sybell swallowed the insult in the Fury's words, for now.

But she'd use them to stoke the fires of her rage during training later on.

Together, they entered the Fate's chambers.

"We should not have allowed her to leave. She was too great a risk, not sound of mind to be left to follow orders!" said Lakhesis, silver hair fanning around her shoulders as she spun. She pointed a finger at her dark-haired sister, as the other, Etropos, watched on. "You hoped that she would find the Prince, save him from Valdis' clutches, and bring him here to be trained, in turn relieving you of your mistakes. But you didn't account for the fact that Ghila Herington is perhaps the least loyal of our entire cohort here!"

Lantern light flickered over half of Klotho's face, casting her severe scowl in half shadow. "I have apologised, more than enough times, for my lapse in judgement."

What had Klotho done?

Sybell stayed still, the hairs at the nape of her neck rising up as an invisible breeze blew down her back, sending a shudder down her spine. The Three Fates shifted their attention to her while continuing their argument, as if her presence meant naught.

"I know that you spent more time with the Wraith than any of us, and perhaps you saw part of yourself in her." Lakhesis' voice eased a fraction, her arms crossing over her chest – the action almost a self-embrace rather than antagonism. "She should have returned by now, which leads me to believe she has failed. She may possess Mind Wielding magic, but that means nothing if she cannot control herself."

So, they'd sent an unhinged Fury assassin to retrieve Elijah. Hadn't they learned that such a tactic didn't work after Ariiaya's failed mission?

"The Gods are unhappy with us," said Etropos with a waver, her head tilted up to the looming tapestry.

Sybell took in the Tapestry of Life, with its woven stories and its tainted edges. It was incredibly impressive, its presence looming over them, its magic humming from deep within, but even Sybell could tell that the thing was sickly. Parts of its surface were glowing and golden, the fabric unlike anything she'd ever seen. The bottom was oily black, like it had been dipped into a pool of tar, spider webs of taint crawling up towards the beautiful, subtly moving images woven into its face. There were scenes of war, clashing weapons and inked blood on a canvas of darkness, but there were dragons flying, people dancing, and forests teeming with life, too. The images were mingled, not separated like she'd imagined them to be. This world, with its chaos and strife, had beauty in it too. Beauty in its wildness, beauty in its secrets. That was what the Tapestry showed, the good and the bad of the world they lived in.

It dawned on Sybell then that there couldn't be light without darkness. There couldn't be grace without inelegance to compare it to.

There couldn't be life without death.

"It's not too late."

Klotho, with her closed-off expression and steel-straight spine, could not hide the look in her eyes at Sybell's words.

Regret.

Sybell again wondered at what she'd done.

Sybell could feel Tora shift beside her, the almost warmth of the Fury's hand at her elbow in warning, but she continued to step forward. "It's not too late to fight for forgiveness."

Klotho's throat worked on a swallow, the only indication that Sybell's words had hit home. Etropos moved to the dark-haired Fate's side, close enough to touch shoulders, and Lakhesis shifted closer too, before casting golden eyes over Sybell. Though Klotho had done something significant to result in the taint on the Tapestry, and the favour of the Gods diminishing, the sisters – despite their Goddess status and belief in suppressing emotion – obviously cared for one another.

And they'd been given this job because they cared for this land on some level. The Gods would not have chosen them otherwise.

She didn't need to know what the Fate had done. The past was the past. What mattered now was the future, and which side the sisters decided to settle on. She prayed to the silent Gods that that side would be theirs.

"War looms, and Sybell Kruel is correct. It is time that we chose a side. Fate is not neutral. It is persuasive, and judges those on their intentions and actions." Lakhesis faced her sisters. "It is time that we chose a side."

Something zinged down Sybell's spine, her lips smiling wide, as Tora let loose a breath beside her.

Klotho remained silent, turning towards the Tapestry once more. Then she said, "That is for fate to decide…"

CHAPTER FIVE

ELIJAH

How long had they been on the move? Days? Hours? Weeks? Elijah no longer had a feeling of time. That had vanished after being forced to view horrific memory after horrific memory until his eyes were sore and his body ached.

While his body hurt, his mind seemed strangely sluggish, as if it, too, was too tired to think.

Elijah felt as if his mouth had been stuffed with cotton wool, the very pores of his skin so hypersensitive that a mere brush of his clothing had him shivering, tense and exhausted.

He pulled his head from the pool of the mirror, gasping and spluttering.

"Enough, Ghila, please."

Ghila's top lip curled as she wrenched him back by his shirt collar, gazing down upon him as if he were an annoying, wriggling worm. "Begging is unbecoming of you, brother."

He bared his teeth. "And torture is unbecoming of you."

Ghila's face twisted with delight. "Oh, but it is now, dear brother. I've had years to plan out how I'd exact my vengeance. Years to figure out how to repay you for abandoning me. To repay you *all*."

His thoughts were a scattering of chaos and grief, and the only way to fight against the mental assault was to grab hold of his focus and latch upon simple words and moments that dredged forth memories from the misty archives of his mind. Gods, he needed water. He needed to wash the taste of bile from his mouth. Elijah darted his tongue across his chapped lips, but the motion only resulted in tasting the copper of his own blood. He'd bitten his lip at some point, between the visions of what he had done.

The blood he'd spilled.

Fae blood.

Ghila's words scraped at the hollow of his insides. No matter how many times he'd tried to reason with her, or how many times he'd tried to explain that he hadn't regained his memories until recently, Ghila would not listen.

Elijah swallowed air, for there was no moisture left in his mouth to draw upon.

The mirror warped, smoothing into a moving image of a worn path brimmed by thick forest. They were on the move again, it seemed. A thatch of yellow flowers hanging like bells across their path, sparked a memory. He grabbed hold of it, desperate to relive something not drenched with blood. The scene in the mirror changed to another memory.

"Do you remember the time when you fell and skinned your knee, tearing the fabric of that beautiful yellow dress mother had made specifically for the Equinox Ball?" Elijah asked, staring at the mirror, willing the chosen memory to stick.

Ghila froze beside him.

In the mirror a little girl appeared, her fingers clutching his own as he helped her regain her footing after a fall. It was late afternoon, and he remembered the sky had been blotted with clouds, all drenched in purple, orange and gold as the sun fell. His little sister had been so excited, prattling on about the Equinox Ball for weeks prior, so much so that Eliverus and Brohem groaned whenever she mentioned it.

"It is the only celebration where father allows the traveling circus to be held on castle grounds! You all think those humans are strange, but I love them! They're so colourful – with their little painted carts and rainbow clothes. And their music is just so… cheery. They have naught a care for what people think, all they care about is providing entertainment!"

Instead of a dress of mismatched colours and fabrics – like Ghila begged and begged for – she'd been placed in one of canary yellow. Elijah had thought she'd be happy with the dress, it was her favourite colour after all, and the girl had seemed relatively content if not a touch disappointed as they headed from the tailor, back to the golden castle. Elijah and Brohem had been beside her, grumbling as she prattled on and on about the circus folk, distracted from the skips of her feet. Then, Ghila had taken a tumble on the gravel road, leaving her new dress soiled and torn. He remembered her bottom lip jutting and tremoring, the rapidly pooling tears in her eyes, and his rotten feeling of shame because he had been so sick of her prattling that he hadn't held her hand as he usually did when they traced this particular rough route back to the castle.

Silent tears had streaked her little rounded cheeks as their older brother moved to face her, his own expression mirroring what Elijah felt in that moment. The three didn't need words, as Brohem clutched the girl to his chest, carrying her back to the tailor, while Elijah held her hand. Brohem had become so serious then that Elijah had seen a hint of their stoic father in him, as he instructed the tailor to fix his sister's dress.

"We haven't the same shade of yellow," the tailor had said, an aging woman with silver streaks in her tree bark hair. She offered alternatives as Ghila sniffled.

"Then improvise, no other dress will do," said Elijah, his little face stern.

That night, as the castle halls opened and courtiers flooded the grounds for the Equinox Ball, little Princess Ghila climbed onto the royal dais in a dress of mismatched colours, the bodice remaining her favourite shade of yellow, the skirts a flurry of light blue, orange, green and purple, almost akin to the jovial guests dancing near their carts in the castle grounds. Her face had been lit in the brightest smile Elijah had ever seen, and he and Brohem couldn't help but feel her happiness. Gods, his mother had been upset, briefly, but thankfully the tailor had only suffered a mild rebuke.

Ghila had always spoken of that night as being the best of her life.

Now, as he watched her within the prison of his own mind, he could see a spark behind the grey storm clouds of her eyes. A spark of memory, or recognition.

He grasped it.

"Brohem and I would have become the biggest thorns in that tailor's side for even a tiny chance of bringing back your happiness. I may only have a small fraction of my memories from then, but I know that I love you, Ghila, and that has not and *will* not change. I love you and I am sorry."

She remained silent, inching away from him as if his words caused her pain.

"Tell me what happened to you," he dared to ask, watching her face carefully.

Ghila flinched again, scooting back, putting an arm's length between them as her hand rose to grasp the amulet at her throat. She spun back to face him as she mumbled under her breath, her words incoherent.

He took a chance and placed a hand upon her shoulder.

Ghila flinched under his touch, recoiling.

The mirror suddenly morphed, and he glimpsed a flash of an image. A memory, one that was not his own.

The crack of a whip. A back hand slamming against a pale cheek. Black hair caked with what he could only guess was blood and soil. A dank, wooden cell. Ghila's high-pitched wailing, her young voice pleading for mercy. Large hands gripping her arms, fingers like claws. A filthy, marred teddy bear resting in a pool of dank water. Or was it blood?

Then there was a voice, low, gravelly, horrible, and *familiar*. It dripped with cruelty, and bile rose to Elijah's stomach as the stranger uttered one sentence.

'Little baby crow, how far from the nest you have flown.'

Elijah's eyes snapped back from the mirror in time to see Ghila's face of fury as she lunged for him. He was not fast enough to avoid her, his movements sluggish from exhaustion, but he brought up his hands just as they collided, grabbing the leathers of her jerkin as she twisted her fingers in his tunic. They spun, his back slamming against the edge of the mirror, making it rattle. Such force would have normally made the thing topple, but in this reality, it held firm as if glued to the spot, the glass within shuddering from the impact.

His sister's face was inches away, teeth bared, eyes so wide that he could see the intricate red blood vessels webbing across the white. "Let us make one thing especially clear to you, brother. You will not touch us. You will not touch us *ever*."

Her nails clawed through the fabric of his tunic, almost tearing at his skin. What he had seen in the mirror had been a tiny glimpse into the horror his sister had been put through, and he had seen it from just one tiny unguarded touch.

The amulet around her neck came free, swinging between them. He chanced a glance at it, seeing a metal serpent curled in a figure eight. He felt a strange sort of power radiate from it, a power that drew his attention no matter how hard he tried to look away. Was it aiding in her restlessness?

Beside his head, the mirror wavered.

"Us? Who are you speaking about, Ghila?" He spoke gently, steadfast in his compassionate approach. "Who is haunting you?"

But he could quickly see he was losing her. Haze drifted over her deep grey eyes, and her features morphed to serene once more. He tried to grab at the amulet, but Ghila was *fast*. She shoved him towards the mirror again, forcing him to watch, but not before he saw the flash of panic cross her face at his attempt to grab the necklace.

It wasn't much, but it was something.

"No!" he shouted, but it did nothing. She forced his face into the mirror.

Remnants of Ghila's memories shuddered around him as he was thrust into another nightmare, the voice of her ghost whispering words through his ears as he fell.

'Little baby crow, how far from the nest you have flown.'

ARIIAYA

Sapphine? Well, either there was a place forgotten from all the maps in Fythnar, or Noct was getting his world lines crossed. Arii had never heard of a place called Sapphine, and before she could demand more of him, he grasped her sleeve and tugged her from the library. He gave her ten minutes to get dressed and pack for travel, telling her to pack light. So, she donned dark brown breeches and a charcoal-coloured tunic, strapping her daggers to the belt and leaving her hair unbound around her shoulders.

Was she ready to fully put her trust in this otherworldly stranger? Was she ready to move forward without Elijah?

She didn't see any other option at this point and wasn't sure whether Kadec knew about this little excursion, or perhaps it was on the sly. She was ready for a fight, honestly, if it came to it – alliances be damned. If finding this Ouroboros meant a huge surge of hope in the war, then she had to take it. Maybe once they found it, it could also allow them to find and liberate Elijah from Ghila's hold.

Elijah.

Gods, she hoped he was alright. Well, as alright as one could be when their body wasn't their own. Her entire being burned from his absence, and she felt all consuming anger at herself for how she had treated him in the days leading up to him being taken. She should never have pushed him away. It was her fault that he hadn't felt confident to come to her with his decision to meet with Lorch. She had been a brat.

Arii met her friends in the meeting chamber, a sliver of afternoon light sheering through the partly closed drapes.

One thing she was glad for was how quickly her companions prepared for a mission.

And how quickly they forgave her.

Krepth eyed Noct warily from where he perched on a councilman's chair, voicing the question shivering on the air. "You have a plan?"

"I always have a plan," retorted the man, a slow grin spreading his face. Emerson and Luc moved from the couches nearby, joining them as they all gathered in the centre of the room.

The Shifter stood. "Well, it better be a swift one, and involve some of your epic ancient magic, because I overheard Kadec speaking about moving his forces to the mainland in two days' time. He received word from the south and east courts, they want to start moving against Valdis before he can amass any more to his army."

Nem perched on the heavy oak war table, silver hair kissing her shoulders as she tilted her head. "Kadec will be meeting with his councilmen in three hours, after inspecting the battalions you have been working with, Arii."

Three hours.

Nocturne straightened the lapels of his suit before cracking his knuckles. "No time to lose then."

He lifted a hand, fingers flourishing in a complicated sign. The shift in the room was swift, the air becoming heavy – damp almost – and at the snap of his fingers a crackling void widened from nothingness, ringed with a dance of crackling sparks.

"Wait, where are we going?" mewed Emerson, his face and everyone else's washed in sudden blue light.

Arii blinked, then blinked again, trying to make sense of the scene in the portal before them.

Fish darted across the void, dark mountains curling like monoliths encasing the yawning mouth of a rippling cave. Trees… no, not trees, towering underwater plants wavered in the murky, filtered light from high above.

What they looked upon was the very dark entrance to a cave at the bottom of The Sapphire Depths. Completely and utterly under water, and completely and utterly unbreathable in their case.

One of the fish broke from its school, pausing to blink at them with beady eyes and shimmering scales.

All of them but Noct blinked back, mouths opening and closing in confused awe.

Noct's laugh broke the silence, "You should see your faces!"

"But that's under water," said Luc. "Unless you are part fish, Noct, we can't breathe under water."

Noct turned to them all, the portal framing his dashing form. He brought forth the little notebook that Arii had seen in the library, thumbing through the pages. "Here comes the next part of my plan. I will warn you all, this may be uncomfortable for a moment, but I promise the discomfort won't last."

Nodding to himself, he stashed the notebook away, before slapping his hands together and pulling them apart. Between his palms sparked magic, rippling blue like the underwater scene behind him. He then thrust his palms out, and threads of magic swirled around them.

The effect was instant.

Something tickled at Arii's throat, like the beginning of a cold, before it became far worse. Pain laced either side of her throat and she gasped, vaguely registering her friends in the same state of distress as she flipped her unbound hair over her shoulder and clawed at her neck. Lacerations formed under her fingertips, rising and parting her skin under the blade of an invisible knife. As soon as the pain began, it quickly subsided, ebbing to a dull ache as all eyes fixed upon the man with a half-moon grin. Noct rolled his head to one side, revealing the same three puckered lines on his own throat.

"What the fuck," gasped Tikkani.

"Gills. Not the most comfortable of spells, I do admit, but now our visit to Sapphine will be far easier."

"We are going to Sapphine? Wait a moment!" growled Krepth, fingers gingerly prodding his own throat. "No one said we were going to the home of the water nymphs."

Dread pooled, weighing like a stone in Arii's stomach.

Noct's expression didn't change - if anything he looked almost smug. "You will be safe; you have my word. If we want to gather more about finding the Ouroboros and saving Elijah – and the land, for that matter – then we must make nice with the women of the deep. We must be quick, though. The spell only lasts three hours, to when

Kadec will hold his meeting. If the Gods are good, and the nymphs are in a better mood than the last time I spoke with them, then we should be back in a fraction of that time, far before we drown – or worse, become a siren's dinner."

Arii didn't like the sound of that. From what she sensed from her friends, they too had no confidence in this quest. They had nothing else to go on, though, no other leads. This was all they had.

Arii turned to them, swallowing audibly before croaking, "None of you have to go, none of you needs to risk your lives for a lead. You can stay here if you choose–"

"We're coming, Arii," interrupted Tikkani, her eyes mirroring the same courage of the people around her. Even Nem had a stern look of determination on her pallid face.

She swore she saw a little hesitation on Emerson's face, but it quickly faded when his fiancé, Luc, grasped his fingers.

With a deep inhale, Arii turned back to Nocturne, and he smiled once more.

"I do love an adventure," he said. "Let's go."

She felt weightless, limbs cutting through the water as they swam through the maw of the cave and into an almost pitch-black tunnel, naught but a little orb of light conjured by Noct leading their way. Breathing underwater was the most bizarre feeling Arii had ever experienced. It was like taking a long, steady drink at first, until the water took over, filling her lungs with a strange heaviness that yanked a moment of panic from within her chest. As quickly as it began, the feeling eased, and she was breathing – long, heavy liquid breaths that chased bursts of bubbles from her lips.

The others had panicked, too, especially Emerson, but the boy had Luc by his side, their hands entwined tight, gazes locked as the spell took hold. Arii's chest tightened at the love... the steadfast confidence in their eyes, clinging on like anchors. Her thoughts drifted to Elijah, the murky seaweed of her anxiety placing a dark shadow over her mood.

Nocturne fronted their floating group, his dark suit fluttering around his lean form as he moved through the water as if he were made from it. He glanced over his shoulder occasionally, ensuring everyone was keeping up, the little orb of light swivelling with his line of sight.

Arii was grateful that she did not suffer from anything like a fear of dark, tight spaces. The tunnel stretched for ages, the tiny pinprick of light at the end slowly growing larger, closer, as they swam on. A gurgled squeal caught her attention, and she saw the silhouette of Tikkani's flailing arms being tamed by Nem and Quinn. "I… I touched som' seeweeeed, ewww," gurgled the elf, speaking as well as anyone would expect while deep underwater. Filtered blue light dashed across a tiny, amused quirk of Nem's lips as they drifted on.

Soon the light became heavier as they neared the gaping maw of the cave, opening to a cavernous space of shivering blue and green. If they had breath, it would have been stolen by what was slowly revealed to them. The remnants of an ancient underwater civilization, veiled by the passage of time now stood as a haunting testament to a forgotten era. Sunlight filtered through the translucent waves far above, casting a mesmerizing glow upon a colossal laneway of ethereal ruins.

They swam down the laneway between towering buildings with elegant archways of white sculpted stone which perhaps once teemed with life and grandeur. Cloaked now in a tapestry of vibrant corals and iridescent shells, the city street shivered between abandoned homes with broken doors and jagged windows. Fish darted in and out, quickly retreating as the group passed. Ahead, Arii spied steps leading up to a cathedral spire, flanked by two towers, adorned with ornate carvings and crumbling statues, stretching upward like skeletal fingers yearning to touch the surface above.

Arii's hair stood on end, the only warning she had before a sudden whoosh of an invisible force hit her from the side like a blast of wind. She spun, hand shooting to the weapons at her hips, but froze as a cold blade tip pressed upon her jugular.

Her eyes followed the weapon to its wielder, a willowy woman with pearlescent white skin that shimmered with the hint of fish scales. Her black hair fanned her face like gossamer, her fins fluttering around her like wings. Her waist tapered down into a double-edged fin, batting against the breath of a current caused by the flurry of commotion. When their gazes met, the woman's jaws opened wide in a smile not unlike a shark's, all jagged teeth as she screeched in Arii's face.

Noct threw up his hands, pivoting gracefully as dark shadows conjugated around them like ghosts.

"Ladies, ladies, it's only me. Place down your weapons, we are here to talk." His voice reverberated around them, bouncing off the empty city ruins.

No… not empty.

Without moving a muscle, Arii glimpsed beady eyes peeking from within a shattered window overgrown with coral. Others began to emerge, all female, young and old, featuring the same smatterings of scales on their willowy, finned bodies that reminded Arii of schools of fish. Curious, staring schools of fish with eyes narrowed in suspicion.

"What would the people of the deep have to say to land dwellers?" said a nymph, drifting from above.

More bodies surrounded them, moving like ghosts in the deep, all holding spears and dressed in barely a whisper of cloth. Flashbacks speared Arii's mind, of the ferocity of these women when the Gods had gifted them legs, on the night of the full moon in Viridya.

They had been fast then. Now they were in their territory, and Arii was quickly losing confidence. This had been a ridiculous idea. These creatures, they cared nothing for the qualms of the above world, why would they help them?

"The last time I visited, your gracious queen was most accommodating," began Noct.

The nymph glared, jagged teeth hinted at behind full lips. "Since then, we have had to tighten the security around our fortress. The taint from above is seeping in, and too many of our own have been plucked from the waters to be experimented on. You cannot enter Sapphine at this time, Nocturne Tempest, nor will we allow any of your ragtag party."

Quinn snorted a bubble nearby, quickly inhaling it back at the jab of a spear tip.

But Noct was not giving up easily. "If you would just allow us five minutes, Lophia—"

The woman prodded her spear deeper into Noct's chest.

"None shall enter," she repeated, the tone of her voice dropping with finality.

Noct's mouth opened again but Arii drew a watery breath first. "We are here on behalf of Prince Eliverus Herington, rightful heir to the northern throne."

Everyone tensed, the guards all swivelling heads in her direction. Under their black eyes and snarls of barbed teeth, she steeled her spine and lifted her chin. The spear tip resting there pressed forward in warning, but she barrelled on, ignoring the bright red blood tinging the water before her. These women were not playing around, breaking skin, but Arii had to test every option.

She spied Noct's small smirk as she said, "Queen Vexia Silverfin of the Deep owes us a favour."

After that declaration, the water guard had been swift albeit reluctant to lower their weapons and escort them into the underwater castle. As soon as they passed the threshold, their feet suctioned to the floor, causing everyone to gasp. Except Noct of course, who remained annoyingly unruffled by the fact they could all be floating into an early, watery grave.

The magnificent structure was unlike anything Arii had ever seen. Under filtered light cast from an array of tall windows as they drift-walked down a high-ceilinged corridor, the place was eerily beautiful. Coral grew en masse from the floor in pinks, blues and greens, emitting a faint glow which created wavering patterns upon the cracked glass floors. Fish darted around them, rainbow hues trailing little bubbles in their wake as they danced around barnacle-rich chandeliers overhead.

Old oak doors laced with rot and flaking filigree stood open like eery, welcoming arms, and beyond lay a sprawling throne room lit with ethereal light.

As they moved into the space, Arii heard Tikkani's awed gasp behind her. Nestled within a cavernous chamber, illuminated by bioluminescent flora, stood a coral throne. It towered high on jagged steps of stone, its structure seemingly forged from skilled hands and aided by nature. Adorned with delicate tendrils of vibrant coral, the throne exuded an otherworldly beauty, colours rivalling a thousand tropical sunsets. The seat itself, fashioned from polished shells, shimmered with an alluring iridescence that seemed to shift and change as if capturing the very essence of the ever-moving sea.

Embedded within the throne were rare and precious gems, sparkling facets winking in the muted light. The throne's armrests, sinuous and curling like gentle waves, were embellished with intricate seashell carvings, each one telling a forgotten tale of the castle's former glory. Within the coral tendrils that adorned the throne were barely hidden barbs, sharp as the fangs of sea serpents, poised to pierce the flesh of the unworthy.

And perched upon it all was Queen Vexia Silverfin.

Her chin was lifted high, long silver hair floating around her shoulders like eels as her black, depthless eyes watched them halt before her. She wore a dress the colour of murky water, and a crown of coral rested on her forehead, the colour of leached bones. Like the last time they met while escaping Viridya, the Queen's expression held barely a flick of emotion, but Arii could tell that the Nymph was scanning the faces of each of their party.

Searching.

"The Prince, he is not with you," she said, her voice a steady tenor, yet embedded with an unmistakable question.

The guards drifted, floating sentries at every point of the room. Arii dipped into the best bow she could manage, the cloth and leathers of her outfit hovering awkwardly around her. The others followed her lead.

"He is why we have come." Arii straightened, pinning the Queen with her violet stare. "He has been taken by the enemy. We need your help."

The corner of Vexia's lips curled up. "And why would we be of any help to you?"

Glancing back at Noct, Arii gestured to bring him to her side. Vexia's eyes seemed to lighten, the change ever so slight, but Arii saw it. "Ah, Tempest! You have returned!"

"As I promised I would," he said, folding an arm over his abdomen, bowing theatrically again. "What can I say, you can't keep me away from your ethereal home of liquid beauty, nor the fair and alluring people who live here."

Quinn made a sound, clearly not agreeing with Noct's words as one of the guards showed him their teeth.

The Queen shifted on her throne, the very slightest shimmy of her hips, and Arii noticed *that* too. Vexia grinned wide then, her demeanour changing entirely with the presence of the otherworldly stranger. Pushing herself from the chair, she drifted upon gossamer wings to join them.

"Ariiaya Trillia, I had thought you dead by now. But I must say that I am pleasantly surprised that you are not." Arii bristled, eying the Nymph Queen's profile as she continued. "Eliverus, tell me what happened to him."

Arii quickly explained the events of Elijah's capture, who they suspected was behind it and where they could be now. The Queen drifted among them as she spoke, pausing before Quinn and pinching a lock of the young man's hair between long, almost claw tipped fingers. Quinn held still, his spine rigid, earning him a light chuckle from the siren. They all didn't miss the way she eyed him like a delicious morsel brought to her as a potential snack, and Tikkani subtly laced her fingers with Quinn's as the Queen moved her attention elsewhere.

Despite the beauty of the room, there was still a sense of forgottenness to the place, the eerie quiet of a secret realm. As her powerful fin propelled her from one of Arii's friends to the other, she swore the Nymph's ribs were more prominent than last she saw her, her cheekbones a little more jagged, eyes deeper set. There was a haggard hungriness to those eyes that remained, one Arii had spied in the people outside, too. A restless energy simmered beneath all of their scales, one that Arii knew came with the full moon, yet the Queen remained here instead of heading to the surface. That thought brought back flashes of the night they had battled under moonlight, weapons coated in sea salt and blood.

The night she'd witnessed Elijah's battle prowess.

She recalled Elijah's hooded form cutting down Nymphs in defence of his home, the deadly grace that had stolen her breath and warmed her to her core.

He had spared the Queen that night, and Arii remembered her words the last time they'd met.

"'A life for a life, partly paid.'"

Vexia swivelled to her, eyes narrowed at the words spoken.

"You owe us a debt–" Arii began.

"I owe *him* a debt, little Fae, not you." Suddenly the Queen was in her face, jagged teeth bared from behind bloodless lips. The guards shifted on gentle currents around them, waiting. "You thirsted for blood, *my* blood, and had it not been for the promised King, you would have bathed in it like you did my sisters'."

Arii glared back, letting her own incisors show, a shiver of adrenaline coursing through her veins. She hadn't been the only one to kill that night, but perhaps the Queen was choosing to forget that. "Yet here you stand," she paused, then amended, "or rather… hover. You live because of us."

"Because of *him*. My debt is owed to Eliverus Herington."

Arii swallowed back her frustration. "Our need is dire. You said for us to find you here." She hadn't understood then, but she did now. "We need your help in the war to come."

"Your little spats above water are no concern of ours."

Arii's frustration spilled over then. "But it will concern you when there is no one left above to conquer, and then who is to say they won't invade you down here, too. He has already kidnapped and experimented on your sisters!"

Vexia was silent, surveying Arii's face with dark eyes. At that silence, Arii surged on. "I'm pretty sure that the undead don't need to breathe, so when all is turned to ruin above, Valdis will continue to let those abominations spread, and I don't think he will limit himself to just the surface. They'll plunge us all into ruin, and then who will feed you every full moon?" The fact was morbid, but true. The people here relied on what they could gather from the surface – blood, food – and they couldn't have those things when everyone above was dead.

Bubbles trailed the silence around them like awkward, dancing fish. Vexia's eyes never broke from Arii's, and she knew better than to be first to look away in this silent battle of wills.

Finally, the Queen said, "What will you have us do, then?"

Effervescence trailed Arii's breath. It seemed she had gotten through. But yes, what would they have them do? She hadn't quite thought that far ahead, focusing on breaching the ice wall that was the underwater Queen. Arii glanced sideways at Noct, and he nodded, drifting forward.

"My dear Queen, you are simply radiant when you're angry," at his words, the Queen broke away, drifting over to him and laying a hand upon his chest. Noct's face didn't betray anything, he simply smiled, and the Queen smiled back. Arii swore she saw the woman's cheeks flush with a coral hue.

Noct continued, tone breezy, almost flirtatious. "The last time I visited you, I mentioned the Ouroboros. Do you remember?"

She smiled, pressing closer. "Of course."

"You know a way into the Dragons Teeth Mountains, one that bypasses Bonemire, one that takes us directly into the heart," said Noct. "If you guide us there, I swear to you that when we obtain the Ouroboros and have used it to save the land, we will bring it to you."

Vexia considered his words with a purse of her lips and a shine in her eyes. "You will release it to me?"

Noct nodded, and Arii felt trepidation in her stomach when he replied, "Yes."

She had no idea what kind of power this Ouroboros possessed, let alone how terrible it would be in the hands of the underwater kingdom. Could it allow them to stay above water indefinitely? Noct knew more about it than the rest of them put together, and if he was prepared to hand it over, it was possible that it was something that, once used, would be made worthless. Looking at this place, it was clear that they were suffering, and desperate.

Desperate enough to cling to the hope of something they didn't understand.

Just like Arii.

"Very well, you may leave and we will guide you on your return. But, should you break your promise, you'll have more to worry about than the mayhem above the surface."

Unease chased Arii as they left, as the group swam back through the empty city street. She propelled herself to Nocturne's side, casting a quizzical look at him. "Are we truly going to surrender the Ouroboros to her?"

Noct's bicoloured eyes swept over to her, his smile easy. "Trust me, little Fae."

That was all he gave her.

Well, she supposed she had no other choice.

"Are we not going into the mountains now?" chimed Emerson from behind, sounding a mixture of curiosity and nervousness.

"We need to prepare first," answered Krepth, his cloak drifting behind him like a wolf's tail. "Kadec's meeting is about to begin and it's important we hear his plans and tell him of ours."

"Will he halt his descent into the North?" said Nem, silver hair rippling ethereally as she moved easily beside Krepth.

"That's the hope," responded Krepth, not looking at her. His eyes tracked everywhere but, and Arii again was sure that something had transpired between them.

Noct swiftly opened a new portal and with a final look at the murky city behind her, Arii swam through to air just as heavy as the deep salt water, mind whirling with questions without answers.

CHAPTER SIX

LORCH

He was surrounded by death. It shadowed him in places where he should have felt safe and steady, and yet as Lorch Kruel sat upon his golden throne, a morbid guard of twitching, soulless bodies flanking him, he felt like a gust of wind could take him from his seat. Memories plagued him, following him like wisps of shadows whenever his mind sought rest. He couldn't shake the sound of Elijah's grief as Lorch's soldiers beheaded his mother. Nor Arii's look of shock and pleading as she reached toward him, a reflex to the sound of the axe falling down.

Now, Lorch was back in Viridya, taking up court as he normally would at the beginning of a new week, hearing the woes of those granted his precious time. But bitterness warred with uncertainty in his heart. He had liked Colleen, hadn't a single qualm against her, so when his father had suggested – no, more like *ordered* – taking her as leverage, he had felt a stone forming in his guts. In the moments prior, Lorch had worked himself up to thinking that he was doing what was wrong, to ultimately make things right.

But things had escalated so quickly that upon reflection Lorch had to remind himself that what he had done was not some sort of horrible nightmare.

Lorch felt the stickiness of Colleen's blood on his hands as if he were the one to deliver the final blow.

He hadn't wanted to kill her; he had thought kidnapping her would have forced Elijah to return to them. But when he had refused, Lorch had done what he had thought would snap Elijah into quick surrender.

The thump of the old woman's head hitting the dirt had been playing on repeat in his mind ever since.

"There are tens of people who are dead, Your Highness, and that number is only increasing. They fall ill with terrible coughs and fire in their chests which they describe as being burned alive from the inside. Just yesterday alone we lost our town baker, then the blacksmith's daughter, all within the span of a few hours. It is ravaging the towns around the city, and I have no doubt it is within these walls now." The man speaking to him was a general, the vermillion of his cloak touching the marble floor. Sweat beaded his forehead, eyes glassy with the horrors he had seen.

This was not new to Lorch, he was aware of the blight racing across the land. But he found that with everything else, it had become a 'future Lorch's' problem'. When another of his councilmen spoke, Lorch felt his father tense beside him.

"People are saying there is a cure, one created a few weeks ago in Colkirk. While it is rumoured to be a cure, it has not had long enough to show its true effects. But everyone in the town claims that it has been positive in halting the sickness at least."

Light from the wall sconces flickered over the man's face, and Lorch saw hesitation there. He knew why, he could feel it in the shift of the room, a particular feeling that often preceded conversations of a banned nature. The councillor continued bravely. "However, this cure has been created with magic."

"Magic does nothing but create problems, Sir Cawsus," began Valdis.

"Please, sir, let us put aside our fear for just one moment and entertain this news," Sir Cawsus barrelled on, his voice containing a strength Lorch knew was forced. He could see the fear in the man's eyes as some of the nearby undead guards wavered, glowing eyes tracking him. "If it is untrue, then we can brush it aside and continue to support the healers who have begun vigorous testing into finding a cure."

Lorch leaned forward on his throne, resting his elbows on his knees, trying his best to remain looking mildly interested. His father drew breath first. "Leave the cure to the physicians and healers, Sir Cawsus."

It wasn't lost on Lorch how hypocritical his father was being, surrounded by the magic they all feared so much, in the form of swaying, decaying bodies.

"If the magic cure eventuates to more than just rumour, Sir Cawsus, then we will consider it further." Lorch added, standing.

His father glanced at him then, a look on his scarred face that clearly showed his acrimony, and perhaps something else that Lorch had no interest in deciphering. A headache was blooming behind his eyes and at the base of his skull, a feeling he was becoming all too familiar with.

"Very good," sighed Cawsus as the council mirrored their king and stood.

"Dismissed."

Later, as Lorch rummaged around the small study adjoining his rooms, his thoughts once again echoed with the screams of those alive and dead. The man he once was would have been able to push aside what was happening within these walls, dash it all behind a veil of silk and skin.

He glimpsed his reflection in the nearby gilded mirror, and quickly looked away. A heavy feeling of self-loathing pressed between his shoulder blades like boulders, his stomach a churning maelstrom that no poultice could cure.

He had to get air, find somewhere he could escape the death surrounding him, just for a time. It had been so long since he had visited the town, the hustle and bustle of the streets could be a welcome distraction from the haunting in his head. A bag, he had a bag somewhere, surely.

As he packed, Lorch tossed thoughts in his mind of how best to slip from the room undetected, drawing upon foggy memories of times he and Elijah would make it a game to get out of the castle without being seen. Lorch had been avoiding his royal responsibilities, laughing at Elijah's scowling protests, for he had never been one to break the rules. Despite this, the young warrior had remained discreet, without alerting the guards even though it would have been easy for him to do so. The memory rose above the fog, making his chest hurt. *"No harm done, Elijah, just a little bit of fun! Now, let's go and sample some of those flaky pastry pies – being so grumpy all the time must make you so very hungry." Lorch said, as his friend's scowl followed him down the busy streets of Viridya's market. Those pies had been so good, and in the end they had sat by the willow tree, gazing at the rippling surface of the pool as they spoke about their day around mouthfuls of stewed beef filling, laughing at the pastry crumbs on each other's faces.*

Now, Lorch's heart clenched at the memory, reminding him of why he had left such thoughts untouched. They were too painful to bear, dredging up doubt about all that he and his father were working towards.

All he needed was a bit of reprieve, away from guards with pity in their eyes – or nothing in their eyes at all.

A break, he simply needed a break.

Lorch donned a simple tunic and grey vest over black travel pants and swept a hand through his hair as the copper strands dangled over his eyes. Gods, he needed a haircut. The only positive about the crown was that it kept his pesky hair out of his face. That crown was now placed in a locked cabinet, its gilded surface reflecting him mockingly.

Lorch turned his back, stalking to his walk-in dresser and rifling through the hangers until he found the old, well-worn piece that his mother had told him to toss ages ago. There was memory within its stitches, and he was far too attached to it to just throw it away. The gold filigree and immaculate, expensive cloth of his other cloaks would make him stick out in the market crowd like a sore thumb.

Muscle memory didn't fail him, thank the Fates, allowing him to quickly follow the familiar path down from his second story window. When his feet found the soft lawn below, he felt a very unfamiliar zing of excitement skitter down his spine. The first time he had felt anything other than a daze in weeks… months, perhaps.

He pulled the cloak around his neck, suppressing a shiver at the unseasonably cool air, and made his way swiftly across the gardens and towards the gates.

The only resistance he met there was one lone guard, sitting on a stool with a scarf double-wrapped to his chin, legs stretched out.

"Business outside the castle?" the man drawled, not even bothering to make eye contact as he leafed through a ledger. Lorch didn't know whether he should be angered at the man's lack of interest in his duties, or thankful that this was going to be easier than he predicted. He had considered scaling the wall to avoid detection, but when he spied the lack of security at the gate, a part of him wanted to do a little test. Were his guards always this… lazy?

"Headin' to the market," Lorch replied, lowering his voice a pitch and tilting his head down – a mere servant. "Need to collect some eggs for–"

"Don't need your life story. On you go," said the guard, still not bothering to look at him.

Lorch bristled. *Well then.*

He hurried on, passing the outer courtyard to the mouth of the upper market. Bodies bustled, but he could feel tension in the air. On a normal day, the market would be teeming with people, stall holders hollering about their wares, people hauling bags and chattering around stalls of fresh produce. Today though, it was unusually quiet, far less people around.

"Cold, unseasonably cold," he heard a woman say, hunched over as she swept the worn steps of her little shop. "And this strange ice ain't letting up, either. What God do ye' think has been angered by those atrocities up in the palace, eh? Ain't been the same for twenty years, not since–"

A young man dropped a sack nearby, stretching out his back. "Nan, you could get arrested with that kind of talk, what have we told you?"

The old lady snorted, continuing to sweep, mumbling under her breath. Her eyes suddenly found Lorch's, and he realised he had been staring like a stunned deer. He ducked his head, forging on as the woman's words lingered. *Ain't been the same for twenty years...*

Someone thumped into his hip. Lorch let a remark slip as the little figure continued without apologising, but the words faded as he turned and saw who they were running to.

Someone familiar to him.

She looked different from when she visited the castle. Now she was draped in a moss green cloak, her hair free in wild brown curls around her beautiful face.

Celadine enveloped the hooded figure in her arms, a smile lighting her face.

Lorch realised then that he hadn't seen the apothecary smile before. It did something strange to his chest. She had been the one to bring him medicinal draughts, their interactions brief and fleeing but not uncomfortable. The sight of her brought a balm to his senses, confusing him. Perhaps it was because whenever she came to his quarters, it was with pain relief.

Or perhaps it was her unwavering look, the absence of sympathy in her eyes that he had noticed in all others recently. What he saw instead was resolve, almost like she was *willing* him to push through his pain.

Push through the invisible walls holding him caged.

Celadine placed her hand on the back of the cloaked figure as they made their way in the opposite direction. Interest piqued, Lorch followed at a distance, feeling odd about his choice to follow them, but they were a touch too far for him to call out now, and he preferred not to draw attention to his identity.

The town was a slither of its former glory, quieter than he had ever seen it. Where there was normally seemingly endless selections of fruits, vegetables and herbs, now sat near empty wooden trays and forlorn-looking stall holders. The canopies above them were stiff with a fine layer of the black ice. Afternoon light pinwheeled across the cobblestones, dappling the scraped piles of ice on either side of the street. He knew the black ice was affecting farmers' crops, but to see those effects with his own eyes had Lorch's stomach clenching.

Celadine and her companion slipped down a narrow alley, one which Lorch knew. Lorch glanced at the wrought iron plaque, unable to hide his smile. Mrs Mulvany's Tavern.

Celadine rapped on the thick tavern door, speaking in hushed tones to whomever stood behind. He caught the words "It's just beginning," in a male voice as the door opened. A doorman? A curious thing for this tavern.

A flash of green light had a sound of delight erupting from the small, hooded person accompanying Celadine, and the doorman laughed, turning to whatever was happening inside. Lorch used the distraction to slip in behind the apothecary and her companion, moving casually to a nearby empty table. He sat and took a breath, letting the familiar scents and sounds of the place wash over him.

The tavern, despite seeming small and quaint from outside, was large inside, with high ceilings draped with banners of gold. The bar stood in the middle of the space surrounded by a generous table and dark oak stools. Barrels of mead hung from the ceiling, fitted with golden taps to pour the establishment's famous mead. The mirrored wall at the back was lined with bottles of all different designs, sizes and colours, sure to be imported.

At the helm, filling a mug with frothy liquor, was Mrs Mulvany herself. Her cheeks were dotted with freckles and her purple hair swept back into a plaited nest atop her head. She was tall, and might have seemed imposing if not for her usual grin. She was the reason scuffles were a rarity here, because Lorch knew that if a patron acted up, she would simply grab them by the scruff and throw them into the alley.

His eyes slipped to the right as another flash of green light drew his attention. The stage normally housed a merry band with instruments but today there was just one young man, dressed in robes of mismatched fabrics.

A maid paused by Lorch's table, and he slid a copper coin across the top, eyes fixed on the man on the stage as he lifted his hands and waved them about. "One mead, please. Small mug will do." The maid nodded, snatching up the coin and trotting to the bar.

Suddenly, the man's hands began to glow, and Lorch felt a shiver of sweet dread.

Magic.

He kept quiet as the light sprang forth, coalescing into caricatures of magical green light. Some patrons sighed with delight, and Lorch now noticed children among them. Sparks flashed above their heads, morphing into figures of people as they danced in the air, shimmering in misty green and gold. The figures twirled to a silent song, and Lorch was reminded of the countless royal balls held at his own castle. The magician waved his hands, drawing excited chatter from the children at the front, faces upturned and bathed in green light.

This male was wielding magic, and that could only mean one thing. He was Fae.

Lorch knew he should leave and carry this news to his father, but something had him rooted to the stool.

"Our land was once a place of inclusion, a place where grand balls like this teemed with races from all over the continent. Humans, Elves, Shifters... and Fae," intoned the magic wielder.

Voices murmured and Lorch stole a quick glance around the room, his eyes finding Celadine in the dim light. She wore a tiny smile, the tip of a pointed ear peeking from the waves of her hair. Not for the first time was Lorch curious about her. He had assumed she was of Elven origin because he hadn't seen her use Fae magic or change form like a Shifter, but he didn't know much from what little interaction he had been allowed. The herbal concoctions she had brought him were standard enough – nothing the usual castle healers wouldn't provide – but he had had the wool pulled over his eyes before.

The people in the illusion danced then warped into something entirely different, and Lorch found himself gasping along with the other patrons as a creature emerged from the sparkles and mist, jaws snapping wide as it belched fire.

The man on the stage smiled, pointed canines glinting as he exclaimed, "And there were also dragons!"

The crowd clapped as the beast splayed its wings and flew about the room, leaving a trail of smoke and sparks in its wake.

"Magic was in abundance, as much a part of the land as the skies above our heads and the earth beneath our feet. There was so much power, so much possibility." The man paused, his eyes sweeping over his audience meaningfully. "But with such power came fear; fear of those possibilities by people who could not share in magic not gifted to them. The ruling Fae families seriously underestimated the humans they shared their homes with, becoming so complacent that they had no idea what was brewing beneath their noses. The humans were scared of the magic and rightfully so. Our history may be rich but it is also bloody."

Lorch's breath came in silent, short bursts as fear and anxiety rose within him. With a hard swallow, he pressed them down, watching the scene unfold despite his instincts waging war within him. This talk was dangerous… forbidden. The man standing upon the stage was a threat to everyone in this room, a threat to his kingdom. His father's voice entered his thoughts, stories of the unstableness of male Fae and their magic playing havoc with what he could see now, and what he had witnessed a short time ago when facing Elijah's outburst of grief.

He could still feel the fine mist of his soldiers' blood upon his hands as they gripped the reins. Could still feel the hot bite of bile as it rose in his throat. But what he was witnessing right now seemed harmless enough. Even he couldn't help a flicker of wonder at the image of the dragon dipping and diving, the majesty of its presence demanding the full attention of the room.

As swiftly as it had appeared, the dragon twisted back into figures dancing, moving through the air with vigour. The children had fallen silent, the air in the room turning tense.

No, the people weren't dancing… they were tangling in the sways of *war*. They swung swords and lifted shields, popping in and out of the scene as if moving just within the magician's view.

"We have been hunted, slaughtered, almost wiped from the very existence of this land. But we remain, we linger, and we wait." More murmuring from the crowd, tones of excitement rising in the warm, sweet air.

Lorch leaned forward in his seat.

This was a resistance. This was what his father was trying so hard to prevent.

This was what *he* should be trying to prevent.

His gaze trailed around the room. Without his Red Guards, he would be a fool to bring attention to himself right now. One glimpse of his copper hair and these Fae would know him instantly.

The barmaid returned with his glass of frothy golden mead, and a tickle of paranoia made him think she was lingering. When she spoke, he was tempted to ignore her over the rising noise. "Anything else? To eat perhaps?"

"No, thank you."

Seemingly satisfied, the maid moved away. He took a healthy sip of mead as the illusion of battle raged in green around them, the cheers and thumps of the crowd ringing like drums of war.

"But soon, we will rise up. We will take back what is ours… a home for *all* of us without fear."

The room erupted into cheers, but Lorch remained fixed to the spot by a mix of emotions – fear of discovery mostly. Despite this, his eyes caught Celadine as she and her companion stood and moved towards the back of the tavern.

Lorch threw back the remainder of his drink before standing and slipping behind the crowd as the magician continued to weave magic into the air, stories of hope and adventure that left the room sighing in his wake.

"Mum," came a small voice as Lorch paused at the doorway to the rentable rooms. He saw a small girl, brown hair wrangled into a braid, a few curls whipping around her face as she turned and clutched at

Celadine's hand. So, Celadine was a mother? Lorch supposed this shouldn't come as a surprise – he barely knew her, really. Now that he could see the girl, he saw their resemblance instantly. Wide evergreen eyes, freckled, sun-kissed face far more expressive than her mother's.

"Not all humans hate us," was Celadine's response to a question unheard by Lorch. It drew him up short as she continued. "Come now, let's collect our order of thimble grass from the cook and head home."

"But," the girl began, moving her hands expressively, then falling silent as her green eyes darted to him, connecting in the firelight. "Mumma," she breathed, a chill in that one word.

Lorch's spine went rigid as Celadine spun, face twisted in confusion, which quickly morphed between surprise and anger. "You."

He held up his palms. "Please, let me explain."

Celadine's lips parted, and his stomach dropped as she said, "Mia, alert Mrs Mulvany that we have been discovered by the King."

CELADINE

He was here. The King. The how and why of the situation was quickly wiped away by alarm, his presence sending her insides churning, panic rising above all else. Her daughter, Mia, began to slip out from behind her.

"Wait, please!" Lorch said, stepping forward.

She gripped Mia's arm to stop her, could feel the weight of her daughter's eyes as they skipped between them, confused.

Lorch suddenly flew forward, but he was human, and Cela was faster. She snatched his cloak with one hand and dragged him into an adjacent room. His sound of panic would have been almost comical if his very existence here didn't posed a grave danger to them all.

But something told her to allow him a chance to explain. If he had wanted them caught, the tavern would be overrun with palace guards right now.

So why hadn't he alerted anyone? Were they on their way here right now?

Lorch's ocean blue eyes were wide, copper hair dusting the rise of his brows as he yelped. "I mean no harm, not to you or your daughter, or any of the people out there!"

"Mumma," Mia repeated, closing the door silently beside them.

Celadine's nostrils flared, her teeth baring in a snarl. "You expect me to believe you?"

The King's hands grasped her wrists, fingers grazing her skin, and suddenly she was overcome. An image flashed before her eyes, one of her daughter kneeling before a fireplace, flickering light on her face. Her hands slowly moved, signing to a man kneeling in front of her. He mimicked her hands, trying his best to copy the language one used when robbed of hearing. Mia laughed, and he laughed too.

The man in the image was undoubtably the one staring at her right now.

"Mumma," whispered Mia again, her voice rising with an urgency that wrenched Cela from the scene. She chanced a look at her, quickly deciphering the flourish of her daughter's signing hands.

"It is too great a risk, Mia. This is the King," she ground out, thumping Lorch's back against the wall for emphasis, as he let out a grunt.

The girl's jaw slid forward in a look of stubbornness that instantly reminded her of herself. She launched into a tirade of complicated signs that were rough and incomplete, but Cela could easily read them. When agitated, Mia was more likely to sign than speak. Her hearing was taken two years ago, and though she could speak, signing her words had become far more natural to her. The guilt of the circumstances that had led to her daughter's stolen hearing tormented Cela with each passing day, but the mix of compassion and hardness in the depths of Mia's eyes was beyond her six years of age. It reminded her of just how far they'd come. What they fought for every day.

Look at him, mother.

She did, taking in the panic, the wide eyes and dishevelled hair. This was an in-between version of the King that she knew, albeit briefly. His skin had more colour than last she'd seen him, yet there was a listlessness in him that reminded her of an untethered boat drifting in unfamiliar seas.

He is just as afraid as we are, signed Mia, her eyes softening.

Cela sighed, long and hard. Her daughter had a good heart, one which sometimes led her without caution. She felt some of Lorch's tension shift as she released him from her hold.

"What are you doing here–" she stopped suddenly, remembering who she'd just been crushing against the wall. She cleared her throat and added, "Your Highness."

Lorch brushed at his cloak, a drab thing totally unbecoming of a king. Now that she was taking him in, his clothing was far more becoming of a peasant, and it led her to wonder if he had been intentionally following them. How long had he been watching them? How long had he known about their resistance, waiting for the moment to tell his father?

The look he gave her was a ghost of the ones she was often greeted with in the flicking firelight of his study. A man misplaced, a man who was losing himself.

"I needed to get out of the castle for a time. I thought the market would bring me comfort like it used to, and I saw you there," he paused, gazing down at Mia. "I wanted to call to you, but I have an overwhelming feeling that I'm not the most liked person in the North right now." He cleared his throat, then squatted to stick a hand out to her daughter. "Lorch Kruel, nice to meet you."

Mia grinned, taking his hand without hesitation, signing a 'hello' with one hand.

Lorch's expression was curious. "Your daughter… she is unable to hear?"

Mia nodded.

He did not offer apologies, as many would. He simply nodded, then stood and said, "And out there, they are all Fae?"

Cela chose her words carefully. "Mostly, but there are humans and elves too. All united in our cause."

"So, this is a resistance?"

The way he said it so casually had her hackles rising once more. "I should kill you. You are the very reason we hide, the very reason we fear, the very reason we all *bleed*."

He moved away then, spearing a hand through his hair in agitation, throwing his hood back. He stood in a ray of afternoon light, his breath clouding before him in the cold room.

"I know."

She hadn't expected that to be his response. Nor his next words.

"Perhaps you should kill me," he said.

Cela straightened, fists bunched at her sides, taken aback. "What?"

Her daughter's fingers found hers, calming her chaos.

"This has gone far beyond anything I could have imagined. My father, his… methods… they go against everything he has ever taught me." Lorch turned to them. "I am no longer in control."

Cela's eyes narrowed. "You were never in control." Her words were barbed, pricking even her own tongue with their ferocity. Mia squeezed her hand again.

"I know. I'm truly sorry."

She believed him. Lorch wasn't the cruel person his surname suggested. He was a boy thrust into a role that he had never understood, manipulated by people who thirsted for power while driven by fear.

Suddenly her hand was encased in his, the smoothness of his skin warm and firm against her calluses. She met his unblinking stare, noting the determination in his narrow jaw and drawn brows.

"I want to make this right, Celadine. Help me see. Help me understand. Help me be able to help you."

This was dangerous. She knew that. Was she willing to risk everything the resistance was working towards? She'd seen him enough times in her duty bringing his healing tinctures to observe the curve that he'd been riding lately. He'd begun so low that Cela was surprised he'd had enough energy to breathe – heartbreak seeping from every pore. Then had come anger, an acrid scent that oozed from his skin, and shone in his eyes. Shortly after he'd become forlorn, wary… his hurts not only in the headaches brought on by anxiousness and stress, but a different sort of pain.

Regret.

Cela's healer's observances had taught her much in her short employ by the castle. Lorch Kruel had been plagued by regret for a long time. His eagerness to repent wasn't very surprising.

Her attention slipped to her daughter, seeing her tiny nod at her unspoken question. Mia had become quite adept at reading lips, too. Sign language wasn't common knowledge in the realm.

The breath Cela took was sharp and loaded as she found Lorch's gaze once more, transfixed in the churning sea of their depths. There was a glimmer of something in his eyes that she had not seen before. It was a spark of an ember within the charred remains of a hearth. Life flickering from death.

"Return here tomorrow night," she said finally, allowing a slither of her anger to go, replacing it with a tiny thread of hesitant hope.

His response was instant, final.

"I'll be here."

CHAPTER SEVEN

GHILA

It all began with a voice, followed by a sentence that had haunted Ghila for the better part of twenty years.

"Little baby crow, how far from the nest you have flown."

Sometimes the memories would catch her unawares, something sparking a scene long buried in her mind. There was a scent on the air now, a sweet smell mixed with something off, like rotting apples. Elijah paced beside her, their footsteps monotonous as they passed a ramshackle farm, with the grunts and rustle of pigs in a nearby pen.

The aroma triggered a memory, and even though she kept moving, the memories took control without her permission. Ghila was used to carrying on as if nothing was wrong while memories flashed before her eyes. They were held scattered behind a wall of anguish after the night her family was murdered, but some slipped through the cracks. One in particular haunted her, night and day.

"Little baby crow, how far from the nest you have flown."

The man to utter the words, ones that repeated in her nightmares like a dark lament, had since been revealed as a man named Valdis – a long standing advisor whom she hadn't known as a child but had seen around the castle. He had been the first person to find her on the night of her family's murder. He gathered her up and promised her safety. She had believed him, for he had a way with words that promised truth while hiding lies.

But then Valdis Kruel handed her to the monsters, setting in motion a series of events that would change her forever.

Ghila began life as someone who smiled often and far earlier in her infancy than any babe nursed in the golden castle before. She wobbled down the halls with laughter, curious and joyous. She cackled at the birds in the garden, grinned a gummy smile at anyone who placed their face before her, and splashed with merriment at bath time. Her smile did not dull even as she grew taller, her chubby infant rolls smoothing to lean limbs. She viewed the world with wonder, particularly magnetised by art and animals.

But she loved her older brothers above all else. She idolised them, following them around like a starry-eyed pup, always wanting to be wherever they were, doing whatever they were doing.

All of that changed the night the castle was bathed in blood.

She'd been thrown into a rickety cart under orders for her to be taken to the School of Fate. But that had not happened right away.

Often this memory came to her, triggered primarily by smells of overripe fruit.

Ghila's gaze remained on their path as a memory surfaced.

A cart, its floor shuddering beneath her cheek, the sound of wheels clattering over gravel and stone. Her fingers curled against the harsh wood, their tips tingling with cold. Nearby were dirty wooden crates, filled with deliveries of apples and melons, the cause of the stench. The cart had been owned by a farmer, apprehended by the guards with the promise that it would be returned.

But the farmer would not be getting his cart back. The old thing would be her home for weeks.

Her home, and her prison.

It was debatable if her survival was due to the weaving of the Gods, or whether it would have been better if she had not fled the screams of people dying in the castle at all.

Perhaps she was destined to suffer far greater a fate than death.

The men commandeering the carriage were guards under her family employ, but these men were tainted by the dark influence of hate, and she would discover so over weeks of physical and emotional abuse. They were the first of their kind, men who had been raised and trained to hate the Fae, to *fear* them enough to want to hunt them and hand them over to their fate while masquerading as guards. Females would be handed over to the Assassins' school, where they would be honed into emotionless killing machines.

Males… well, male Fae with even a tiny spark of magic were killed for fear of their power, for it was thought to bring about madness, and in turn, death for all who were weak.

Humans.

She'd lain, shackled, smelling the rotten fruit and listening to the creaking of the cart in between pitstops along the road, and as the hours, days and weeks passed, Ghila feared she would never smile again. The screams of those she'd loved, the castle halls in disarray, the sound of metal severing flesh, haunted her dreams nightly. That was when she was even able to sleep. Every little sound, every pass of a shadow by the door of the cart had her anxious and afraid, unsure of what the men wanted with her, or where she was going. Her gentle mind began to conjure monsters from the shadows, things of smoke and breath, until she'd met the worst of them all.

"Such a pretty little bird, a prize that should be savoured."

Ghila Herington had not known true cruelty until she was placed in the presence of Tonix Wrath. The leader of a small band of tainted Red Guard soldiers.

"You are a scourge upon this world, Fae."

Ghila was young, having not long turned seven. She didn't understand this man's hate, nor did she understand how the actions of a few Fae towards humans in the last few centuries had sparked the beginning of an uprising. She would probably be dead had Valdis not promised Tonix another hefty sum of gold at the other end, upon her delivery.

But this did not specify that she had to be wholly intact upon arrival.

Normally it did not take long to travel along the winding road to the school upon the bluff, but Tonix and his crew prolonged the journey, keeping her in the cart with no windows, but she could see glimpses of the forest through uneven slats in the wall.

In the beginning, she'd fought. She'd battled as hard as her body – her mind – would allow, using the most powerful words and arguments she could muster in order to bargain her release. When the abuse began, it did not take long for her mind to fray, for she was naught but a child. They tied her to a post, a place where ropes normally held down cargo. Why they had needed to tie a child down, she would never know. She had fought, in the beginning, jerking against her bonds until her wrists chafed to bleeding, and bit at anyone who neared like the rabid animal they thought she was. It was unbecoming of a princess, but she'd become desperate, afraid, in pain.

"I am Princess Ghila Herington, and you will let me go–"

Crack. His hand connected with her face, breaking her nose, and with it, the last slithers of her pride. Tonix glared down on her as if she were a dog, one that needed to be put into submission. His face held a sneer, his eyes wide with savage glee.

"They will take you, mould you, make you a killer. A rat in a society of cats."

Crack.

"Sing for me, let me hear those sweet screams. Caw little bird, caw."

She hurt, she bled, she caved, until the abuse in his strikes, in his words, faded to a whisper like dust on the breeze. The princess lay, crumpled, body battered, mind pulverised beyond repair – bruises pocking her porcelain skin in blotches as dark as blueberries. When she could no longer feel her limbs, and she could hear the clomp of *his* boots approaching, she began to retreat to a place within herself that she'd only ever glimpsed a few times before. A sanctuary made of smoke, a place where she sought refuge whenever she was experiencing pain, a part of her consciousness that, honestly, scared her. Every day, she drew in a little deeper, let the smoke curl around one finger, then two, then three.

Until she no longer feared it.

Despite the pain and agony lacing through her bones, Ghila still *lived.*

When he was done, the sound of boots growing fainter was like music to her ears. She slid to the wooden floor while her body shook with raw, heaving sobs.

She reached for her smoke sanctuary, but one day, something else called to her.

It began as a distant whisper, a breath by her ear. Ghila moved her head, blinked, but nobody was there. She swallowed past the vomit but no words came. Pleading tipped her tongue, just as pain blackened her vision. With the last ounce of effort, she wrenched herself up, swaying, gasping a breath. A voice whispered then, one which emerged deep from within her own mind.

'We do not break.'

She cocked her head, listening, a whimper sliding from her lips. The voice... no, voices, for there were more, became the tiniest bit clearer. They were a crescendo of tones. Cries of pity, calls of anger, peals of laughter, and then one voice topped them all. One monotone yet fierce.

One deadly.

'They may throw you to the wolves so that they may feast.'

Slowly, Ghila's lips began to curve, blood staining her teeth.

'But it is the wolves who should fear the poison in the meat.'

Ghila smiled wildly, until that smile fell away, and something else stood in its place.

'Become the poison, little bird.'

After a time, the pain faded, and Ghila retreated fully into the smoky depths of her own mind, into a vision of beautiful chaos. As time yawned ahead, whispers echoed through the corridors of her mind, their ethereal voices reverberating with urgency and confusion, echoes of her own self, fragmented and entangled. She focussed on them until whatever insults to her body were but fading etchings on frosted glass.

The voices intertwined, harmonizing at times, only to dissolve into dissonance the next. Rationality and delusion danced together, inseparable in her mind. The voices usually came in threes if not more, flurrying around her like moths on wings of brittle dust. Sometimes they came in whispers, gentle, incoherent, and then sometimes they came in rolls of laughter, finding a joke where she had said nothing.

Then they came in screams.

Heart wrenching, gut rendering, mind shattering *screams*.

"Well, our destination is in view, and our little adventure is coming to an end." Tonix smiled, a sadist's smile. *"We will miss you, little bird. Enjoy your fate."*

Tonix continued his inflictions until two days before her handover – enough time for her Fae healing to cause her injuries to fade. With the voices' help, Ghila committed his face and each of his crew's to her memory and vowed to become a poison.

Her mind was fragmented yet intact enough to remember that vow.

She held on to it long after her transfer to the School of Fate.

A short time passed, and her difference became noticeable, so the Sisters had her looked over by a resident healer. They watched her for a while, saw how she interacted with the other students as it rapidly became clear that she was... damaged.

Over time, the healers came to understand that she was experiencing emotional turmoil and confusion, due to her family's murder, they assumed. During their observations, they noticed that Ghila was not overtaken with distinct personalities, but instead tormented by haunting whispers and traumatic memories, leaving her mind fragmented. Ghila did not tell them about her terror enroute to the school, but by this time, almost everyone who possessed pointed ears and magic knew of the blight of bigotry blooming across the North.

After a time, Ghila stopped trying to make sense of where or who the voices belonged to, or how they had found their way into the one place she had been able to retreat to when the pain of reality became too much to bear. So, the young Fae weaved her own reality, one where she wasn't alone, where the voices multiplied and eventually became familiars. Almost like family.

Naming her new family, Ghila opted for basic emotions that suited each of her invisible friends' voices: Sad, Happy, Fear and Anger.

Ghila often clutched her most cherished possession, a serpent-shaped pendant on a fine steel chain, which she discovered fallen behind a crate inside the Red Guard's cart during the endless journey.

The whispers told her to keep it hidden, safe, a *secret*.

The pendant became like an anchor, something to hold on to while a tornado raged in and around her. It was hers, and hers only. If anyone around her sensed its presence, they did not let it show. The place was teeming with magic, the pendant concealed. It became something precious, the serpent's tiny red ruby eyes speaking to the hopeless loneliness she felt outside. It kept her company during long, lonely days kept in her rooms. She hadn't anything but what little training the Fates gave her, fuelled with seeds of promise that someday she would find a purpose.

Until now, until all she craved was *revenge*.

Ghila was as brittle as dried flowers. Her body was thin and only possessed part of the strength that others her age and species possessed. She was the quiet girl who spoke to herself, who passed the tasks set by the Fates by the skin of her teeth.

The girl who could not conjure magic.

The magic that was supposed to leap to her palms at her command never made it past the initial thought. She tried but could not focus, couldn't rein in her thoughts enough to satisfy the Sisters.

Until one day while attempting to grasp her magic, she had found a fellow student's mind instead, passing through the barriers they had erected, taking hold of their body as well. She had felt a semblance of power then, one that had felt *good*.

And after that, the Fates kept her separate from the others, training her in matters of mind, focusing on the muscles there instead of her body. The long stretches of loneliness caused her to become bitter and discontent within herself. So Ghila took a blade to her long hair, feeling as if she was shedding some of her previous self – the weak girl who had been a malleable prey for monsters. It left her with an uneven bob of black hair, but her soul, and mind, felt just that little bit lighter.

Ghila was kept separated, until her presence was forgotten by all except for the Sisters and a few assassins sworn to secrecy.

Only called upon when needed, often for interrogations with those who refused to cooperate with the assassins, she spent her time alone. Until a few months ago when she'd learned that her brother, Eliverus, had survived. He was whole, unharmed… and working for the very people who'd slaughtered her family. He wore the same red uniform as those who had almost *destroyed* her.

She stewed in her thoughts, listening to the voices, and slowly thirsting for revenge.

Ghila was a Mind Wielder, a kind of magic that was revered as much as it was feared.

She had become the Wraith, breaker of barriers, master of minds, causer of chaos.

And all the while the voices whispered, cried, screamed, demanded retribution for her suffering.

She would become poison. A trap for the wolves, a bane for the monsters.

She would have her revenge.

ELIJAH

Travelling unwillingly with his sister was something far beyond what Elijah had experienced during his trial set by Kadec Brolikian in the West Court. The illusionary world shown by the Prince had felt disconnected yet real, but he hadn't felt the heat of the apocalyptic wasteland, nor had he felt the flames of the dragon's fire.

Now, he could feel sensations upon his skin while watching his own point of view through the mirror, as if he were right there. A cool breeze brushing against his arms, the smell of sulphur and the sea, telling him they were headed west. Elijah wasn't sure how long it had been since they began their trek back towards the coast, perhaps three or four days. They'd passed a farm at one point, and he'd noticed a change in his sister. She stared straight ahead and fell silent, deep in thought, speaking little in comparison to the ramblings he'd endured for most of the time they'd been travelling. Elijah tried to pinpoint the cause of his sister's sudden quietness, but not being in control of his body made observing his surroundings difficult.

They had stopped at one point to rest, after what felt like days of gently convincing his sister that despite them being Fae, they were not invincible, and if she were to use him in any sort of plan of vengeance, then he would need to be at full strength... well, his *body* needed to be. So, they had rested, his body leaning with arms crossed against the trunk of a tree while his mind lay on his childhood bed within the dream bedroom, his feet poking over the end of the mattress. It was so strange. He remembered the bed being so much larger when he was a child, so that whenever he shifted under the covers, his limbs had found pastures of cold, making him feel like a curled-up ball of warm dough on a bed of icy feathers.

Ghila had left his bedroom through the door he had tried countless times to open. He guessed that was her exit from his mind, and she was resting fitfully while also keeping watch over his body in the real world. Despite the torment she was putting him through, Elijah hoped she was getting some sleep.

He slept for a short while himself, before a reflex within his mind drove him awake on his own. Looking at the mirror he found his body on the move again, the overhang of trees slicing pre-dawn sunlight over the gravel road, which stretched before them, uninhabited save for a cart far ahead.

Elijah moved, resting his hands on the mirror's edge, glancing towards the door where his sister had left. His sister was... boundless with her energy, skittish and almost paranoid, constantly murmuring with darting grey eyes, waiting for something, or someone. The glimpses that he had seen when her guard was down had his guts churning with regret. He should have sought to find her after regaining his memory... He should have sought to learn more about his original family and the likelihood that any of them would still be alive, for if he had survived, there was a chance another may have as well–

The whinny of a horse drew his attention back to the mirror and the forest road scene. They were drawing closer to the cart now, and four soldiers dressed in gold and red came into view. It was larger, sturdier than a normal cart, with a hint of cage bars glinting under the corner of a heavy tarp. The thing shuddered, and Elijah swore he heard a guttural hiss from beneath the covers.

The two horses drawing the cart stomped their feet and jerked about, clearly in distress. One of the soldiers tugged harshly on the reins, uttering curses at the beasts as the other men crowded around their cargo while keeping a safe distance from the thing under the cover.

The two Fae approached, two lone figures on a quiet road. Beside him, Ghila smirked.

So, this was it. Valdis was finally about to have him in his clutches, and there was nothing Elijah could do while under Ghila's control.

He pounded his fists against the mirror's frame, clenching his jaw in frustration, glaring at the scene in the glass, calling to his sister.

"Ghila, we have to turn back. Please, turn back now!"

If she could hear him, she didn't make it known.

"Stop," yelled one of the guards, hand on his sword's pommel.

Elijah could feel his muscles bunch, anticipation coursing through him, a ghost of what his body felt in reality. The soldier neared, and something registered across the man's features, his hand hesitating on his weapon.

"Wait a minute, I know you, you're–" Before he could finish, Elijah's arm struck out, sword drawing so swiftly it was but a flash of silver. The soldier's lips opened and closed like a fish, before his head slowly separated from his shoulders.

The other guards kicked into motion, rushing at them with shouts.

Beside him, Ghila let out a howling laugh, and stepped back.

"There is no escaping your final fate," she called as the scene erupted into bloody chaos.

He glimpsed the reflection of his own face in the polished pauldrons of the man's uniform, the man he'd murdered, as he tipped backwards. His own face was hard-cut granite, eyes as flat as stones.

Beyond the mirror, Elijah gaped. What… what was *happening*?

With absolute precision, his body, under Ghila's command, cut through the soldiers as if they were nothing but annoyances made of meat, placed in the direct path of his sword. No matter how loud he called, telling his body to stop, the massacre continued. He was outnumbered but the guards were no match for him, not when his vessel called upon magic, blasting two men against the carriage.

The heavy linen covering on the cargo flew away, and a claw reached out of the cage, seizing a soldier and tugging his shoulder and head between the bars. The Kryvern within began devouring him with such ferocity that Elijah wished he could turn away.

All the while, Ghila cawed in delight.

As the last soldier slid off the end of his sword, Elijah surveyed the carnage. He tasted something on his tongue, and a feeling manifested from his vessel and into his consciousness beyond the gilded mirror. He tasted… rage, satisfaction and elation, then… familiarity. But this scene was not familiar to him. Murdering soldiers, dressed in his old uniform, was not familiar. He'd done so much that he now regretted, but this kind of pointless violence? No, that feeling of familiarity was not his own.

Elijah, shocked and confused, gasped as realisation dawned.

The feeling of familiarity was *hers*.

Ghila's.

The landscape shuddered, then flashed between the scene in front of him and what appeared to be a shadow-framed memory. Elijah fell back from the mirror's enchantment, his entire body shaking.

So much death.

As the scene began to fade, the bedroom door flew open and his sister strode in. Just like in the real world, her pale skin was spotted with tiny specks of red, but he knew it would not compare to the amount that would be covering him – or rather his body outside of his mind.

"Those men, they were innocent," Elijah rasped weakly.

"None of the Red Guard are innocent," Ghila shot back, her wide smile remaining as she came closer, a look of pure entertainment brightening her features. Elijah's jaw slid forward, adrenaline still shivering through his limbs.

"I worked with those men for years – I'm not defending them, not entirely, because I know many had unsavoury pasts that some regretted. But sister, they didn't deserve death. They didn't deserve to be *slaughtered*."

She was close enough that he could smell embers on her, a lingering scent that never seemed to dissipate. Ghila brushed a strand of hair from Elijah's forehead, and he suppressed an outward flinch, surprised at her sudden willingness to make physical contact, however fleeting. She clucked her tongue, surveying his face as she said, "We gifted them a kindness."

Shadows danced in the depths of her silver eyes, reminding him of murky waters with beasts swimming within. Just past her shoulder, the mirror began to shiver.

"They deserved far worse than a swift death by your sword. Think of it as merciful. We could have made it *far* worse."

"But do you not work in alliance with Valdis? Aren't you supposed to hand me over to him?"

Ghila grinned. "Hand you over? Nonsense. You're ours to torment."

With effort, he stumbled backwards, eyeing the mirror as if it were gilded with poisonous snakes. Ghila shifted, hands on hips. "Your discomfort brings us so much joy!"

"You're…" he swallowed his words, because her hand rose to clutch at the pendant around her neck again.

That damned pendant. He had to rid her of it. It was the only thing he could think of that could grant some sort of reprieve from this nightmare. It could be nothing, a trinket with no power save for the comfort it seemed to give his sister, but he had to try. She was playing with him, either for some secret motive or for her own sick and twisted enjoyment. He was running out of time.

He had to get back to her… to Ariiaya.

Thoughts of her were perhaps the only thing keeping him from collapsing into pure insanity. He imagined her there, her hands on his face, gentle yet sure, her lips on his, confident and passionate. They'd only just begun to truly puzzle each other out, when he'd made the mistake of thinking his best friend may have wanted to extend an olive branch. Would she still love him, knowing the extent of what he'd done? Only she could answer that.

He'd been such a fool.

Elijah imagined Arii's stubborn scowl and beautiful, fiery purple eyes, telling him, *"I love you. Don't let go. Or I'll kick your arse."*

He deserved that, truly. And he was going to make sure she'd get the chance to make him regret his choice to face Lorch without her.

Elijah sealed his memories of Arii in a gilded box, keeping them safe from Ghila's probing gaze.

Flashes of memory that were not his own came back to him. "Ghila, were the people who harmed you royal guards?" Parts of the puzzle of her history clicked together. "Those guards should have protected you after all that happened to our family."

Ghila froze, her eyes narrowing. "Not as silly as you look," she replied.

He could see a shift in her. The very slightest of change in her eyes, as if a veil of gossamer drifted behind her irises.

A sick feeling rose in his stomach. Valdis had his poison-tipped claws in more places than Elijah had originally anticipated. His family had trusted Valdis with matters of importance, he had been the King's Hand. All the while he had been waiting in the wings, carefully organising treason, placing criminals with like-minded beliefs within the ranks of their palace guards.

The gilded mirror rippled, and another scene began to play.

Ghila turned slightly, staring at the mirror, sucking in a startled breath as Elijah slowly rose to his feet. Ghila shuddered, enraptured by a new scene, unaware of the flicker in the walls – in the entire bedroom around them. Like a rapidly thinning veil, the setting of Elijah's bedroom winked in and out, changing from gilded walls to wood ridden with mildew. Then it winked back, his bedroom walls standing solid once more.

Elijah held his breath, dreading what memory was about to play. They had only grazed the surface of his misgivings, and Ghila's excitement radiated from her in waves.

Within the mirror, bodies lay around a cart, and hands unfamiliar to him rose before them, soaked in blood.

This was not his memory.

The sound his sister made was a mixture of delight and fear, her hand clutching at her pendant once more. A soldier had just laid waste to his own men, before placing himself upon a stool, blood-drenched sword resting on his knees.

This was her memory.

It was the man he had spied in earlier flashes of Ghila's memory, when she had let down her guard for a split second. She hadn't known, of course, of the flashes of memory he'd seen. Of the man with little hair and a gap-toothed smile.

They watched on, as Elijah scurried for ideas on how he could end this. He had to ease her terrors somehow, perhaps then she would let him go. He knew her past could never be erased, the scars upon her body, her mind, could never be erased. But he had to show her that she wasn't alone. She no longer needed to seek revenge. She needed to realise her strength, her resilience. She was a survivor, and surviving did not mean she had to be alone in her trauma any longer.

Ghila's hand crept to her throat once more, and Elijah knew. He had to get hold of her amulet. Perhaps then he'd have a chance to escape.

CHAPTER EIGHT

ARIIAYA

After telling Prince Kadec and his advisers about their journey to Sapphine, there was a furious discussion about the broken laws that demanded punishment. Arii understood the frustration – they'd left when there were newly laid orders that no one was to leave the island. They'd flouted the rules, but she and Nocturne did their best to communicate that the object of power they were now seeking could help them. Even if she really didn't know what it was they were looking for.

Finally, Kadec agreed to hold his forces for a few days more, allowing them to explore their lead.

Three days. He gave them three days.

By the time Arii fell upon her bed hours later, crunchy salt water cleansed from her hair and skin, sleep quickly claimed her, and dreams swiftly found her. She'd expected to dream of floating through ethereal underwater kingdoms and negotiating with fish-tailed sirens, their hair drifting upon watery wind.

Instead, she dreamt of a memory.

"Once upon a time, there was a girl who longed for a place to call home."

There was an echo in the voice that spoke, deep and gentle, as it whispered from parts of her memories long buried, a disconnect that felt like the memory could just drift away at any moment. She clutched it like a lifeline, so desperately that his voice brought pain mingled with comfort. And it became stronger until the memory resembled reality.

"But no matter how hard she yearned, how hard she hoped, the home she longed for was always just out of her reach, drifting backwards as she moved forwards."

Suddenly, Arii was a child again.

Her wide, young eyes lifted to the strong, angular jaw of her father. They had often sat like this, she on his lap as he reclined in the plush settee in his private study. A mild flame was stoked in the nearby hearth despite Viridya's balmy climate. She suspected that magic dampened it, its presence only there for ambience. Magic was something she was used to, if unable to wield it herself yet. All in good time, her father assured her, despite his own lack of magic.

She couldn't wait for her power to manifest, had dreamed about it often.

"Why did she not just grab it, father? Make it stay?" Arii said, her voice light, sweet and young. A long-forgotten stranger's voice.

"There are some things we cannot force, little Violet." Her father chuckled, flipping the page. He spoke of more than the story, although at the time his meaning had been lost on her.

She pouted. "Why not?"

The dull thud of the book closing sent a puff of air into her face, making her start. Her father laughed again. "You certainly are like your mother. Determined and headstrong." He gave her a squeeze, his shoulder-length chocolate-coloured hair tickling her cheek, making her laugh. "You'll understand someday. Time for bed."

"I bet I could get rid of bedtime too if I could grab it and throw it."

Father flicked the tip of her nose. "Now," he chided, but there was a grin in his voice.

She slipped from his lap, twirling in the musty light, fingers twining in her skirts. "Well, I know where home is for me. It's right here in this castle with you, and Mumma. This is where I belong."

She gazed up as her father stood, placing the book on the pile on a nearby table. A collection they were making their way through. He had read a book to her every night since before she could remember, and it was a part of their bedtime routine which had never slipped. Mother told her once that he'd begun reading to her within hours of her birth, nestling her in blankets by the fire to allow her mother reprieve from her newborn wailing. It had soothed her from the start, the sound of her father's gentle voice spinning words she would one day understand.

Arii pressed her face into her father's robes, inhaling his dusky, woodfire scent. "Goodnight, Papa."

"Goodnight, sweet Violet."

She skipped to the door, her father's chuckle resonating. Her hand found the warm door handle, but her father's voice paused her. "Little Violet?"

She turned to him.

"What the girl in the story eventually realized was that home was not just a place, but the people who filled it."

His face began to segment, as did the room around him, fragmenting into threads of mist. As it did, so did Arii's heart. When he spoke again, Arii felt it in the present, in her active subconscious, as if he were beside her, a ghost of a hand touching her shoulder. His smile skimmed away like drifts of smoke, but not before he said, "Find your *home*, Ariiaya."

With a blink, her father was gone, and in his place was a familiar expanse of rippling water reflecting stars. Immediately Arii tensed, staring across the star-smattered dream world. Her hand now clutched thin air, and she whirled, heart racing with anticipation of what she was about to be shown.

Before, when she had found herself here, she had seen her mother, and a hooded figure whom she had assumed was her father at the time. That felt like a lifetime ago. Perhaps she hadn't slept deeply enough to touch this place since. It was still a mystery, perhaps conjured up just to spite her, a place where her overactive subconscious thoughts could roam.

Willing her panic to subside, she took a breath and closed her eyes. As always, there was something in her chest, a pinch of weight, a tug of a thread. She focused on it now, and suddenly she found her thoughts slipping to him. To Elijah.

Warmth tingled in her ribs, encasing her heart, and she slowly opened her eyes. As if those thoughts reached across an expanse of space and time, Arii drew her gaze up into Elijah's partially shadowed face.

"Elijah?" she breathed, reaching for his cheek. Her fingers passed through, and she startled. "Where are you?"

Elijah's face turned sad. "I can't stay long." He paused, his form ethereal. "She's heading west, she means to attack the Fates."

She?

"Wait, she… your sister, Ghila?"

Why attack the Fates? That was the last thing Arii had expected.

His image wavered, "This is the most bizarre thing that has ever happened to me, and that's saying something after the last few days… weeks… erm." His image flickered again as his head tilted, "How are we speaking like this?"

Arii pressed a hand to her chest, but paused. "I have an idea why," she said, "but I'll tell you after I rescue you."

She couldn't explain the concept of mates to him, not yet. She was still trying to process what that would mean for their future, particularly his future, if it were true. They wouldn't know until they took the final plunge and slept together. Skin to skin, nothing between their bodies–

Elijah's smile remained sad, his hand lifting to hover near her cheek. Stardust teased at his hair, dark strands shifting over his handsome face. He was dressed in the black travelling leathers she'd last seen him in, the details subdued to a faded shade of dark grey, as if she were seeing him through a covered veil.

"I'm so sorry," Arii rasped, shaking her head. "I'm sorry about Colleen, I'm sorry about Lorch. I left you there, I didn't fight for you as I should have." She wished with all that she had that she could touch him, feel his reassuring warmth. The folds of her gown fluttered around her ankles, touched by a ghost of a breeze. She absentmindedly fingered embroidered gold filagree stitched into deep blue fabric. They were communicating via a dream, and it seemed anything was possible here, except that they couldn't touch one another.

"I promise you that I'll fight for you now," she whispered, placing steel into her voice.

His image flickered again, fading slightly, when Elijah glanced down. Panic welled within Arii as wisps of black smoke curled around Elijah's arms, becoming solid like threads made of darkness. They toyed with his hair, caressed his neck as he attempted to step forward, expression forlorn. The darkness tightened, pulling him back.

Weight pinched at her wrists, and Arii gasped as delicate threads of gold light wrapped over her own arms. The threads spun around them both, clashing as if sunlight warred with midnight. Fighting them, she looked at Elijah once more.

She could see the dark threads pulling him away, but still he spoke. "Ariiaya, you have been fighting for me from the very start. None of it was your fault, my heart. I made a mistake facing Lorch alone. It is a mistake I will *not* make again." He glanced at his arms, biceps tensing against the strain. His image flickered. The rumble in his voice, the steely finality in his words, had the hairs on her arms rising. "Never again."

"I'm coming, Elijah. They can't stop me."

"I know," his hand hovered above her cheek again, shaking against whatever force pulled him back.

She fought it too, desperate for his touch, desperate to remain with him, even if it was all an illusion. His fingers whispered over her skin like the kiss of a ghost. "I'll wade through darkness and hell to be with you, Ariiaya. It'll take more than this to keep us apart."

He was right. It would take far more, for she knew he was fighting for her, too.

His grey eyes were unblinking, dark, determined, "Go west, get to the school before we do."

Like dust on the strengthening breeze, Elijah's skin dissipated until he was nothing more than whisps of dark smoke.

"No!" she cried, and with a final yank, the golden threads curling around her tore her backwards.

Arii's eyes snapped open, greeted by the sheer curtains of her four-poster bed. Her body hummed, her limbs roused from rest.

Her beast rose from its slumber, its magic sparking to her fingertips as she threw herself from the bed and stormed from her room.

GHILA

Ghila remembered the first time she had been strong enough to extract revenge, but seeing flashes of those memories now, on the mirror, had her hesitating. Her brother would see part of the poison she had become. For a breath she was unsure if she wanted him that, for fear of what he would think.

But that was silly, she didn't care what anyone thought of her.

Not anymore.

Ghila briefly wondered what roused such a feeling of anxiety – perhaps it was witnessing her brother's distress, his agony over his past actions. Perhaps she felt a little bad for making him relive those memories.

No… no he'd left her in the cart with her monsters, as much an accessory to her torment as Valdis was.

The feeling of unease remained, even as she glanced back to the man grown from the boy she used to know. Those feelings were perhaps shadows of her past, the girl she used to be, which seemed to hold on like annoying little parasites, no matter how hard she tried to shake them free.

Leaning towards the gilded mirror, she felt a sweet wash of anticipation with the new scene playing. For a split second, she snuck a glance at her brother, but his grey eyes were narrowed at the mirror, a sheen of sweat on his brow.

Ghila almost trembled with anticipation, for the memory on the mirror was one of her own.

She saw the moment Elijah realised, his face remaining stoic except for the confused pull of his brows.

Should he see? What would he think?

Did she care?

'Let him see this memory,' cooed one of the voices. It was Happiness, mixed with the tiniest dash of Bitterness.

Her anxiety drained away, as if someone had pulled a plug in the soles of her feet.

A slow smile curled her lips. This memory *was* her favourite.

The siblings watched the scene play out in the mirror, as if through the eyes of another.

A body lay sprawled over the rungs of a cart, another at the feet of two anxious mares harnessed to it. The legs of another guard poked out from the drapes of the cart, a rickety thing decorated with the red banners of the North. The symbol embroidered on the cloth was not her family's, though, it was the head of a serpent, the mark of the Kruel family.

Male hands shook in their viewpoint, blood already drying beneath his nails. "I killed them," he cried, his voice shaky and strange, as if spoken through a tunnel. There was a sound, and his hand flew to his sword, his lips curling against his will. Everything was against his will, all of it had been. He had killed his men, slaughtered them like useless cattle, but he hadn't wanted to. Someone was inside his head with him, pulling the strings of his body like a marionette. His horse whinnied, stomping a hoof, then his body jerked into motion, heading towards the door of the cart.

"Stop, please, let this end."

Ghila remembered considering allowing him to live and continue on with the knowledge that he had killed his friends and brothers in arms. She had considered allowing him to pay for his actions, no doubt he would be arrested and thrown into the dungeons to rot for his treason. But she could not allow him to harm any more Fae, for she was sure that she wasn't the first, nor the last.

Tonix, her torturer, clambered into the cart, passing over the body of his comrade. He grabbed a chair and dragged it to the post in the middle, the very place where she had been chained, battered and abused so many years ago.

He sat heavily, placing the sword on his lap, face expressionless save for the tiniest hitch in his brow.

Why hadn't Ghila wanted her brother to see this? She couldn't remember. He should be proud that she had ended the men who abused her. She had done what her brother had not.

The haggard face of her abuser shifted between a snarl and a wide smile, as memories lay one over the other, like thin paper.

That smile had her shuddering, hand flying to the pendant around her neck. The voices murmured in her ears as usual, telling her to be wary of the man who subtly moved to her side, watching the mirror, and her memory.

Her brother.

She glanced at him

And immediately wished she had not.

He watched her with guarded eyes, and as he did, other memories slipped free of the vault she had shoved them in. Ones of her childhood, laced with light and love. Her brother, her best friend growing up, the vision of him as a boy mixing with that of the man before her, tore her already fractured mind in two. She loved him, she hated him, she wanted revenge yet what she wanted above all else was… silence. To simply exist in a world with no sound – just for a moment.

She was distracted, her gaze floating from Elijah to the mirror once more.

She did not see him shift, ever so slightly. Did not see him eyeing the pendant swinging from her neck as she drew forward, her eyes wide and reflecting the face of Tonix, a face that was once full of arrogance, sick pleasure and fierce hate. How many Fae had he killed? How many had he tortured? How many had he *broken*? The questions had poked at her mind, amongst the chaos, for a long time. How many hadn't made it to the school like she had? How many hadn't been spared because they weren't princesses or from a powerful line, like her?

The man's face warped to one streaked with blood, his bottom lip trembling, sweat and blood pebbling his forehead and cheeks, fear now the only thing twisting his severe features.

The voices in her mind were a riot of sound, and Ghila grasped hold of the memory and willed it into stillness. This was her favourite, one her brother had to see. She remembered this moment, remembered that she allowed just a little of her abuser's consciousness through, just enough to express his fear in his final moments as he lifted his own sword to his neck.

'He deserved this; he deserved to know that his death was near, at his own hands, and he earned every ounce of fear. The monster was his own undoing. You became his poison.' The voices chanted, cheered, jeered, and cried.

"I was his poison, in the end." Ghila said, gaze never leaving the death unfolding on the glass. "As I shall be for all of them."

"Ghila," Elijah shifted beside her, his voice soft and careful, as if she were a frightened animal. "You have suffered much, and for too long. Perhaps it's time to change that. I can help you. Let me help you."

His throat worked, and she looked aside for a moment to focus on it, before moving to his eyes. Tempered grey, heavy, unblinking.

He whispered, "Please."

Sounds of gurgling death echoed from the mirror, but she turned to face her brother fully.

Elijah stared at her, his eyes – so much like her own – dropping to the pendant hanging around her neck.

She could not stand the look of pity on his face. It called forth Anger, a voice that was deep and usually male. *'He thinks we are weak!'* it bellowed now, causing Ghila's hands to clench at her sides.

She must have let those words loose because Elijah lifted his hands in a placating gesture. "I do not think you are weak." He remained calm, almost stoic, as Ghila's breaths quickened, hand rising to her pendant.

It pressed into her palm, seemingly heating with her emotions.

He had seen. He had seen what they had done to her. Nothing else would have put that look deep into his eyes. The healers had worn the same expression after studying her; some of the students too, when she'd arrived at the school.

She should have been more careful, concealed her darkest memories from the mirror, the ones of her suffering and abuse. He'd seen her at her weakest, and that just would not do.

"There is nothing that you can show me, willing or otherwise, that could ever make me see you as weak, Ghila." He took a step forward, causing the voices to rise. She shook her head, like a mangy dog, the uneven bob of her hair whipping about her cheeks.

His voice… it was so deep and soft and… reminded her of their father.

Father had cared for her.

The voices pitched in crescendo, and for once, she ignored them.

"You're my sister. You're my blood and part of my heart, and we are the only ones who remain that can truly seek vengeance for what was done to our family." Another step. "To our *people*. I am truly sorry that I wasn't there to stop what they did to you… what *he* did to you."

She swallowed, eyes fluttering closed.

"Sing for me, let me hear those sweet screams. Caw little bird, caw."

There was a sudden tug at her neck and her eyes flew open.

Elijah grasped her pendant, and the voices began to scream. Despite the feeling of revulsion that came with any form of touch, Ghila clutched at his arm, spewing, "No! Let *them* go!"

Her words jolted him. "Them?"

She used his momentary surprise to draw a crescent moon dagger from her belt, cleaving it towards him. Elijah let go of the pendant, throwing himself backwards.

Ghila moved on the offensive, teeth bared as the voices bleated through her skull. She blinked against them, anger causing her to shake.

How dare he try to take what was hers.

How dare he try to take *them*.

A hand trapped her wrist, halting her weapon a breath from his face. Ghila threw a punch at his stomach but was quickly barred by his other hand. They grappled for a moment, her limbs screaming in time with the voices. He was physically stronger despite all she'd put him through.

That fact drew forth a frustrated cry.

It wasn't fair. How had she, a Fae, been left with such a weak body? How had she been so unlucky to have her family ripped away, to be betrayed by her brother, who'd somehow survived, when so many had not.

How had she been so unlucky not to die along with her parents, and Brohem.

Ghila's cry warped to a sob, tears blurring her vision.

'You are weak, and the fate you have been dealt is because you... are... weak!'

A gentle touch upon her cheek had the voice of Anger fading, replaced with the deep, gentle tone of her brother's. A sound that tugged her back to reality, back to a sense of *home*. The voices faded; their cries slowly pushed behind a barrier of silver light. Was this her brother's doing?

During her distraction, she had dropped her weapon to reach for her amulet again.

Elijah placed a hand gently upon hers.

Suddenly he yanked, tearing the pendant from her neck.

It was as if a tether snapped. The voices... stopped.

Utter silence.

Ghila gasped, as if the breath was her first in years, as if until now her head had been under an ocean of water. Tears sprang and she let out a sob, choppy waves of hair falling around her face like curtains. She shook, unable to process the pure and strange... silence.

After what felt like an eternity, she looked up, wide-eyed at the man before her. Her heart, long cold, warmed with the tiniest bit of true recognition.

"Eli?" she breathed, and this voice was wholly new. This one was purely *hers*. She could not stop the tears as they rolled down her cheeks, the weight of her ghosts easing from her shoulders as she sagged.

Warmth bloomed across her cold skin as his hand cupped her cheek, her eyes shuttering closed as the sounds of the forest came alive around them. The dream bedroom faded away, leaving them standing alone on the road. As if awakening from a nightmare, she inhaled deeply, registering smells and sensations that had been veiled. The voices were still there, but muted now, swapping sides with her sense of self that had been slowly pushed away over the years.

Tears lined her big brother's eyes with silver, and he smiled, "Hello, Ghila-bila."

CHAPTER NINE

LORCH

Lorch tried his best to focus on the happenings around the castle, but often found his attention shifting to what he had learned of the Fae resistance, and his pledge to help them. He felt… different. He felt focused for the first time in what felt like years, just not on castle affairs. Courtiers fluttered about him, dresses skittering across his marble floors, faces glancing his way with looks of curiosity and hunger. But he saw through them all, as if they were nothing but annoying shrouds of mist.

"The governor's daughter is of a suitable age for marriage, and the family is wealthy. They own the majority of crops and farmland between Colkirk and The Wastes, and I think of all the suitors, she may be the prettiest. She's here tonight, you know. Perhaps we can re-consider their proposal."

Lorch blinked, catching the last of his father's drawl as he straightened upon the throne, stretching a crick in his back. "Sorry, what?"

His father scowled. "What preoccupies your mind, son?" His words were clipped, wary.

Lorch made a show of throwing one leg over the other and pressed his palm to his cheek. A nonchalant, well-practiced mask that he slipped into like a second skin. "You know, just the usual. How can so many dance and play while surrounded by the stench of death?"

His father stiffened further. "The guards are hardly noticeable."

"This room reeks like roast chicken and rot," Lorch sighed and stood. "I think I'll retire."

"In the middle of a ball? You know how that will look," his father growled.

Lorch glanced at his father over his shoulder. The golden crown upon his brow shifted, unsteady like his thoughts. "Any queries can be handled by you in my stead, as usual, father. Tell them I have a headache."

Valdis remained silent, but his hard expression relayed his anger.

For once, Lorch did not care.

He slipped from the dais and made his way to the doors at the rear. A small procession of guards followed him to his chambers, the clink and shuffle of boots filling the awkward silence. He could tell which of them were alive, and which were dead. The dead, although adorned in guard regalia, dragged their feet with an odd jerkiness, which he knew they had been ordered to mask as best they could.

There were four dead amongst the six that accompanied him now, which irked him because he had demanded there be none near his quarters. It was obvious how little his demands truly meant.

He dismissed the guards with a flick of his hand, before shutting the door.

Lorch spun, pressing his back to the wood and inhaling deeply. Determination sparked his limbs as he flung himself at his armoury to pull his shabby disguise from under a rainbow of royal outfits.

Dusk drew a cloak of orange shadows across his chamber floor as he swiftly changed into his peasant clothes, before following the same path as the night before. Music thrummed from the golden castle in his wake as he pulled up the hood of his cloak, sticking to the shadows and opting for the gate to the town when he saw the same guard lazing on his stool.

As he approached, Lorch pulled a basket from his cloak, and the man yawned, "Eggs… right. Off ye go."

Lorch almost cackled at how easy escaping his own clutches truly was. As he passed through, he noticed a trailing scratch down his exposed forearm. When had he done that? Perhaps when climbing down the wooden lattice from his window.

As he rounded the corner towards the tavern, two cloaked figures turned towards him.

"You're here," said Celadine, the flickering lanterns throwing light over her profile. At her side, Mia smiled, signing a jovial 'hello'.

Lorch tried to mirror her action, which earned him a muffled laugh. He smiled. "I said I'd come. I meant it."

"Good."

Celadine turned and rapped her knuckles on the heavy door. The eye slat opened, then snapped shut and the door creaked open to allow them entry.

The tavern was only a quarter full compared to the night before. The stage was occupied by a lone woman playing a flute to a small audience who sipped mead and picked at meagre serves of cheese and cured meats. They passed unnoticed, heading to an unoccupied room at the rear. Once inside, Lorch removed his hood, glancing around the neat little room.

Two satchels sat propped at the foot of two single beds which took up most of the room. There was a hearth stoked with a small flame in between, and a little desk and chair by the only window, its surface scattered with brown paper bags, sprigs of herbs, a pestle and mortar and some empty vials.

"Do you live here?" he asked as Mia threw herself onto the bed, face-planting the downy covers.

Celadine hung her cloak on a hook, expression guarded. "No, it is a temporary in between while I work in the castle."

"Fair enough," he mused, approaching the table of supplies and picking up the mortar, weighing it in his palm, eager to do something with his hands. After a beat, he placed it down, and when he turned back, Celadine wore a strange, thoughtful frown.

Lorch unclipped his own cloak, keeping his gaze locked with hers. Something in his stomach told him that this moment – as mundane as it seemed – was the beginning of something important, solidifying mortar in a brick wall riddled with cracks. The ember in his chest flared to life, and he absently draped the cloak over the chair and said, "Tell me about the resistance."

Celadine hesitated, glanced at her daughter, "What do you want to know?"

"How many of you are here in the city?"

"Roughly three hundred."

"And you all have… magic?"

Her eyebrows rose comically, as if his question was the oddest he could ask. "No, only a fraction are magic wielders."

"And you?" He asked the question casually, but with it came a weight, lodging in his throat. He couldn't help but recall a face, one with purple eyes above a full lipped smirk. "Do you wield, too?"

He wasn't sure when she had moved, but she was beside him, the brush of her shoulder against his arm sending a little shiver through the fabric. She smelled of lavender and herbs, and something else… sweet and soothing… chamomile, perhaps?

"Magic comes in all sorts of forms." At Lorch's blink, she sighed, tilting her head, the wildness of her curls slipping over her shoulder. "Unlike the entertainment by the man on the stage last night – a wielder of outward magic – mine is a little less obvious."

He flinched as she took his arm, turning it to expose the long, shallow scratch on his skin. He had forgotten it already. Now though, it was like the wound was re-awakened, pin-pricking under her probing fingers. Her skin was warm, perhaps overly so, as she cradled his arm in one hand, and passed her fingers over the wound with the other. The warmth built to little licks of fire, and Lorch watched with wide eyes as the wound began to close behind the path of her fingertips. Every instinct within him was screaming for him to pull away, to *run*, but he fought against them, silently mesmerised by the speed of the healing. It wasn't completely gone when Celadine pulled back, just a faint pink line remained. But the sting was gone.

Elijah's voice echoed through his mind, some of the last words he spoke before Lorch took away his mother. *"Lorch, listen to me, the Fae are not a threat."*

Those words warred with what he had witnessed when Elijah ruptured, annihilating half his battalion in one explosion of magic. At times, he could still taste the copper mist of his soldiers on his tongue.

Now, seeing Celadine's magic heal his wound had doubt rising. Perhaps not *all* Fae were a threat…

Her voice brought him back from his thoughts. "My magic is limited to healing ailments. Mending of the flesh and of the mind."

She released his arm after a drawn-out moment. He wasn't sure why, but the knowledge made him feel easier, less afraid.

"That's incredible," he whispered finally.

A curl in her mouth was the only tell of her amusement, "You didn't know magic could heal?"

"No one focuses on the positives of magic," he sighed. "All we are told is of its destructiveness."

Healing magic suited Celadine. But perhaps that was because he knew she was an apothecary. She had always soothed his hurts. He wondered idly whether that was why she hadn't been recruited by the Fates, who only wanted those who could use external magic.

He paused, letting the knowledge settle, thoughts spindling across his mind like rapid frost over glass. "What about Mia? Her hearing, could magic not heal her?"

Celadine was quiet momentarily, fingers trailing the now faint scar across his skin. He suppressed another shudder – this time it wasn't one of fear.

"I haven't told you how she lost it, have I?"

Lorch wordlessly shook his head, watching her fingers.

"Her father joined a rally several years ago, protesting treatment of the Fae. It was a peaceful protest, that quickly turned violent. The guards used a bomb with iron pellets inside, and when it exploded, Mia was near her father. He shielded her, but…" her voice trailed away, eyes shifting to her daughter, who rummaged through a rucksack, seemingly oblivious to their conversation.

"That was how he died. The bomb was so close that it was a miracle she wasn't killed, too. But it took her hearing, and iron shrapnel entered her body in several places. Most we were able to take out through traditional means, but one still remains, far too close to her heart that removing it could risk killing her." Cela's voice hardened, dropping a touch. "The iron prevents me from healing her eardrums with magic. If a wound or ailment is left unhealed for some time, it becomes harder to fix with magic. If the iron shard is ever removed, too much time would have passed to properly heal my daughter's hearing."

Lorch's gaze shifted to Mia, as she leafed through a notebook with charcoal sketches inside.

"I am not surprised by your lack of magical knowledge, Lorch. Destruction is all you witness in its presence. I never thought the return of magic to the North would be in the form of tainted, necromantic conjurings." She added, "They are here in the town now, did you know that?"

Lorch startled. "What?"

She busied herself pouring a mix of herbs into the mortar. "Your guards, the ones without souls, they move through the streets, but none have attacked. They're looking for something."

Lorch's brows furrowed, and a murky memory of his father's orders to the guards danced forth.

'There is resistance, and we will find it. Send them to search the town. Send them to Amberbourne, to every single crevasse of this court. If there are Fae here, we will find them.'

At the time he had thought the order was for live guards, not the dead.

He would have to be far more careful than he had initially thought.

Mia made a sound on the bed, and Lorch saw the terror etched on her face. That same terror coiled his insides when he was anywhere near one of his father's undead soldiers. The quiver in the girl's lip brought him forward, and she shifted across as he sat on the bed beside her. She made a sign, quickly, and Lorch glanced at her mother, but found himself guessing what the girl said.

He shifted to face her fully, pressing a hand to his own chest. "You fear them. I fear them too."

Mia's look of surprise spurred him on, his words meant for both daughter and mother. "I know that you don't trust me, I have not earned anyone's trust. I have been a shocking king, and I know it has taken me far too long to realise this, but I hope it is not too late to make amends."

Both Fae were silent, the snap and crackle of the hearth the only sound.

"Perhaps I can begin by learning your language, Mia. Will you teach me?"

Celadine glanced at her daughter, but didn't need to translate – the girl had been watching Lorch's lips intently. She perked up, nodding enthusiastically. He offered her a smile, before glancing back to Celadine. She frowned, deep green eyes wary.

"I don't expect you to divulge the secrets of a broken society to me, Celadine. I know I've had a hand in harnessing the monsters that brought you all down." He saw a flicker in her expression, the skin around her eyes and mouth softening so slightly that he would have missed it had he not been fixated on her face. "But I'll do whatever it takes to help."

She whispered, "You will be aiding in the demise of your own house... your own family."

"My family has always been broken."

"What could you possibly gain from helping us?" Celadine asked.

"Atonement," Lorch replied, that one word shivering in the air between them.

They were so close that he could feel the warmth of her breath, could almost hear the thunder of her strong heart. It could have been his own, he wasn't sure, for his heart had been silent so long that he had forgotten the feel of its beat. "Perhaps I could change the fate meant for me. Or die trying, at least."

Celadine's smile was wry, her voice but a breath. "Fate? You believe in fate?"

"Maybe," he replied, the word dying on his lips as Celadine's eyes dropped to his mouth. Whatever he had planned to say about fate flew to the back of his mind as he took the moment to study her features. The fine hairs of her thick brows, the expressive indent between them. Her lashes were unbelievably thick, with a tinge of auburn when the firelight reached them. Freckles sprinkled her cheeks, tiny kisses from the sun that hinted at time basking in its rays.

When green eyes flicked back up to meet his, he found he was holding his breath. Releasing it, he said, "Fate brought me you, I think."

He regretted the words immediately after they left his mouth. He saw the shift in her again, as if a door had begun to open, but then violently slammed shut. She moved away, attention solely on the pestle and mortar, pulverising the herbs inside it with vigour. Mia sighed, offering him a sympathetic shrug.

Clearing his throat, he retreated towards the young Fae. He sat on the edge of the bed, surveying her little face and wild curls, her eyes – as green as her mother's – dropped to his mouth. So, Lorch spoke clearly and slowly, but not enough for it to be deliberately noticeable.

"Let's start with the basics, Mia. How about hello and goodbye?"

The girl grinned, and the King began to learn.

Several hours later, Lorch slipped into the dead of night, hood pulled over his head. The dank alleyway was dimly lit with one flaming sconce, orange light jumping like fireflies. There was no moonlight tonight, the sky was a flatland of dense, darkly shredded clouds, and the air held a chill that misted his breath.

Time had escaped him, but he hoped his lack of presence back at the castle wouldn't be noticed. If it had been, though, he had a story ready. One of the women at the party had finally taken his fancy, and he'd lost time in the sheets of her bed. A pretty no-name, the second daughter of a wealthy merchant. Not an unlikely story, and he could blame forgetting her name on the drink. The lack of witnesses he could blame on the quite literally dead silent guards who would have been lumbering in his wake if he hadn't given them the slip.

No one could really question the King, right?

His shoulder thumped against another, and Lorch stumbled on the cobblestones. His hand automatically flew out, gripping the arm of whoever he had bumped in his mindlessness. His fingers encircled an arm far too thin, bone draped in cloth. The apology that had sprung from his throat halted as Lorch glanced up into eyes sunken above cheeks like jagged peaks. Glowing blue eyes stared back, lids long dried into place below sparse brows and a hairless head.

Drawing his hand back swiftly, he sprang away, desperate to put distance between him and the mindless, dead soldier. His pulse was in his throat, hammering franticly. He had to get back to the castle, and quickly.

Behind him, cracked lips stretched in a not-so mindless smile.

CHAPTER TEN

NEMESIS

Nemesis had previously survived on less sleep than the three hours she'd just had, and she had read books with less light than the poorly candle sputtering beside her bed. Try as she might, rest eluded her once again, restless thoughts leaping between what she had seen on Death's door; the emotional maelstrom warring through the bond between herself and Ariiaya; the ancient magic used to catapult them to an underwater city.

And ever present was thoughts about the dark-haired, emerald-eyed wolf Shifter who was in a room one door down.

Once she would have just turned it all off, like slamming home the lock on a door to an overflowing closet of skeletons. Now though, that was practically impossible. Between her own emotions, which she had allowed to develop without restraint, and those of her impulsive and emotional best friend, she found she no longer held a tight leash.

Nem's eyes slid to the open window, gossamer curtains fluttering on a warm midnight breeze. She slapped the book shut, no longer interested in its stories. Her feet met the floor, toes flexing upon the soft fibres of a downy rug.

Sensations. There was so much that she now allowed herself to feel.

She padded to the window to open it. Her room was elegant but a little smaller than the others and without a balcony, but that was no matter to her. With the agility of a cat, she hopped onto the window sill and peered at the roof just below, the dark grey ceramic tiles overgrown with thick, curling vines. Climbing out, she sat cross-legged on a thick gathering of greenery, the perfect perch even with her impeccable balance.

Nem sighed, staring up at the moon – full and haloed. Clouds drifted lazily through the midnight sky towards the mainland on the horizon, leaving the stars to watch upon the sleepy, spring city below. Dressed in a light blue sleeping shift embroidered with gold filagree vines, Nem felt placid as the warm air swept across her skin.

Her thoughts were unreasonable things, though, as insistent as hungry newborn babes. When she had danced with Death, listening to its whispers as it tugged her towards a golden horizon, she had seen figures haloed in light. She hadn't spoken to anyone about it yet, about who they could have been, if they had been anyone at all. No memories of her past had returned to her over time – despite her fierce hope they would.

A deep, gentle voice graced the silence. "Beautiful, isn't it?"

Nem spun, crouched, whipping out a half-length golden knife and pointing it at the man's throat before he could draw another breath.

Krepth balanced on the tiles, hands raised, wearing his usual wolfish grin. "Where in Fythnar did you pull that from?"

"Doesn't matter – are you spying on me?" Nem growled, glaring.

His shoulders shrugged, but his eyes never left hers. "The night is warm, and my window was open. I heard you."

"No, you didn't," she spat, knowing that she hadn't rustled a single leaf under her bare feet. His wolfish hearing was good, but not *that* good. She pressed the tip of her knife to his chin and forced his face up. Despite his height, she used all the power within her glare to seem twice as tall.

"Fine…" Krepth sighed, watching her down his perfect nose, thick lashes touching his chiselled cheeks in a slow blink. "I smelled you, alright?"

"Another stalkerish trait?" she said, removing the knife, watching his Adam's apple bob.

"Another *wolfish* trait," he corrected, tapping his nose. She made a sound of disgust, but it was half-hearted. Nem twisted and returned to her perch, folding her legs beneath her.

"I thought you could use some company," Krepth said, shifting to the space beside her, hardly big enough for two. His shoulder brushed hers, hip grazing her thigh, and she could feel his radiating heat through the sleeping tunic and pants he wore. She threw him a side eye, and despite herself, watched a gentle breeze sweep his hair over his forehead and into his eyes.

Eyes that were fixed on her, eyes the depth of a forest and the colour of emeralds.

Stupid, roguish male.

"I don't need company," she groused.

"Perhaps a want, then?"

"Don't want it, either."

He shifted a tiny bit, brushing her arm again, and she cursed the tingles that erupted on her skin under her shift. There was a small silence where they both stared at the moon, and that silence, as much as she hated to admit it, was not as uncomfortable as she wished it to be.

Like the changing of a season, Krepth's voice dipped. "Do you want to talk about it?"

There was a timidness in his tone that she was unfamiliar with, and it got her attention. She surveyed his strong profile, from the tip of his neatly-pointed ear, to the proud tip of his nose.

The lack of eye contact told her that he was allowing her to shut him down again, that he wouldn't be surprised if she did. Thankfully it meant he would not see how her eyes softened, how just a hint of her animosity slipped with his concealed concern. What harm would it do, to tell him about what she'd seen during her brush with death? She could lie, tell him she only experienced pain, and saw nothing beyond the promise of eternal darkness.

But Nem was slowly coming to realise that being alone had never worked before, hadn't given her the answers she so desperately sought.

She inhaled and scented him, pine and spring water with a dash of forest wilds. Heady, and wholly distracting, just like his face as it tentatively tilted to her. She could shut him down again, could tell him to go away but instead she whispered. "Yes, I do want to talk about it."

Krepth waited, allowing her time to retract her words. After a moment she continued, gazing once again at the swelling moon.

"Right before I was pulled back from death by Arii and Elijah's magic, I saw figures in a golden halo of light. I think… they may have been my family."

His long fingers toyed with a tiny, unopened white flower bud. "Have you remembered anything about your past since then?"

She shook her head, silky silver strands brushing her cheeks. "No, nothing."

"Perhaps this object we seek… the Ouroboros. Perhaps it could help unlock your memories too?"

She hadn't thought of that. She supposed anything was possible, especially with the discovery of interdimensional travel.

Another idea came to mind, leading her to say "Perhaps I should speak with Nocturne?"

Krepth stiffened.

She tilted her head, brows rising at his shift, and she allowed her face to morph into something close to… flirtatious surprise. "You're not a fan?"

"The strange void traveller may have Ariiaya's trust, but he is still earning mine."

She smirked, "Is this a matter of trust, or a misplaced sense of possession, Krepth?"

He shifted to face her and her smirk dropped at his serious look. "I don't trust anyone when it comes to you, not when I almost lost you."

She swallowed a lump at the mention of her near-death experience. She didn't need to be reminded of her throat being opened, her blood coating the snow, nor the risk that Arii and Elijah had taken to forge the life bond that saved her.

Krepth's hand rose slowly but halted in the air on its way to her cheek. She watched his face intently, the way his eyes tracked his own hand, the way the corner of his mouth twitched and his throat worked. He looked as though he were about to put his hand into a viper's nest, risking a touch of scales or the wicked bite of fangs.

Was he *scared* of her? It suddenly hit her that she didn't want him to fear her. She didn't want him to treat her like an unpredictable, fickle beast anymore. She hadn't earned anything less, she knew that, but her earlier thoughts returned, about seeking help rather than pushing it away. Krepth had never done anything but respect her – even though he stoked the fires of her irritation just to see her react. He desired her, that much was explicitly clear, and yet he still handled her with care.

Perhaps it was time to allow herself to take risks, make mistakes. Allow herself to *feel*. Maybe then the revelations of her past would show themselves, and if they did not, then she would continue as she had been, looking out for her friends, watching their backs. It was what she was good at, she realised.

Nem placed her hand upon his and pressed his palm to her cheek.

His skin was warm, roughly callused in velvet like the pads of a wolf's paws. The sensation of skin against skin had her pulse skittering and her own skin heating. She sighed; eyes fluttering closed as her body finally relaxed. It felt like so long since she had allowed herself to relax.

Krepth inhaled, gently as if he were tasting her escaped breath, and he too was finally relaxing without the threat of a bite. His thumb coasted the bow of her lips, and she rested her fingers against his wrist.

"Far more beautiful than the moon…" he sighed reverently. His gaze circled her face but he did not move closer, still tentative. So, it was she who covered the last slice of distance between them.

Their lips met in a press so gentle, so diffident, that shivers of unfamiliar, sweet sensation rushed down her spine.

His warmth and the gentle way he brushed his lips over hers had her intoxicated. Despite her lack of experience, Nem pressed forward, deepening the kiss, feeling a thrill when his mouth opened willingly to her. She moved on instinct, exploring what felt best. Unlike her skills with a blade, in this she felt totally out of her depth, but he guided her gently, moving in harmony, like an instructor adapting to a pupil on a dance floor. Bliss heaved in her chest, and sparks ignited in her blood, and it felt *good*. Was this what she had been missing? His tongue swept against hers and she gasped.

"You and that damned moon," she whispered finally, but her tone lacked bite, only breathlessness, and to her misty-minded horror, desire.

Krepth smiled against her lips, "Me and my damned insatiable *hunger* for you."

The unexpected warmth pooling low in her belly had her beast awakening, tilting its head and swallowing with hunger.

So engulfed in the moment was she, that she only just caught the whisper of Krepth's next words.

"You're… glowing."

Nem's eyes flew open.

Unbeknownst to her, her free hand had tangled in his tunic during their kiss, and that hand was indeed glowing. She lifted it, twisting it between them, watching as the glow beneath her skin touched the handsome features of his face. The glow was silver, like moonlight, and at the realisation, her eyes jerked up to his.

"Silver moon," his voice held such awe, such reverence, that she couldn't bring herself to feel demure. Instead, she felt… beautiful. Confused, but beautiful.

"How?" her breath trailed away, speechless.

"Well, this is a positive step in uncovering your past, Nem." He grazed his fingertips down her arm, watching the magic shimmer on her skin. "You're Goddess-touched."

Goddess-touched?

"Remarkable…" he murmured. "According to legend, when you feel pleasure, your skin glows and sparkles like falling stars. Have you never felt true happiness before, Nem?"

No, she hadn't. The revelation of her origins was mind-boggling, yet the discovery wasn't the first thing on her mind. *He was.* She would find an explanation later, but for now, she wanted to revel in the feelings he was giving her. She tentatively rested her hands on his shoulders, then firmly clasped the muscles bunched there as she leaned forward. His hands found her waist, guiding her to straddle his lap. He exhaled something unintelligible, a bittersweet curse or a soft prayer – she couldn't be sure. Nem's mind was a whirlwind, her body a beacon of passion-fuelled light.

"I've never burned for anyone as much as I do you," he whispered against her lips.

She could feel that fact quite evidently against her inner thigh. Nem shivered with need, and she glowed brighter.

"Then show me," she breathed.

Krepth hesitated, and she noticed. Nem leaned back, studying his face. His brows were tilted, a look of uncertainty she was sure she had never seen him wear before.

"What?" she began, a warm breeze brushing her hair across her face.

"This…" he ran his knuckle down her arm, and the light glittered a path down her skin. "We should probably discuss *this* before we go any further."

Was he serious right now? After years of chasing her like a dog with a bone, she was finally relenting, and he wanted to… talk?

Her disbelief must have shown on her face, causing Krepth's expression to change. "I wouldn't be stalling if it wasn't something incredibly important. Even though you've always kept me at arm's length, I swear upon the Fates that I have never kept the truth from you, Silver Moon. I am not about to begin now."

Nem swallowed her disappointment, waving away the fog of desire that clouded her mind. "Is it about this?" She lifted her hand, the light beneath her skin beginning to fade.

Krepth paused, moonlight once again gracing his handsome

features. "I'm going to guess that you haven't been taught the history of demi-gods and goddesses, judging by your reaction."

Nem shook her head. "No, I guess it was never beneficial to my assassin training."

"To be Goddess-touched means you were born from the union of a Fae and a deity. Offspring of this union were named demi-gods. They were bred long ago for one thing." He paused, the weight of his words sitting between them. "You were born to hunt Shifters… my kind, Nem."

Waves rolled upon the shores in the distance, and a night bird cawed nearby, the only sounds in that moment.

When Nem found her words, they were breathy, disbelieving. "What?"

"You are familiar with the story about the Fae who stole the objects of power from the Gods? The ones who were cursed, the first of the Shifter people? Well, when the Gods saw how those Fae embraced their animal natures, they were enraged. They were weakening, on the cusp of slumber. A few with enough strength to do so walked among the mortals, and bedded them with the intention of planting seeds, which could remain in the mortal realm. Those seeds were born as demi-gods, and they knew their purpose as soon as they could gather coherent thought. To hunt for the stolen artefacts."

"But I haven't any instinct to find artefacts, nor hurt you…" she paused, pressing her tongue to her teeth. "Well, not beyond warning your curious wolf nose away from me."

Krepth smiled, but it did not reach his eyes. "I think your amnesia wiped away your demi-god instincts. That's my theory, anyway."

It was a lot to take in, not just the glimmer of hope for discovering her origins, but also the weight of what this represented for them.

"Your destiny is to be apart from me, Nem. You're Goddess-touched. Created by the Gods to kill me."

Nem swallowed, heart in throat. Krepth's expression was pained… sad.

She fought to keep her temper – no, her fear – from her voice.

"I don't understand," she tried again, lead pooling in her stomach, weighing her down.

The Shifter touched her cheek, before letting his hand drop.

"It means things just became undoubtably more complicated between us."

CHAPTER ELEVEN

SYBELL

Tora was busting her arse, and Sybell had to admit that she was feeling stronger for it – in body, mind and skin. The Southern Fae's methods were harsh and emotionless, as was the way of the assassins, and there was no room for sympathy, no time for rest, and no compassion for petty mistakes. It reminded her of the short lessons she'd had with Arii, and she appreciated them perhaps a bit more now after the fact. As time passed, Sybell found that her Fae school mates paused to watch less with callousness, more with mild curiosity. She was beaten down often, but when she was, she stood back up again, and no matter how hard Tora forced her back down, she rose. Again and again and again.

The thrashing was not just physical, but mental, too. When she wasn't training with Tora, she was chasing the Fates, or attending classes. The education was complex and heavy, but Sybell was used to absorbing thick texts and information like a sponge. The moth-eaten notebook provided to her by the sisters was nearly full of scrawled notes, and she had already demanded a fresh book twice. It was the only way to acquire anything in this place.

Sybell was used to being demanding.

She clutched Tora's offered hand, before spitting and swiping at her split lip with ink-stained fingers.

"You've eaten more of the dirt of this courtyard than any other female here, and yet you still do not yield," mused the assassin, eyeing Sybell's swelling lip. Maybe she'd knocked something loose in her brain with the number of times she had collided with the floor, but she could have sworn Tora sounded almost… impressed.

"You'll find though my skin is soft, my resolve is not."

Tora huffed a rough laugh.

"Can we have breakfast now?" Sybell whined, rubbing her hip while eyeing the cloudy sky. "We've been at it since before the sun rose. I can't even tell how long it's been, but I'm sure it's been hours."

Tora tsked her tongue. "It has been naught but two hours, princess."

Two hours?

Sybell's stomach groaned just as she did.

A horn sounded, signalling a party approaching the gates, and the sound had everyone snapping into action. Roused and hunger momentarily forgotten, Sybell watched cloaked women bustle about. The Fates had not sent out any more search parties recently, she knew, so whoever was approaching was not their own.

Sybell replaced their training weapons as taught, then looked up as Tora paused silently at her side, grey eyes focused elsewhere. She was listening to sounds close but too soft for Sybell's human hearing to pick up on.

Tora spoke before she could ask. "Red banners… a battalion approaches from the east flying the Kruel house crest."

Sybell's entire body tensed, warring between fight and flight.

"Head to your rooms, they need not know you are here. You have my word."

Oddly, Sybell trusted her. But something deep in her aching bones told her to *stay*. Perhaps it was the remnants of her adrenaline-fuelled training, or perhaps she really had dislodged something in her brain. "No," she whispered, unsure why her voice dropped, but she knew her Fae guardian could hear her as clear as crystal. "No, I'll remain out of sight, but I want to see. I want to know what they have come for."

Tora stared, full attention on her now, and it made her want to fidget.

"Alright," she finally relented.

"Honestly? Just like that?" Sybell gasped, fighting a grin.

The woman grunted in response, yanking a startled laugh from deep in Sybell's chest. Gods, she hadn't laughed in so long. She moved swiftly to the sheltered outer rung of the courtyard, ducking behind crates of supplies. Tora stationed herself nearby, arms folding over her chest.

The gates rumbled open, and a group of thirty men entered. Three were on horseback, including one who headed the procession, his blonde hair cropped short to his scalp, his face a haggard mask. As soon as his feet hit the floor, an order flew from his mouth.

"Stable our mounts and alert the sisters that we bear news from the North and require an audience immediately." The Commander clicked his fingers in a motion that rubbed Sybell the wrong way. It reminded her of the way many back in the castle treated servants, and the women of this castle were *not* servants. Not to him, anyway.

He stared down his nose as if they contained parasites. All of these women could tear this man in two and hardly break a sweat. She wished it wasn't against house rules to murder someone for rudeness alone.

A Fury marched up to the armoured Commander, her hair long and wavy, the colour of dried lavender. "The sisters are not to be disturbed, they are preparing for a ritual," She barked. "What is your business? I will pass the message to them once their ritual is complete. In the meantime, we will have your battalion fed and horses seen to, and you can return home by the time the sun hits the horizon."

Sybell watched the soldiers on the outer circle of the battalion. They stood straight backed and lightly armoured, but she knew something wasn't quite right. Some of them swayed oddly, as if tired, yet it only took hours to march from Viridya. Some cast bored gazes over the castle walls, some stood with mouths open as if dumbfounded. Some wore helmets, but most did not, dirty hair framing dirty faces. All-too bright blue eyes met hers, and a shiver of dread coursed down her spine.

"Tora," she whispered, moving forward and tentatively placing her fingertips on the woman's leather vambrace. "I think we need to be on alert."

"The message cannot wait," snapped the Commander. The bodies shifted restlessly at the rise in the man's voice, but the movement was so slight that Sybell almost missed it. Some teeth clattered, and boots scuffed. Were they… excited?

"Tora," Sybell tried again, her whisper rising with concern. "I think we need to alert those on the rise."

"No one, not even the King of the North, can halt the Fate's ritual," the Fury shot back, her hand sliding to her waist. "I'll say it again, you will have to wait."

One of the soldiers turned his head towards an elven stable hand as she bent to tend one of their horses' hooves. His unclean hair fell forward as his head kept turning, unnaturally so, body unmoving, lips parting over yellow teeth in a warped grimace.

"This is preposterous!" shouted the Commander.

"Tora…"

"You came without first sending a raven. I believe *that* is preposterous, Commander… what did you say your name was?" Lavender Hair stepped forward, eyes narrowed. She displayed her fangs, and with it the air became tense, almost charged.

The hairs rose on Sybell's arms.

"Fucking Fae scum, the lot of you." The Commander's hand twitched to the pommel of his sword as he uttered, "If they will not see us, then we will *make* them see us, and our message will be written in blood upon these filthy walls."

"Tora," Sybell hissed again. Grey eyes finally slid her way, and Sybell was about to curse the slow brain in the woman's thick skull, when her attention was diverted back to the exchange.

The Commander's arm snapped out, steel flashing in the overcast light. His sword was met with Fae steel, but the tip hovered inches from the lavender-haired assassin's outraged face.

Suddenly, the soldier eyeing the elf stable hand broke from his battalion, flinging himself upon her, sinking his teeth into her neck.

She screamed as the horses reared, hooves flailing in the air as pandemonium consumed the inner ward.

The Commander let loose a war cry, swiping his sword. Lavender hair flew as the Fae swept into a backwards dip, barely escaping the blade. She struck back with immortal swiftness as she and the Commander clashed swords.

Tora whirled, grasping her upper arm, grey eyes alight with manifesting magic. "Arm yourself, it is time to put your training to use."

Sybell nodded, but grasped Tora's hand before she could pull away. "Those soldiers are dead. They're reanimated. They don't fear death or feel pain. As far as I know, the only way to put them down for good is by severing their heads from their bodies. Or removing their crystal heart."

Tora nodded, squeezing her palm. Her irises ringed with glowing silver, and the Fae's lips pulled back to hint at her fangs in a small smile. "Thank you, princess." She turned, drew her sword, and entered the fray.

The sight took Sybell's breath away.

She sucked the stolen breath back sharply, swallowing it with her fear. Throwing herself towards the steel weapons across the yard, Sybell leaped over a body severed from its arms, twitching along the ground like a demented slug. She slammed against the rack, fumbling for a sword as a long-winded wail sounded behind her.

Sybell whirled, just as something collided with her, jarring her back against the racks. Weapons clanged to the ground like bells of chaos as her arms strained, sword poised between herself and an undead soldier. As her eyes darted up to her attacker, his blue eyes glowing under a helmet, she forced down her terrified scream. Half his top lip had been torn away, cracked teeth widening in a twisted grimace. The blade of the sword neared her face and she gasped, throwing up a hand to press her bandaged palm against the tip, tilting her head back as the steel touched the leathers covering her breasts. Steel ate into the tourniquet wrapped around her hand, slicing into her flesh. Pain spiked her adrenaline as she bared her teeth, shaking against the overwhelming smell of decay. The soldier's bare hands held the blade, pushing, black blood cascading from his palms, yet he did not relent.

Sybell's muscles heated in protest. She had to dislodge him, lest he drive the blade into her chest, slicing her ribcage in two.

This was *not* how she intended to die.

With an enraged cry, she threw herself sideways, the leather of her armour tearing. The undead's momentum wasn't balanced and he drove forward, falling headfirst into the racks with a howl. As soon as he emerged, Sybell swiped her sword in a downwards arc, slicing his helmeted head from his shoulders, black blood spewing like a cracked water pipe over her trousers and boots.

Gagging, Sybell moved, scouting the bloody pandemonium in search of Tora.

Streaks of magic and fire bolted every which way across the space, and Sybell saw undead soldiers scale the walls to the second floor, like spiders in speed and agility, engaging with the assassins stationed there.

A sickening feeling stabbed her stomach, and it wasn't the smell of death and decay that had her reeling. Her mother, her father, where were they? She wasn't one to pray, but she did anyway, throwing a plea to the Gods for their safety as she saw a blip of dark blonde hair and an elaborately tattooed profile.

"Tora!"

The Fae turned to her; face set in a harsh scowl.

"We have to find the Sisters!" Sybell yelled.

Tora beheaded another soldier, spitting on his corpse where it fell. "The Fates will survive. We must continue to defend the front gates. There could be re-enforcements incoming, and if there are, we will meet them here. We are the rocks on which their surf will break."

Nodding, Sybell let determination flood her fear, and threw herself into the chaos.

ELIJAH

They arrived to the sound of distant screams. The school stood like an obelisk upon the bluff, framed by angry grey clouds. Waves crashed, mingling with the faraway clangs of steel meeting steel, causing Elijah to quicken his steps. Beside him, Ghila kept up, raven hair whipping around her solemn face.

She had remained quiet, contemplative and uneasy in the hours that had passed since he had broken her hold, but she seemed to have been freed from whatever violence whispered in her mind. Elijah couldn't determine whether she was fully free of whatever haunted her, though. She had been through much too much for everything to just be wiped away, and even if the amulet had most of the impact, he was certain some of her problems had been engrained as well. She no longer wore the trinket, instead keeping it deep in her pocket.

They had continued towards the school once Elijah was convinced that the fire of Ghila's revenge had cooled to embers. Since he had told Arii that they were headed there, he believed it best that they keep going. He hadn't seen Arii in his dreams since, and his gut churned with anticipation.

He was hoping to meet with the Sisters and give them the chance to explain; and to find out what side they were on in the coming war. They had kept Ghila safe, when he hadn't, and he felt he owed them a chance to explain why they'd kept her secret. Surely, they'd known her true identity.

As they drew closer to the old castle, Elijah prepared himself for resistance, steeling himself with magic in his limbs.

What he hadn't expected was the sounds of battle clanging on the wind when they came within range.

His sister's shoulders tensed, fists clenched at her sides. "Those are not typical sounds from the school…"

He hadn't thought so.

They passed through the wide-open front gates and straight into the fray. Elijah's eyes swiftly assessed the scene. Soldiers dressed in the red uniform of the North clashed against leather-clad assassins, some soldiers moving with trained precision, some in mindless, murderous vigour.

Elijah's tired mind quickly pieced things together. The fact that these soldiers were attacking the assassins clearly marked the Fate's stance in the war, but it wasn't yet clear if they stood on the grounds of neutrality, or on the side gathering upon the promise of a future under his rule.

The smell of death hit his nose right after the salt and sulphur did, and he chanced a quick glance at Ghila, "We have to find the Sisters," he said, hand moving to his sword. At Ghila's slightly upturned lip, he quickly added, "If they live, they aren't to be harmed."

Ghila made a sound that reminded him of a hissing cat, before tearing her crescent moon blades from their sheaths and lurching at the back of a toppling red guard, burying her weapon to the hilt in his back. The man spat blood, before slumping to the ground, revealing a woman with mint green hair shorn to her scalp. Blood flecked her face, pointed ears startlingly sharp against her profile. "Ah the allusive Wraith. You've returned," she called, weapon trained on his sister. Ghila yanked the steel from the fallen man's back, wiping the blade on her thigh.

Ghila's cool gaze cast back to Elijah, before dancing back to the Fury. "We are here to help. Where are the Sisters?"

The Fae hesitated, then nodded, pointing towards a nearby archway. "In there. They guard the Tapestry."

They dodged clashing bodies, Elijah covering his sister as they dashed down the sconce-lit hall. A few bodies lay fallen, most dressed in crimson, some missing limbs. Elijah couldn't tell if they'd been missing them before the onslaught or after.

He followed Ghila's swift steps, keeping close, until a thrum of power jerked him to a halt. Gooseflesh raised on his arms, and his own magic rose to the surface in answer, static crackling to his fingertips. Yells sounded ahead, and his sister's fingers tugged on his own. "Quickly," she grumbled.

The last time he'd been here, he had felt the dull pulse of power, but he hadn't connected with his magic at that point. At the time he'd thought it was left-over adrenaline from rescuing Arii from Bonemire. Now though, as he followed his sister into what would have once been a throne room, its ceiling high and overgrown with tendrils of ivy, his attention was pulled straight to the enormous glowing, golden cloth draped upon a gilded frame on the dais.

The base of the Tapestry of Life was faded, a shade of dark brown that looked as though it had been dipped in grease, spiderwebs of darkness climbing ahead of the taint. Despite the sickly look of the thing, Elijah could feel the hum of its power, drawing his chest as if a rope was lassoed around his ribcage.

Three women, flanked by a handful of cloaked Fae, fought under the Tapestry. Books burned around them, sending acrid smoke into the air, reducing visibility. They were severely outnumbered, soldiers alive and dead tightly packed in the space but held back by the magic sundering their front line.

Elijah called upon his magic, dredging it up from deep within. It sang, rising up with an eagerness that had his heart flying. It had been suppressed for too long. He cast a hand towards a nearby plume of fire, and it jumped to his command. Outside, thunder rolled and lightning snapped, heralding the maelstrom rising within him. He sucked in a breath, keeping it in check, fighting against the pure, unrestrained power that writhed with the awakening of his beast.

It felt *good*.

His magic… it was rested, agitated and eager to burst.

Elijah thrust his arm out, aiming directly down the middle of the battalion. His magic roared, twisting in a snapping tornado of wind and fire, engulfing all in its path. The ranks parted, charred husks leaving a smoking path directly up to the women on the dais.

Ghila let out a snap of laughter, one reminiscent of when she had him in captivity, and the sound drew him back to focus.

"Incredible!" she laughed as all eyes turned to them.

Elijah gripped his sword with both hands. Ghila licked her lips in anticipation and twirled her crescent moon daggers.

Three glowing-eyed undead attacked first, uniforms streaked with blood and ash.

His sister thrust forward then dropped, skidding between the legs of one of the soldiers. Its eyes were not upon her though, they were upon Elijah, skin flaking as it wailed and arced its sword.

Elijah dodged to one side, sword swiping upwards to quickly dispatch the soldier, as shapes converged on him. Years of battle-honed training rose and even though severely outnumbered, Elijah kept his movements precise and calculated.

He counted his breaths, lungs inhaling and exhaling in time with his sword strokes.

Elijah punched a pulse of magic to clear a momentary path. He scanned the flail of bodies, before ducking a clumsy strike from an undead soldier sporting one arm. The man wailed; the sound abruptly cut short when his head toppled from his soldiers.

Elijah's gaze became a little more frantic.

Ghila, where was she?

He whipped around, catching her sprinting towards the Tapestry. He followed, blasting four men back, blocking out their screams as they hit the floor. His sword stopped one soldier in his tracks as he neared Ghila, while his sister dipped and slashed her daggers through another soldier's ankles, knocking him down. They moved in rhythm, Elijah deflecting the brunt of the onslaught and while Ghila deployed fast attacks to finish those reeling from his blows. The attackers were mostly already dead, vessels with eyes like flashing blue lights, wails like the keening cry of dying animals.

The siblings burst through the crowd and landed on the dais, where they were met by three pairs of golden eyes. The Tapestry stood behind, its power draping over their shoulders like a shroud.

"Wraith, you have returned, with Eliverus Herington in tow. You took your time, but I suppose late is better than never," sneered Klotho, landing a punch on a soldier who broke the line of their defending

Furies. Elijah noticed that the sisters were unarmed. Odd.

"What has happened to the Tapestry?" called Elijah, hoping to deflect the barb of the Fate's words. Klotho blinked rapidly, mouth opening to speak, but her red-headed sister beat her to it.

"Ah, so he comes willingly." Etropos smiled, veiling the cunning in her eyes. "Your talents were underestimated, girl. You come just in time to help us."

"We did not come to help; we came for revenge," Ghila snapped, digging the serpent pendant from her pocket. It snagged her fingers, swaying in the strobing firelight.

"Where did you get that?" Lakhesis' voice was spiked with fear mixed with awe. All three sisters stopped, bodies tense, chests rising and falling with rapid breaths as they stared at the necklace, eyes following it like pendulums.

Ghila's own eyes narrowed. "You know what this is?"

"That is the Locket of Dreaming, and it has not been seen in hundreds, if not thousands of years."

Ghila inspected the pendant with raised brows. "Is that so?"

"How long have you been in possession of it?"

"Long enough for my mind to be forever altered," Ghila shot back, rolling her shoulders and tipping her head to the side, and Elijah wondered if the voices had returned. "Do you want it back?" she continued.

Klotho visibly flinched.

"I have you all to thank, you know. For nurturing my skills, strengthening my magic, stoking my hunger for revenge against those who wronged me."

Elijah shifted, attention torn between the fight at his back and the tense scene before him. He stepped forward as Ghila's fangs glinted in a slow spreading smirk which dimpled her cheeks. "Tell me, Sisters, have you pulled the strings of your own fates from the Tapestry? Or do you wish for your deaths to come as a sweet surprise?"

Had his sister lied to him? Was she still plotting to hurt those who had raised her? Elijah had no reason to trust the weavers of Fate, but he also did not believe they should die. They had raised Ghila, as they had Arii, and Nem.

Ghila took a step forward, and a shiver of panic shot down his spine.

Magic rose at his command, quick and eager. Elijah turned, hand raising, lips parting to tell her to stop, when a rush of magic smacked against his side, tearing his feet from the floor and launching him into the air.

CHAPTER TWELVE

ARIIAYA

Plans swiftly changed as Arii explained to her friends that she had met with Elijah in a dream world which may or may not stem from a bond they may or may not share. So, with a few hours' sleep, the group were once again headed south, under the watchful gaze of a sky ablaze with the remnants of dawn.

"Fates be damned," murmured Emerson, chewing some cheese from a hastily-thrown together breakfast nestled in the folds of a burlap kerchief. No one pointed out that the utterance was ill-suited, as the Fates could well be damned if they didn't get there in time.

With the existence of void travel, Arii once again found herself wondering why they were trudging across this Gods-abandoned land when they could simply fly to their destination with a wave of Noct's hand. The man in question pinched the bridge of his nose, swaying atop his rugged, blue-black stallion.

"Once again, I'll say it for those who had trouble processing it the first time. Magic such as mine needs time to replenish, especially after casting the breathing-underwater spell on *all* of you. Besides, life isn't easy, sometimes you have to travel."

Quinn's mouth snapped shut on what was most likely another query of why they couldn't just 'jump' to the front gates of the School of Fate. The boy's brows drew over his expressive brown eyes and a pout. "Righto."

Tikkani smiled sympathetically, pressing her cheek to his back atop their buckwheat pony.

"We aren't far, anyway," said Luc, petting the neck of his silver mount. "And besides, I've only just shaken the sensation that I was floating in water rather than walking."

Emerson shuddered behind him, recalling the strangeness of moving through the underwater city.

In her star-flecked dreams Arii had seen Elijah, whole, unharmed, and it gave her enough hope to believe he was still in some control of his consciousness. When she had recounted the strange dream to Nem, the Fury had reiterated that there was a connection between them, and not to throw the dreams away as her own overactive imagination conjuring up false hope.

If they arrived and the Sisters waged further war, then they would deal with it.

Several hours later, when they rode up the bluff towards the crumbling castle, dread hit her like a punch. The doors were thrown open and sounds of battle rang out. Knocking her heels into her steed's ribs, she raced ahead.

The courtyard was a frenzy of battling bodies, Fae, humans, and undead. Rain began to fall, as if the heavens themselves wept. Fork lightning streaked above, clouds rolling angrily as Arii leaped from her mount, boots splashing in crimson puddles. The others followed, drawing their weapons.

She scoured the scene, spying familiar faces in amongst the chaos. The women she had called sisters were clashing with men clad in the red armour of the North. A red banner lay on the stone floor like a pool of blood, the gold filagree jaws of the Kruel house crest glinting under the light of flickering spot fires.

A body fell from the battlements, almost landing on Tikkani, but Quinn was quick to pull her out of the way.

"Guess fate is no longer neutral," said Nem, silver hair whipping around her stoic face.

Arii's eyes narrowed, twirling her blades. "It was *never* neutral."

A pulse of magic shook the ground just as lightning struck the peak of the tallest tower, sparks showering over them like rain.

"Go find the Sisters, we will lend our aid here," called Krepth, shrugging his heavy cloak, rolling his shoulders and head. His eyes glowed with magic; his teeth wicked sharp in the breath before his Shift. He and Nem shared a look, one long and full of unexplained tells, before he turned and leaped. Shifting into his wolf midair, he slammed into the back of a red-clad soldier who was seconds from lodging a blade into an overwhelmed Fae assassin's chest.

The others flew to the aid of the assassins against the onslaught of the undead.

A face came into Arii's view, wet golden hair flying around dirt-flecked features.

Sybell.

Her sword cut through the air as the rain fell in earnest, drenching the steel as it whipped through the torso of a soldier. The woman yanked her sword from the man's corpse, eyes widening upon seeing her. "Arii?"

"Where are they?"

She didn't need elaboration, Sybell knew exactly who she was seeking. "The throne room. Valdis has decided to rid himself of the Fates."

Well, that answered one question. The Fates had always considered themselves neutral even though they resided on the cusp of the North and West realms, placing pawns in dangerous games while weaving fates. But now they had to choose a side, and Arii was adamant it would be with them.

Arii clapped a hand on Sybell's shoulder, smirking. "Good to see you alive and using everything I taught you, Princess."

Sybell slapped her hand away, but her face was set in a smirk that Arii found she'd missed, "Stay alive to teach me more later, Assassin." Thunder rolled again, quaking the wet stones beneath their feet.

"Arii," Sybell held her breath for a minute, eyes softening but heavy with meaning. "He's here."

It took a moment for her mind to catch up with the speeding gallop of her heart.

Elijah was here.

"Let's go!" called Nem as she freed a man of his head.

A tall, broad Fae female stood over Sybell's shoulder, her demeanor almost protective. Arii nodded to Tora, who nodded back in silent understanding. *Protect her.*

Arii and Nem headed for the throne room. They leaped over fallen bodies as they rushed towards flickering orange light, one of the heavy doors crooked on broken hinges. When they entered, the stark smell of burning flesh slapped them. Magic sizzled across the floor, and flames licked up the walls, catching on dry ivy to create an archway of fire.

Arii's breath punched from her lungs when she saw the scene.

It was utter chaos.

But her gaze was drawn to the dais, to the towering, broad-backed man who stood there, his gaze fixated on the three Sisters of Fate and a thin, leather-clad Fae female. Klotho pointed an accusatory finger at Ghila, her hand shaking, "How long have you been in possession of that trinket?"

"Long enough for my mind to be forever altered." Ghila shot back, rolling her shoulders and tipping her head to the side. "Do you want it back?"

Klotho visibly flinched.

"I have you all to thank, you know. For nurturing my skills, strengthening my magic, stoking my hunger for revenge against those who wronged me."

Elijah shifted but remained silent. Arii could not see his face, only the tip of a pointed ear and a hint of jaw, covered in dark beard. The side of his neck was creased with dirt and blood, and he was in the same clothing as when she had lost him. He took a step forward as Ghila's fangs glinted in a slowly spreading smirk. "Tell me, have you pulled the strings of your own fates from the Tapestry? Or do you wish for your deaths to come as a sweet surprise?"

Arii moved, pushing wailing, scrambling bodies back and cutting through them as quickly as she could manage, her movements desperate. Nem fought beside her, covering her back. She didn't know how long the Sisters had been fighting, and she didn't want any of them to die before she obtained answers or claimed Elijah back.

Then, Ghila took a step forward and Elijah shifted, his hand rising. Magic stirred life in the acrid air, causing Arii's ears to pop. She could feel the chaos manifesting in her bones, could taste it in the air amongst everything else. Elijah's magic had become as familiar as his kiss, charged, claiming, unpredictable. Arii recognized the peril in the untamed magic he wielded and sensed the danger of facing him under Ghila's influence. Time was slipping away, and she had to act swiftly.

Arii unleashed a blast of magic straight at Elijah, propelling him backward through the air. Her chest ached as she watched him land on the floor and come to a stunned halt against a stack of tumbling books.

Ghila's attention snapped towards Arii, eyes wide with alarm. Arii channeled her rage into her actions, flinging her blades at the Fae's chest in an attempt to put a stop to whatever she was doing to the Sisters and Elijah. Weapons clashed and sparks flew as she stared down into narrowing orbs of quicksilver, her irises flecked with dark spots much like her brother's. The resemblance snatched at her breath.

Ghila's arms shook in her effort to keep Arii's blades from her chest, and Arii felt that if she pushed just that little bit harder, she could plunge her weapons home, straight into the female's sick and twisted heart. The Fae's strength felt akin to a human, and that fact had Arii unintentionally holding back. "Let them go! Let *him* go!" Arii snarled.

Ghila's arms strained under Arii's onslaught, "Ariiaya! You're just in time, he is—"

"Arii!" Nem called, and Arii reluctantly glanced her way. When the Fae pointed, Arii followed, watching Elijah slowly get to his feet. The distraction cost her. Ghila's fist slammed into her stomach, and Arii keeled over.

Ghila turned and ran back towards the Tapestry.

Shit.

"Ariiaya!"

A shadow fell over Arii, just as her head tipped up. A blur of movement and a glint of steel, and Nem was before her, weapons arcing towards an undead soldier who had burst through the line of warring Furies. She twirled, blades severing cloth, making quick work of her opponent who had lost their armour long ago. The creature wailed then slumped as its head detached and rolled across the floor.

"Go to him!" Nem called over her shoulder before heading towards the Tapestry too.

Arii launched to her feet, daggers singing as she dodged another soldier, spearing towards Elijah. He was up, staring, heavy lashes hooding his silver eyes. She had no idea if he were still under the influence of Ghila's mind-wielding, and she wasn't going to leave an opening to find out. He'd nearly killed her before, and a shadow of pain bloomed behind her nose in memory of him breaking it.

Subdue, restrain, and ask questions later, that was her objective.

Like the countless times she'd headed into a mission, Arii pressed her emotions back behind a hastily erected wall. She glared at the man she loved with naught but a twisted snarl.

They clashed, Arii's daggers against the swift rise of his sword.

"Arii!" he grunted, and her muscles bunched against his strength. There was the tiniest waver in his stance, a pinprick of a slide in his boot as she pressed harder, his face inches from her own. He was filthy, marred with dirt and gore. Was some of it his own? What had Ghila made him do? It was obvious he hadn't rested much – or more likely, Ghila hadn't let him rest, or bathe. The mistreatment had fire erupting through her. Seeing him alive, though, flooded her with relief.

"It's me!" he said, a tick in his jaw marking his irritation. What had previously been an amusing little tell on his handsome face had her hesitating. The last time they fought, he had nothing on his face, no expression. Was this a trick by his sister? Was she able to take hold of not only movements, but speech and facial muscles, too?

Her hesitation lasted but a breath before she was whirling, blades singing, boots scraping. She knocked back his sword, not allowing herself to process how easy it was to do so, before sheathing one of her weapons mid spin, throwing her fist into his stomach.

Elijah grunted but held his ground.

Pain sparked in her fist, racing up her arm. It was like punching a wall of rock.

He dropped his sword, one hand catching her wrist, spinning her so her back slammed against his front. Beneath the smell of travel, death and dirt, she smelled him. Pine, steel and the faintest hint of forest.

"Stop, listen!" he growled into her ear as she bucked against him.

She hadn't forgotten how strong he was, nor had she forgotten the reaction such a stance triggered in her. This exact one, his chest pressed to her back, the dash of breath against her ear, his arm encasing her, reminded her of when he'd gotten the upper hand when they'd first begun training. She'd been cocky, thinking him human, believing him easy to best. Warmth bloomed down her neck, his panted breaths spearing fire down her spine, igniting her core.

A warm hand found her neck, cupping forcefully, turning her head to look at him. The fierce way he handled her only further warmed her more intimate parts. He'd always been so gentle, handling her like glass even when she told him to stop holding back. His heart thundered against her back, and her own matched its tempo, as the hand slipped to her collarbone. She suppressed a shudder of desire.

She heard his swallow, and knew he felt the same fire at the contact of skin, too.

Could he truly be free from Ghila's influence?

If she allowed her guard to fall and this was an act, she'd pay dearly.

Arii relaxed ever so slightly, and his hold eased a fraction. Then, she whirled, taking a step back, gasping.

"It's me," Elijah said again, hand reaching for her, but she thumped it away and bared her teeth.

"You can prove that when I have you bound in rope," she growled, striking with her dagger. Elijah was *fast*. His hands somehow avoided the sharp edge of her steel, grasping her arm, the tip quivering an inch from his face. Her gaze slid past the hilt to catch his silver eyes fixed on her.

Then the resolute look on his face broke way to exasperation and his eyes rolled. "For Fate's sake. See through the anger that blinds you for one moment and truly *look* at me, Arii."

She pressed on her weapon, and his foot skidded back another fraction. She stared, really stared, and he returned it, unblinking and severe. "I broke her hold. It was the locket she wore." He was first to look away, in search of his sister. "Ghila has suffered a lot, and even though the locket's influence has been removed, she will be forever altered. She's… damaged, and misunderstood, but I have to help her." Elijah's eyes moved back to her, and they softened around the edges. She knew him though and could see shadows of lingering ghosts behind his eyes. Her anger began to fizzle, like water hitting hot coals. The reverberation around his magic had dissipated, and while he was fierce without it, she could feel that he wasn't trying to fight her. "I never once stopped trying to get back to you, my heart."

My heart.

Ghila wouldn't know how those words tugged at her own heart, at the invisible force around her chest. Ghila was not manipulating Elijah's words.

"You're really… back?" Arii's voice was a rasp, the words curling around her dry tongue, her press upon him easing. One hand held her back now, the other moving to her face again, his fingers touched her chin, gliding to cup her cheek, and with the touch she truly relented. Her gut feeling was that he had found his way back to her. Arii allowed her emotions to unlock, and they sang with his return. She could stop fighting, just for a little while.

He smiled then, a slow curl that she knew too well.

"You look like crap," was all Arii could manage, relief flooding her muscles.

A hint of teeth as Elijah replied, "I can't argue with you, I look and definitely *smell* like crap."

There was an explosion from behind, and a triumphant cry. The assassins were picking off the remaining few undead, while Etropos and Lakhesis quelched nearby spot fires with magic.

They had survived, this time.

With her last blade clattering to the floor, Arii lurched into Elijah's arms, and he embraced her fiercely. "I thought I'd lost you," she whispered.

"It'd take far more to sever me from you, Ariiaya. Are you alright?" Elijah said, brushing a damp strand of honey-tipped hair from her cheek. The featherlight pass of his knuckle painted her skin with fire.

Nearby, Nem held Ghila by the arm, dagger hovering at her throat. The Wraith did not fight her captor but watched the exchange between her brother and the Fury with interest.

"I'm fine... now," Arii blew out a breath as they turned to the Tapestry, where Klotho and her sisters now stood, flanked by a handful of Furies. Sybell and Tora had arrived at some point, and Arii was thankful to see them alive and well, albeit battered and bruised. Tora leaned heavily on Sybell, who supported her with an arm looped around her waist.

Arii's gaze skated over the remainder of her friends as they joined them, inwardly sagging with relief. Luc was supported by Emerson and Nocturne, a sizable gash running from his forehead and curving around his cheek. Tikkani held hands with Quinn, who surveyed the carnage with wary eyes. Krepth stood with Nem, his dark hair unkempt with what Arii guessed to be gore.

Hacking coughs drew their collective attention as a scar-faced Fury dragged a man clad in bloody armor to the front. His hair was shorn short, half of his face covered in blisters. The half that wasn't mutilated spiked a memory in Arii. This was the man who flanked Lorch, Hawke's replacement, when they had faced Elijah outside of Border Town.

Klotho was first to speak, "Keep this one alive, Tyan, he could prove of use should he answer some questions." The Fury nodded.

"The King's Hand, Lord Valdis, sends a message. Your usefulness is at an end. Even the Fates cannot escape death," the soldier gargled, vermillion-stained teeth flashing between a smirk and a pained grimace. "This land will be cleansed of your kind soon enough, and a new era for humans will begin."

Klotho, Etropos and Lakhesis watched the man with varying expressions of disgust. "Take him away."

Suddenly his hand flew to his mouth. Tyan jerked the soldier up, but it was too late. He began to convulse, pink froth oozing from his lips, eyes rolling back.

Krepth growled, "Poison."

The man slackened in death, and Tyan let the body drop.

"Guess he didn't want to be interrogated," said Luc into the unease of the room.

The Commander's final words left them with a sense of disquiet, and within Arii the sense of urgency renewed.

They were quickly running out of time. They needed to find the Ouroboros, and to gather whatever forces they had accumulated. And prepare for war.

Sunlight peeked through the high windows, blessing them with an unusual hint of blue sky and warm sun. The battle here had ceased, but as Arii set her sights on the slim, dark-haired Fae with eyes the colour of a storm, she knew it was far from over.

GHILA

Ghila heaved a breath, the vice-like grip upon her arm dredging up unpleasant memories. She didn't enjoy contact, especially strong touch; it made her feel like she was back in the carriage. Back in the monsters' hands…

Swallowing her revulsion, she shifted, but the silver-haired Fae – Nemesis – did not relent, remaining as still as stone. Ghila eyed her sideways, for she'd heard much about her stellar, violent record. She was one of the Fates' favourites, along with…

Her.

Ariiaya.

The one she'd used to try to get to her brother. An ex-favourite.

Nem's blade remained at her neck, but it was hovering, not quite touching her skin. There was hesitation there. The air radiated with tension, and Ariiaya's intense violet stare never left Ghila's face, making her feel uncomfortable. She glanced away, the whisper of voices prodding deep behind her consciousness like worms.

Something snapped over her wrist, and Ghila jerked, bringing her arm up. A slim iron manacle ringed her wrist like a bangle. Weight on the other arm told her there were two.

The voices were gone in a second, as was her magic.

She should have felt angry, threatened; but instead she felt… tired. Bone-shakingly *exhausted*.

Perhaps it was time she stopped fighting, just for a little while at least.

Slowly, the blade slipped away, and Nemesis stepped back.

"You took him from me," Arii finally said, eyes narrowed, her voice echoing about the room. The legs of a chair scraped the marble nearby as a blue-haired Fury righted furniture. The others moved about, avoiding their small circle and the obvious anger simmering there. While the assassins weren't averse to violence, they knew their purple-eyed sister's anger wasn't one to be trifled with. Even Ghila knew of Ariiaya Trillia's legendary short temper.

Ghila swallowed, her throat working around words, unsure where to start.

"I'm sorry," she managed. "I'm so sorry."

Her eyes slipped to the towering frame of her brother. She wouldn't blame this woman if she wanted vengeance for the pain Ghila had caused – she herself would have been the same.

Arii remained silent, her eyes speaking instead. Her silence was weighted, barbed, making Ghila's skin tingle, a feeling worse than if she were to yell and scream.

A deadly silence.

"She was in possession of this," Klotho reluctantly lifted the locket, taken from Ghila and handed to her by Nem. "The Locket of Dreaming. An age-old piece that we believed lost long ago. You kept it well hidden, child."

Lakhesis whispered from her sister's side, white hair marred with splotches of blood. "Cursed souls were harvested into the fibres of the material it's made from. It was created with the intention of allowing its user to traverse the dreams of others, but in the hands of one with those powers already, it would do naught but curse them."

"That could have been the voices plaguing you, Ghila," offered Elijah, crossing his arms over his chest.

She was sure that the thing had aided in the voices, but even now that she was rid of it, she felt them somewhere deep in her mind, veiled behind her consciousness. After Elijah had taken it, she'd explained the voices, and how they'd helped her. He hadn't seemed convinced that they'd be anything more than a curse on her, but they'd kept her company for twenty years, had been there during those dark nights in the cart. Had been there when *he* had hurt her.

Her pain had been their pain, and their pain hers too. She owed them, yet loathed them, in a way.

"This trinket was stolen from the Gods long ago," said Etropos, taking it from her sister. "Along with two other artefacts."

"I remember that story, the one about the Fae who stole three precious items from the Gods that resulted in them being cursed. The origin of the Shifter people," pointed out a bright-eyed elf, her hair falling in tendrils from her ponytail. "Krepth?"

The attention of the room shifted to a male with hair as dark as raven's wings, and eyes as green as a forest. Ghila was sure she could smell the earthy scent of an animal in the air.

The man held up blood-stained palms. "Far before my time, so I'm exempt from blame here." Krepth pointed an accusatory finger at the swinging pendant. "Is it not the thing we are seeking, Noct?" he said, tipping his head. Ghila wasn't sure if she could learn all their names, but now with silence in her head, she felt it would be less of a challenge than before.

"Its resemblance to the Ouroboros is purely coincidental," answered a man in immaculate, foreign clothing. Noct, she presumed.

The Sister's brows rose in tandem, and their outward curiosity flared to life inside Ghila, too.

"There was a cloak and a sword, too, right?" continued Tikkani, glancing up at the Tapestry. "Speaking of curses, the Tapestry isn't looking too great–" she hesitated, looking back at the Sisters. "No offense."

Now that it was mentioned, Ghila had to admit that the magic in the room felt strange, a little off in comparison to previous times here. When she had been allowed into the room, she had always felt the mighty weight of the Tapestry's power. Now, it felt weaker, and she noticed the last quarter of the glowing gold fabric looked to be dull and lifeless.

Nearby, Ariiaya's lips were a tight line, her face emotionless as she hitched her chin at the Tapestry. "What is happening to it?" she asked warily.

Klotho sighed, roping her long, dark hair back with a tie as she replied, "Perhaps this is an explanation best given over wine. Lots of wine."

Ghila read Arii and Nem's exchanged glances without having to probe into their minds. The Fates seldom indulged, nor did they give information easily.

Klotho eyed the Tapestry sadly, before turning to them fully.

"The Gods are abandoning us," a weighted pause, "because of me."

There was further silence as even the Furies cleaning up paused at the explanation. Ghila surveyed every face in the room, taking in the varying states of wariness. Something twinged in the back of her mind, perhaps it was remnants of the voices that had plagued her for so long, so she allowed them a tiny gap to speak through.

'The land is dying, and your Gods do not watch over the dead.

There is only one who does that, and they do not suffer the living above. Only balance will restore the God's faith, their presence, and their magic here.'

Ghila shivered, pressing the voices back. She reached for the empty space at her neck, fingers brushing her skin as her eyes found her brother. Into the tepid silence she spoke, her shoulders curling inward at the attention coming her way.

"The souls in that trinket plagued me for a long time. They filled me with so much hate, their thirst for revenge insatiable, mingling with my own. But sometimes they would tell me things that I didn't understand. I think I understand them now, they speak of balance needing to be restored."

She had initially thought that balance was relating to her own life, culling those who brought her harm, but now she was coming to realize this was far beyond her. It was about her bloodline, about what once was, and what was meant to be. She drew breath as the last words seemed to spill from her.

"My brother needs to become the King and restore balance once more."

Klotho's eyes narrowed. "Much relies upon his claiming of the throne, it seems.'

Elijah shifted uncomfortably in her peripheral vision. Not once during her time in his mind did she get the impression he wanted to be a king. Even as a child, she remembered him being reluctant, whereas her other brother, Brohem, had been excited by the premise of being next in line.

Lakhesis and Etropos flanked their sister as Klotho spoke again. "In order for us to aid you, the Sisters will no longer be neutral. I will prove my service to the Gods, and right my wrongs."

Ghila had been kept separate from the happenings of the world, so whatever the dark-haired sister had done was a mystery to her. What was done was done now, though, and she thought she best learn from this. If one of the Fates could atone for her misconduct, perhaps she could too?

Ariiaya stepped forward, her face a scowl which didn't quite meet her eyes. "And how can we trust you? You aided Valdis in the creation of his undead army. How do we know you aren't continuing to aid him?"

The dark-haired Fate rolled her next words over her tongue, her eyes drifting to Ghila. "I will show you what happened. Why I did what I did."

Arii crossed her arms, glancing between them. "By using *her*?"

Ghila tried not to outwardly flinch at the bite in the female's words.

Unperturbed by Arii's obvious venom, Klotho began to answer, "If I allow the Wraith access to my mind, she can see–"

"Then pass the vision on to us," finished Elijah, the deep timbre of his voice gentle.

Arii shot him a glare. "Fucking *no*."

Ghila did flinch at that.

"The choice if yours, Violet Assassin. To seek the truth is to seek it in its entirety, not just in pieces."

Elijah and the remainder of their group were silent, contemplative.

Finally, a voice broke through the stale, sulphuric air. "I think we should see her side, Arii."

It was the other elf, the male with inquisitive, upturned golden eyes and a gentle yet curious disposition. A dark-skinned boy stood beside him, blood peppering his cheeks and tunic.

Ghila understood Arii's hesitation. She didn't think she'd trust the one who took Elijah away... But this could help in beginning her amends for what she'd done.

"Think on it and let me know. Until then..." Klotho said, turning on her heel, gazing back at the Tapestry. It hummed, iridescent magic flashing over its surface, as if it were opening an eye and awakening from slumber.

Without speaking, Lakhesis knelt at the base and pinched a thread, tugging it gently free. The thread looked sickly, and the Sister held it in cupped palms before handing it to Etropos, who pinched either end and tugged the string tight. She then turned to Klotho, who ran her fingertip over the dull thread.

Her eyes shimmered as she cast them back over the group, then spoke, her own voice wavering with another, unearthly voice. It reverberated around the room, weighing it with a divine presence.

"Should I not fulfil my duty in aiding the rightful heir, Eliverus Herington, to his throne, Ariiaya Trillia – the Violet Assassin – shall take my life and choose another to stand in my place."

Chapter Thirteen

SYBELL

Sybell was surprised by how light the body was as she dragged the slumped form of one of the undead soldiers towards the arrangement of flat-laid bodies. The man couldn't have been much older than herself, but his skin was mottled, limbs spindly, hardly a muscle on him. Dead for a time before his reanimation, obviously. Dragging him was like dragging a sack of bones – well, she only guessed so, as she'd never dragged a sack of anything in her privileged life. He reeked, the smell stinging her senses, but she didn't show her disgust. The old Sybell would have turned up her nose and demanded a servant do the heavy lifting, but they were no longer in a castle, and she no longer had servants.

She was no longer a princess.

Sybell was an assassin and had to get used to getting her hands dirty.

She was getting good at disassociating herself from her feelings, like a true Fury. The stiffening young man beneath her palms was no longer a person to her, but a vessel that once carried a life. Before, she would have felt ill at the feeling of stony, dead skin under her fingers, and squirmed at the way his head lolled against her bicep. But now, she brushed away all thoughts to get her job done.

There would be no mentioning the cavern in the middle of his chest, skin butterflied open to reveal insides, and the lack of a stone heart that she'd witnessed Tora quite literally tear from his chest.

The old Sybell would have vomited long ago, had she not learned how to press her feelings back into a gilded chest in her mind. Besides physical training, she'd been tossed headfirst into honing that skill, too.

"Place him there, princess. Good, on his back, and rest his arms over his chest."

Sybell's stomach lit with flutters at the voice.

Alright, not all feeling had gone *just* yet.

She did as instructed, gently crossing the man's hands over his chest, before glancing at the neat arrangement of bodies around the burial pyre. Others had their hands over their chests, and she felt a twinge in her own at Tora's attention to detail. This one had been attacking them earlier, and despite his violent end, Tora placed his hands so that they folded over his chest. The warrior squatted, placing coins over misty eyes.

Sybell straightened to look at Tora.

"They may have been puppets, but they fought valiantly for their cause. They will be farewelled with respect." Tora murmured; her accent particularly thick in the moment. Sybell wondered whether, despite her lack of emotion, she was impacted by the amount of death more than she let on.

Sybell motioned a hand towards the coins, placed upon the eyes of the dead, glittering like a small sea of dragon scales in the mid-afternoon light. "What are the coins for? It's not a custom I've seen used here before."

Tora rose to her feet, dusting her palms on her thighs. "'Tis a custom where I come from." After a pause, Tora continued. "In the South, when one travels from this world and on to the next, they must pass through a purgatory – where they are greeted by a ferryman, their only way to cross the sea of the dead." She nodded at Sybell slowly. "No payment means no means to cross, and without passage to the beyond, those souls linger at the water's edge until the end of time."

"That's… sad." Sybell breathed, as Tora paused and winced as she tried to shrug. Sybell took a step forward, alarmed. "Are you hurt?"

"Nay, it is only a scratch—"

Sybell, despite Tora's small sound of protest, scooted closer, examining the jagged tear in her mentor's fighting leathers. She prodded the fabric, eliciting a sharp inhale from Tora. "Scratches don't run that deep. Come on, let's get it looked at." She grabbed the Fae's callused fingers, tugging her towards the portcullis, and up a flight of stairs.

Sybell expected resistance, but when Tora sighed and trailed along, fingers limp in her own, she kept her triumphant grin at bay. The warrior didn't resist, even as their boots thumped dusty floors towards the medical ward. The closer they neared, and the longer Tora held her silence, the more Sybell began to worry. If Tora wasn't fighting her, perhaps she was in more pain than she let on.

Those disturbing thoughts remained as the physicians – human women, she noticed – removed the outer layers of her armour to better inspect the damage. The fabric of Tora's cobalt tunic was almost black with blood, and the healers scurried about, retrieving alcohol and tools. There were others here too, hidden behind curtains. Sybell could smell the herbal medicine being used, its potency burning her nose.

Sybell paced, her tone so gruff that she was sure Tora's demeanour was rubbing off on her. "Can magic not heal you?"

The Fae craned her head, watching the healers work, wincing as they poked a needle and thread through her flesh. "Mmhmm, but then we would not have scars to remind us. There is learning in our failures, lessons to be learned from our wounds. The scars remind us of what not to do next time."

"That is just ridiculous." Sybell whirled, tossing her hands.

Tora winced, holding the soiled garment away from the wound, "Calm, *dunga*, you'll wear a path in the stone, or worse, give yourself a headache."

"How can you care about a headache when your skin is being stitched together like a quilt?!"

The healer, a young woman with tawny hair, shot her an unimpressed look as Tora murmured, "You stitch very–" a wince, "–

neatly, Silvana."

Sybell wasn't sure why the thought of Tora's skin being ravaged by a jagged, unsightly scar bothered her. The Fae was an assassin, sure to have plenty of other scars hidden on other parts of her body that Sybell would never see or hear about. Unbidden, Sybell's eyes skirted the expanse of Tora's stomach that she could see, toned from training, and apart from the wound, smooth and the colour of sun-kissed sand.

Sybell's cheeks heated, and she looked away.

"Your concern is flattering, princess, truly," Tora said, her tone gentler than Sybell had ever heard it. It brought her gaze back, and though she tried to look anywhere but the grey eyes of the woman, Sybell found her attention drawn straight into their cool depths. "You fought well today." Tora added, breaking eye contact as she did.

A compliment? Well, she'd be a Kryvern's uncle.

Silvana tied the last loops of stitching, before handing Tora a small flask. Tora murmured a thank you and the human bobbed a curtsy before moving to another patient.

Tora gingerly rested the fabric down. Sybell sank to the mattress beside her and said, "I've never seen so much death."

"One becomes accustomed to death in the company of assassins."

As Tora downed the contents of the flask, Sybell found her tired mind wandering back to a time when all she cared for was the gown she'd be wearing, and was it different to the one she'd worn at the last event. Was a single hair out of place? Were her nails clean, the polish without blemish? How far she'd come from those trivialities, from what she now considered to be a simpler existence in comparison to this.

She'd gained a whole lot of perspective since then.

Now, Sybell picked at a tear in her fingernail, the last one remaining past her fingertips. She inspected her hand, the blood-stained cuticles and grimy creases of her knuckles. Once, the dirt would have bothered her, but now… just like Tora's scars, the imperfections were a reminder of what she'd just gone through. One day perhaps she'd have her own scars with stories to tell. Would she forget those stories once the skin healed?

Hands just as stained as her own gently covered hers, startling a breath from Sybell.

"But just because we become used to death does not mean we are unaffected by it, Sybell."

She wasn't sure if she were more surprised by the contact, or that Tora had finally addressed her by name. She stared at where their hands met, and although Tora's was larger in width, and slightly darker of skin, their fingers were about the same length, nails in the same chipped condition.

Different, yet almost completely the same.

"It gets easier? The killing, I mean," Sybell said, her voice just above a whisper. Her eyes lifted, meeting grey ones, normally hard like stones, but right now slightly softer around the edges.

Tora mulled over the words before replying, "It does."

"But being from the South would have hardened you before arriving here, right? I heard from a merchant once that you are sent into the snow forests as soon as you can walk, to tame bear cubs? Or else you're not allowed home?"

"Dire Wolf pups," Tora corrected, a sound escaping her that was a meld of a laugh and a grunt. It gave Sybell warm tingles, and her face twitched into a smile. They were so close that their shoulders touched, and the tips of Tora's curls tickled Sybell's cheek. The assassin's skin was so smooth, she noticed, and her eyes held a hue of blue that she hadn't noticed from afar.

"Right, how silly of me to get the two mixed up," Sybell sighed.

Tora bumped her shoulder. "Do not worry. The pups share our fear. If the child isn't worthy, they are left with a few scratches and an even more damaged pride. The event is so ancient, that even the adult wolves stay back, knowing that should their pup bond, it is the will of the Goddess, and they shan't intervene.

It is the family waiting at home that the children need to worry about. If they are unsuccessful in taming a wolf, they are sent back into the forests until they are. And if they cannot make a connection, they are cast from the Court, to enter an existence without purpose… or they seek another fate. Make something out of their failure and learn from it."

"Families abandon their children? That is… barbaric." Sybell noted, brows scrunching, which coaxed another gruff sound from Tora. The silence wasn't uncomfortable as she thought it might be, and as the cogs of her clever mind turned, she landed on a thought that she would have kept to herself just a few days ago.

"Wait… is that how you got here?" Sybell voiced her thoughts timidly, unsure how the Southern warrior would react.

Tora's lips pursed, a slight tell that she was once again mulling over her words. Sybell gazed away, not expecting an answer, so when Tora spoke, her heart clenched.

"Yes."

Their eyes met again.

Sybell felt anger for a little girl cast out from her home, all because a silly wild dog hadn't the good sense to choose her. Fate was unfair to throw such unfortunate luck upon such a strong person. Tora had a good heart, Sybell decided. She'd had plenty of chances to stop training her, or to belittle her, and look at her the way all of the others in the school had. But she'd continued to train her, despite her frail human body.

Not only that, Tora had protected her during the fight, when she could have – no, *should* have – headed straight to the Fates or to any of her sisters. But she'd fought alongside her. Sybell knew that the Fae's strength wasn't only in her body, but in her heart and soul, too. She'd always been a good judge of character, and her gut was telling her that Tora was *good*, against the occupation she'd found herself in.

Why would a wolf pup not be drawn to that?

She was drawn to that.

They were close enough to share breath, caught in a moment drawn purely between the two of them, one as fragile and thin as angel's hair, and Sybell wondered if she'd regret crossing that delicate space to chance a kiss. She had naught a clue how Tora would react, or if she felt that way inclined, but with her grey eyes fixed on her now, she wondered....

Tora tilted towards her, eyes dropping to Sybell's lips, a miniscule thing that had Sybell's heart kicking up a beat.

Sybell was stronger now, in both body and mind. If the warrior were to reject her, she could take it. It would give Tora a fresh reason to up her training and call it progress, while in reality punishing her for a weak moment of emotion… but Sybell thought it was worth the risk–

"Oh thank the Goddess you're alright!"

Sybell jerked away, thoughts sundered like torn cloth, turning to see her parents entering the room. Dust coated her mother's robes, and she was sure the soil on her father's wasn't simply muck from the stables, but blood too.

"I'm fine," Sybell muttered as her mother cupped her face to tilt her head from side to side, inspecting every inch of her exposed skin. Luckily, Sybell hadn't sustained any injuries save for a few bruises and small cuts.

Perhaps a Goddess had been watching over her, after all.

Or perhaps it had been the stoic Fae assassin whom she had thought about kissing mere moments ago.

Shame heated her cheeks – she hadn't even thought about her parents. Now, relief made her sag into her mother's embrace. "Where were you?"

"Your father and I protected the stables. Lucky for us, those abominations only seemed to care about those in the castle." She glanced back at Hawke. "There were only a few who broke away to the stables. The horses must have drawn them."

"It won't take long for Valdis to notice his battalion has not returned." Hawke said, crossing his arms. "We should alert the Sisters to the possibility of another attack."

As the ex-commander of the Red Guard army, Sybell knew his warning was not a guess. He knew how Valdis ticked and could very well predict the tyrant's next move.

Before they could turn back to the silent warrior beside her, Tora stood slowly. Sybell dashed to her feet too, to ensure Tora was steady. It was instinct, her body angling before she thought about it, and she winced, awaiting a scowl from Tora.

Instead, cool eyes assessed her, softening as she nodded gently.

Thank you.

Sybell looked away, hiding a blush.

Tora cleared her throat, taking on the air of an assassin once more. All eyes in the medical bay, wounded and not, remained on the Fae as she said, "I will alert the Sisters. Prepare yourselves, because tomorrow we will begin heading East."

GHILA

Ghila stood before the Tapestry, her fingers teasing at the manacle around her wrist. It had been so long since she'd laid eyes upon the Tapestry of Life or been within touching distance of its magical fibres. And longer still since she'd had an uncrowded mind to let thoughts stir. With it towering over her now, a quarter of the fabric covered in a sickly darkness, Ghila reflected upon her time kept hidden away, inside secret chambers buried beneath the old castle structure.

Not many knew of the existence of a small network of tunnels and rooms under the school – the perfect place to train a Fury in secret. The dark, dank rooms became her home, the lack of light aiding her growing vendetta against those who had taken her in. Klotho had been the one to see to her personally, teaching her in in the ways of magic and strength – as was her responsibility. History and knowledge were left to Etropos, the red-haired Fate who gravitated towards the books held in their small library. Lessons in stealth and subterfuge were left to Lakhesis, whose cunning mind and keen eyes saw through to Ghila's soul. She supposed she should have been grateful to have not been left in the light-haired Fate's charge, but after spending time under the condescending lift of Klotho's angled chin and the narrow of her otherworldly golden eyes, Ghila found herself wishing she'd been left with the latter.

She'd been left with the least kind of the three, and as time snaked on and her lessons became harsher, Ghila felt the acidic burn of her anger mingle with the voices within her necklace. Their anger became hers, amping up the already burning need to be free… to be *more*.

There were times that Ghila was sure that Klotho knew of her possession of the locket, the Fate's eyes holding unspoken accusation and curiosity, but the Sister never asked. Why? Surely, she had felt it, or sensed it?

Ghila had been curious once, enough to use her mind-wielding in an attempt to satisfy that curiosity.

The last time Ghila had tried to take hold of the Fate's mind, it had been during training. She hadn't succeeded, and had paid for it dearly.

'Useful, on the right target, little Wraith. But not upon a Goddess.'

She'd nestled in her blankets that night sporting magical burns and purple bruises, her fingers latched around her locket, listening to the voices whisper. She'd vowed never again to attempt to dive into the Fate's minds, not unless she was strong enough to take hold… take possession… make the next attempt *final*.

Whether Ghila was strong enough for that now, she didn't think so, for she lacked the drive she once had. She felt listless, a boat without a rudder at sea, the waves of dozens of consciousnesses lapping against her mind, while staring up at the foundation the School had been built upon. The manacles kept things at bay, but she could still feel their gentle touch.

The Tapestry of Life loomed over her.

One consciousness remained a few feet away, watching her silent reflection, the Fury with silver hair. Nemesis hadn't left her, but kept sentry, probably to keep Ariiaya happy.

Footfalls sounded behind, and slowly she turned.

Klotho stood below the dais, accompanied by Elijah, Ariiaya and the other two Fates. Ghila kept her lips firmly sealed, casting her eyes over each of their faces in turn.

"If you'll allow it, Ghila, we wish to learn of Klotho's side of the story," said Elijah, a slither of afternoon light casting a crack across his dark leather armour.

After a breath, Ghila tilted her chin in a nod.

Klotho approached, lifting her long-nailed fingers to encircle Ghila's shackled wrists. Her voice was low, dangerous, as she whispered, "This memory is all you will see."

The weight in her words, the meaning in them, was not lost on Ghila.

Don't go digging where you are not supposed to. You will only see the memories which are given to you.

Ghila didn't much feel like tempting fate today.

The manacles fell away, and the return of her strange magic felt like a whisper upon her skin. Ghila took in Klotho's face, the flawless smooth skin, the striking golden eyes framed with thick, black lashes – as dark as her hair, shiny as a waterfall of oil – and her blood-red lips, pulled into a stoic line.

Defensive in her outward composure, when Ghila's mind tentatively probed hers, the door to Klotho's consciousness was unlocked.

Ghila entered the mind of a Fate, unsurprised when she stepped into a room made entirely of gold.

The space was unfurnished, a room as large as the throne room she'd just stepped from, the walls like polished gold mirrors. Even the floor consisted of it. It reminded Ghila of Viridya, and she wondered if it wasn't entirely a coincidence.

Her reflection gazed back at her from four angles, and she glanced at each in turn until she met Klotho's strong, beautiful profile, standing beside her where she had not been moments ago. Klotho nodded towards the wall ahead, and Ghila followed her motion, seeing a memory begin to play – much like those she'd shown to Elijah in their gilded mirror.

As the face of Valdis Kruel began to manifest, Ghila felt the sour taste of terror coat her tongue.

No, not him. Anyone but him.

A firm grip encased her bicep as she turned to flee. Klotho's steely voice rattled the revulsion from her bones.

"Watch... *see*."

She hadn't expected this. Not him. She didn't want to hear his voice agai–

"I gave you all that you wanted, filled your coffers with as much magic as I could muster, and yet you still keep me at arm's length. Did we not have a deal, you and I? Did we not have an understanding, Valdis?" Klotho's voice reverberated from the moving image, one of her cloaked and standing almost nose to nose with the fiery-headed man. Valdis, with the severely scarred face and an even more severe scowl, stepped back from her.

"Our deal was just that... a deal. Never did I allude to anything more. This love you feel towards me, it makes you weak. Compromises you." His lips curled in disgust. "Never did I think a Fate would succumb to the emotions that plague the very mortals you despise."

His hate of anyone who wielded magic was shockingly clear to Ghila, and the fact that Klotho had thought he'd change because of her was extremely perplexing.

Klotho followed in his backward steps, hands reaching out. "I can still be of use. I have a plan, to retrieve the Prince and bring him to you – pliant and malleable. There may be no more magic that I can source for you as I did before, but with him in at your disposal, you will not need any more."

Valdis' look of revulsion remained. "I will always need more."

So, this wasn't about using Eliverus? This was about obtaining more magic... more power. Would he not try to take it from her brother?

Unless Valdis had found another, more effective way to absorb magic.

Ghila's blood chilled.

"Is there someone else?" Klotho whispered, a bite to her breath.

Valdis' eye ticked, but he answered, "What I have discovered will open an entire *world* of possibilities." He nodded to someone unseen, and Ghila heard the clink of armour. "I have you to thank, but now your usefulness has come to an end. Escort Sister Klotho back to the School. We are done here."

For the first time ever, Klotho's features twisted, emotions passing over her face so clearly that Ghila could see the moment her heart broke. The Fate had been… in love with Valdis Kruel.

Even Goddesses were susceptible to heartbreak. And he'd used her feelings for him to gather power, with no intention of ever reciprocating her love.

Ghila had always known the man to be heartless, and this revealed memory did not come as a shock to her.

What came as a shock was Klothos' heartache; her body as it slid to the floor; and her weeping, flanked by silent guards. She'd expected the Fate to react with anger, but instead she let her emotions spill forth.

Klotho had gone against all they taught at the school. She'd let her emotions cloud her judgement.

She'd helped Valdis unlock a new kind of magic, of which they were yet to discover the true extent.

Unable to look away, Ghila watched as a series of images flashed on the wall.

Children, taken from their families, tiny hands reaching through the bars of cart-drawn cages.

Valdis, raising his glowing hands in supplication to a jagged monolith of Nexus Crystal, its depths strobing with red light.

Blood reflected on golden walls. Bodies unmoving.

Fire rose in Ghila's throat, bile and disgust at what she saw.

"I may be proud, and stubborn, but I am immortal, and forever is a long time to wallow over a broken heart or fester in self-hate." The images faded, leaving Ghila and Klotho side by side, staring at their reflection. "I was weak. I made an extreme lapse in judgement. I allowed my heart a moment to take control…"

"Why did you not seek revenge for the hurt he caused you?" asked Ghila, watching Klotho's golden reflection carefully.

She could have killed Valdis and prevented a war. Could have prevented so much death.

"Why do you think my sisters and I guide and train others to do what the Gods bid? Why do we not mete judgement ourselves?" At Ghila's silence, Klotho sighed. "My sisters and I… we are unable to use our own hands to change fates. The Gods do not allow it."

Shocked, Ghila turned to face the Fate.

"We were given immortality to be messengers and weavers, guides to the whims of the Gods. Nothing more."

"What happens if you… try?" Ghila asked.

"We simply cannot."

Ghila began to understand. Unable to strike down Valdis herself, Klotho had begun a delicate weaving in order to atone for what she'd done.

"You threw my plans into disarray, abducting Eliverus, but you have returned, with the Prince unharmed. All is not completely lost," Klotho sighed.

Ghila did not apologise for her actions. She couldn't. She still hadn't forgiven herself for them.

She said instead, "I will show them what I've seen, this proof that you are no longer in league with Valdis."

Klotho's smile was strained and did not reach her eyes. It was as if the muscles of her face were unused to the action. "Good."

Ghila turned, leaving the room of gold. She did not look back.

CHAPTER FOURTEEN

ARIIAYA

The waning sun bathed the crumbling castle in cascading orange light as the disarray from the battle was cleared away. By the time the sun set, the bodies were piled neatly upon a pyre, arms on their chests if they had them, coins upon their eyes.

Darkness and firelight washed over a crowd of solemn faces as they stood silently watching the bodies burn. Even though none of the dead polluted by Valdis' necromancy were known to them, they were farewelled with the dignity of soldiers. The Sisters used old language in a burial fit for fallen assassins, praying that the souls found peace in what lay in the afterlife.

Ariiaya watched impassively, thoughts flickering like the wildfire licking over their charring bones. Elijah had relayed the scenes shown to him by Ghila, leaving a sour taste in her mouth. So, the Fates weren't exempt from emotion, it seemed, nor were they as heartless as they'd made themselves out to be. Klotho had let her heart decide her actions, and while the thought of someone lusting after Valdis turned Arii's stomach, she now understood the lapse in judgement.

Love was a strong emotion, a manipulative and powerful magic on its own.

The Fates were on their side now, a powerful ally, and they had Elijah back. Arii let her guard fall for just one moment, pressing her palms to her eyes and sagging her shoulders. They could cease their hunt for the Ouroboros. They didn't need to take a trip into the Dragon's Teeth anymore.

She sniffed against the thick smoke as it blew her way, squeezing her already closed eyes. "We could follow Kadec to the east if we head out right now."

"I'd strongly advise that we continue our search for the Ouroboros," voiced Nocturne, standing from his squatting position beside a fallen soldier.

Elijah's deep voice rose before Arii's protest could. "We haven't time to delay. Enough has been wasted during our time apart."

"And we have Elijah back now. He has power enough that we no longer need your Ouroboros," added Arii, letting her hands fall.

"Don't you think placing a few days into finding something that will greatly turn the tide in the war is worth the delay? You saw what Ghila showed us – Valdis has found a new way to amass power, a way that may just overthrow all of our efforts up until now." Noct's voice rose, wavered a little, and Arii blinked at the slip in his composure. He knew more than what he was letting on. Was this something he'd seen before? In another world?

"Why do you continue to help us, Noct? Why do you not just open a portal and return home?" She sniped, the question picking at her for a while.

"I won't see another realm fall to corruption… not again. If there is even a tiny hint of hope, it should be grasped, because that tiny pinprick of light could be the thing to ultimately turn the tide."

Silence ensued, the nearby sounds of a horse's whinny breaking the tension.

Elijah angled towards her; brows drawn. She predicted his words before he spoke, but scowled when they drawled in the air anyway. "He has a point…"

We can't just solely rely upon me.

The words were unsaid, but she sensed them. Elijah still doubted, still felt as if the world was on his shoulders.

They needed every ounce of hope they could get. She couldn't deny that fact.

"Alright, as long as you can take us east as soon as we've found it."

Noct's shoulders slumped in relief, while Elijah nodded. She hoped she wouldn't live to regret this choice.

A messenger arrived from the west, carrying an update from Kadec. Elijah placed a signed letter in the young man's hand, detailing his return and that they would meet them in Evergrave in four days, if all went to plan. With Kadec's forces scattering on the western fringe of Viridya, as well as Jero and Thogan's taking place in the southern border, they still had time to use their favour from Sapphine and take a day or two to explore the Dragon's Teeth. They would be dangerously close to Bonemire, and the others agreed that they shouldn't linger there longer than necessary.

So, as quickly as possible, they prepared with as many supplies as the Sisters could part with.

Arii still did not fully trust Klotho, but the Tapestry was dying, and she knew that the Sisters lived to serve the Gods. They would be on their side, for now. Pressing her thoughts aside, Arii turned to their group, the castle gates a yawning mouth behind them.

Nocturne rubbed at a spot of ash on his almost immaculate lapel, his face creased in a frown. "I have enough magic to take us back to Sapphine, and if we allow time for rest, I should have replenished enough to take us to the edge of Evergrave - if I use my magic sparingly. I'm not like you Fae, I don't charge back up again like a toddler with a sugar-high right on nap time."

Luc snuffled a laugh, clearing his throat and murmuring, "Is it too soon for humour?" as he eyed the funeral pyre behind him.

Noct shrugged. "Sometimes humour is all I have," he said, turning to help the others.

Arii absently wondered if Noct were missing his home.

Luc shook his head before helping his fiancé lift a pack, grunting, "Have you packed for the whole party in one pack, Emer?"

Emerson shook his head. "Better to enchant fewer packs to keep them from getting drenched. And you know me, always have to pack the things that everyone else forgets." He stared pointedly at his sister, who waggled her fingers back.

"Always thinking of everyone else," Luc laughed, eyes glittering with affection.

Arii made a face. Deciding she no longer needed to witness the couple's public affection, she turned, only to thump into the solid wall of Elijah's chest. A sound like a squeak erupted from her as she wobbled back.

"Gods!" She should be used to the preternatural quietness of his Fae steps, as he ducked around her to take the heavy pack. Emerson sighed in appreciation.

She wasn't the only one to be thankful for the return of his solid presence.

Arii burned to speak to Elijah in private about what he had endured under his sister's influence, but they had not yet had the chance. Not only was there fire in her veins for him, but the rage she felt when she gazed at his sister was just barely in check. She'd voiced her displeasure, to which Elijah insisted Ghila deserved a second chance, rid of the curse as she was.

Arii wasn't so sure. Nor did she trust the Mind Wielder with a ten-foot poleaxe.

"Are you ready?"

Elijah's voice cut through her thoughts as she glared at the back of Ghila's head. The small Fae was standing silently by the pyre, watching the flames dance into the sky. As Elijah's words registered, a phantom bloom of pain chased across Arii's neck, and she touched the skin there, reminded of the spell allowing them to breathe under water. Elijah's eyes followed her movement subtly, attention on her fingers.

Arii swallowed. "The real question is, Elijah, are you?"

Arii enjoyed the transformation even less the second time around, but thankfully that and the swim to Sapphine passed swiftly.

Unlike the last time when they had floated down the laneways of the ancient underwater ruins, there was more movement. Nymphs floated around the entryways to their homes, some with children in tow, watching with cautious eyes. The children's presence unnerved Arii, their willowy forms bobbing in the current, eyes far too large for their slender faces, fins more translucent than the adults'. After the last time they'd come here, Tikkani had wondered about the lack of male Nymphs, and Krepth had explained that there were none. Water Nymphs were an all-female race, with reproduction similar to that of hammerhead sharks. Arii had once read about parthenogenesis in a textbook; the concept of reproducing without having sex was something she found exceedingly boring.

Where was the fun in that?

The castle loomed, coral spires casting rippling shadows across the sands underneath as they swam to the entrance. Arii and her friends were greeted by stoic-faced Nymph guards who wordlessly opened the doors for them.

Tikkani's head craned as their feet suctioned to the floor by magic, bubbles trailing from her lips as she said, "Still exceptionally beautiful, and still exceptionally creepy."

Arii had to agree with her. Despite the ancient, ethereal quality of the coral-laden city, there was a sense of sadness and desolation, a shadow of the bustling city it perhaps once had been.

Before long they were before the Queen, her silver-spun hair drifting like loose spider webs on an invisible breeze. Her attention was fixed upon Elijah, as if she weren't fully convinced it was him.

"Did you bring it?" The Queen finally asked, nails curving on the armrests of her throne.

Elijah tilted his head to Noct, who drifted forward and bowed before speaking. "Luck was on our side, and we were able to get the Prince back without the Ouroboros."

Vexia's chin lifted, scrutinising the group. "Did you think that returning without what we agreed upon, while still anticipating passage, would prolong your good fortune, Tempest?"

"We are still seeking the Ouroboros, and our promise in returning your generous favour still stands," answered Noct, his words smooth as silk.

Seemingly satisfied for the moment, Vexia nodded, lifting from her throne and floating the current down to them. "Very well. My guards and I will escort you to the caves which lead into the mountains. It has been quite some time since I visited the caves. Come, it is a short swim from here…"

During their swim towards the caves, Arii couldn't help but wonder about the Queen's reaction to the locket, and if she would accept it as the object they were seeking. She presumed – if they were to survive the war to come – that Vexia would be angered that the trinket was not the actual Ouroboros. Would their deception begin another war? That wasn't something she wanted to worry about right now.

As they prepared to enter the yawning caves, Queen Vexia said, "Bring the item of power to us when the battle is over, Eliverus. Once you have used it to win. We shan't need it if this world falls."

Just as Arii was beginning to feel claustrophobic, their heads broke the surface inside a cavern sometime later, Fae light bouncing in ripples on the ceiling and rock around them.

"There," said Noct, chin pointing to a rocky shore.

Once out of the water and sure nothing awaited them in the darkness, they rested for a few moments as Nem and Arii, aided by Elijah, used a small burst of magic to help dry their sodden clothing. When damp, instead of soaked, clothes pressed against their skin, they traversed on, entering the dark caverns with no end in sight. The magic-made Fae lights whizzed about, revealing nothing but misty cave walls ahead, pools of dank water rippling underfoot.

"Surely there are Kryvern in here… this looks like a place where they would sleep," Tikkani whispered, as if the beasts themselves might hear.

Emerson nodded in agreeance as Luc traced his hand along the rocky wall, to which Krepth replied, "Where do you think those beasts reside when they aren't picking away at the farmland just south of here? The Dragon's Teeth is where the Kryvern originated. I wouldn't be surprised if we come across a nest of them at some point."

Tikkani's worry weighted the air and she gnawed her lip as if it were hard candy. "Way to set the mood, Krepth."

The Shifter bowed mid-step, a grin plastering his face.

"*So* not funny…" Tikkani chided.

Arii had to agree. She didn't think running into a Kryvern nest would be amusing either.

Beside her, she felt Elijah's attention shift to the cavern roof, and she followed his gaze. Above them, sprinkled like stars, were glow worms. They began sparingly, but as the party drew deeper, their numbers grew larger, until blue Fae light mingled with the purple and green of their little glowing bodies.

The tunnel began to sprout deviations, smaller openings chiselled into the larger cavern like doorways. Arii felt as if they were inside a tree, a labyrinth of roots curling off in many directions. Nocturne steadfastly led them through the main passage. Deviating down one of the smaller tunnels would only take them to dead ends, so he claimed. How the man knew where they were going was anyone's guess, but he seemed confident, and none knew any better, so they had no choice but to follow.

Here, under the earth, it was impossible to know the time of day, and after what Arii believed was hours of tramping the damp, rocky terrain, she decided it was time to take a break. The sigh of relief that rippled through their party was a tangible thing.

"I am starving," moaned Tikkani, groping for the pack on Elijah's back.

They set up camp, fashioning a fire pit from cave stones and lighting a fire with dry kindling from their packs. It had been Emerson's idea, although Quinn had argued that packing kindling would take up precious space, it was chilly, and everyone was glad for the warmth.

But when Tikkani pulled a steel pot from Elijah's pack, Arii had to stifle a laugh at his expression.

"What? Couldn't leave without some way to make soup." Tikkani said, fishing out a few ingredients and a large flask of water.

"I get lectured for packing kindling? You packed a cooking pot!" cried Emerson.

Elijah rolled his shoulders. "No wonder that pack was so heavy."

Tikkani loaded up the pot with herbs and stock powders, before pulling out three sizable potatoes and yanking out her knife. "You'll all thank me when your bellies are warm and full. Besides, it was Quinn who lectured you about kindling, not me."

Quinn paused while laying his cloak on the floor. "I would have been happy with the ration packs that Nem gathered for us back at Ayrith."

Nem nodded sagely, sitting cross legged by the fire with her eyes closed.

"No, you wouldn't, you'd be complaining about hunger pains twenty minutes after devouring two!" Tikkani said, plopping chopped potatoes into the pot, before whipping out a thatch of leeks.

Beside her, Elijah blinked, casting his eye back at the bag.

Arii flopped back on her pack, her stomach grumbling loud enough for all to hear. She didn't care where the food came from, she just wanted to eat.

"I'd be chucking in some of those mushrooms I found outside the school walls." Quinn said, rummaging through the pack.

"I wouldn't let you add those, they could be poisonous," said Arii, pressing a hand to her raging belly to placate it. "Actually, I wouldn't let you cook for us full stop."

Quinn pointed an accusatory finger. "You're… you're mean when you're hungry!"

Arii tsked, staring at the glow worms speckling the ceiling. "You haven't seen mean, not really."

"The mushrooms around the school aren't poisonous… in fact, they tend to grow larger than normal due to the residual magic hanging in the air around the place," said Ghila, her voice gentle yet rough with disuse.

The group stopped abruptly, casting curious glances at the girl, her large, grey eyes shy. Into the silence, Nem said, "She's right, and

Ariiaya knew that. She just doesn't like mushrooms."

"How can you not like mushrooms?" yelped Emerson, the tension evaporating to chatter.

The tension remained in Arii's chest though, for she didn't trust the Wraith still. She noted the way Ghila's eyes tracked each face in their party, except for hers, her lips twitching around unspoken words. Did the voices still plague her, even now, without the cursed pendant around her neck?

"Something that grows in the shit of others shouldn't be considered a vegetable," continued Arii defensively, her attention remaining on Ghila. Surprisingly, she saw the Fae nod.

"They aren't considered a vegetable, they're a fungus," said Emerson, his voice taking on a tenor reminding her of lessons with the Sisters of Fate. She'd always been more akin to the practical assignments, rather than sitting in a musty classroom.

Tikkani stirred the contents of the pot as the smell of herbs filled the space. They argued some more about mushrooms, and Arii gleaned that Ghila disliked them too. Something in common after all. That wasn't enough for her to redeem herself, though.

Emerson took a breath from his lecture on the nutritional benefits of mushrooms, to which Arii stubbornly murmured, "Still don't like them."

Elijah rustled elbow-deep in the pack beside her, finding some battered tin bowls and spoons. His face still held a look of bewilderment. "How much did you fit in here? This pack has to be enchanted."

"Of course it's enchanted," grumbled Arii snippily.

Elijah didn't look affronted, only perplexed and intrigued as he gazed down into the pack once more.

"Tikkani, what did you call Arii earlier?" Nocturne asked in a stage whisper.

"Bad-tempered or irritable as a result of hunger – hangry!" laughed Tikkani, ladling thick soup into bowls. Arii jolted to a sitting position faster than a snapping bowstring.

"It's true, I've been both witness and victim to it many times," exclaimed Krepth, blowing on his spoon before shoving it into his mouth. "Oh, this is *really* good!"

"I do not get hangry!" Arii exclaimed, before inhaling half her soup, grimacing against the heat.

Krepth said around an open mouth of potato, "You are the epitome of the term, Little Fury."

Beside her, Elijah nodded, eyes closed as he blew on his soup. Catching him agreeing, Arii made an indignant sound, slapping his spoon away.

Elijah sighed before continuing to eat.

"See!" cackled Tikkani, blowing the wisps of heat over her bowl.

The murmuring echoes of their voices and laughter danced around the cavern, stirring the glow worms above them.

Once sated, they plotted their next course of action.

"I vote Arii does the dishes while we rest," said Quinn, raising a hand. "There was a spring back there which would be perfect."

From where she relaxed, head on Elijah's lap, hands on her soup-swollen stomach, Arii groaned. "Fuck off."

"Only fair after the hangry disrespect you showed earlier," piped Tikkani.

Arii shifted her head, glaring at the elf, "Do you want to die in this cavern?"

"I'd prefer not, but doing the dishes is the least repayment for such a lovely, wholesome meal," said Tikkani, laughing. The others voted in agreement.

Arii watched the show of hands. When had they all begun to stop fearing her? This just simply wouldn't do. She pouted but paused as Elijah said, "I'll help you."

Arii grumbled to her feet, grabbing the small tower of bowls and spoons. Elijah retrieved the pot and some soap.

"Great, and when you return, I have some herbal teas I procured from Kadec's kitchens," grinned Tikkani, handing a small, labelled satchel to Ghila who sniffed it curiously.

Her eyes widened, and she smiled dreamily. "That smells lovely."

"There are many more," said the elf, showing Ghila. "Here, smell this one."

Arii snorted as something ugly rose up in her, something with wicked teeth and fire on its tongue. She'd had enough of everyone treating Ghila as if she was innocent.

"Are we to speak of what you did or will everyone continue to act like nothing happened?" she snarled, planting her feet before the dark haired, cross-legged Fae. Ghila looked up and as her hair fell back from her face, Arii expected a look of shame, or perhaps regret.

Instead, Ghila's grey eyes were narrow, jaw set stubbornly in a way that was incredibly like her brother's.

"Arii…" Elijah warned.

"She is right, brother. It's about time that we spoke about what happened." Ghila said, returning the tea to an uncomfortable Tikkani.

"Ah, so you'll talk to me in person now? No speaking into my mind without my permission?"

Ghila rose, a head shorter than her aggressor. "You are angry, I get it. I deserve your ire."

"You fucking deserve far worse than my *ire*, Mind Wielder."

Nem subtly shifted to Ghila's side. Arii was far too agitated to feel betrayed by the move, she understood why Nem did it. Her closest friend was used to cleaning up after Arii's short temper. And she knew Nem could feel the tension through their life-bond and had felt it since she'd dragged Arii away from Elijah's emotionless vessel, Ghila's catlike grin flashing over his broad shoulder.

That smile had been haunting Arii ever since.

She leaned forward, voice like the growl of a wolf. "You have no right to be here. You should be rotting in the cells under the School of Fate. You may be cured of your curse, and you may have everyone plus your brother fooled, but I don't trust you, Wraith. Valdis wants Elijah dead… he wants all of us dead, and I wouldn't put it past him to plant a poisonous seed in our ranks."

Ghila blinked, arms folding over her chest. "Don't you think my brother would be dead already if I were in league with Valdis Kruel?"

Arii didn't miss the bite in Ghila's voice as the name rolled from her teeth. She had to admit that the same thought had crossed her mind, but she couldn't rule out the possibility that she may be gathering information to feed back to Valdis, before taking her pretty crescent moon blades and lodging them into their backs.

Ghila continued. "You have no clue what torment I endured before. My revenge was the only thing that kept me going, the only reason I continued to breathe and to fight, rather than toss myself from the bluff into the sea. I've apologised to you and will continue to do so until you believe me."

She inhaled shakily. "I want to help, I want to make up for the hurt I caused you…" Her gaze slid over the others, standing with solemn faces to listen. "All of you," she added, throat working. Ghila's eyes found her brother's, before landing back on Arii.

Words heated on Arii's tongue, but couldn't seem to pass her clenched teeth. She felt Elijah's hand at her elbow again, but shrugged him off. Her bones filled with molten lead, her jaw ached as she inhaled through her nose and out through her teeth, watching Ghila's stormy grey eyes shutter.

Into the awkward, bated silence, Ghila finally said, "What would you have me do, then?" Her gaze slipped to Arii's boots as her shoulders curled, the slightest tell that she was cracking. Her choppy hair fell forward, curtaining her face, and as Arii studied the young Fae, her mind leaped back to when they'd crossed weapons in the hall, the memory of the sound of the undead and the smell of smoke assaulting her senses, cracking through her red haze of anger.

Ghila was physically weaker than the other Fae that Arii had spent years training with, and not once had she used any outward magic.

It hit her that Ghila's ability to wield minds was the only magic she possessed. In a physical fight against Elijah, Ghila wouldn't stand a chance. Arii could draw her knife and slit her throat before the Fae knew what she was doing. But she wasn't about to kill her, though. Elijah was the only reason she stayed her hand. He had forgiven his sister.

She let that thought sink in, allowed it to cool her fire somewhat. It did little to ease her suspicion of Ghila though, nor did it deplete much of her anger. Arii held on to anger like a dog with a bone. It would take time, and a lot of action, to earn her trust.

She drew a deep breath and hissed. "You do what you promised, and help us. You prove that you have changed. Use your magic for good. If you even so much as breathe the wrong way around my friends, if you even look at Elijah in a way I deem suspicious, you're out."

As Arii spun to march away with the dishes, she heard Ghila say, "I'll die before I break that promise."

CHAPTER FIFTEEN

ARIIAYA

Arii made a sound in the back of her throat, spinning on her heel and storming in the direction of the spring. She couldn't stand to be in The Wraith's presence any longer, memories still strangely raw of the darkness-laced words entering her mind unbidden. She'd invaded her space, her innermost thoughts, and then taken Elijah, and inflicted who-knew-what on him.

Now Ghila acted as if all was fine?

Arii couldn't dredge forgiveness from her heart. Not yet. She was not one to forgive and forget so quickly.

Her footfalls thumped, echoing in the cavernous space, disturbing the glow worms illuminating the small spring. The pool gleamed, its bottom so polished by the running water that the light seemed to emanate from below as well.

"I know you don't forgive her," said Elijah from behind, the sound of his own footfalls superseded by the brutality of hers. "But I have, and I think you should open your heart to doing the same."

The gentle steadiness in his deep voice – the patience within it – had shame heating her cheeks, making her feel suddenly foolish. Perhaps she'd been a little harsh on Ghila.

But what she'd done still hurt.

Arii crouched by the water, placing the bowls down with a little too much force. Her blood was a riot in her veins, bubbling like boiling acid, filling her ears. Her words burned up her throat, but when they emerged, they were softer than the jagged harshness she felt on their way up, "How can you just… forget what she did?"

Elijah crouched too, placing the pot in the shallows, crystal water lapping at his boots. He was silent for a short time, choosing his words carefully. "I forget that you didn't see what she went through, why she did what she did to me… to us. My sister was abused by those who were supposed to protect her. She suffered under brutal fists while I was mended under gentle hands. While we were connected, some of her control slipped, and I saw glimpses of her past. It was…"

Arii watched him, swirling the mint-scented soap and water in the pot. There was a waver in Elijah's voice, a fragile thread keeping his words together. She pressed her anger down, swallowed it until the heat slid painfully down to her stomach. Holding Ghila hostage to her past was similar to what Arii did to herself, condemning her own demons and blaming them for the lack of forgiveness she couldn't even offer herself.

"She's free of the curse but she'll forever be altered, a shadow of the self she could have been. I don't expect you to forgive her overnight, but try to… accept her, even just a little bit?"

Arii sighed, tipping sudsy water back into the pool, watching the bubbles swirl against the basin of rocks. She shifted, facing him fully, placing the bowl down. His gaze met hers, ripples of light from the pool feathering across his features.

"I'll try," she finally said, meaning it. She would, for him. For the fact that he was back, alive and whole. Ghila hadn't tried anything since, nor did she show signs of corruption anymore. If anything, the girl was timid in her interactions with the group. The elves had taken her in, making conscious effort to include her in conversations and jokes even if the girl wasn't quite sure how to react. She seemed slightly eager, but intimidated. They didn't press her though.

As hard as she tried, Arii still felt a flicker of acrimony. Instead of dwelling on it, she decided to instead try to understand.

"We haven't really spoken about what happened to you. What she did to you while you were under her control."

His smile was sad, "You're less likely to forgive her if you knew,"

Elijah sighed, placing the pot aside to drip dry, before placing his attention on her fully. Light mingled with the black flecks within his silver eyes like courtiers on a dance floor, emphasising their depths like a churning sea. They had never pushed each other to divulge the ghosts of their pasts, and she wasn't about to now. When he was ready, if he ever was, she knew he would tell her. If she had learned anything over the last few months, it was that the past was the past, and nothing could change it.

When his fingers grazed her chin, fluttering over her bottom lip, Arii's thoughts slowly melted away. This male… he had the strangest effect on her. With just a touch, he silenced her thoughts, yet her heart raced as if she were confronting her deadliest foe. Her insides rioted with barely a graze of his fingers, a fact that she knew was apparent to him now, by the subtle flare of his nostrils. His grey eyes dropped to where his fingers paused, and he drew his bottom lip between his teeth. In contemplation? In hesitation? She had to admit that things felt… strange since they'd reunited, as if something weren't being said that probably should have been. It was almost as if they'd cycled back a few months, to when things were more volatile yet more fragile. Her memories drifted back to when they'd met on the dream plains, wrenched apart by threads of darkness and light. His words had remained with her ever since.

"I'll wade through darkness and hell to be with you, Ariiaya. It'll take more than this to keep us apart."

Ghila's abduction hadn't changed how she felt for him, but a tiny part of her wondered if something had changed on his side. He did seem ever so slightly closed off, but perhaps it only felt that way because they hadn't had proper time alone until now.

Alone. They were alone.

Arii swallowed, watching Elijah's throat work too. He seemed to be working towards saying something, so she waited expectantly, her eyes never leaving his.

"There were moments I was a breath from breaking… on the cusp of giving up the fight, but what held me together was you, Arii. Every second I spent within that nightmare realm, I was thinking of you, and how I could possibly see you, and speak to you, one last time."

She leaned into the palm of his hand as it cupped her cheek, eyes fluttering shut, touched by his words, for they mirrored her own thoughts. Not for one moment had she thought of giving up, either. A gentle, warm caress of his breath brought her eyes open a crack, as he said, "And kiss you, one last time."

Elijah's deep, gravelly voice and whispered breath brought warmth to her core, bringing alive her slumbering desire. She drew a shaky breath, unable to find any other words apart from "Is that *all* you wished?"

Gods, she sounded pathetic to her own ears.

Her words drew a huff of a laugh from him. "Definitely far from all that I wish to do with you, Ariiaya."

When he murmured her name in that gently dropped tenor, as if promising passion – or pleasure – it made her toes curl in her boots. But as he kept speaking, something in his voice held her pinned, kept her from closing the distance between them.

"I vowed from a young age that I'd always remain in control, after my past was taken from me. I remained in control, fixated on it as I grew in the ranks within the Red Guard. That first day in Viridya's throne room… when you felled a beast with nothing but a kitchen knife, I knew things were no longer in my control. When you slaughtered those bandits with a snarl on your face; and then when you bought me that basket of paints… I knew I was no longer in control. In Bonemire, when you looked at me with those fucking beautiful purple eyes like I was a miracle sent by the gods, I knew then I was no longer in control."

She held her breath as he continued. "When you told me you were falling for me in Ayrith, I began to finally *accept* that I was no longer in control. Fate has a way of weaving its threads in different directions, whether we have hold of them or not. It wasn't until I was taken by my sister that I realised that we only have so much control over our fate."

His voice shook ever so slightly, but Arii heard it. It wasn't a fearful tremble, nor was it one of anger. It was one of barely contained desire, as if he were moments away from losing the control he fought so hard to hold.

"I've never had control around you," he finally said, dark eyes fixated on her lips, on the rise and fall of the slight reveal of her breasts at the vee of her tunic, "and that frightens me."

Arii knew the words he left unsaid. He was afraid of the deep instincts gnawing at him, of what his Fae beast wished to do.

She rolled her words around her tongue, tasting them, savouring them, before she glanced from his lips and back up to his eyes. She saw raw hunger there, swirling within the quicksilver, like eddies inside a wildfire, tossing heat in its bid to consume.

Then Arii whispered, "You know you've never had to hold back with me, Elijah. Loose control with me, let your barriers fall. I'll catch you, I'll hold you, and then I'll watch you rise. Your demons are my demons, your darkness is mine, and when you're ready, we will set this world afire." She shifted, and she saw a change in his face. She drew nearer, gaze unblinking. "I'll watch you incinerate your enemies, stand by your side as you take back your destiny – and all the while I'll be burning inside for *you*. Wanting *you*, no matter what. Needing you over *everything* else."

With each word she spoke, with each breath she took to deliver them, the air around them thickened with heat. The depths of his silver eyes shone, a vortex of whirling emotions as the ring around his iris shone blue with residual magic. That was new, and it was striking, a sign of his inner power – power that she knew he was fighting to control.

"I'll fight for you… in war, in court, I'll fight for you until there is no fight left – and then I'll keep fighting."

Before she could take a breath in the wake of her speech, something snapped, her words taking up the last slither of heated space between them as Elijah's lips crashed against hers.

All the tension that had been building, the strain pulled of their time apart, finally torn asunder.

Arii's hands flew into Elijah's hair, burying into the thick strands of darkness as their tongues warred, teeth clashing in their eagerness to drink each other in, to consume each other like wildfire through dry forest. Pots and bowls splashed into the shallow pool as Arii straddled his hips, pressing as close as their traveling clothes would allow, wishing – no – needing to feel his heart close to hers. The compulsion to have skin against skin was maddening, and when she felt the strained press of his arousal pulsing against her inner thigh, it took all her willpower not to tear the clothes from him like a wolf tearing meat from a bone.

Gods, it had been mere weeks – a speck in a Fae's lifetime – but it felt like far longer now. Elijah kissed her like a man starved, and she met each kiss with equal vigour to show him how much control she had around him.

Which was a slither to none.

She ground her hips upon him, their collective gasps swallowed by their kisses.

"Gods I missed your fire," Elijah rasped, taking her bottom lip between his teeth. "I missed everything about you, my heart."

She grinned against his lips, "Not as much as I missed you."

For emphasis, she ground her hips against him again, eliciting a very satisfying, very low groan.

She whispered, "But if you want, you can show me exactly how much you missed me, using what I can clearly feel beneath me right now."

He made an unintelligible sound against her teeth, causing her smile to widen further. The shake in his shoulders, the tentative way his hands slid to her bottom, told her he was still holding back.

"They'll hear," he finally ground out, placing a kiss on her collarbone. Arii's head tilted back, eyes tracing the glittering stalactites above. She hadn't forgotten how close their sleeping friends were, nor that this time and place weren't ideal to take their relationship further, but with every hot kiss against her skin, she burned, and thoughts of anything else but the man beneath her were quickly dissipating.

"We will just have to keep quiet, then…" she murmured, unable to hide the thrill that zinged down her spine. When their gazes met again, his eyes were smouldering, their depths reflecting the pool by their side.

Wordlessly his fingers moved to her front, gently tugging at the laces of her leather corset. Right now, her comfortable travelling clothes felt all too tight. Her breasts felt heavy, nipples pebbling, her breath shearing out as the corset loosened. Elijah removed her clothing slowly, meticulously, his eyes coasting every inch of her skin as it was revealed to him. Corset, blouse, support, all carefully laid aside. His fingers swept back a thick strand of honey-tipped hair from her collarbone, the meagre touch tingling across her skin.

"You're even more beautiful than in my dreams," he whispered, voice low and laced with desire. From this angle, with his head tilted up, silver irises watching her from beneath dark lashes, his lips a breath from her nipples, she felt exposed… vulnerable… shaky with need.

He took one of the sensitive peaks into his mouth and she moaned, head tipping back as his hips drove up. The friction upon her most sensitive parts elicited rich, powerful waves of pleasure, coursing from the crown of her head to the tips of her toes. He treated each breast equally, squeezing gently, teasing each nipple with his teeth, sending her beast into an absolute frenzy. Her head dipped back again, waves of hair caressing her lower back as Elijah kissed each visible scar, tasting her flesh as if for the first time.

She held his shoulders, nails clinging to his tunic, the heat of him radiating into her palms. When his kisses ceased a moment, she took a deep breath, yet felt his absence like a wash of ice.

Then his hand cupped the back of her head as he laid her down upon her discarded clothes. About to speak, her words halted as Elijah pulled his tunic over his head to reveal what she'd been so eager to see again.

Her hair splayed around her like water as she drank in the sight of his battle-toned torso. "And you're even more beautiful than in *my* dreams," she gasped lamely, eyes dropping to the bulge in his pants. "They betrayed me though, because you were wearing clothes."

His chuckle was deep and dark, a smile tugging his lips as he hooked his fingers in the waistband of her leather pants. She leaned back on her elbows, teeth pinching her bottom lip in anticipation.

"Do you taste as good as I remember?" he asked, head tilting ever so slightly, a hungry predator sizing up its prey.

Arii gulped, toes curling as memories of previous 'tastings' made their way through the fog of desire. Like always, before their moments of intimacy, Elijah paused, allowing her time to tell him to stop, to change her mind. He considered her boundaries, respected them even after the times she'd left herself bare, allowed him through the barriers of her mind… her heart.

There was no hesitation now, but her heart squeezed in response.

With her small nod, Elijah removed the last of her clothing. Her skin pebbled, anticipation warring with the cavern's cool air.

"It's so hard for me not to fuck you right here, in this cave, on this filthy molten floor," he growled, dipping his head to nip at the crease of her belly, trailing kisses along her abdomen. His words, the coarseness of them, sent a thrill surging through her, pooling further heat into her centre.

She writhed. "Then do it."

"Perhaps we can try something else?"

Skin heating despite the cool cave, Arii followed his gentle beckoning, until he was beneath her again as she straddled his hips. He held her gaze a moment, the blue light shimmering over his chest as he leaned back, his large hands gripping her thighs, gently guiding her with him. She wriggled, shimmying her hips with his guidance, curious at what he was playing at. His callused palms stroked her curves, splaying over her bottom, further pressing her up.

When her core was hovering dangerously close to his face, she held herself aloft, staring down past her breasts to see a wicked glint in his eyes.

Was he serious?

"I stand by my oath to take you, Arii, *properly*… but not here or now. That doesn't mean I won't take you in other ways."

Her blood sizzled, sparks ricocheted down her limbs as her sluggish thoughts caught up.

On her knees…

With the hottest, most sensitive part of her on his *face*.

Oh Gods.

His fingers squeezed, bringing her closer until she hovered a hair's breadth from his lips.

Elijah's hands gripped her thighs, and when his tongue pushed into her, the intrusion alone almost sent her to the precipice of release. The heat of his mouth, the pressure of his tongue as it explored, had her almost praying for mercy. She tasted blood, suggesting she'd bitten her lip to remain quiet so that the mountains above would not hear.

She shook, thigh muscles burning, as he guided her with gentle hands into a rocking rhythm, all thoughts fleeing through her feet.

"This… feels… blasphemous," she panted, laughter in her voice. "I need… to pray to the Gods… right *now*."

She felt him smile against her sensitive flesh. "Won't be the last time you'll find yourself on your knees around me," he purred.

Arii smirked. "Spoken like a man destined to be King."

Wicked, wicked male. Her tease earned her a twist of his devilish tongue.

She felt the graze of his teeth against her flesh, and a deep, rumbling growl that sent her hips rocking, the tip of his nose rubbing against her swollen bud. He groaned in approval, wholly and eagerly at the mercy of her undulating hips.

Arii suddenly felt *powerful*. She had all the control at this angle, could set the pace, the intensity of his penetrating tongue, the pleasure she could wring from him… all purely selfish. His grip on her thighs held her, spurred her on as she moved faster, harder, as if the beast within was moments from severing its leash, frenzied in her pursuit of pleasure. The intensity rose, fire pooling until she was dripping with primal need.

Release hit like a thunderclap.

Spine rigid, head tossed back, she let loose a cry, his name mingled with an animal curse.

As always he remained a selfless lover, wringing every last drop of pleasure from her body as she shook with the last of her release. Her hands slapped the slate either side of his head as she shakily removed herself from the vicinity of his wicked mouth. Her hair curtained them as they shared each other's breath.

"I…" she began, but halted, unable to process coherent thought in the moment.

Elijah's hand cupped her face. "You are even more exquisite when you come undone."

That utterance alone had the fire returning to her blood, igniting fuel that had barely cooled.

Arii scooted down and he slowly sat up, eyes locked as she hovered at the apex of his thighs, anxious to make him feel the same ecstasy he'd given her.

His eyes remained dark, the ridges of his body bathed in flickering light as he rasped, "You don't have to–"

"I know, Elijah, but need… that is wholly different. I *need* to do this for you. Will you let me?"

She spied his throat working, while his stormy eyes grew darker still. His chin dipped in a silent nod, biceps rippling as his hands splayed on the stone behind him, as if bracing, and she couldn't help a small, wicked smile.

Unbuckling his belt, it didn't take long for him to spring free, jutting forth impressively.

He sucked in a sharp breath.

So did she.

Arii curled one hand around the base, feeling the soft skin quiver under her touch. With her other hand, she pulled her hair back, her tongue darting over her lips as she looked up at him. He stared, mouth slightly agape, shoulders shaking. How long had it been since he'd allowed someone to pleasure him? That thought didn't rise further, because she promised herself she'd do her best to see him undone. It wasn't often she orally pleased a man, so she took her time to understand what movements of her lips and teeth caused his deepest sighs and strongest quivers.

She took him as deep as she could, using her palm to cover the rest. His arousal became impossibly thicker, a ground-out groan sliding from between his teeth. Arii glanced up to see Elijah's head tilt back. Her gaze glided over the strong column of his neck, his chest rising as his panting escalated, the sheen of sweat across his skin. She swore she heard him utter a stifled, drawn-out curse.

Gods, he was divine, and in this moment, he was *hers*.

She devoured him, sucking forcefully, rippling her tongue along the base as she felt his hips rise.

Her name on his lips in that moment was both plea and curse.

Magic rippled around them, rising from the rocks. Arii saw the tightening of his abs, the way his breath hitched, signalling that he was barrelling towards release. His hips jolted up as he came, and she swallowed his spend as if it were wine. He tasted like her kisses on his skin, with something wholly more complex, musky and purely *him*.

He fell back, and she climbed the length of him to nestle by his side, watching his chest rise and fall, placing her palm to savour the thundering beats of his heart, their mixed breaths a song of their pleasure. After a time, he spoke, his voice satisfyingly husky. "You have a wicked mouth."

Arii grinned, eyes fluttering closed. "Something we have in common."

Silence stretched, the only sounds a gentle drip from the overhead stalactites meeting the water, along with the easing of their breaths.

While tangled in each other, Elijah began to tell her about his true demons, the memories he'd seen while he'd been away. She listened, while her mind fluttered lazily back to the golden thread from the Tapestry. Their shivers of pleasure subsided, and they lay spent on the cool slate, gazing up at the light-specked cavern ceiling.

Arii vowed that no matter who the thread belonged to, she'd burn the world down just to see him come undone like this, one last time before the end.

CHAPTER SIXTEEN

LORCH

Lorch could get the hang of this. Mia's language wasn't so difficult to grasp, although he did keep getting a few signs mixed up. The little Fae was patient, though, taking his hands in hers to help him correct the flourishes of his fingers and the placement of his hands.

Celadine was always near, and he was aware of her watchful gaze like a weight upon his nape.

Mia giggled when he once again muddled up what should have been a simple sign for 'drink, please'. Lorch's hand rested on his leg and he grinned, the simple sound of laughter unusual to his ears. It was… a welcome sound. One that had him feeling more human. Quite often he found himself forgetting that mother and daughter were indeed not human, but apart from their small physical differences and… well, the magic – they weren't so different, really.

Mia sighed, placing pinched fingers to her mouth, motioning a chomping action. A universal sign for hunger. Her hand moved in circles over her stomach, causing Lorch to laugh. "Hungry?" he guessed. He was sure that wasn't the technical sign but appreciated her simplifying the motion after such a long afternoon.

Mia grinned, nodding eagerly.

Her mother placed down her utensils and stretched her back. "Let's visit the kitchens, and once we have eaten, we can discuss the movements of your father's search battalions. You mentioned earlier that he had doubled the amount of undead… seekers?"

Lorch rolled his head from side to side, stretching as he rose from their makeshift cushion seats on the floor before the fire. "Right, that's what he called them. He claims they have slightly more intelligence than the others, purpose bred–" he shuddered involuntarily, "to track. To look for signs in the world around them. To observe."

"We will relay this to Yarn. He'll want to alert the families in lower town, and those in Amberbourne. How many have amassed in the castle grounds now?"

"Thousands, I'm sure of it. Yarn? Is he your resistance leader?"

Celadine and Mia exchanged a curious look. "You could say that."

As they left the room for the warm, smoky corridor to the kitchens, Lorch had to ask, "Cela – may I call you that?" She nodded assent, although still wary of him even now. He continued. "Cela, can we trust this Yarn to be… okay with me being here?"

"I have spoken to him already."

Lorch's brows pulled in worry. A small smile tilted Cela's lips. "It took some time to calm him, but I have convinced him to give you a chance."

Thank the Gods.

As they entered the kitchen, Cela added, "He did say he would remove your dainty fingers and the jewels which adorn them should you give him one reason to fret about allowing you here."

Startled, Lorch held his hands in front of his face, twisting them this way and that. He had left his rings back at the castle. "Dainty?" he repeated.

Cela laughed.

The sound had him grinning, despite the threat in her words.

A towering woman turned to them, her brow dotted with sweat from the ovens. Mrs Mulvany waved them in while tossing four plates on the counter. "Come in, come in. Just pulled a roast from the oven. Are you all hungry?"

Mia bounced on her toes, eager to see as Mrs Mulvany loaded their plates with slices of lamb, chunky potatoes and lightly charred broccoli. Strands of purple hair burst from the braided nest on her head, winding around her smile-dimpled cheeks.

At Lorch's slightly-wrinkled nose, she brandished her tongs at him, her voice a motherly boom. "If you leave your greens again, Your Highness, ain't no royal decree gonna save you from them being forced down your pretty throat."

Lorch crossed his arms defensively, but a small smile remained. "Now I have a pretty throat? You all need lessons in delivering proper insults."

Mrs Mulvany chuckled, drizzling a red wine jus speckled with finely-chopped thyme over the dish. Lorch's mouth watered. Sure, the dish was perhaps simpler than those served by the royal cooks, but he enjoyed the heartiness of the tavern owner's cooking. Everything about his life had become so complicated lately, that even the food's simplicity made him feel less overstimulated. As if life, like the hearty food, could be just a little easier – even if just for the short time they shared this meal.

Mia signed to the cook, to which Mrs Mulvany replied, "Chocolate? With a roast dinner? Girl, you are a strange thing."

Mia signed again, and the cook chuckled. She poured a steaming mug of hot chocolate, passing it to Mia's grabby hands. Mrs Mulvany muttered something about a 'riot on your tastebuds, and not in a good way', shaking her head, but Lorch saw the twinkle in her eye.

"Take a plate to Yarn, he's been hounding me for dinner since lunch!" she ordered.

"Typical Yarn, forever hungry," said Cela, balancing two plates.

Lorch thanked Mrs Mulvany, and again, like every night, offered to pay, to which she waved him away. She had known him since well before he had begun spending time with Cela and Mia, and she had always treated him with kindness, as if she could see the boy beneath the drapery of a forced king. She saw the young man who just wanted to escape, drink mead and watch the local entertainment like anyone else, free of judgement and responsibility – just for a night.

Lorch held the door for Cela, and they headed to the main room. A bard played his lute, singing a melodious tale about a girl who fled her wealthy, controlling father to board a pirate ship and sail the seas.

Lorch knew that one – the father had promised her to a marriage she didn't want, a life of expectations and servitude. The girl longed for adventure, she didn't want a husband, nor children. She wished to be free from expectations. He liked the story, felt it all too closely.

Cela chose a table up the back, tucked away from the hubbub of feasting and drinking tavern patrons. Mia plonked down her meal and slid along the bench seat, nestling next to the man already there.

Lorch took a moment to study the man.

Yarn looked a little younger than his own father, sporting a thick, dark beard and short, cropped hair the colour of chocolate, roots peppered with grey. His eyes were heavily creased with laughter lines, but when those deep green depths met his own, he saw a harshness derived from years of survival.

He also looked… familiar.

It was hard not to shift under the man's weighted gaze. Lorch kept his feet planted, his own gaze unflinching, face open. The man's perusal was arduous and swift, and when the silence began to stretch taught between them, he wondered what was wrong.

Until Yarn spoke, voice coarse as stone under wagon wheels. "What's wrong, boy, Fae got your tongue?"

Mia winced, cheeks distended around a mouthful of lamb. Even Cela wore a guarded look.

Lorch opened his mouth to speak, but Yarn continued, "They say you have a golden tongue, always know what to say to please those around you. Your silence leaves me… disappointed."

Lorch's fingers curled around the edge of his dish, the only sign of his discomfort. "With all due respect, sir, you'll find those stories aren't entirely true." He paused, contradicting his next words. "To be honest, sir, I don't normally think before I speak, but I'd rather keep my fingers on my hands until I've had the proper chance to show you why I'm here."

The man eyed him wordlessly, sceptically, so Lorch continued, "I know I have not earned your trust with my history, but I'm here because I want to help right the wrongs that I have caused."

Elijah's anguished face, the blood pooling from his mother's headless body, Arii's screams.

Yarn eyed him for a little longer before he let loose a long sigh.

"Good answer," groused the man, motioning to the seat before him. "Sit, eat before it gets cold."

With that, Lorch felt his shoulders loosen just a touch. He sat, and as gentle conversation rose between the resistance leader and Celadine, Lorch relaxed, taking a fork to his roast. He remained straight-backed though, not allowing his guard to fall.

Music kicked up as they ate. Mia played with her broccoli, using her fork to swim it through her gravy, butting it against a potato chunk in mock collision. Lorch couldn't help but smile through his own broccoli, watching her. He could feel bits of food in his teeth, so he grinned wider until Mia caught his eye and let out a hawking laugh.

From the corner of his eye, he saw Cela place a hand over her own mouth, shifting to hide her amusement. He saw it though, and so did Yarn. The man leaned back, dropping his cutlery with a soft clink.

"So, my daughter tells me you're the one passing intel to us. We have been better able to hide a few families after learning that seekers were placed in certain areas. We have you to thank for helping keep them safe."

Daughter?

At Lorch's puzzled look, Yarn let loose a deep chuckle, placing a thick-fingered hand on Cela's shoulder. "You didn't tell him I was your father?"

Cela shrugged. "Didn't see it as important."

Lorch begged to differ – he would have tried far harder to impress him. And he *definitely* wouldn't have been making silly faces at the man's granddaughter.

Yarn shifted, leaning in for his fresh mug of beer, and as the light of the candles flickered over him, Lorch noticed the man's ears.

They were tattered, the tips torn into rugged arches.

Horror roiled in his stomach, warring with his dinner.

What had happened to him?

Yarn began to drink, then paused on seeing Lorch's face. He set the mug down.

"Just noticed the ears, heh?"

"I… well, yes, but please don't feel you need to explain–"

"I do not need to sugar-coat our world for you, Your Highness, for I'm sure it's revealing itself now that you're outside your golden walls. But this–" he pointed to the side of his head, "–is the product of cruelty. This is when individuals let their fear drive them to do terrible things."

Lorch shifted in his seat, sensing a dark story coming.

Yarn's gaze held his, assessing his reactions closely. Lorch remained impassive, knowing that showing sympathy would not earn him any favours. Instead, he leaned forward. He needed to hear this. He needed to see the bloody dirt under the nails of the society he was supposed to be leading.

"I was arrested and held in the dungeons on suspicion of aiding an attempted poisoning assassination. Yours."

Lorch recalled the incident clearly since it was the first of several subsequent attempts on his life. His royal taster had keeled over before his very eyes, foaming at the mouth, eyes rolling back as he writhed in the throes of death on the lavish crimson rug meant to warm Lorch's feet during breakfast. Blood had flowed like tears down his face, blending seamlessly with the red of the carpet. The poison had killed him quickly, but mercilessly. Painfully.

The poison meant for Lorch.

He had tasted his first tang of fear then: fear and realisation that not everyone loved the boy King.

"The roots of our family tree have always been dipped in the waters of healing. We come from a long line of apothecaries, who have done nothing but serve their Kings and Queens. I own the only herbal grocer in the city, so naturally the suspicion was thrust upon me. They questioned me, demanded I tell them what the poison was, and who I sold it to." Yarn sighed, tugging the lobe of one mutilated ear, perhaps a habit. "I told them I don't sell poison. They didn't listen."

Of course they didn't listen.

"Your men in red sheared off the tips of my ears in hopes of persuading me to spill secrets, but honestly, I think it was really for their own sick amusement. I had nothing to give them. I knew nothing. They had a boy there in the dungeons, too, the one who served you the tainted food. Though they mutilated me, they did far worse to him. I believe it was your personal bodyguard who was given the order to kill him."

He remembered that vividly, too. Elijah, though stoic as always, had definitely been changed by that order. They hadn't spoken about it in depth, only that it had been done, but Lorch would forever remember what Elijah had told him afterwards. *"I would do it again, if it meant you remained safe."* His eyes though, their deep silver depths, had been haunted. How could you not be after killing one so young?

"They let me go, bloody and filthy, once they determined I had nothing to do with the plot, and that I was... no longer a threat. I was a message, I think. What I had witnessed and what I had endured was a message to our kind: that the time of magic was over."

Lorch's lips parted, a question burning his throat, though he wasn't sure it was appropriate to ask. Yarn paused and motioned for him to speak. So he did, thinking of the warm touch of Cela's fingers as she healed his arm.

"Could you not have healed yourself with magic? Or used magic to escape?"

"Go and watch the bard, Mia, he's about to tell the story about the princess and the sword in the lake," Cela whispered to her daughter, shooing her further into the dining hall. Lorch's stomach clenched in apprehension.

Yarn's smile was sad as he watched his granddaughter's wild curls disappear between two patrons lingering near the stage. "They shackled me in iron when they arrested me, and to ensure I, nor anyone else, could heal me, they made me swallow a few iron pellets."

Cela's fingers curled into fists on the table, and her father curled his pointer finger into a claw. "They were hooked, ensuring at least one would catch in my stomach lining somewhere. The others passed through… eventually." He shook his head.

"Iron pellets?" whispered Lorch, unable to hide the note of horror in his voice. He had no idea that such barbaric torture was happening under his castle, by his guards, the men tasked to protect their people. When it came to eliminating threats, he had assumed the orders were to simply 'kill', not torture. Thinking on it now, though, he realised how naive he was.

"Iron nullifies magic, but I'm sure you are aware of that. Even now, my magic hasn't returned, leading me to believe there is still iron inside. I could have it removed with surgery, but I made the choice to remain like this. Severed from my magic, reminded of why I continue to fight, for the Fae, and for the humans caught up in all of this bigotry and hate. Not all humans see as you do."

Beside her father, Cela's jade-green eyes flickered with flames of fury. His breath felt too tight in his chest, thoughts of little Mia with an iron shard near her heart entered his mind.

Hot emotion roiled in his stomach, rose to his throat like dragon's breath, and Lorch's next words wavered.

"I am truly sorry for what happened to you, and for what has happened to all of you, now and in the past. You have no reason to trust me, but I'll do my best to earn it, to help all of you."

Yarn's gaze locked with the young King's for several moments, before he nodded as if satisfied, and took a long swig of his drink.

Lorch blew out a breath.

"Continue to feed us information, as much as you can, and we will continue to skirt in the shadows of your father's seekers, trying our best to survive. At least until the true heir returns with his army."

That had Lorch pausing mid-swallow of his own beverage.

"Eliverus lives?"

"He does, and as we speak, he is heading East. The forces have begun trickling in from the West and South, dispatching the forces wreaking havoc there."

Lorch absorbed his words on the surface, but deeper down, he was thinking about Elijah. His brother. His best friend. He hadn't forgotten the look in his eyes the last time they had seen one another. There was an emotion he had never gleaned before, fiery, tremulous, embers of hate mirrored in catastrophic silver.

Lorch knew the next time they met, Elijah would try to kill him for what he had done to his mother. For all he had done in aiding, or not preventing, the rise of his father's evilness and allowing the hate to further spread.

He had to make sure that all he did until then would make a difference.

Yarn's report of the movements of the armies of the other courts was extremely useful information, of which his father would be keen to learn.

He would not be the one to enlighten him though.

The rebellious notion had a tingle running down his spine. This wasn't exactly great news for himself. He was the King, after all. The one the armies would be gunning for. But perhaps if he played his cards right, and placed his pieces carefully, he may just be able to prevent an all-out obliteration of his family. Perhaps Elijah would exile them instead of staking their heads on pikes.

The barbaric thought didn't sit right. He didn't imagine Elijah to be the sort to pike heads at the front gates. That was something his own father would do.

Elijah was nothing like his father, and that was why Lorch knew that his reign... well, his father's reign, was almost at an end, and it was for the better.

He knew that now.

A short time later, when the world had darkened to pitch outside the tavern windows, and the crowd roused with drink and stories, Mia leaned against his side, fighting the pull of exhaustion. Lorch looped an arm around her, keeping her from toppling as they stood watching the stage, listening to tall tales of wonder. He turned his head, seeking Cela, finding her close. Her face was already upturned towards his, eyes narrowed and contemplative. She startled, perhaps broken from thoughts as deep as the Endless Sea.

"Time to go?" He asked her, smiling as Mia let loose a huge yawn. "I'll walk you to your rooms."

The room was pleasantly warm, filled with the lingering scents of dinner and Cela's herbs. Cela placed her daughter in bed, tucking the thin blankets to her chin. The girl was already out, brown curls spinning over her white pillow, snoring softly.

While Cela kissed her child's brow, Lorch busied himself retrieving his cloak. Cela met him at the door, as she did every time he left. Tonight felt different though. Perhaps it was just him, or perhaps a side effect of the longer time spent together. But there was a heaviness to the air, a charged feeling, that had him feeling… bold.

"There is something else." Lorch said tentatively, watching her face. She was getting that look again – the one where he knew she was sliding up barriers, ready for the unexpected. She angled her head slightly, tucking her hair behind a delicately pointed ear.

"Oh?" was all she said, a wisp of wild hair springing free across her cheek – a particular strand that always seemed untamed. His fingers moved before his mind had a chance to think, fingers brushing her warm skin, brushing the unruly hair back into place.

His breath hitched, and so did hers. Lorch swallowed, hard, while grasping at the floating tendrils of his thoughts. "I think there is someone else helping him, my father. Someone with immense power, with magic."

"Really… but, who?" she muttered, somehow closer now, when normally she would be retreating. Her nearness, and the fact that she remained so, kept his heart thundering.

His stare held hers as he murmured, "I'm not sure, but I'm going to find out."

ARIIAYA

The cool air of the cavern grazed her heated, tingling skin like a balm as they returned to the sleeping group, but the bliss that melted through her body like chocolate soon turned to ice as a voice cut through the snores like a knife.

"Did you have fun?"

Nemesis lounged off to the right, arms behind her head, brows raised, with a knowing smirk.

A blush climbed up Arii's neck and speckled her cheeks.

"We… ah," Arii fumbled.

Elijah cleared his throat and knelt by his pack to busy his hands with his sleep roll, seeming calm and collected, except Arii could see his pointed ears were blushed pink. She stared at the back of his head with a look divided between betrayal, embarrassment and murder while she directed her words towards Nem.

"I have a feeling you already know the answer."

The silver-haired Fae grinned, aqua eyes bright in the sleepy embers of their campfire.

"Damn this bond and its lack of privacy," Arii growled, replacing the clean bowls and spoons before unpacking her bed roll and looking anywhere but at Nem.

"Hm, I've learned to mute the bond somewhat. These though," she pointed to her ears, "They pick up a little more than you think."

Goddess have mercy. Arii had bitten her lip in her efforts to stay quiet. "Fucking creep," she hissed.

Nem laughed, a bark of sound that burst unbidden from her lips.

Arii counted her lucky stars that Krepth had remained asleep. He wouldn't let it lie like Nem would. He'd probably insist they speak about the birds and the bees, while glaring at Elijah.

"Get some rest, we'll be moving soon enough," advised Nem, her grin remaining as Arii settled into her blanket, eyes narrowed at traitorous, broad back.

She swore she saw his shoulders shaking with silent laughter.

In a few hours, the group began to stir, and soon they were up and armed with torches and an orb of Fae-light.

The caverns remained large enough for all to walk comfortably, and Emerson's claustrophobia remained reduced to light trembles, but there was a sense of foreboding, as if they trudged down the gullet of a never-ending serpent. The smell of earth became more potent as they continued, and rogue stalactites dripped lazy condensation into crystal puddles underfoot, the ominous *drip drip drip* following them through the darkness. Thick clusters of crude amethyst became more abundant, emitting a faint glow which cast gentle blue and purple light across their path.

"Stop here," Noct said suddenly, lifting his torch.

Tikkani cursed, and Quinn groaned loudly. "A dead end."

Arii eyed the rugged barricade, a strange shininess catching her eye. It wasn't like the crude stone walls surrounding them. It looked… different.

Noct raised his hand, running his fingers over the wall.

Something wasn't right.

Magic loomed heavy in the air, and Arii snuck a peek at Elijah beside her. No… it wasn't him.

"Are those…" Emerson began.

"Scales," finished Noct, taking a step back and raising his torch once more.

Before them was a wall of midnight-black scales so perfectly polished that light flashed off the peaks of the tiny, pointed plates like diamonds. Something shimmered in the ethereal light, and the wall of scales began to shift, uncurling from their path like a door opening. Colossal claws clicked against stone floor. Wings uncurled and lifted, the membranes between pitch-black wings glittering with strange patterns.

It reminded Arii of burned cloth, the edges still laced with burning, orange embers, glowing like a second layer of skin. The scales coasted together like plates of slate as the wall moved. As their torches threw light over colossal beast, it turned its serpentine head, lips curling in a draconic smile.

Their party shifted, weapons drawing, murmurs rising as they battled with the instinct of fight or flight.

It couldn't be… could it?

Standing before them proudly was a beast of legend, of ancient history, a beast now only residing in the faded parchments of story books.

A dragon.

The grand head lifted and piercing red eyes swept over them as Noct's voice cracked their slowly rising panic. His voice was contrite, as if admitting to a secret sin.

"Everyone, say hello to the Ouroboros."

CHAPTER SEVENTEEN

ARIIAYA

"Don't run," called Noct, raising his hands. "He won't hurt us!"

"The thing we have been searching for, the apparent magical artefact to help turn the tide of war, the one depicted as a serpent eating its own tail… is a literal, living breathing Godsdamned *dragon*?" shrieked Tikkani, her face filled with terror like the others. The elf took the words right from Arii's mouth, outrage and betrayal palpable.

The beasts' jaws widened, heated breath exploding out over their faces, reeking of smoke and ash. Elijah instinctively thrusted an arm out, placing himself in front of his friends. Arii's hand found his back, before stepping around him, head tilting back. Her heart pounded, the thrum hitting her ears. Above the apprehension though, she felt a curiosity so visceral that it outweighed her fear.

Serrated teeth flashed and the beast's lips rippled as it growled, bright red eyes wide under a thick brow of wicked spikes.

Arii halted, watching the lithe creature unfurl, massive wings flaring out as its chest rumbled in a… laugh?

Was the dragon laughing?

"In my own defence, I never *specifically* said it was an artefact." Noct spoke as if a fire-breathing monster wasn't unfurling behind him, its lips tipping up at the sounds of disbelief amongst their party.

Said non-magical artefact was *enjoying* their surprise.

"I was right, he can't be trusted," exclaimed Krepth. "He's led us to our deaths!"

Arii wasn't well-versed in dragon behaviour, but she was sure that if this beast hungered for their flesh, they would be dead already.

"If it wanted us dead, we would be ash already," said Elijah, voicing her thoughts.

The party shifted, still uneasy.

Suddenly a voice spoke into her mind, undoubtably male, deep and smooth. *"Place down your weapons. They are not needed here."* The voice held a laugh of amusement, and Arii cast a startled look up at the beast. She wasn't sure what she'd been expecting, but telepathy hadn't been the first thing to come to mind. She hadn't really considered how dragons communicated.

"Did you guys hear that?" squeaked Emerson, as Nem shook her head as if to rid it of buzzing flies.

"You'll have to forgive them, they have never seen your kind in the flesh," Noct reasoned, looking up at the creature.

The Ouroboros huffed a cloud of smoke, rustling his gigantic wings. His voice was like silk, edged with daggers. *"Enter, should you find courage in amongst your jitters,"* he said, wings lifting as he tilted and dropped out of sight beyond them.

The group moved as one to gaze over the edge of a sudden drop, staring in collective awe at the sprawling cavern before them.

It was if they had ventured into another world.

The earth dipped down into an underground realm with no visible end, a maze of rivers flowing through it that appeared to be made of starlight. Stalactites hung like dragon's teeth from above, meeting craggy sloping walls studded with clumps of amethyst glowing with blue, purple and warm gold light. Additional clusters flashed like star constellations on the enormous ceiling. Rock formations stood sprinkled throughout, jagged and tapered, a forest of primitive, ancient stone.

Despite the otherworldliness, Arii found her curiosity overwhelming her fear. She stepped forward, and the others followed her lead as they trekked down into the cavern.

In the very centre stood a castle, spiky turrets reaching for the ceiling. The castle was half the size of the gleaming gold one in Viridya, with flying buttresses, high arched windows and a bell tower, ancient embellishments with so much detail it left Arii wondering who had built such a structure down here. The entire place exuded a look of dark, rugged, ethereal beauty of which she was sure none of them had ever seen before.

They took the long expanse of road leading to its huge front door, mindful of their steps on the crushed stone floor.

As they approached, a shadow swept over, momentarily blocking the light. Wings thrummed the air, wind rushing against their faces as the titan dragon landed, the earth rumbling beneath its feet. Ouroboros' head lifted, angling towards them before his wings folded against his scales and his entire form began to warp. Magic doused the air, raw, heavy and ancient, before the beast changed shape in a shower of crackling sparks.

Suddenly before them no longer stood a dragon, but a man instead.

"Holy tainted dragon's breath," breathed Tikkani, clutching Quinn's arm as she whispered, "The dragon is… sinfully handsome. I'm not sure if I'm scared shitless, or strangely attracted."

Residual shock remained in the air, and not even Emerson reacted to the inappropriate timing of his sister's humour.

Arii eyed the man with fascination.

His hair was black, flecked with a glint of residual magic, the top half pulled back while the remaining length tumbled to his shoulders. High cheekbones framed a severe, angled face and strong jaw covered with a neat beard; one of his thick brows curved in a curious look. The man looked to be in his forties, but there was something timeless about him, about the way he moved – slow and precise – and the way his voice travelled, deep and melodious. Garbed in a simple moss green tunic and dark pants, draped in a high collared cloak that swept the heels of his boots, The Ouroboros turned to them fully, lips curving in a smile.

Everything about him had changed, seemingly human, all but the vivid crimson of his eyes.

"You all look as if you've never seen a dragon shift into a man before," he observed, laughter coating his words.

Arii's lips opened with an audible pop.

The Ouroboros laughed openly then, teeth flashing. They were straight and square, no hint of serrated dragon teeth, as were his rounded ears human-like. Had they not just witnessed his transformation, she would assume him human. Strangely, despite his dramatic shift, the instincts that normally plagued Arii in the presence of danger were non-existent. She trusted him.

Was this a trick of magic?

Ouroboros pressed a long-fingered hand, tipped with stained nails, against the heavy latch of the castle doors. They opened with a groan as he said, "We have been expecting you. Come, come inside, we have much to discuss."

Arii glanced back at her companions, meeting a mix of uncertainty, stoniness and fear. They seemed to be waiting for her, silent until she determined what they should do next. They'd come too far to turn back now, and she knew better than anyone not to let their guard down.

Arii sucked in a breath, rolled her shoulders and nodded, before leading them through the castle doors.

The receiving room featured high ceilings of arched crown moulding detailed finely with gold filagree. The walls themselves were black marble, intricate gold patterns weaving across the surface, reminiscent of delicate vines or ripples of water lapping a shore. The floor was polished in the same material, cool and spotless, a complete opposite from the rocky, dusty cavern they'd just come from.

As they gathered, Noct clapped hands with their host before introducing each of their party, speaking with a familiarity that clearly showed he and the dragon shifter had met before. Well, she was planning to grill the otherworldly stranger later for not being more forthright about what they had been seeking, and that interrogation would probably involve her knives.

"Please, call me Ouro," said their host, as charming as Nocturne, which didn't lessen her suspicion. "Welcome to our home."

"Wait, he said *we*… and *our*," whispered Luc, craning his head to take in the impressive room. "Do you think there are more like him here?"

Curious, Arii turned her attention back to the man, thinking the same thing. He pressed open another set of doors, ushering them into a grand hall lined with tall, thin windows. Charred iron chandeliers hung over their heads, throwing flickers of Fae light across the room. There was no throne, instead in its place stood a large, jagged cut of amethyst lined with quartz. A hum filtered through the room in time with the gentle light flashing within it, as if the thing had its own heartbeat. The only other furniture was a lone table with seating for twenty people. Beyond the glass around them, the cavern glowed in a purple and blue twisted sunrise.

When Ouro turned to them, his smile remained. "Unfortunately, no, there are no others here who can take the form of a dragon. It is just me and my companion," his voice rose, calling, "Aellan."

Arii stiffened.

That name.

Elijah moved closer, as if he sensed something wrong.

"Are you alright?" he murmured, voice guarded, as footfalls echoed from the receiving chamber.

Arii swallowed audibly, answering, "Aellan is quite a unique name. I haven't heard it since… since I was a child. It was the name of my–"

A tray clattered to the floor, glasses and porcelain smashing at the neat black shoes of a man with eyes of such a deep shade of blue they were almost purple. They were wide and incriminatingly familiar.

"Ariiaya?" the man gasped, almost painfully.

Arii's voice tapered off as she concluded. "–father."

⸙

The stillness was uncomfortably lengthy and tense as Arii's gaze swept over her father's face, her heartbeat steadily thumping in her ears. This couldn't be. He was dead. Long dead.

She took a step forward, and instinctively Elijah's hand followed, hovering near her elbow.

"Father?" she rasped, as he came forward tentatively. He was exactly as she remembered. His hair, long and the colour of rich chocolate, was pulled back in a tie, a few loose tendrils framing his strong face.

Confusion roiled with disbelief, overriding any semblance of happiness at the unexpected reunion. This was a trick. This was surely a trick, or this place was a home for long dead ghosts.

Her companions were silent behind her.

"Little Violet, what are you doing here?" Aellan said, shaking his head to expel his own look of confusion. He eyed her openly, sweeping from her crown down to her boots and back up. "Gods, you are all grown up. And… you look so much like your mother."

She ignored his words, lips curling back over her teeth.

"What am I doing here? What are *you* doing here? Alive? All this time!" Slowly her voice rose in pitch, relaying the emotions now bubbling inside her chest. A pain ached there, and she rested her palm over it. "You're alive and you never… you never came for me. Never came for *us*."

Her mother's face flashed before her eyes, healthy and golden with life, and then suddenly on the throes of death, pallid and pale. Arii's mother had never gotten over her husband's death – supposed death – her mourning a constant shadow in her eyes, right until her end.

Once young Arii had understood that her father wasn't returning, she'd mourned her loss in a different way. With anger, with bitterness, with regret. Why hadn't he fought harder? Why had the Gods decided to take him away? Why hadn't she been just a little older? Perhaps then she could have saved him.

Her regrets and self-loathing chased her long after her mother was gone, a dark companion ever present in the back of her mind.

Arii could feel Elijah's presence beside her, warm, steady,

grounding. She leaned towards him instinctively, seeking him like a tether in a storm. She knew, without looking, that his face held a brooding scowl.

"I... I have a lot to explain," her father sighed, shoes crunching on shards of porcelain. He winced, "Sorry about the mess, my lord."

Ouro waved a hand, "What have I told you about using titles here, Al?"

The man winced again, "Sorr–"

"And about apologising. Honestly, you paint the picture to our guests that you're here as my servant – which, you are not."

He wasn't this shape-shifting male's servant. Well, that was one question answered, but there were many to go.

Ouro cleared his throat before motioning to the table nearby. "Take a seat, you are all tired and perhaps mildly in shock. Please, I insist."

Tikkani was first to move, followed by Quinn, Emerson, Luc and Ghila. Krepth and Nem followed as Ouro led them to a thick porcelain pitcher already sitting in the middle of the table.

Arii's feet were glued to the floor, her stare fixed on her father.

"You all have questions, and I have my own. So, allow me to first explain who I am, and how dear Aellan here came into my care." Ouro tilted his head, directing his voice across the space. "And why he has been unable to leave..."

That snagged Arii's attention.

So, he wasn't *able* to leave. A touch of her anger fizzled away as her father awkwardly sidled past her and Elijah, joining their host in preparing the table.

Warm fingers slipped around her own, squeezing. She looked up into Elijah's steel-grey eyes, reading his wordless expression. Anger would do no good now. They were best to remain open to hearing her father's story. She knew better than most how everyone deserved a chance to tell their side.

Arii blew out a breath and they joined the others.

With a twist of Ouro's hand, a small, crackling portal flared open beside his elbow. Aellan leaned into the crackling window, retrieving some slate-grey teacups. Arii could see what looked like a glimpse of a kitchen over his shoulder.

"Twenty years ago, I found Aellan gravely wounded and barely conscious, slumped over a pony saturated in his blood. They found one of the secret entries to my castle, and to this day we still wonder how, but that isn't relevant anymore." Ouro threw a look at Aellan, and Arii saw affection there. He took a seat at the head of the table, but Aellan remained standing, shifting to the space to his right. "We now accept it as fate."

"I was able to save him, but only by performing a life bond." Ouro's startling red eyes landed on Arii, and his lips curled in a knowing smile. "Much like yours."

Could this creature… man… sense her life bond with Nem?

Arii tilted her head curiously. "And what has this to do with him not being able to leave?"

"Arii," began Aellan, his tone taking on a fatherly chord.

Ouro tapped his fingers on the slate tabletop, nails clicking on the surface like a metronome. "Your question is warranted, Ariiaya. How much do you know of a life bond's limitations?"

Arii glanced as Nem, meeting unflinching aqua eyes and a frown.

"When you successfully forge a life bond, your souls are tethered to each other. The only way to sever the bond is by powerful magic, sacrifice, or death. You also cannot be too far away from your life-bonded person, or else they will be subject to immense pain the further you part. Stay away long enough, and the one originally saved by that bond will die."

Nem's eyes slid to Ouro, and Arii swallowed a lump in her throat. They hadn't been apart to discover that, and now thinking on it, the thought of being parted from Nem brought on a strange kernel of pain, directly in the centre of her chest. Arii touched the space, and subtly, Nem did too. So, if they were apart long enough, Nem would die?

"You are bonded to the Ouroboros?" said Noct, directing his question at Aellan. The man shook his head, and there was a jitter of confusion around the table. Aellan motioned to the colossal jag of pure amethyst in the place of a throne upon the dais, glowing with magic within.

"I am soul-bound to the ancient magic here, to this castle, hence why I cannot leave. I am forever in service to this place, and it is a service I do not squander." Arii drew her eyes back to her father, feeling suddenly small and childish for her earlier anger. "I am thankful to be alive, but do not mistake my thankfulness for happiness. I have thought about you and your mother every single day since we were parted, Ariiaya. I have long wished to come and find you, but because of my tether, I was unable to do so. Instead, I had to settle for second-hand reports of what Ouro gleaned from the chatter of people in nearby towns. You made quite the name for yourself."

Arii shifted in her seat.

"I have my reasons for staying secluded here, also," sighed Ouro, sipping his tea. "I can visit the towns, which I do on occasion, but being who I am, I must tread lightly. The balance of this land is severely misaligned, and if I am not careful, I could cause far more damage. This is my refuge when the limbs of the tree become too heavy and my magic too restless."

"Kind of like a holiday home, without the sightseeing," surmised Luc, to which Ouro smiled.

The picture of the tree that Noct used as a metaphor for the realms and how they interlaced came to mind, and Arii took a stabbing guess that perhaps Noct and Ouro were from the same realm. Something else pinched at her mind though, overshadowing the metaphorical tree.

"Why didn't you find me and tell me that my father lived?"

Ouro quirked a brow her way. "If a dark stranger approached you and told you that your father lived, would you have believed him?"

Arii paused. "No…" She would have probably stuck him with the pointy end of her blade.

Ouro nodded sagely at her answer, turning to Elijah. "This land is in turmoil, its own magic unbalanced. I have been waiting, Eliverus

Herington, waiting for you to find me."

Elijah's eyes bordered on a brooding glare as he sat rigid in his seat. "Why would you wait for me? Could you not have done something about this long ago?"

"Balance is found not by one person alone, but by the strength of those they gather around them. The only way to bring about lasting change and balance is for you to reclaim your family's throne."

Elijah was silent, his brows pulled in a look of contemplation.

Quinn leaned forward, making a show with his hands. "You couldn't have flown to Viridya, gone undercover as a human, waited until Lorch walked his gardens with Valdis in tow, and then flame-grilled them both until nothing but husks were left?" he said, punching a fist to a palm, before leaning back on his chair, as if he hadn't just suggested murder by dragon fire.

Tikkani gasped and slapped a hand to her mouth in shock, muttering his name against her fingers.

Ouro's brows rose, but it was a look of amusement, like the thought had indeed crossed his mind. "Their followers are many, woven through all of the towns in the North. Their sudden demise would have caused mayhem – especially by a beast thought to be extinct."

Arii winced at the mention of burning Lorch. She was sure no one had noticed, except for Nem, who watched her carefully.

Ghila eyed their host with open curiosity. "Your likeness was on a pendant around my neck for twenty years." The shackles on her wrists clicked together as she brought her hands to the hollow of her throat, a habit she'd not yet shaken. "It brought me comfort in times when I had none, but it also bestowed me with the voices of a thousand cursed souls."

Ouro sighed, cupping his palms either side of the pitcher. Seconds later, its base began to glow under his fingers, and steam whispered out of its tapered spout. "My likeness has been used all over the realms, young Fae, and I am apologetic to hear of your experience. I trust the pendant is no longer in your possession?" He began to share the tea, pouring each of them a steam-curled cup.

"It's alright… and I still have it, but it's tucked deep in Nem's bags for safekeeping." Ghila whispered, and even though Arii still felt hate towards her for abducting Elijah, another slither of her anger slipped away. Nem had taken the locket from Ghila in the tunnels shortly before they arrived, whispering that she would be the one to relieve her of her burden. Ghila sounded… tired, apologetic, defeated almost. She hadn't had the strength to dispose of the locket yet.

"So, you can just… shift into a dragon at will? Or is it a curse of some kind?" voiced Emerson, sipping from his cup. His brows shot up. "Is this strawberry tea?"

"Correct – to both. Strawberry is a favourite of mine, and you could say my ability to change is indeed a blessing and a curse."

"Well, I think it is bloody awesome," said Tikkani against her cup. "Scary, but bloody awesome."

Ouro smiled wide at that. Then he said, "Now for a question of my own, how did you find your way here?"

Elijah explained their deal with the Queen of Sapphine, gliding over the part where Noct had agreed upon giving the Ouroboros to the Queen once they were done.

Ouro's look was comical. "You did what?"

Noct rubbed the back of his neck, "I also left off the information about you being a *person* rather than an object of power. I figured I would give her something in your likeness if we won the war. If we didn't win, then it would be a moot point." He tilted towards Ghila. "Perhaps we could give the Queen the Locket of Dreaming?"

Arii couldn't help but glare, envisioning looping the chain of said necklace around his neck and yanking, hard.

Reading her murderous expression, Noct said, "I didn't think you'd all follow me here if I'd told you we were in search of a living, breathing dragon," he admitted, his voice tinged with a hint of apology. The words hung heavy in the air, weighted with the burden of deception. "I knew you would feel apprehension," Noct continued, his bicoloured gaze steady despite the tension crackling around them. Arii spied a brace in his shoulders, perhaps preparing himself for backlash. "Besides," he added, his voice softening with sincerity, "I didn't think you'd all believe me."

It was Emerson who spoke to the silence. "We have been through too much not to forgive you, Noct."

Each of her friends nodded in shared understanding, and though she still felt a sting, Arii folded her arms across her chest, letting her silence and shifting attention show that she'd let the matter of his deception slide… for now.

The table was a mix of murmurs, of planning and discarding ideas. Arii listened, yet the words didn't quite sink in. Her thoughts were elsewhere – tossed across mountains to the golden city just to the south. She sat and stewed for a time, taking a few sips of the tea, until her thoughts grew to a pitch just below a scream.

"Will you help us?" Arii's voice cut across the room, and the blooming chatter sizzled to silence. There was no use delaying any longer, they were now in a race against the clock, its tick a constant metronome in the back of her mind.

Ouro eyed her, his expression turning serious. "Yes, I can aid your realm, and help restore it back to its former glory. But first, I have some things to teach your future king." He paused as the table collectively shifted to look at Elijah. Arii couldn't help it, she stared too as Ouro said, "Do you have the stone, Eliverus?"

Elijah brought forth an object from deep within his pocket, settling the egg-shaped stone before him. Everyone leaned forward, taking in the slumbering swirl of dull magic in its glass centre.

The dragon shifter's face was stony, his voice dropping an octave as he breathed the words, "Open the stone, and bring the dragons home."

Chapter Eighteen

ARIIAYA

Despite the lack of people in Ouro's castle, and the dark and mysterious décor of the place, Arii had to admit that there was a beauty in the silence surrounding them. They'd been enveloped by so many people lately, courtiers, castle employees, soldiers, Furies, that she had become used to the constant hum of movement and voices. Aellan guided them to the western wing of the castle, to a cluster of neat little rooms there. But as her friends chose their quarters, Arii tagged along with her father for a tour of the castle grounds. She left Elijah to chat with Ouro, not missing the weight of a message in his silver eyes.

I'll come right away if you need me and *try not to kill your father.*

Arii wanted to spend time with Aellan, who was both familiar and unfamiliar to her. Her anger had fizzled, drained away knowing he couldn't leave the castle without ultimately dying, and understood why he hadn't fought to get the message to her. If anyone had approached her, especially years ago when she had switched her emotions off, she would have probably killed them thinking their tongue held lies. She'd be the first to confess that she'd been a little unreasonable back then.

Okay, *a whole* lot unreasonable.

She cleared her throat and nudged her father with her elbow, attempting to pierce the awkwardness between them as they approached a heavy oak door at the end of a hall. "So, what do you do here every day? Twenty years is a long time to spend alone in a big empty castle in the guts of an underground cavern."

Aellan chuckled, the sound reminding her of nights they had spent reading books together, when she would invent tales of inconceivable whimsy while they sipped warm milk mixed with cinnamon in the light of the hearth. Her heart clenched painfully, a feeling of loss overwhelming her, as if her biggest giver of comfort wasn't strolling right beside her. Twenty years was a long time, so she supposed the feeling of disconnect wasn't so unusual.

Aellan held open the door for her as he said, "It may look desolate, but this castle has magic, a force I can tap into, being bonded and all. I spend most of my time tending to the crops and animals we farm here, and when I'm not doing that, I'm learning about other realms from Ouro, or I'm reading in the library."

They descended a flight of stone stairs into a large, walled courtyard. Picket fences divided the yard into sections, some filled with thick crops of leafy greens such as lettuce, spinach and silver beet, along with larger plants like grapevines, tomato plants, and fruit trees. Secluded a short way from the plants were animal pens, one attached to a medium-sized barn and a little chicken coop. She could hear the happy cluck of chickens, their feet foraging at the ground, and as they moved closer, she made direct eye contact with a hawk-wing coloured cow, lazily munching away on a thick wad of hay. Two goats and a cluster of sheep stared as they neared.

The farm was thriving, and as Aellan crouched to pluck a sizable orange from one of the neatly sectioned trees, Arii glanced up at the cavernous ceiling far above, blinking in confusion.

"How does all of this survive without sunlight and rain?"

Aellan held the fruit out to her, a small smile on his face. It felt like a tentative peace offering, so she took it, holding it to her nose to inhale the sweet, citrusy scent.

He turned and raised his arms towards some nearby apple trees. After a few moments, nothing happened, and Arii leaned her elbows on the wooden fence, tossing the orange from one hand to another as she studied her father's profile. Ridges sat over his unblinking eyes, a few tendrils of hair loose against his cheek.

Slowly a breeze began to pick up, and with it the scent of a coming storm. The hairs on her arms stood up, her skin rising with goosebumps. Suddenly, electricity snapped above the crop, as if an invisible storm cloud had arrived. With a pop and a crackle, a portal yawned to life, and from within it came a steady downpour of rain directly above the plants on which her father had set his sights.

Arii stood to attention, surprise flickering through her. Her father had not had magic before, so when he had mentioned tapping into the borrowed magic of the castle, it hadn't registered that it was he who would wield it. She had thought the magic was residual, feeding the life here, but she supposed she had been wrong. Her father was keeping this farm going by conventional means, albeit cheating just a tad.

Incredible.

When the crop was watered enough, Aellan waved his hands, and soon the portal snapped shut, a shimmer of magic sparkling in its wake.

"So, you can open portals like the Ouroboros now?" she quizzed.

Aellan rubbed his hands together, and she noticed a few beads of sweat on his brow. "Not as quickly and easily, but yes. My magic is tied to the castle, and I can only use it while on its grounds."

"Have you tried to leave?" Arii asked, peeling a piece of the orange's skin, her eyes dropping to her task. Had he *tried* to leave, to find her? She hadn't tested the limits of her bond with Nem, they hadn't been separated by much distance since, but she had to admit that when Nem wasn't in sight, she did feel... odd. Like she was missing a limb, albeit a small one. She hadn't asked Nem how she felt, though. The bond was stronger, more potent to the one who had been saved, right? So, her friend could very well be feeling discomfort, even some pain right now, even though they were only half a castle length apart.

"Of course I've tried." His answer was gentle, and when she lifted her gaze back to him, he was frowning slightly. "More than once.

I got to the mouth of the cavern, and I stared into the depths of the tunnels that would lead me back to the land above. But that journey alone cost me. The pain was… terrible. Like a ball of acid, the pain grew and grew in the pit of my stomach until I keeled over, curled up and howling with pain. Ouro brought me back, and every time I tried, testing the limit before I became too encumbered, he would retrieve me again. He never stopped me from testing my limit, despite the pain I felt."

Arii bit into a wedge of orange, and spoke around it. "You've become firm friends, haven't you?"

"Yes, he's unlike anyone I've ever met before. Unlike *anyone* has ever met before, I'd wager."

Well, except Nocturne. The two seemed to know each other, a fact she was eager to grill the man over.

She followed her father towards the barn, where stood a few short, thick-based trees, bulky with wide green leaves. Bushels of red berries clung to the branches, weighing down the limbs so the trees looked as if they were bowing. Aellan squatted by the plant to pick some of the berries before rising to show them to her. They varied in colour, most were dark crimson, some lighter, and some an olive green.

"You've got quite the abundance of food here. These berries don't quite look ripe, though."

Aellan's smile revealed his teeth. "These aren't berries, Arii. These are coffee cherries."

Coffee?

Arii inspected the little fruit-like spheres as Aellan dropped them into her outstretched hand, rolling them around her palm.

"In the world where Ouro is from, this little cherry, once stripped of its skin and roasted, can be ground into a powder that is brewed into a hot drink. It's a strong, bitter sip, but mixed with some cream or milk, and a teaspoon of sugar or two, it's quite the pick-me-up."

"Like… tea?" she guessed.

"Far stronger, and some would argue, better," he surmised.

She stared at the coffee berries with open curiosity.

"I'll brew you a cup when we return to the castle, I think you'll like it."

Feathers fluttered nearby, and Arii's head snapped to the right. The cow in the pen huffed around its mouthful of hay, tail whipping as if at invisible flies. She could have sworn there had been a… shadow. In the chicken coop.

Before she could speak, Aellan sighed. "Albert is playing with the chickens again," he said, a note of warmth around the words.

Albert?

There was an enraged squawk, then a flurry of wings, before two chickens scrambled over the fence, leaving trails of feathers in their wake.

A shadow, far larger than chickens, suddenly sprang their way.

Arii let out a startled cry, dropping the berries to draw her daggers.

"Wait!" called Aellan, and something in his tone had stopped her instinct to stab, to defend. A mass thumped against her chest, sending her sprawling back onto the grass. Her arms shot up to cover her face as hot breath blasted her, a wide, jagged-tooth smile inches from her startled eyes.

It was a Kryvern, rather smaller than those she had faced before.

"Albert!" chastised Aellan, swatting at the stumpy horns on the juvenile beast's head. "What have I told you about chasing the chickens! They stop laying."

Arii panted, her pulse thumping and adrenaline shooting through her limbs. "Albert is a Kryvern?" she gasped.

The young Kryvern lumbered back and thumped onto his backside, tongue lolling between his jaws like a big puppy. A scaled, carnivorous, jagged-toothed puppy. Arii moved to her feet, unable to look away from the creature. She'd only ever seen adult Kryvern, never a baby. He was the size of a large hunting hound, his thorned head reaching her hip, all gangly limbs and soft scales, still in the process of growing. His eyes were a rich amber, verging on the crimson that most adults of his kind bore. His claws were short, and made of bone, not the terrifying iron tips that had been bestowed upon the ones she had fought. She tilted her head to study him, and the juvenile mirrored her action curiously.

"His tail…" she murmured, watching the stump where a long tail should have been wobbling from side to side.

Aellan patted Albert's head, and Arii jolted, about to shout a warning. But the beast simply closed his eyes and butted her father's palm eagerly and she swallowed it down.

"Albert was the runt of a litter. He was smallest, and less formed than the others. He was so weak that his mother left him in the nest, perhaps thinking he wouldn't make it, and moving on to find food for her other hatchlings. Kryvern are hardy creatures but surprisingly emotional – their instinct to feed their young is strong, and there isn't much in these caves. She mourned Albert before moving on, and Ouro heard it. He brought him back here and we have cared for him ever since."

Arii looked at the Kryvern again, a mixture of fascination and awareness ribboning through her. "So, they nest here, in the caves?"

"Yes, and then either head north, beyond the mountains and Fythnar, or travel south, to the forests surrounding Bonemire, and sometimes further down. They're surprisingly cautious, and don't normally head too far into the populated lands–"

"Unless they've been manipulated to…" whispered Arii, recalling the anger and bloodthirst of the iron-clawed beasts she'd encountered.

Albert lumbered on gangly legs towards her, and she lifted a tentative hand. He snuffed her fingertips, before butting his nose against her palm. Arii's face broke into a smile. "Sorry, Albert. We got off to a rough start, didn't we?"

Albert huffed, blinking up at her curiously. Then he nudged at her leg, sniffing, seeking something.

"Ah, he's probably hungry. Hang on, Albie."

Arii chuckled at the fatherly tone. Well, she supposed this beast had become part of her father's family, perhaps a stand-in for the little girl he had lost. She felt strange comparing herself to a Kryvern, but appreciated her father and Ouro's drive to save a beast that many would have either killed or left to rot.

"Frightfully misunderstood creatures," her father said, as if reading her thoughts. He pulled a heavily wrapped parcel from his bag, unwrapping a layer of cloth then some soggy parchment from a hunk of meat.

"You mentioned a library earlier?" squeaked Arii, leaning away from Albert's very sharp teeth as his stumpy tail wagged violently against her hip. When he saw the meat, an excited growl snapped out as he threw himself onto his belly.

Aellan smiled wide, not holding back for the first time since they'd reunited. "I knew the library would interest you. Come, I'll show you."

Albert let out a high-pitched sound akin to a dog begging for a treat.

"Here you go, you rascal." Aellan laughed and tossed the chunk. Albert snapped the meat in mid-air, throwing it back whole like a big, scaley bird. A rumbling burp erupted and he was done.

"Charming," Arii said, unable to hold back a grin. She *had* to tell Tikkani about this. The girl would flip.

"Good boy, now off you go." Aellan thumped the beast on its scaly hide before Albert nuzzled his snout against Arii's hip and turned to leap back in the direction he'd come from.

Arii rested her hands on her hips. "You just let him terrorise the poor animals here?"

Aellan laughed again. "No, he'll head off looking for bugs in the cavern somewhere. Kryvern love to forage for their food, contrary to the belief they'd rather bring down sheep and cows on farmland. This place teems with large, juicy bugs, possibly enhanced in size because of all the magic here. Not enough for fully grown beasts to live on, but enough for him." He looped the bag over his shoulder, nodding towards the castle. "Let me show you to the library, and possibly begin your long love affair – and possible addiction – to a liquid gold squeezed from beans."

ELIJAH

It had taken all Elijah's willpower to allow Arii to go off alone with her father but there were years of questions that needed to be answered, and they deserved their solitude. They had twenty years to catch up on, and he wasn't really sure what Aellan knew about the world outside the cavern. Things had drastically changed since the events that tore their families apart, and though Arii was upset, Elijah felt she wouldn't take long to calm.

Now he accompanied Ouro as they walked the halls of the castle. From what Elijah had learned, this place was a temporary home between the realms he visited, doing who-knew-what. Ouro wouldn't elaborate. He itched to know about the place where Ouro had come from, but for now, the man's previous words still echoed, a statement he'd been mulling over.

"Open the stone and bring the dragons home."

"Your bloodline contains some of the fiercest dragon riders of our history," said Ouro as they passed through open doors onto a wide balcony, one which reminded Elijah of the Dragon Landing back at castle Viridya. "That potential is within you, too." He gazed out over the stone trees dotting the cavern like a dark forest.

Elijah eyed the starlit lakes, before bringing his attention back to the tall man beside him. Ouro had a few inches on him, and despite him being amiable and friendly so far, Elijah couldn't shake the knowledge that the man could transform into a beast almost the size of this very castle. One that could swallow him whole.

The words caught up with him, and Elijah crossed his arms over his chest. "How do you know so much about my family?" He had to ask. He knew Ouro was an immortal being, one who had probably seen the beginning, and end, of many worlds and bloodlines. But he was still curious. He was also becoming slightly bothered by the fact that almost everyone else knew more about his family history than he did.

Ouro leaned back on the railing. "I was the one to introduce the first of your line to their dragons. I was also there when your grandfather sent the dragons back. He was a brave man." Crimson eyes swept over his face, and Elijah suddenly felt self-conscious at the admiration in the gaze. "You look much like him in his youth, albeit a tad scruffier."

Elijah cleared his throat, but a warmth had flared in his chest to war with other feelings. To busy himself, he fished the Void Stone from his pocket, lifting it between them. The stone glowed from within.

"Can you tell me how to open the stone? Or teach me?"

Ouro's red eyes lifted from the stone. "I can point you in the right direction to do so, but it is something you must do on your own." Ouro's voice was steady, but a slight pull in the corner of his mouth betrayed him. He was not telling him the entire truth, or was unable to.

"You can't just tell me the spell to open it?" Elijah pressed, agitated.

Ouro shook his head, looking regretful. "It's not something that can be taught. It is an instinct."

Elijah shoved the stone back into his pocket with less decorum than normal, trying and failing to hide his disgruntlement.

"I may not be able to aid you in opening the stone, Eliverus, but there are other things I can teach you."

A whip of air suddenly rose around them, drawing their cloaks into a dance. Ouro stepped past him to the centre of the balcony.

"I can teach you how to ride a dragon."

As he spoke, magic doused the air, and Ouro's form began to shift. Power skittered across Elijah's skin, caressing his flesh with fingers of familiarity, and pressing weight upon his shoulders like a heavy blanket. His head craned back as swirls of crackling chaos spun around the unfurling wings of a giant – black scales sliding together as the dragon's long, lithe body stretched over the marble balcony. Claws clicked as Ouro's long neck arched, bright crimson eyes blinking with the dip of his serpentine head.

He paused once they were eye to eye.

Now that there wasn't an immediate threat, Elijah could examine him properly. Majestic horns tapered from a long-snouted skull, spikes running along his eyebrow ridges and up along his long neck. He was all black, scales like charred ash. The membranes between his wings shimmered with a pattern akin to golden embers glowing and shifting.

Power emanated from him, leaving Elijah speechless.

Ouro's lips quivered, serrated teeth glinting in a serpentine smile, voice rising forth from the surface of Elijah's mind. *"It is time."*

Seeing a dragon in the dreamscape conjured by Kadec's magic, or illustrated in the pages of dusty old tomes, was nothing compared to witnessing one in the flesh.

Nor did it compare to actually riding one.

Elijah's thighs clenched hard as he perched between Ouro's shoulder blades. Even though he wasn't equipped with saddle or reins, the spot was moulded to him, seemingly made for a rider. Ouro's scales were warm beneath his palms, shifting like liquid as the dragon lifted himself from where he'd crouched to allow Elijah to mount. He had been hesitant at first, of course, to which Ouro had snorted a cloud of smoke into his face.

He had only known this male for a few hours, but his instincts told him that he wouldn't be harmed. Ouro had insisted that he listen to those instincts, and it felt right.

The dragon shifted, claws scraping the balcony as he turned his sights to the cavernous land stretching beyond.

"Hold on," Ouro said into Elijah's mind, his neck lowering slightly as his wings unfolded.

Vibrations began to rumble beneath him, and Elijah shot forward, gripping two spikes perfectly placed as handholds. He sucked in a breath, fighting an edge of hysteria as Ouro began a lumbering trot towards the edge of the balcony – now just a small lip at Ouro's clawed feet.

Panic rose like a raging tidal wave, squeezing his lungs.

He couldn't do this.

Ouro's head suddenly disappeared, and they were tipping forward.

The glowing cavern yawned before them, erasing any opportunity to back out.

Elijah's stomach dipped, and he leaned back, swallowing his panic.

He couldn't do this.

Then they were falling.

A yell rose and burst from Elijah's lips, his thighs clenching so hard that his muscles heated in pain. Air whipped past, whistling like a hail of arrows, plastering his hair against his skull and stinging his eyes. But he held on, folding at the waist, making himself as small as possible against the pull of the wind.

Ouro's wings folded close to his body, gravity snaring them in a freefall past the cliff at his belly. The cavern floor with its thin glittering lakes enlarged as they fell; the stone trees rose swiftly to meet them like spikes in a trap.

Elijah fought the overwhelming urge to squeeze his eyes shut, tears pooling at the rush of air.

Then, even though he knew he shouldn't, Elijah closed his eyes.

And quickly regretted it.

Ouro banked into a violent turn that had Elijah halfway out of his seat, momentarily weightless as his fingers scrabbled for hold. Just as quickly, the dragon banked in the opposite direction, slamming Elijah back into place hard enough to whoosh the breath from his lungs and elicit a pained groan.

Then they were again descending, and Elijah couldn't help but feel that his mount was trying to test him.

A lesson, but a trial as well.

At the last possible moment, Ouro's wings snapped out, snagging the air, billowing like sails on a ship. Gravity hurled a weight against Elijah's back and he grunted, his chest momentarily pressed against warm scales as the world righted and his mount levelled out. The speed in which the dragon flew did not relent as they entered a labyrinth of stone walls. Elijah held on, jaw clenched, as Ouro tipped to the right then the left, following along the snaking valley of slate and starlight.

The dragon jerked from side to side, skirting so close Elijah feared his head would collide with the valley walls. He could feel his thighs slipping, his body teetering from side to side, his nails scrabbling for purchase on the spikes, as fear rose acidic on the back of his throat. Fear, bright and hot, burned its way behind his teeth, threatening to char his courage. He dug his heels in, desperately clinging on as the dragon whipped through the glowing junctions at breakneck speed. Gravity yanked him at every turn, weighting his limbs, his body feeling as if it had no centre.

He felt like a beginner again, shaky on an untamed steed, trying desperately not to be thrown. Not only did he fear broken bones, but failure itself. Unlike the time he'd first ridden a horse, Elijah wasn't being scrutinised by a nearby commander, knowing that his performance would shape his future as a soldier.

This time, he was under scrutiny from someone far more important. Someone who needed proof that he had what it took to shape the very future of the land.

He'd never had the opportunity to discover a fear of flying – and that fear was swiftly unlocked.

He let loose a yell, incredibly grateful that none but Ouro could hear, then his body jerked so violently that his jaw clacked together, shutting off his scream. He was unable to hold on any longer as he felt his hands slip, the mass beneath his thighs turning to nothing but air, Elijah realised that all fear he had felt up to this point was nothing.

Nothing compared to the fear of failing everything and everyone he held dear.

Elijah crashed into the river, the force of the water slamming into him and tearing the breath from his lungs.

He sank for a few feet, dazed, trailing bubbles up to the rippling surface. He'd fallen only moments into the test, and self-doubt warred with the overwhelming sense of failure. His magic pulsed in his chest, judging, almost bitter.

Within his mind, he heard his own mocking laughter.

That tiny hint of the madness that haunted him caused him to push back to the surface, defiant of the darkness, pushing back towards the light.

He'd failed… *this time.*

"You held on longer than I thought you would," called Ouro, his dark shadow passing overhead with a beat of wings. Elijah threw his head back, blinking water from his eyes as he watched the dragon bank into a turn, heading back his way. Ouro's talons cut through the water, before snatching around his biceps, scooping Elijah from the water.

Elijah fell four more times, and each time he managed to hold on just that little bit longer. Enough water flew up his nose and into his mouth that he was sure his brain was becoming waterlogged, and his clothes were soaked enough to become a second skin. Try as he might, he couldn't quite shake the fear, and perhaps it was that fear that made him lose his hold time and again.

"It takes courage to continue at something you're trying to master, but it takes even more to know when to stop."

"I'm not giving up," Elijah panted, holding on tight as Ouro dipped into a sweeping turn, dagger-shaped head twisting back towards the towering castle.

Ouro huffed a smoky laugh. *"Not give up, young Prince. I'm merely suggesting you take a break. We can try again tomorrow."* If Ouro had any idea of Elijah's fear, he did not let it show. A stubborn fire ignited in his bones, but as his gaze dropped to the rushing river beneath them, it was quickly doused at the thought of hitting the water again. Perhaps a break wouldn't hurt – well, far less than hitting the water face-first, which he'd done at least twice. Elijah thanked the Gods he hadn't broken his nose, or anything else for that matter.

His shoulders slumped, exhaustion taking hold as Elijah conceded. He wanted to find Arii and see how she was holding up after her time with her father. Mostly he wanted to talk with her, knowing she'd want to hear everything about his first time on dragon-back.

As they headed back towards the castle on the bluff, lit by otherworldly light, Elijah felt the fear level out to something else.

Excitement.

Elijah wanted to tell her every detail, but also tell her about the fear. He needed her strength… her steadfast belief in him. He wanted to hold her, his feet solidly on the ground, and her lavender scent in the air.

He wouldn't be done until he could hold his own on the back of the beast, but Ouro was right. Slow and steady won races, not mad dash sprints. Just like wars weren't won overnight.

CHAPTER NINETEEN

ARIIAYA

She wasn't sure what she'd been expecting of a dark, ancient library encased within a lonely, desolate castle, but what greeted her across the threshold was unlike any library she'd ever seen before.

Like the gigantic place which hid the castle itself, the library was cavernous. The walls were lined with wood shelving so dark that it looked black. The shelves weren't all straight and orderly; some sloped up and down, and others even curved, the flow of the place reminding Arii of water. Long, thin, rippling glass windows allowed filtered blue light to scatter against the golden glow thrown from the oil lamps, painting the spines of countless books in a wild spectrum of colour.

The shelving reached up to a twisting, high ceiling. Magical mist hung in the air like clouds, obscuring her view of the library roof, and she swore she saw flashes of blue light, like electrical storms raging deep within their depths. There were small balconies rimmed with intricately-carved dark oak railings, oil lamps throwing flickering gold light against plush couches, cosy reading nooks not dissimilar to the viewing boxes in Viridya's grandest theatre. Magic was everywhere, weighing heavily on the air, so potent that Arii could taste it. It was much like the magic she'd experienced while falling through one of Noct's portals, different and ancient, like rich, aged toffee.

Arii's head tilted back, mouth dropping open as she spun slowly, absorbing the library's magnificence, and feeling very much insignificant.

"Welcome to the Library In-between."

Arii couldn't stifle the little gasp of awe that escaped her.

Her father headed past her towards a little kitchenette inside the shallow enclave under a curved bookshelf. He opened a dark tote bag to draw out a strange barrel-shaped glass with a bowl-shaped bottom, almost like a large decanter. Aellan poured a soil-like black powder from the tote into a mesh metal cylinder. The wire cylinder was then slotted into the glass. Then, he placed a pot on a thick metal rack, clicking his fingers. The pot filled with water, which boiled almost instantly and he poured it over the powder. He worked quickly and deftly, having done this many times before, it seemed.

Arii padded closer, her awe of the library changing to fascination as she watched her father take a metal plunger, slotting it into the glass tube, before pressing down.

Dark brown water pooled in the bottom of the glass. A rich, earthy scent drifted in the air, not unpleasant.

Finally, Aellan grabbed two thick black and white painted porcelain cups with curving handles, like two little impatient maids with fists resting on their hips. "Coffee is a complex thing, full bodied and aromatic, but not always everyone's favourite drink. It's stronger than tea, and far more personal. If straight black isn't to your liking, you can try different combinations of milk, and even sugar, until you have a concoction that brings you warmth, comfort, and a little kick."

Aellan filled the cups, steam wisping lazily from them, pushing one towards her before gesturing towards a moisture-pebbled pitcher of milk and a pot of sugar. "I'd start with a splash of milk and one sugar, remembering your fondness for sweetness."

Arii complied, adding both before taking a tentative sip. The sugar balanced the bitter, strong earthiness of the coffee.

Her father let out a laugh at her expression, which she hadn't realised she'd been making. "You like it?"

"I… think I love it." Arii said, smiling over the rim of her mug, inhaling the rich scent. "One sugar and a dash of milk is perfect."

Aellan smiled back, jerking his chin to the shelves. "Let me give you a tour. I think you'll find this library to be far more fascinating than any you've seen before."

They moved into the thick of the library, their shadows dancing over the spines of countless books. Arii cradled her mug, lifting it to her nose every now and then, before taking a sip. It warmed her from the inside, like home in a cup, hitting deeper than any tea she'd ever drank.

"So…" Her father's voice began timidly, drawing out the word before leading her towards a small reading nook by two tall windows, closely encased either side by bookshelves. Two plush seats flanked a coffee table, an oil lamp flickering lazy gold light over the space. Taking a seat, Arii looked at her father curiously. Despite the time they'd spent apart, she couldn't recall a time her father had ever sounded… apprehensive while speaking to her before, even as a child.

It put her on guard instantly, and when the next words tumbled from Aellan's mouth in a rush, Arii brought the coffee closer to her chest, almost like a shield.

"You seem close to him. To Eliverus, I mean. You were young when we were separated, I never had the chance to talk to you about… well, I'm sure you're all caught up with what can happen when two people become fond of each other and–"

"Papa, no–" Arii began, alarmed.

"You're grown up now, I know that, but I still can't help feeling it's my duty as your father to make sure you're… safe. Making the right choices."

Arii buried her nose in her cup, coughing around a hurried sip of coffee. A conversation like this needed something stronger. *Far* stronger.

"I…" a whispered curse. "I'm being careful," she finally summarised, hoping the flame of her cheeks wasn't so obvious.

When her father remained silent, his gaze holding the weight of twenty stolen years, Arii's shoulders slumped in defeat. "We are close. It didn't begin that way. But that doesn't matter now. I know a future with him looks uncertain, but I'm determined to see him where he is meant to be. On the throne, making this world a better place. I'll figure out the rest later."

Her father's smile held pride, "Be sure not to throw your own destiny aside in place of someone else's, Arii."

She shrugged. "I'm still trying to figure out my part in this."

"I must say, when I learned he was still alive, I was overcome with relief. What happened to his family was…" he searched for the right word, before continuing. "Abhorrent. And his sister, Ghila. She isn't the little girl I remember. Something hangs in the air over them both. A darkness, a light, a feeling… a story."

That drew Arii up short, and she looked at her father. His look had turned contemplating, distant, just over her shoulder.

Arii blinked, following his gaze to the shelves behind her, before casting her attention back. Twenty years was a long time, she wasn't surprised there was an awkwardness and a scatteredness to her father.

He suddenly stood.

"Spending many years in this library has given me the gift of countless stories. Stories that are a mixture of fable, of extraordinary imagination, and some narrative truths, but most of all, stories made of magic," he smiled widely. "Of this world, and others – ranging from new to as old as time itself."

A shock of blue light snapped over his face, cast from something behind her. The hairs on her arms rose in response to magic, and she turned around to see a small portal open and hover before the shelves.

Suddenly a hand emerged, delicately tapered with skin a strange shade of blue. The nails were long and pearlescent white, polished to a shine, as the hand coasted along the shelf.

What in the world?

"Were you not curious as to why this place was called the Library In-between?" said her father with a grin.

Arii examined the hand with fascination, catching a glimmer of blue robe linked to the host's arm, and a slither of bookshelves so pure white that the contrast to the dark library she was in was almost blinding.

"I hadn't thought about it."

Her father laughed, to which a voice echoed from beyond the small opening. "Hello, Aellan. I hope you're well today."

"Very well, Xi. Found what you're looking for?"

The hand swept a finger in the air in contemplation. "I believe so, after a cosy fantasy today. She's a touch over adventure tales."

"Good choice. Your little bookworm will have this library entirely read soon." Aellan chuckled, pinching his chin.

The person beyond the portal – Xi – laughed too, the sound light and tinkling like bell chimes. "Not too far from it. *Sayoi noi*, dear Aellan. It was good to hear your voice."

"*Sayoi noi*, Xi. Happy reading and say hello to Yui for me."

Arii shook her head, speechless, watching closely as the hand halted on a book's spine, tapping the gold filagree in triumph. It then slid the tome free and retreated into the portal, which closed with a static snap.

"Sa... ya..." Arii paused, and let her poor imitation of the beautiful, otherworldly language drop before she could truly butcher it. "What... who was that?"

"*Sayoi noi* means farewell in Xi's language, one so beautiful and complex that I still haven't scratched the surface of learning it. They are from another realm, one with technology that makes our world seem extremely archaic, but they still love to read from paper and ink."

Another small void popped into existence nearby, and another hand emerged. It was far different to the one she'd just seen, with thick fingers covered in what looked to be scales the colour of cherries, with nails of pure black. Another void snapped open, another hand, aged and seemingly human, placed a book back on the shelf before retreating from this existence. Blue flickers of light snapped up further, and higher in the shelves, where beings from other realms broke through to browse the countless shelves of books from the Library In-between.

A library in-between *worlds*.

"Incredible," breathed Arii, instantly curious about each and every portal opening in their vicinity. "Can anyone reach this library, from anywhere?"

"Not quite. Only those bestowed with a special kind of magic can reach it. And those who have it know how sacred the stories and information contained here are. There are bedtime stories but there are also books of prophecy, knowledge of things that have yet to happen, and spells that – if they were to fall into the wrong hands – would be catastrophic for the realms they relate to.

This place isn't just a library, Arii, it's a sanctuary of knowledge, and a weapon in hands that would shape it that way. When my life was bound to this place, I found myself drawn here, and in time I was made a caretaker. I can sense when the voids open, and if any of them bring a feeling of threat, I can close them instantly before anything with ill intentions can enter."

A slither of pride wound its way into her heart, and Arii realised that her father hadn't just been sitting in this big dark castle, trapped without purpose. He was doing what he could with the fate given to him, and she couldn't help but appreciate that now. Her anger over his forced abandonment slipped through her fingers like desert sand.

"It's getting late," Aellan said, stretching.

Arii glanced at the windows as her father spoke, blinking. She hadn't a clue what the time was, but once it was mentioned, she did feel tiredness in her muscles. She found herself quickly longing for the plush king bed she'd spied in her rooms, and for Elijah's steady embrace. At the thought, she heard the distant boom of wings.

Arii turned to her father as she set down her empty cup, her mind focusing on something she'd been dying to learn more about since flipping through the dusty pages of *The North: Past and Present* in Viridya. She knew Elijah's family history contained dragons, and people who rode them – some of the most legendary in fact – but the old book hadn't given her as much detail as she'd hoped, nor had she had time to properly read it.

She inclined her head towards the twirling shelves and asked,

"Don't suppose there are some stories about dragons and their riders in here somewhere?"

Aellan grinned, grasping the spine of a thick book, gently tugging it from its place.

"My dear, if you're looking for a story, or looking for a truth, this place will most certainly have it. You just need the determination to *find* it."

Arii followed her father's lead, her eye drawn to a tome with a symbol pressed in gold leaf on the spine.

One with a serpent curled in a figure eight.

NEMESIS

From this vantage point, Nemesis had an uninterrupted view of the valley and its snaking streams of starlight, as well as the enormous length of the hazy cavernous world beyond. Unlike her previous perch overlooking the spring city, this one was far quieter, allowing her an ideal place to sit and think.

Nem balanced on the rooftop just below her bedroom window, the ancient tiles rough with a layer of build-up, almost like barnacles on a ship's hull. Her shoes easily gripped the slate as she sat, arms holding her legs to her chest, chin propped on her knees.

The air was still, naught a breeze nor the sound of birds to keep her mind from straying, inching back to eyes of deep green and a smile ending in a wicked dimple. Often her thoughts strayed like a hound back to Krepth, to the situation they'd found themselves in, and in turn the revelations of what she'd learned about her past. Try as she might, the memories were still just out of reach, tantalizingly close, but not enough to have a clear lead as to where she had come from… or *who* she had come from.

Part of her whispered to be grateful that she had any information at all about herself, even if it hinted at the possibility of being bred for a purpose not unlike that which she'd been raised to do. A bloodhound with an affinity for stolen divine objects… one who was supposed to hunt down the very beings who had taken those objects.

She retrieved something from the breast pocket of her blue silk tunic.

As of yet, Nem hadn't felt any kind of 'pull' towards the Locket of Dreaming, one of those said objects, no matter how hard she glared at the trinket in the cup of her palm. She did feel *something*, though, and knew that it was the power infused within the very fibres of the metal.

It felt… not wrong exactly, but not right either. Something in between, something else…

With her curiosity came another feeling, one that tickled the nape of her neck and subconsciously caused the hairs on her arms to rise.

The feeling of company, and not just any company.

His.

"Some would call your behaviour almost creepy, Krepth," she said, her attention remaining on the swaying locket.

The male's laugh was forced… timid almost, as Krepth rested his arms on his window sill, a few feet from her own. "I wasn't watching you," he said, gesturing at the valley below. Nem caught the muted beat of wings as Elijah and Ouro once again chased the paths flowing around the cavern. She'd lost count of the amount of times Elijah had fallen and commended him for continuing to try. Goddess knew she wouldn't have lasted anywhere near as long.

"Guess that is pretty entertaining," Nem agreed, tilting her head to see Krepth's languid smile.

His gaze did not meet hers, and the void caused her chest to tighten.

Awkward… things had become awkward, whereas they'd never felt this way before. Before, things were dancing a border between heated and chafing, a mixture of longing and unexplained dislike. Her feelings for Krepth had always been a strange tangle, one she couldn't quite puzzle, but now, with the revelation of what she was, she had thought that perhaps they could move forward. Perhaps they'd grow closer, push against the fate meant for them. He had knowledge of what she was, and she'd thought he'd be inclined to help figure out *who* she could be. But instead, they'd become distant.

Was it him who had brought on that feeling? Or was it her?

She'd never been one for guessing games, had never had the patience nor the drive for puzzles. They irritated her, and perhaps that was because of her murky past. She returned the necklace to her pocket.

Nem's heightened hearing caught the sound of a distant splash, and her attention slid to the valley where Ouro twisted and dived back towards a speck bobbing in the water. She had to hand it to Elijah – he was as stubborn as the female he pursued. Nem was sure she'd have given up learning to ride by now.

The figures rose into the air, heading back towards the castle. It was about time Elijah took a break.

Krepth was laughing to himself when Nem twisted back to him. "I'd like to see *you* try to ride a dragon," she quipped, irritated.

"I'm not stupid enough to try," was his chuckled reply.

Irritation morphed to anger like the snap of a whip as Nem snarled. "You're a fucking coward."

She sprang to her feet, heading back through her window, leaving Krepth blinking in her wake and craning his head after her. "Hold on, Silver Moon."

She hardly heard him speak as she dived into her room to search her closet for clothing which she didn't mind soiling. She needed to let out some frustration, because as she cinched her belt and tied the laces of her silver blouse, she realised she'd perhaps been a little harsh – a consequence of the other things weighing on her mind.

When she yanked the door open, he who occupied her thoughts stood in the doorway, arms crossed and dark hair hanging over his forest-green eyes.

"Come on." Nem sighed, claiming his arm and dragging him down the hall. "I need a sparring partner."

Krepth followed without protest, but she could hear a note of hurt in his voice as he jokingly said, "Fine, I'll be your punching bag. So long as you don't aim for my face."

Oh no, wouldn't want to mar that frustratingly beautiful face.

Sounds of weapons clashing and bowstrings *thwang*ing met their ears as they entered the courtyard, a small expanse of gravel nestled in the protection of high walls. As they approached, Tikkani let her bow drop, swiping her nose with the back of her sleeve. "Are we about to witness an arse-whooping?"

Quinn paused mid-parry as he and Luc turned to stare. Emerson sat cross-legged nearby, striking a whetstone over his short sword. On the outskirts of the makeshift arena, Noct and Ghila sat together. Noct whittled a piece of oak, while Ghila oiled the crescent blades of her weapons. Their hushed conversation paused upon Nem and Krepth's arrival.

Nem let her hand drop, stomping from Krepth who took up his previous pose of arms across his chest, blowing a strand of hair from his eyes. Nem waggled her fingers at Emerson impatiently until the boy's expression changed from confusion to understanding, tossing the sword towards her. Nem snatched the sword mid-air, before twisting her wrist to make the metal sing.

Quick as a striking snake she turned, her movements a blur as she charged the short distance and brought the sword down.

Metal ground against metal as Krepth, grimacing, barred her attack with a sword hastily thrown his way by Luc.

Still his eyes did not meet hers.

Instead, they fluttered to her hair, hanging in silver curtains around her face.

Fuelled by her anger, Nem bore down, before shoving back and twisting on her heel, striking low and fast. The male's parry was just as swift.

Krepth was a master of spies, but he was also an ideal adversary. He'd trained in combat, and though he was perhaps lacking in technique beside her, he knew how to defend himself, and what she needed in that moment was someone who wouldn't be a pushover within minutes.

She really did need a punching bag.

Perhaps she should have called for Arii, but she knew her best friend would be suspicious of her mood right away. Arii had become far more curious of late, sensing Nem's disquiet. Nem wanted to tell her about what she'd learned, and her conflict of emotions regarding Krepth… but Arii had a lot on her plate as it was. Nem didn't want to pile more on top of her, because Arii had become a sponge to the problems of everyone around her – wanting to alleviate the suffering of her friends.

Nem was grateful that their bond was a one-way tether. It was easier to hide her heart that way.

Krepth met her blows with smooth parries, her anger making her strikes rattle the bones in her arms. No matter how quickly she moved, or how viciously she struck, he was there, taking the assault yet never moving to retaliate. Their friends drifted away, reading the situation quickly. They'd born witness to many similar moments, because this was exactly how Ariiaya dealt with her frustration. They knew better than to hover when there was a pissed-off Fae.

When Nem's breaths heaved and sweat rose to the surface of her skin, she panted, "What else do you know about the stolen objects of power?"

Tikkani, Quinn, Emerson and Luc continued their training, but Nem knew their attention wasn't fully on their tasks. Nem caught the twitch of Tikkani's ear as she tilted towards their conversation.

Real subtle.

Krepth pushed back, and Nem allowed it, giving him a moment of reprieve to answer. "There is the Locket," he tipped his chin at her breast pocket, somehow knowing she'd stashed it there. "Then there is the Cloak of Protection, made of material said to be untearable, and unsusceptible to magic."

Their swords clashed again, and Nem couldn't help but glide her gaze over the column of Krepth's neck, chasing a stray bead of sweat as it tumbled down. His forest and cedar smoke scent washed over her, lighting parts of her that she did not want to awaken right now. Gods, everything about him sang to her, coaxed her forward, teased at her resolve – and her patience.

She wanted him, perhaps always had, but right now, the sight of his perfectly angled jaw and his slow-rising smirk had her teeth clenching, pressing back the desire and allowing her hurt… and her anger, to burn the brightest.

Why wouldn't he look at her?

"Lastly, there is the Sword of Power, said to be a conduit for magic, and said to empower its wielder. Most would say it's the coolest of the three, but I honestly think the cloak would be far –"

"The sword and the cloak, do you know where they are?" Nem cut him off.

"If I knew that, Silver Moon, I'd have gone to find them myself instead of following Herington across the continent." He drew the blade of his weapon along the length of hers, but still his eyes didn't meet hers, despite her questioning. His gaze was fixed where the blades met, possibly absorbing his own wavering-eyed reflection or avoiding hers.

Look at me.

"Perhaps with them, I could have saved my mother."

His mother. She had been taken to Bonemire, along with countless other beings to become the soulless soldiers filling the northern army. Nem knew that every time they clashed with Valdis' forces, Krepth was searching the faces for his mother. He hoped to see her face amongst the chaos, but also seemed relieved when she never showed.

Nem's stance faltered, seeing the flutter of his lashes as he blinked, and the tug on his mouth as it pulled down. She felt sympathy for him, of course, but that hadn't anything to do with what was happening between *them*. Right? Was there a part of him that was disappointed, knowing what she was, that she no longer had the instincts to discover those artefacts that he believed might have given him a chance to save his mother?

Please, look at me.

"Three artefacts stolen, and an entire race cursed. So much spite over a few little trinkets, when they are probably a drop in the treasure trove. Did the Gods ever show their faces? Try to get their precious items back themselves? Or did they place that burden upon others, before burying themselves away?" She couldn't speak about the Goddess-touched, not in front of their friends. It was her secret to carry, until she was ready, and she felt strangely protective of that, at least until she knew more. He was the only one who had any knowledge of what she was… maybe even *who* she was, and he was the best chance she had of uncovering more about her past. She didn't trust the knowledge to anyone else. It felt… intimate. Something they shared, just the two of them.

Look. At. Me.

The ridges of his knuckles grazed her arm as their blades kissed, and Nem pressed forward, lips pressing together with the riot of her thoughts. Buzzing filled her ears, the magic beneath her skin roiling at the points where their skin almost touched. Almost, but not quite. Her body was frustrating her, but most of all he was frustrating her. He'd hardly said a word to her since Ayrith, and he hadn't looked her in the eye since then, either. His disconnect wounded her far more than she thought, because when his eyes skirted her cheek and then moved away, she felt the tether on her emotions snap.

"Why won't you look at me?!" she finally bellowed, the clang of her dropped sword echoing around them.

Krepth's gaze finally slid her way, head angling as he frowned. "What?"

Nem swallowed, feeling separate from her skin as his thickly-lashed eyes blinked almost in slow motion. Her voice sounded tinny to her ears, like she was speaking through a funnel, "You…" Her voice fell away at the sound of footfalls.

In that moment of awkward silence, Arii and her father arrived nearby, a book wedged under her friend's arm. Curiosity radiated down the bond, and Nem internally cursed at her lapse in concentration. She should have felt her best friend's arrival.

The way Krepth looked at her now… his deep jade eyes shining with… something. Hurt? Concern? Anxiety?

Fear?

Did he fear her?

"Never mind. I… I think I need to eat something." Nem stepped back, running her gaze quickly over the concerned eyes of her friends. "Thank you for the spar." Her gratitude was half-hearted, a feeling of unfamiliar anxiousness fluttering through her chest like birds spooked from their nest.

"Nem," Krepth began, but Nem didn't pause to listen. She twisted to pick up the sword and return it to the weathered steel racks, before heading back to the castle, head bowed under the weight of her thoughts.

Maybe seeking more about her heritage would only end in hurt. So far all it had done was drive a wedge between her and Krepth, and she feared that uncovering anything further may spread more unease towards the others who had become important in her life. So far, having anything to do with the Gods only seemed to hint at seclusion, at her being *different*.

Maybe she was supposed to keep to the shadows and remain nameless. Perhaps she wasn't meant to shine bright at all.

Because what was the point when there was no one to bear witness to her light?

CHAPTER TWENTY

GHILA

Ghila watched the throwdown between Nem and Krepth from beside Noct, the gentle scraping of the man's knife pausing at the rising voices. He'd been carving a shape, and until a few moments ago, Ghila had been trying her best to decipher what he was trying to create. Now, just as the wolf shifter and assassin clashed in the middle of the training area, surrounded by their friends, Ghila finally made sense of the little triangle ears, short snout and snaking tail.

A cat.

The guy was whittling a cat.

"Why won't you look at me?!" Nem bellowed, voice bouncing off the old castle walls. The pain in that one sentence drew a flush across Ghila's cheeks. There was something charged between the two, and Ghila wasn't educated in the tells of attraction, but there was something there… something that left them gazing longingly at each other's backs while also spitting insults at their faces. Did they like one another, or didn't they? It didn't make sense to her. You either liked someone, or you didn't. Right? This dancing around their feelings thing was awkward and strange to her.

A tingle zinged down Ghila's spine, and her gaze swept to the archway leading from the makeshift training arena, where Ariiaya and her father, Aellan, had entered. Her Fae senses felt a threat, making her arm hairs raise and her skin tingle, and she knew that was because of the assassin's keen-eyed, purple stare, which grazed over her, hardly stopping in their perusal of the scene.

That awareness, that awkwardness, that strange sense of fear… it seemed to remain when Ariiaya was near, and Ghila knew it was because the female's dislike of her was so strong that it manipulated the air around them.

She needed to work on atoning, and earning some semblance of acceptance from her, or else she would wind up with a dagger in her back. Ghila paused, keeping her eyes on the tense exchange happening before them as she thought, *"Not in the back… Ariiaya would shove the blade into my chest so that she could watch the light leave my eyes…"*

As the last word left her mind, their eyes met, and a long moment passed before Ghila chose to be first to wrench her gaze away.

"I'll go after her," said Arii, pacing in the direction that Nem had fled.

Shadows danced ominously across the walls of the ancient castle, and a tense chill seemed to permeate the very air they breathed as the group remained silent.

"Ahem, well, you have all travelled far and been through much, so I would hazard a guess that you're all a little stretched beyond your limits." Aellan's voice was gentle, his demeanour kind and caring, a far stretch from the characteristics shown by his daughter. Ghila idly wondered if Arii's mother had been as fiery as she. With that, her thoughts drifted to her own mother, her gentle grey eyes and her heart-shaped face, the way she had held herself – regal, yet attentive. She had wanted to be exactly like her mother when she grew up. *Had.* That was far from a possibility now.

There was too much blood on her hands to become a queen.

"If any of you wish for something to eat or drink, the kitchen and dining room is through the archway just to the right of the throne room. Whatever you need, whatever you want, the castle will provide. Just call for me and it will pass the message on." With that, the man nodded, and returned inside.

"I like him," said Tikkani, scooping up some arrows that had missed their mark on the target. "He's far more chill than Arii."

"He said that the castle will 'pass on the message'," Emerson said, the elf twin who never seemed to miss a thing, as he helped his sister pack up their archery gear. "You don't suppose…"

"This castle is magical; I mean you saw that big-arse chunk of glowing crystal in the throne room," added Quinn, dashing hair back from his face as he rolled his shoulders, swinging the training sword in practiced motions through the air.

"Yes, it was pretty hard to miss," chuckled Luc as Quinn swished and stabbed his weapon against an invisible enemy, imitating the sounds of swinging and clanging through pursed lips. "Wouldn't surprise me if the castle could speak."

Noct spoke without looking up, "Not speak. Well, not in the way you and I do, but in other ways. Sentient buildings are not abnormal where I come from. Some use objects in the house to communicate – old diaries, clippings of words from old books, writing on a foggy mirror. Some send images to their occupants, direct to their mind. Some send thoughts and feelings to communicate, too."

"That's some haunted house shit," said Tikkani, eyeing the castle warily.

Ghila didn't like the thought of a sentient castle watching their every move, either.

Nocturne lifted his whittled cat, using the tip of his knife to carve tiny little eyes into its face, a hint of amusement in his voice. "The castle doesn't think as you do, it only exists to make sure its occupants are cared for."

That didn't sound so bad. Much like a big, stone guardian.

She must have voiced her thoughts, because Noct turned towards her, his lips curled in a grin. "Yes, kind of like a stone guardian."

Ghila dropped her face to her daggers, surveying her reflection in the rose gold metal. She thought about how nice it would be to feel truly *safe*, to live in a place where there was no fear of being taken from your home against your will, or your family slaughtered in their beds.

Movement around her suggested that the others had finished

packing away their weapons, so when her head lifted again to see the recruits and Nocturne watching her expectantly and Tikkani's hand offered to help her up, she couldn't help but feel a weight forming between her ribs.

"We're going to go take Aellan's offer and ask the castle to make us something impressive. You coming?"

Ghila stared at the offered hand, blinked twice, before willing that little weight of anxiety to ease. She could feel the voices, slinking their fingertips across her subconscious, as if beckoning to let them come forth. She wondered what they'd make of this, what they'd think of where she had ended up. What was their purpose, now that she had none herself?

If her hesitation annoyed Tikkani, the elf didn't show it. She waited patiently as Ghila's eyes passed her to her friends behind. The wolf Shifter looked uneasy, but she wasn't sure if that was remnants of the strange situation he'd been facing with Nemesis, or if he too was still debating trusting her. Before she could think on it further, the Shifter excused himself, and slunk away.

The others spoke softly between themselves, relieving some of the pressure from watching and waiting for her response. She felt her chest tighten with unexpected gratitude.

After another beat, she took in a breath and whispered, "Sure."

She took the offered hand.

⸸

The dining hall was immersed in dark grandeur, deep blue velvet draped over arched stained glass windows and the same hues extending to the antique but well-maintained tabletop décor. The room contained dark, intricately carved furniture, each piece bearing the weight of centuries of history. In the centre, a massive mahogany dining table commanded the space, its polished surface reflecting the flickering light of torches mounted on the walls. The chairs surrounding it were adorned with velvet cushions, their deep blue hues matching the draperies.

As the group took their seats, Ghila paused at a painting, its frame carved from the same dark wood as the table and chairs. A rendering of the Dragon's Teeth Mountains in the dead of night, the skyline lit with the last remnants of a falling moon, stars scattered in constellations which hadn't changed for an age. It was beautiful, so much so that she couldn't take her eyes away.

Ghila was about to look for the artist's signature when Noct spoke from over her shoulder, "Strange to think we are under those very mountains right now, isn't it?"

She turned, angling her head at the man, her voice escaping her throat like a rasp. "I had forgotten, actually."

Noct joined the others at the table. Ghila surveyed them for a moment, silently, like she had done for days now, a strange feeling returning to her chest. Her feet stuck to the floor and her fingers moved to the manacles again, running her nails along the metal, using the coolness to ground her wandering mind, keep her in the present rather than her past.

Tikkani looked around the room. "Erm… castle? Could we please get some food? Perhaps some tea, too?"

The floor rumbled, subtle at first, until the vibrations picked up, and a streak of blue light passed over the table, then the entire room, causing them all to jump. It looked like a pebble being dropped into a still pool, the reverberations scattering across the surface.

The rumbling and light subsided, replaced with silence.

Tikkani tapped the tabletop with her knuckle, before pressing her ear to the wood. She straightened, about to speak, when another figure entered the room.

Aellan greeted them all with a smile. "Didn't think you'd all stay away for long with the promise of food. Here, let me whip some things up." His hands flourished, opening a portal upon the surface of the table, in which platters of food began to rise. Excited chatter rose from his guests as they watched the castle's magic work.

"Ghila! Tell us more about your gifts. Is it true that you can make people do your bidding? Like, could you make Emerson lick my boots – for example?" Quinn asked, leaning in his chair and thumping his boots on the table.

Ghila had just taken a seat when the boy's question startled the room silent.

Emerson waved his hand in the direction of Quinn's boots, lost for words, pointing an accusatory finger at the silt dusting the polished wood.

Tikkani, her face flushed with shock, lifted her hands. "Oh Ghila, I'm so sorry about him. Quinn cannot keep his thoughts from running through his mouth sometimes! You *do not* need to answer that." She threw Quinn a glare, mouthing the words '*What the fuck?*'.

"No, it's alright." Ghila replied, shifting awkwardly. She folded her hands on the tabletop, the metal manacles clinking together. "Though I wouldn't call it a 'gift', as you phrased it, because a gift shouldn't bring such misery and pain. This power, though rare, is a curse." The smell of food drifted on the air, rich and delicious.

But she didn't feel hungry.

Luc leaned his cheek against his palm, jade eyes warm. "You're being a bit harsh on yourself, don't you think?" he said, dragging a plate of pastries towards him.

"I've done a lot of things that would make you change your mind." Ghila said hesitantly. She fingered the manacles, a ghost of fire and fury burning in her throat as her tormentor's faces flashed across her mind.

Luc leaned across the table, busying himself with reaching for an apple and passing it to his fiancé. His voice was light as he continued, "I think you'll find this land is riddled with people who have done questionable things because of a past they couldn't control. None of us judges you."

Ghila's voice was icy. "Nothing about my abilities is positive. All they bring is pain and torment, which I give back to those who inflicted these things upon me."

"I don't believe that," said Emerson, his golden eyes intent.

"You've been so focused on revenge up until recently that you haven't had the chance to see what else your powers can do. Why not try to use them for healing?"

She wasn't sure how much they knew about her past, but Ghila assumed Elijah or Arii had divulged enough that they'd put some pieces together. She'd been *The Wraith*, a shadow upon consciousness, the collar and leash around those who decided to defy the Fates. There hadn't been many who'd opposed the Sisters, but there had been a few, and it hadn't taken long for those to come quickly back to heel. She'd inflicted torture, much like that which was done to herself, and at the time it felt justified. Those who deviated from their designated path were not to be show mercy – or so she'd once believed.

She'd been filled with so much anger then.

Now though…

Ghila wasn't sure what possessed her, but she found her lips forming the words, "I could show you, if you like."

The table was silent for a beat, the sounds of cutlery clinking and soft chewing the only sound as the group quietly assessed her. She regretted her words the instant they left her mouth. They may not outwardly show it, but she was sure they all had the good sense to fear her, no matter how welcoming they all seemed.

Finally, Quinn lifted his hand. "I'll do it."

Mask falling, Ghila cast the young Shifter a look of surprise.

"Why don't we open our minds to you. Show you that not all is pain and torment. You could use your power to see the good inside a mind, see positive memories, try healing, or chasing away bad thoughts? You could use us for practice," Quinn suggested, taking a bite from an apple.

Could that be possible? She'd never thought to try, nor ever had anyone 'volunteered' before.

"We could test you by thinking about what scares us, and you can attempt to press the fear away," Emerson suggested.

That didn't sound so hard…

She didn't dwell on the thought about how they could possibly trust her with this, but figured Noct was perhaps strong enough to be their failsafe. Instead of asking whether they were all sure, Ghila glanced at each of their faces in turn, all smiles and chewing, as if they were discussing the weather rather than her digging into their minds and maybe discovering all of their secrets.

All except for Nocturne.

He didn't meet her eyes, but he didn't argue against the plan, either.

"Very well," Ghila said, straightening in her chair, manacled arms resting on the table before her. She wasn't sure if the others could see the hesitation in Noct's movements as he moved his hands to hover above her wrists, or the way his breath hitched as he signed a spell to relieve her of her binds. It could have been her Fae hearing, her hypersensitivity to every sound of the room.

Giving Quinn a moment to decline, Ghila rubbed at her wrists. "If at any point you wish to stop, I will not resist if you push me out."

Quinn nodded, leaning forward.

She closed her eyes and pressed her mind towards his.

His door was slightly ajar, and Ghila pressed through gently.

Her boots clapped against a stone floor, a wall of heat and the smell of soot hitting her first, followed by the sound of a mallet on steel clanging in rhythm. Ghila cast her eyes over the humble blacksmith's shack, taking note of the skinny young man who worked on a knife at the forge. Barrels of crudely-made weapons sat around the place, blacksmithing utensils hanging from fixtures upon heat-stained walls. Quinn turned from the forge, pushing his sweaty hair from his face, greeting her with a timid smile.

The door through which she'd entered thumped shut.

Quinn chuckled at her expression. "You weren't expecting this, huh?"

Well, she was still getting to know all of them.

"No, definitely not," she mused, gazing around the workspace. "This place brings you comfort, obviously. Most minds, when awake, tend to be somewhere that brings them comfort – or a place of fond memories. Were you a blacksmith before?"

Quinn's expression turned to something unreadable, a shadow passing over him like cloud cover on a summer's day. It was so out of character from what she'd seen so far that it made her whisper, "What is it?"

Just as she spoke the words, the door behind them banged open again, causing Quinn to jump and Ghila to twirl to face an intruder. All she could see was the silhouette of a woman, a thick cloak and cowl hiding her features, a bundle of blankets in her arms. Ghila didn't need to move closer to know what the woman held, for the bundle let out an upset cry.

A babe.

There was a sound of distress behind Ghila, and she angled herself so that she could see Quinn but keep the woman in her sights. After a tense moment of silence, while Quinn clenched his mallet and worked his throat, it didn't take long for Ghila to place the pieces of his fears together.

"Why?" Quinn croaked, mallet falling to his side, his shoulders slumping. "Why did you leave me?"

The faceless woman in the doorway remained silent.

An odd twist wrung in Ghila's chest. Had Quinn been abandoned as a babe? Sympathy curled low in her belly despite the whisperings in her ears.

'How easy it would be to take hold of this mind. How easy it would be to make him fear.'

Suddenly, Quinn let out a laugh, the sound choked and forced, snapping her voices to silence. Ghila eyed him carefully, keeping her face an impassive mask, observing. The young Shifter masked his pain and fear of abandonment with humour, a tactic he seemed to fall upon even within this dreamscape. "She won't do the same as you. Tikkani won't leave. None of my friends will."

'Remember why you're here,' whispered a completely new voice, one that overtook those chattering in her own mind. Ghila's own voice was soft, almost unfamiliar.

Blinking, she swallowed a breath, lifted her hands, and reached for her magic.

Ghila had seen the way Quinn and Tikkani interacted, with laughter and flirtation, but she'd also seen the way they looked at one another, eyes shining with affection. Perhaps it was love? Ghila could only guess.

She knew nothing of love.

Her brother's features flashed before her mind's eye, followed by that of her family. Brohem, his wide grin, her father, face stoic but eyes shining bright, and her mother – her warm embrace, her gentle fingers in Ghila's hair.

No… she *did* know love. She'd had it once, a different kind, but love all the same.

Drawing upon the emotions rising with her thoughts and a new sense of determination, Ghila weaved her magic around her fingers and willed three figures to form, white mist twisting into the smiling faces of Quinn's friends. Tikkani, Emerson, and Luc.

The woman in the doorway held out the bundle, and the babe cried anew, the sound loud and distracting.

Quinn flinched, hands slapping over his ears.

Ghila flinched too, her magic slipping as the figures wavered, becoming translucent. She bit her lip, using the sting to ground her, distract her from the rising wails of the baby.

"Quinn, do not look at her. Look at your friends instead," Ghila said as the figures became solid, and she willed them to his side. The shifter glanced up, his hands still clapped over his ears, but his face gentled a touch at the sight of his friends.

She knew she had to keep him distracted, however long it took for his fears to subside.

The cries of the baby increased, their urgency making tingles shoot down Ghila's spine. The sound was distressing, even to her ears, but she fought, keeping the images of Quinn's friends solid, kept them around him, kept them speaking words of encouragement that she couldn't quite hear herself.

The spectre of Tikkani gently removed Quinn's hands from his ears, and the boy clutched her fingers as if they were a lifeline. His gaze fixed on hers, lips forming her name.

The woman in the doorway lowered the babe, the cries fading upon a sudden, cool breeze. She backed away, before slipping into the night, and the breeze met Ghila's heated cheeks.

Gone.

The fear was gone.

She'd done it. She'd used her abilities in a way she'd never done before, tapped into a skill she didn't know she possessed.

Ghila looked from the door to the group, to the way they comforted each other without words. Quinn's eyes met hers over Luc's shoulder, and she could see gratitude in their deep woodsy depths. Ghila offered him a tentative smile, before turning back to the door, where a compulsion tugged at her limbs to move.

Leaving the blacksmith behind, she passed through to a star-speckled night, stone giving way to soft loam. There were other doorways a short distance away, open so that she could see the consciousnesses beyond, scenes of memories moving inside them.

But Ghila continued to move, following a feeling that drew her straight on.

She passed scenes of lapping shores and fishing villages. Passed the sounds of laughter and deep forests. Passed the declarations of love and the sweet whisperings of fussing siblings.

A compulsion pulled her further, until she was in a field of scattered wildflowers, the sky almost completely white.

She came to a double door, standing on its own in the middle of the field, the grass fading from green to brown the closer she approached. It had an arched top with the carved image of a tree inside, with many limbs and a thick trunk twined from black iron – a startling contrast against the deep, almost red wood. Hinges snaked like vines from the sides, curled into symmetrical patterns that reminded her of the entrance to an old cathedral. The handle knobs were smooth and polished black.

She placed her hand on the wood tentatively, avoiding the iron, and felt it shudder beneath. Ghila peeked around it, seeing the same door on the other side. She straightened, biting her lip, for the scent emanating from it reminded her of ancient magic.

Otherworldly magic.

She knew who *this* door belonged to.

She did not hesitate long, for she knew she didn't have much time.

Like leaning on a door that wasn't quite closed properly, Ghila fell through with a *push*.

Ghila tipped forward and fell into darkness, a cry rising in her throat, bursting into a scream with no sound. She fell, through hollowness and space, through stars and mist, until something wrapped around her limbs, suspending her in nothingness.

'I was afraid you'd gravitate here,' a voice said, as soft as dark silk. *'I knew you would feel the pull and wouldn't resist letting it take you.'*

Nocturne.

The darkness around her shook, stars warped, and a cool breeze pressed against her skin, rushing against her body until she began to rise, heading back the way that she had come. Ghila angled her head, her attention snagging on clouds of flashing memories moving by.

'You're stronger than you think, Ghila, but some secrets aren't meant to be uncovered.'

Secrets? Was he speaking of his own?

He hadn't fortified his defences enough for her to be locked out, and if he truly did not wish for her to see his mind or memories, then she was sure he would have kept her out. Ghila's first thought was that the man didn't wish to look like he was keeping things from her, allowing a tentative level of trust. A careful game of honesty and mystery. This place was not the full depths of his mind, merely the surface, like the shallows before a mighty lake.

She threw her consciousness out, drawing upon the compulsion until scenes began to flash before her eyes. They came tentatively at first, as if they were pieces of silk snagged on stones.

A male hand, reaching longingly to twin suns as they slowly faded behind a thick wall of mist.

A dark sky, with two moons side by side.

Noct, standing beside a young woman, a streak of blonde in her hair, her eyes the perfect mirror to his own. Her pale face mournful, her skin pearlescent, lacking warmth. A sister? A twin? Their resemblance to one another was uncanny.

'Alright… that's enough,' came Noct's voice, trying and failing to mask his strain.

Her view twisted, streaking to a bird's eye view, revealing Nocturne and his sister, standing in the centre of a gigantic footprint, humanoid but not, pressed deep into dead, sodden earth.

'Time to go.'

Ghila's body was wrenched backward, *pushed* from the scene before she could fully absorb what was before her eyes. Her back hit the chair in the underground castle dining hall, her breath whooshing from her lungs as her eyes adjusted back to her reality.

She blinked to see Noct's hands moving away from hers. The manacles were once again around her wrists, staunching the flow of her magic, and silencing her mind to a drone, but Ghila didn't care.

Her curiosity was a raging fire in her veins.

Ghila stared up at the man, his face was schooled, calm and collected, a hint of a smile at the corner of his lips. But she could see a sheen of sweat on his brow. Could see the shudder behind his bicoloured eyes.

For the first time in so long that she could remember, she was curious. Curious to know more about what worlds could exist beyond theirs. Wanted to know about where he had come from.

And curious as to what unexplored potential her abilities truly held.

CHAPTER TWENTY-ONE

ELIJAH

Galaxies swirled within the stone, roused by Elijah's fingertips as they grazed the glass surface. This simple, yet enchanting stone was the key to unlocking a doorway to another dimension, through which the dragons that had inhabited their land had been transported to keep them safe. He once again pondered all he'd learned about it, and why it was *he* who was apparently the only one who could call the dragons home.

Despite what he knew so far, it still wasn't enough to solve the riddle to open the stone.

Elijah lay on his side on the bed in their quarters, head propped on his palm, watching the stars wink and spin in the stone, following the trail of his finger. Beside him, Ariiaya watched while lying on her stomach, chin squished on her palms as her bare legs kicked the air behind her. Her hair hung in waves, still lightly damp from her bath some time ago, golden-tipped ends tantalisingly within reach. She smelled of lavender and soap, and something else that was just… her. He wondered if anyone else could scent that about her, the warm almost honey sweetness that lingered close to her skin.

He hoped not, he couldn't imagine anyone else being close enough to find out.

"So Ouro didn't tell you anything?" She asked again, thick lashes sweeping her cheeks as she watched the stone.

He took in the moonlit curve of her face, the peak of her nose and crescent moon of her cheekbone. The stone, the impending war, seemed to steal all focus since their reunion, and though they'd shared some moments since, he couldn't help but feel his attention was divided between her and his responsibilities.

Not to mention the darkness curling at the back of his mind, a darkness he was finding harder to keep confined to that small part of his consciousness.

He'd take himself out before allowing any harm to come to her, especially from his own hands. Perhaps those thoughts were aiding in the disconnect that he had begun to feel from not only her, but his friends too, as if his warring subconscious was pre-emptively trying to protect them all.

"I've heard dragons are hoarders of treasures, and I'm coming to realise that also extends to information. I think he knows how… but whether he's unable or unwilling to tell me for one reason or another remains to be seen."

Arii's lips formed a line as she looked up, letting her hands come to rest on the bed between them. He stared at them, seeing the scabs around her nails. That anxious habit of gnawing the skin only looked worse since before they'd parted. The scabs were solid though, a good sign, showing she hadn't picked at them for a little while.

"We could ask Nocturne," she began, drawing his attention.

"I'd rather not." Elijah interrupted, earning him a raised brow.

He placed the stone on the nightstand as Arii chuckled. "Is that jealousy I hear in your voice, or caution? Stubbornness, perhaps?"

He clasped her arms and pulled her up onto his chest. She squeaked, an adorable sound of surprise that made him grin. They were heart to heart, her hair a curtain around his face where he felt he could hide with her for just a few minutes. "One is only jealous if they doubt themselves. I don't doubt myself when it comes to you."

Her tongue propped her bottom lip, tugging at his attention as Arii said, "So confident."

Elijah's mind cast back to the time they'd met on a celestial plain, the connection between them spanning deeper than anything he could truly understand. Even while separated, they still found each other somehow. That was what gave him his confidence because his heart knew that kind of connection was beyond anything they shared with anyone else. It was something special, something sacred.

Elijah pinched her chin, drawing her face to his as he muttered, "Let's leave thoughts of the stone to tomorrow…"

He took his own words to heart, casting all thoughts aside except for those focused on the woman whose lips met his, whose heart thundered against his, whose scent swept over him, casting him into a world where no one existed but them.

"Thankfully Fae are some of the most stubborn creatures I've ever met," commented Ouro as Elijah hauled himself onto the dragon's back for the umpteenth time that hour. They'd met at what would be dawn outside the cavern, judging by the way his body naturally awoke from sleep and the way the insects quieted in their singing. Ouro had been waiting for him at the same place they'd met yesterday, and they'd quickly dived back into practice. Elijah was aware of how little time they had left and was determined to conquer his fear before heading East.

If he hadn't possessed the strength of a Fae, Elijah was certain he would have drowned by now, or broken most of his bones. Every inch of his body felt bruised and tender.

Ouro twisted his head, large oval eye blinking slowly. *"You would not be quitting if you had another rest, Eliverus."*

Elijah speared wet hair from his eyes, shaking away the droplets from his face. They sprinkled the dragon's cheek, causing the beast to huff a laugh.

"No, I want to keep going," he replied, ignoring the chafing on his thighs and the raw skin of his palms.

"As you wish."

Ouro's wings billowed, body tilting as he banked into a turn, sailing back towards their starting point.

Elijah felt his confidence growing as he began to learn the ways in which the dragon moved, the ways he needed to shift his weight, to place his hold and when. There was an art to flying on a beast such as this, to accepting that you were not in control, but only along for the ride. He did not dictate Ouro's movements, but he could influence them with a slight lean or a shift in his posture, and once he began to understand that, Elijah began to understand everything else.

They dropped into freefall, speeding towards the mouth of the valley once again.

Elijah lowered himself further, practically folding his body in half, his heart thumping in his ears. Gravity clawed his limbs with thick fingers, seeking to pull him into the underrealm.

Ouro's wingtips clipped the starlit water as he yanked to the right, whipping around another stone wall. Like riding a thundering horse around a narrow course, Elijah kept himself low and let his mount guide his movements, trying his best to keep his unsteady weight centred. Ouro rumbled approval below him as they dipped to the left, leaving the snaking valley to fly over a wide, open lake.

Ouro's wings levelled out into a glide. As the shock wore away, Elijah allowed himself to take everything in, sitting up and stretching the kink from his lower back. He inhaled deeply, eyes moving over the expanse of water before them. Rare gems dotted the shore, flickering like multicoloured candlelight. The water was clear below them, the lake floor covered in a sheet of pure white quartz. He chanced a slight lean and glanced down from Ouro's back, watching the water speed in a glittering blur below. That explained what made the lakes here look to be filled with starlight.

Breathless, Elijah sat straight once more, closing his eyes to the feel of the wind in his face, in his hair, upon his skin. His magic was awake, too, humming in his chest and warming his veins.

It felt… right.

Ouro's claws skimmed the water, leaving glitter shimmering in their wake. The dragon's chest rumbled, and his head lifted, one crimson eye blinking back at his rider. *"You are a natural, as expected."*

Elijah huffed a laugh, not admitting that his thighs were still locked in a death grip, the ache of which he knew he'd feel tomorrow. "Don't give me too much credit, I've fallen enough times to consider me a novice to the art."

Teeth flashed in a draconic grin, *"Let's go higher."*

Elijah couldn't help the smile that cracked across his face. They rose above the lake, climbing towards the misty cavern ceiling. Gravity pulled him backward, but he held fast, revelling in the powerful boom of Ouro's wings as he propelled them higher.

Perhaps he could do this.

Ouro's jaws snapped open and a stream of fire fanned out before them.

The dragon's roar shook the cavern, its thunder filling his ears like the storms which had once plagued him during sleep. They had frightened him then.

Elijah let go of Ouro's scales, thrusting his arms out, welcoming the heat and flames as they flew into a raging inferno.

The difference now was that he was no longer afraid.

LORCH

Lorch had not felt at home in the castle for some time. Its cool golden walls, though beautiful, only served to throw his hard-faced reflection back at him, and that of his stone-faced father over his shoulder. Black ice continued to build on the outside of his bedroom window, a slow climb of dark frozen fingers, now framing the glass so thickly he could hardly see the cloudy sky beyond.

The parties had slowed down, the courtiers now far and few between. He avoided the throne room, its cavernous space dark and unused, save for when his father conducted meetings in there. He insisted his son wasn't needed, and when Lorch voiced that he should be present, his father's eyes took on a suspicious edge that had Lorch swapping back to his usual mask of nonchalance. He wanted to learn more about his father's plans without raising much suspicion, but his lack of attention and drive in the past now made that difficult.

Whatever he did learn, though, he relayed back to Celadine and the resistance.

Thinking about the green-eyed Fae and her daughter had warmth blooming in his chest. They filled him with a sense of purpose, a new meaning. They made him feel something other than self-loathing and anger.

They made him feel *human* again.

He saw Cela in passing, tending to duties around the castle, their gazes fleeting yet perhaps lingering a touch longer than necessary. He remained stoic, aloof, in her presence so as not to give away that their relationship was anything other than what it was meant to be.

A healer, duty bound to her king.

A man who cared for little but himself.

Nothing more.

Every moment he spent in the castle made him long to be beside her, no prying eyes of expectation or suspicion. Every night since he had agreed to help them, he had been back in the tavern, relaying whatever he knew, learning sign language with Mia, hearing Cela's rare little laugh, the small smiles into her herbal concoctions when she thought he wasn't looking, and of course filling the gaps in his knowledge about the Fae and magic. He was understanding more, finding himself thinking of ways to better all their lives, Fae, elf and human alike.

By the time he returned to his rooms, he had only a few hours' sleep before the sun rose. He remained curled in the covers of his bed well into midday, as was not unusual for him, and when he did decide to arise, he found a cooling tray of sliced venison and potatoes on a golden platter left over from lunch.

Lorch haunted the castle, idling by the outdoor training yards where a small battalion of living, breathing soldiers trained with those who were dead. Lingering on the outskirts, saliva dripping from jaws, prowled three Kryvern, glowing blue eyes darting restlessly, iron claws leaving divots in the gravel. Lorch kept well away from the beasts, watching the proceedings with a mask of mild interest.

He wasn't sure what point there was to training mindless beings, but they were tough adversaries, their movements wild and unpredictable. In some instances, Lorch was afraid the undead would lose the tether of their magical leashes and start to attack anyone, wild as they were in fulfilling their orders, but somehow they held back, and Lorch was sure it was by just a hair's breadth. Their eyes were wide, swirling with magic, the sounds they made like human moans mixed with the savage growls of rabid dogs.

There was only so much of this Lorch could take. The sounds plus the stench had him quickly moving on.

He bypassed the fields, the expanse of which was once perfectly maintained green grass. Now, it was dredged-up mud, slopping under the boots of soldiers and wheels of countless carts. Thousands of soldiers. Lorch knew this wasn't the entire force of *his* army. Some had been dispatched to their towns, and some even over the border, laying foundations for the war to come.

Stone-faced, he moved on.

The clap of boots followed, as they usually did. He had three guards now, two alive, one dead. They gave him space enough, but their presence had his teeth grinding. He had hoped to escape a touch earlier tonight, his longing to see Cela and Mia like a persistent itch on the back of his neck.

He headed south, towards where the sound of the waterfall was normally loudest. Oddly, it didn't seem so loud today. The rumble and boom of the torrent of water below the castle was, on most days, a hum he was used to, but now more than ever, Lorch found himself standing on the expanse of the Dragon Landing, seeking the roar of sound to drown out his thoughts.

But now, silence greeted him, causing the hairs on his arms to rise.

After a muttered order, his guards remained near but allowed him space to walk out to the tip of the landing.

Lorch's eyes coasted the overcast sky, clouds darkest over their heads, lightening out into the distance.

His attention lowered, and suddenly his breath caught.

The lake, normally deep blue and sparkling even when the sun sat behind the clouds, was dark and still, as if the water had been drained and replaced with dark, veiny marble. His human eyes could not detect any motion on the water's surface, no gentle lap of docile waves, no crash of waterfall, and hardly a whisper of mist on his face. It was… frozen.

The entire lake, all of it, even the waterfall.

Lorch sucked in a breath, placing his palms on the railing, but as soon as they made contact with the surface, he jerked back, stung by biting cold.

The balustrade was covered in a thick layer of black ice, just like his bedroom window.

The entire Sapphire Depths was covered in it… frozen with it. It was ice, yet it was different, colder… harsher… other. This was not natural; the North had never been cloaked with ice and snow. The air had a cool bite to it, but it was not frigid enough to freeze water, surely. The cool air in question picked up, toying with his copper hair, making gooseflesh rise upon his exposed skin. Wrong… all wrong. The North was a place of summery days, blue waters, expansive cerulean skies and bursts of wildflowers.

Lorch ordered over his shoulder. "Prepare my horse, I wish to go for a ride."

Two soldiers stood to attention, while one continued to slump. "Your Highness, your father… Lord Valdis, recommended no one leave the grounds until further notice."

"And his word overrules mine?" Lorch queried with bite, storming towards them.

"Well, no, Your Highness, I–"

"Ready my horse, and wipe that look of fright from your face. I merely want to visit the pool."

The soldier visibly sagged with relief. "I suppose that isn't outside the grounds," he said, more to himself.

It took longer than Lorch would have liked, but within an hour he was atop his horse and galloping down the gravel path that he had not travelled since that day with Ariiaya and Elijah, which now felt like a lifetime ago. The willows sagged under the weight of ice upon their limbs, the leaves tainted with an odd dark sheen.

He pushed his horse faster, uncaring of the guards in the dust of his wake, and as the trees sped past, dread boiled in the depths of his stomach. The path was familiar yet different, as if a long expanse of time had elapsed. Hooves thundered under him, his thighs clenched, and his mount leaped the small incline that he usually took slowly. When they landed, the horse threw its head back, whinnying to the sky, and Lorch gripped the reins, patting the beast's neck, its muscles twitching with adrenaline under his fingers.

"Hush now, hush…" he whispered. His comforting words died as his eyes found the pool, its surface frozen, its shores crusted with glittering obsidian.

The reality of it all crashed down on his shoulders, and Lorch felt his heart break as he gazed at the sad remnants of his place of solace, towered over by a dark grey sky.

As light rain began to fall, Lorch decided enough was enough.

Valdis had to be stopped, no matter what.

Even if it was *he* who had to deliver the knife into his father's heart.

As soon as night fell, Lorch wrapped himself in a cloak and followed the well-worn path from the castle, quickly making his way downtown to the tavern. The dining area was quiet, hardly a patron in sight. He practically shivered with adrenaline, his fingers clenching as he knocked on the door of their room.

Cela opened the door cautiously to him. Mia lay sprawled on her stomach upon the worn rug, a semicircle of wooden figurines around her. Her legs flailed in the air as she moved one carved into the shape of a dragon towards some soldiers on horseback. "Rooarr!" The dragon and soldiers collided, and it was safe to say the little toy men were not the winners in her little war.

"You're later than I thought you'd be," said Cela.

Lorch could hardly grasp his own words. "It's frozen." He gulped, pausing at Cela's blinking stare, barely gathering himself. He inhaled deeply, forcing his hands not to shake. "The pool. The Sapphire Depths, everything. All… frozen. Soon, the entire North will be frozen too. It is not ice, it's something different, something unnatural. The people will freeze soon too, I'm sure of it." His voice shook as he added, "What have I done?"

Cela moved, approaching him as Mia craned her head, concern painting her face. The apothecary grasped his fingers tightly, firmly, and Lorch found his scattered attention quickly magnetising, though the shake in his hands wouldn't cease, and the rapid gasps of his breath wouldn't slow. Cela swiftly signed something to Mia, who nodded and flew to her feet. She wrapped Lorch's waist in a hug, then silently slipped from the room.

Cela tugged on his hands, motioning him to sit. The bed creaked under their shared weight. A fire flared brightly in the hearth, warming his skin but not the ice gathered deep inside him.

He couldn't slow his breathing. There was a weight in his chest, like a monster digging its claws in, refusing to let go.

"You're having a panic attack," said Cela, her voice gentle and firm.

"A… what?" he gasped.

"A panic attack," she repeated, shifting to face him fully, still keeping her grip firmly on his hands. "You need to steady your breathing. Listen to my voice and breathe in deeply. In through your nose, out through your mouth. I'll count to three, count with me in your head, alright?"

He couldn't slow his breathing. The monster remained.

"Breath in, now. Through your nose. Slowly. Good. One… two… three, let it loose."

He did as she said, eyes trained on hers, fixed on their green depths.

Firelight reflected in them, golden flickers washing over half of her face, highlighting the gentle dips of her feature and the scattering of freckles across her cheeks.

"In…. out… gently now."

A tiny bit of the tension began to ease.

"In."

He inhaled, eyes dropping to her lips as they formed an O, letting loose his breath in time with hers, expelling the monster of his anxiety.

"Out."

A ripple of his discomfort remained, but it was slowly pressed back with the distraction of her beautiful, strong face. He branded that face to memory, and everything about her. Her voice, the colour of her hair in the firelight, her scent of camomile and sage. Her kindness, resilience, beauty, her steadfast gaze.

"Are you alright?" Celadine whispered, the first real look of concern he had seen flickering over her face.

Yes… no… perhaps.

He only felt right when he was with her. There was a pull, like she had her own centre of gravity, and he was being helplessly pulled right into it.

Unable to stop himself, he leaned forward, but it was Cela who closed the distance between them.

When her lips met his, tentatively, the remnants of the monster in his consciousness fizzled away. In its place was silence. Blissful… blessed silence. And a slowly gathering heat in the depths of his chest, thawing the ice, sending tingles of warmth to their joined hands. The tentativeness with which she kissed him dissolved when he did not move away, and their kisses became more. Heated, frantic, passionate. Lorch's hands explored her face, her neck, the thick tresses of the hair at her nape while her hands tangled in his tunic. She tasted of salt and mint; a combination he'd never thought he would be at risk of becoming intoxicated over. That and the scent of herbs and camomile, had his head, and his heart, kicking up in a frenzy. It was a coalescence of sensation on his senses that he was sure he wouldn't stop wanting, wouldn't stop *craving*.

He'd known he had felt something for her for a while, but now he was certain.

Lorch wanted Celadine with a ferocity that scared him. A need. Perhaps it was because war was looming, perhaps it was because something between them was ultimately forbidden, or perhaps it was because it just felt... right. Nothing had felt so right in a long time. Not since...

He shoved that train of thought away before it could track too far, instead drawing his attention into his movements, the feel of his knuckles brushing a thick curl from Cela's collarbone. He drew his lips across the spot, chest tightening at the sound of her sharp intake of breath. Her head tipped back, and he smiled against her warm skin when he caught her whispered prayer. He kissed her chin, ran his nose along her jawbone, inhaled the duskiness that was *her*.

She was his healing, his banisher of pain. She was his salvation and could very well be his future, should they survive the events to come.

Cela's hands ran along his back, tugging him closer, and he felt a burst of relief that she wanted him as much as he wanted her.

"Celadine..." he whispered, and she sighed in reply. "Where did you send Mia?"

"The kitchens..." she murmured, moving to kiss him, her body languid under his eager hands. Her fingers slid up his tunic, grazing over his abdomen. She made a sound of appreciation that had him grinning against her mouth. Cela's fingers began fumbling at his buttons, and he fumbled to help her, all the while their lips locked. His skin tingled in the wake of his tunic sliding from his shoulders, and he shucked it away before cupping Cela's cheek, guiding her to lay back on the bed. The old mattress squeaked as he braced himself above her, eyes drinking in the fan of her hair around her head, the flush of her cheeks and swollen lips in the firelight.

His look gave her pause, her chest rising and falling deeply. "What is it?"

"It's not often I'm lost for words, but I can't find the right ones to thank you for healing me, Cela. You've healed me of hurts far deeper than those on the surface of my skin."

Her jade eyes were soft as she leaned up to kiss him. This kiss was different, gentler, sweeter. "Sometimes we don't need words," was all she said in reply, and those words spoke to his soul.

Suddenly, there was a muffled thump beyond the door, one that caused them both to still.

Her hand flew to his chest, and they sat up, sharing a look before Lorch glanced back at the door. Was it Mia, returning from the kitchens?

Cela's fingers dug into his biceps as her head tilted sharply, listening with her heightened hearing. Lorch's mouth opened to ask her if they should stop, if Mia was returning, when she suddenly hissed "I can hear something."

"What?" he murmured, to which she hushed him with a gentle squeeze, her Fae strength making an appearance. He knew he'd have bruises tomorrow, but he didn't care. Her expression had thoughts of bruises quickly tumbling away, for he too heard something now.

Voices.

The thumping of boots.

Mrs Mulvany's yells for them to respect the paying patrons of her establishment.

The unmistakable skids and thumps of a tussle, and the muffled rumble of a voice that he knew as well as his own.

They had been discovered; his father was here.

Cela was on her feet in a flash, and Lorch followed, uttering a very un-royal curse. He threw his gaze around the room, first to the window. They could climb out, flee into the town. No… no, his father would have soldiers outside. He was cunning, he would cover all points of exit.

Cela threw herself towards her table, swiping a knife, her knuckle white around its grip.

His heart thumped in his ears as he turned to the door, a shadow cancelling the light from the space beneath.

"Check every room. If he is here, we will find him," boomed his father's voice.

"Fuck," Lorch growled, spinning to Cela. He couldn't allow her to be hurt in his father's pursuit of him. He couldn't live with himself if...

His eyes stopped on the small, upright closet in the corner of the room. It would be a squeeze, but perhaps it could serve as a hiding place.

"The closet," he said, grabbing Cela's hand and pulling her towards it.

"What?" she squeaked, offering no resistance as they hurried.

Lorch yanked open the double doors, thrusting aside the few cloaks and tunics hanging there.

"It's only big enough for..." she sucked in a startled breath, twisting to glare at him. "Only big enough for one of us. Lorch, no!"

He cupped her face. "You cannot be captured, they will not show you mercy, I know that now. If I go without a fight, they won't bother to look for anyone else. They only seek me right now."

Her hands gripped his wrists, tugging. "We could both fit... or I could fight them, we could fight them, then escape. There is a family in Amberbourne who will take us–"

He shook his head before she could finish. "I'll be the first to admit that I would not last a few minutes against them. I'm not a fighter, Cela."

There was pain in her eyes, wide and dazed. He kissed her brow, then her lips. "Let this be the first thing I can do to repay you for everything. Let this be the beginning of my amends to the North."

"Lorch..." she pleaded, as he pressed her back into the closet.

"I'll find you, both of you," he whispered, placing as much promise as he could muster into the words.

As the doors to the closet closed, the one to the room burst open, and Lorch turned towards the shadow in the doorway, lips curling in his usual smirk. Firelight played across his bare torso as he drawled,

"Hello, father. Guess you found me."

CHAPTER TWENTY-TWO

ARIIAYA

"I can't believe I'm saying this, but I think I'll miss this place," said Tikkani, running her hand along the smooth, polished obsidian marble of the receiving room. "It's quiet. I think I've been missing the quiet lately."

Arii had to agree, she too had felt peace in the silence of the place.

"And I was getting used to watching Elijah fly around on Ouro's back every morning and evening. That was definitely a sight to see." Tikkani added, grinning.

That she had to agree on with her friend as well. Elijah was fearless perched on the back of the beast, at home nestled between towering wings and shifting scales. So much so that when Ouro educated them on the history of Elijah's family, and the history of dragons in their realm, Arii didn't doubt a single word out of his mouth. She'd read it in the tome she'd found in the Library In-between, and even if she hadn't, the proof was in front of them now, in the way Elijah held firm as Ouro's dragon form whipped through the starlit valleys.

He was born to dragon ride.

Once the shock of her father's emergence had worn off, Arii forgave him for his absence. Perhaps if he had been able to free himself of his bond and find them, she would be different. Perhaps they could have taken up residence on a little farm somewhere, together, away from the blight of the land. The thought was a fickle one, for if that had happened, she never would have gained her skills as a fighter or met her friends… or Elijah. She wouldn't have liberated Elijah from Valdis' clutches, wouldn't have started the chain reaction of his memories awakening and his magic surfacing. Her father had said as much after she had related their adventures. She hadn't delved much into her relationship with Elijah, but he had guessed it by observing their moments together, even though fleeting. Elijah had spent most of his time with Ouro, and puzzling over the stone.

She could tell that he was frustrated, there was a hardness in his shoulders when she held him at night, and a tiny twitch in his stubborn jaw when she watched him in sleep, forever present even when he wasn't conscious. He was tired, weighted under the burden of his future; the future of their land should he fail.

When he kissed her, when he touched her and set her blood alight in the glow of the ethereal cavern beyond the windows of their rooms, she could tell his mind was not fully present even then. There was a listlessness in his deep grey eyes that made her chest hurt. She wished she could absorb his burdens into herself like the crystals scattered around the cave, absorb his woes like they did the magic in the earth. When she asked him why Ouro didn't just open a portal himself and call the dragons through, Elijah explained that the portals that Ouro and Noct created were only large enough for people to move through. They were not able to make larger ones.

"You are all welcome to return whenever you wish. It has been nice hearing the sounds of voices other than my own and Aellan's." Ouro said, smiling at his friend.

Her father smiled back, "Yours does become particularly droning after a time."

Ouro chuckled, clapping Aellan on the back. "I will be back before you know it."

Aellan's eyes locked with Arii's as he said, "I'll hold you to your promise, my friend. Look after my daughter." His words reached not only the tall, cloaked man beside him, but the warrior by her side too. Despite being the promised king, Elijah hadn't escaped Aellan's fatherly interrogation. Tikkani had laughed at the shade of red that Arii's skin took on as her father lanced Elijah with hard-hitting questions about his planned future with his daughter, while nestling mugs of coffee with their friends in the library. It had been meant as a last shared moment before they were to prepare to leave but instead it had turned into an interrogation.

"I can assure you, Mr Trillia, your daughter is in safe hands with me. You have my oath."

Her father had been satisfied by the conviction and unwavering look in Elijah's molten silver eyes. She'd told her father she was more than capable of looking after herself, but Elijah's words still brought a warmth to her heart.

"I promise. Remember, dragons cannot lie." Ouro said, placing a hand to his chest.

"Is that a fact?" asked Krepth curiously.

Ouro nodded in reply.

Sadness welled up inside her. Arii didn't want to leave her father behind, but she considered it a blessing to see him again when she had thought him dead. When the war was over, she would find a way to free him of his bond and bring him home.

Her father pulled her into an embrace, stroking a hand through her hair like he had when she was a little girl. Arii pressed her face into his neck, feeling unusually fragile. He'd be okay, he would be far away from the war, sheltered in this cave with his magical library. She'd see him again, she swore it.

Aellan held her at arm's length, eyes coasting over her, before absent-mindedly straightening her cloak. "Oh, I forgot to mention – this cloak you are wearing. Were you aware that it is enchanted?"

Arii blinked, looking down at what had become her favourite cloak. "It is?"

Aellan pinched the fabric, studying the way it glittered in the lamplight. "Absolutely. A rare treasure, I can feel its ancient power. It must be… thousands of years old yet it looks like it was crafted yesterday." He smiled, "I'd hesitate to guess that it's one of those objects of power I heard your dear Shifter friend talking about."

Arii looked at Krepth, who blinked back in surprise, before

answering, "You think it's the Cloak of Protection?"

Nem sucked in a startled breath, audible to Arii's keen ears. Arii hadn't spoken to her friend about her outburst on the training field the day before, thinking it best to allow her space. She'd been meaning to though, but her thoughts had been so preoccupied with her father, Elijah and opening the stone, that it'd fallen to the wayside.

She shared a look with the silver-haired Fae, who looked at the cloak with fiery interest.

Aellan nodded, causing Arii to think back on each time she'd engaged in combat while wearing it. It hadn't sustained any damage, no tears or nicks while battling cursed foes, even though she was sure it'd been grabbed and torn at by teeth and claws. Curious, she fingered the fabric, before a shadow fell over her.

Ouro brought forth a blade, handing it to Aellan, who took a sizable pinch of the cloak, pulling it out between them. A protest rose to Arii's lips as her father slipped the blade down, but as the steel gave way, and not the fabric, her protest became a little sound of disbelief. Shards of steel clanged to the marble floor.

The group collectively gasped, inching closer.

"That's amazing! Up until now I thought you were just a badass in combat, never sustaining many injuries, Arii, but now I see it was your cloak protecting you all along!" Tikkani cried.

Arii threw her a blazing glare.

Krepth murmured. "What a steal for one hundred silvers…"

"It's said to be unpierceable by mortal blades and untouched by time, never to fade. It won't protect you from death, but it will provide you with another layer of armour, young Arii," said Ouro, picking up the pieces of the fractured blade, before melding them back together with his fingertips, using his magic. "I'll get a better knife when we get to Evergrave."

Luc, while struggling to close his overstuffed pack, said, "So you're coming with us?"

The dragon Shifter hadn't agreed to join them outright, but Arii had assumed he was coming with them. The evil brimming in Viridya was as much a threat to Ouro's realm as it was to theirs.

In the glow of a newly opened portal, Ouro grinned wide. "I'm ready to finally leave my cave and venture east to follow you into war."

ELIJAH

Elijah was becoming used to the warp, tug and pull of void travel, despite the few times he had done it so far. The experience felt… familiar, somehow. It was a brief slither of time between the lift and fall of a boot as it stepped from one place to another, but within that time the very fibres of his body changed, passing through a split second of magic so ancient he felt it in his bones.

When he hit the earth in his destination, those fibres were once again back to normal.

Elijah no longer feared magic, if anything, it left him in awe of its possibilities. To get to this point had taken less time than many would have thought, but he hadn't travelled there alone. He'd seen the dark side of magic, and the light, had seen how it could twist a person, and how it could save a life.

Soon it would turn an empire to rubble, then forge it anew.

Elijah had had plenty of time within himself to become familiar with the ebb and flow of his pool of magic, and the dark, unseeable bottom. His acceptance rippled like the waves of magical water, and along with it he'd had time to accept the darkness that encroached, spindly wisps tugging him tentatively back.

Ouro had been exceptionally knowledgeable when it came to Elijah's lineage, and with that, some questions had been answered. The Herington line had always possessed strong magic, and there had been an uncle on his great-grandfather's side who had been driven mad by it. When he asked if there had been more, Ouro had alluded to the possibility, but the look in his crimson eyes told Elijah that he knew why he questioned him so heavily on the matter.

"Do not fear your fate, Eliverus."

How could he not fear the very real possibility that he may descend into one worse than that which he was trying to prevent? The madness that would come with such exceptional magic could not be stopped, it seemed.

The knowledge weighed on his mind, a lingering little demon that clutched the nape of his neck, not allowing him to fully rest. It was present when he performed particularly strong spells, a little peel of laughter that tinkled from the depths of his mind, eager for him to press harder, to let go of his control, to cause calamity.

Even now, as he and his friends alighted on the mossy ground of the East, near the towering trees at the entrance to Evergrave, his hand firmly linked with Ariiaya's, his skin tingled with an eagerness that came from the ancient magic at his back.

He swallowed it back as figures emerged from the cover of the trees.

A familiar face was revealed as Iniq dropped her hood, a smile spreading over her beautiful, dark-skinned features.

Luc broke from their pack, throwing himself at his sister with a cry. "Iniq!"

The warrior embraced her brother fiercely, "Thank the Gods you're all okay." She leaned back, holding her brother at arm's length, surveying him critically. "No injuries?"

"No, we're alright," Luc replied, grinning.

Iniq glanced over her brother's shoulder. "Few more of you now," she added, eyes narrowing at Nocturne, Ouro and Ghila, unable to hide her natural suspicion.

"We have a lot to catch up on," said Arii, and Elijah heard a tired note to her words.

"We sure do," Luc piped up, gesturing to their group. Emerson's cheeks turned crimson as he lifted his hand, a silver ring glinting starkly against the dark skin of his finger.

Iniq sucked in a gasp, and Elijah couldn't help but smile as she let loose a cry of delight, throwing her brother to the side and leaping towards the elf. "You finally said yes?!"

Emerson's smile was timid, but there was a sparkle in his golden eyes. "Think we have time to organise a wedding?"

"There is always time for a wedding; wars and impending doom be damned!" cried Tikkani.

Iniq waved to her soldiers, and they shot to attention. The warrior's eyes met with Elijah, and there was something within them that hadn't been there before. Relief, and respect.

"Notify Freya of the return of the Prince, and that we have a wedding, and a war, to plan."

The afternoon sun cast rays of gold light over the carved wooden throne, the light catching on the elk horns and silver-painted filagree. The grand room in the heart of the ancient tree looked as it had the last time he was here, but there was a different feel to the air this time.

Elijah moved through the crowd; elves, Shifters, Fae, humans – there was a riot of scents in his overly sensitive nose and a cascade of different faces watching him as he made his way towards the dais. They parted for him like water, some reached to touch his black sleeveless tunic, touch his bare arms and the shimmering tattoo of the bear on his bicep. There was reverence and awe in their whispers, hope in their eyes, a far cry from the hesitation and distrust when last he moved among them.

Arii walked behind him, her movements lithe, her presence giving him strength. He clutched the Void Stone in his palm, its smooth surface warming his skin. He kept his expression impassive, even though his stomach was a boiling pot of nerves.

Freya awaited him before the throne, standing in robes made of white moonlight. Head angled, she watched his progress, the inky depths of her eyes stricken with stars. A heavy gaze, assessing.

Off to the side he could see Noct, Ghila, Nem and Krepth. Ghila twisted her hands in front of her, grey eyes watching the mass of people warily. Nem touched two fingers to her arm, and Ghila seemed to calm. Elijah felt a flare of appreciation for the Fae, it was a tiny gesture, but one that held grand weight.

Across the way were his other friends, Tikkani, Quinn, Luc and Emerson, who watched him with confidence, and lingering nearby was Ouro, partially in shadow, eyes bright like embers.

He had successfully completed the tasks Freya had set for him, now there was only one left, the one which would earn him the support of the last court in Fythnar. What challenge she would put him through was anyone's guess, but Elijah felt he had come too far to fail now.

Elijah halted before the Queen, and she spoke, her voice projected for all to hear.

"Welcome back, Eliverus Herington, true heir to the North. You return bearing the acceptance of our border brothers, for which I commend you."

As she spoke, three more people parted the mass, stopping just before the dais and turning to face him.

"I also welcome Jero and Thogan, Prince brothers of the South, and Kadec Brolikian, Prince of the West. After many years, we are all finally united under one cause, to bring our land back to balance."

The sight of their familiar faces had warmth spreading to his chest. Freya stepped from her place, standing side by side with the other rulers, all on even ground. Then, as one, they each bowed.

His knowledge of court protocols was still undeniably cloudy, so Elijah followed their lead and bowed too, and the crowd applauded.

As they righted, Jero inclined his head in a respectful nod, which Thogan stoically mirrored. Kadec cast him a toothy grin, waggling his fingers in a subtle wave while his personal guard, Roarke, stood stoic faced behind.

Elijah nodded back to the princes with a small smile.

Freya continued, aiming her speech at the crowd, a mixture that Elijah was now realising was made of Shifters, Southern people and Western folk. Some wore the mid-class clothing of his own court, people who have braved leaving the North to be here. Escapees from the blight of his home. An array of different clothing, different accentuations, all mingled together, gathered as one. This wasn't everyone, there were surely others outside, awaiting news of the proceedings, but the room was filled with a blending of faces. The people brought from the other courts were warriors, soldiers, fighters, all recruited to fight in the battle to come.

"Against all odds, you stand here now, your destiny within reach. I never doubted you, Eliverus, and though I did say you would need to complete my test to earn my support and that of my armies, I have decided that you have proven yourself enough. We are on the cusp of war, on the cusp of change, and though you have completed many challenges up until this point, your most pressing challenge is still yet to come."

Arii blew out a breath beside him.

Freya wasn't going to test him? The news had tension leaking from him, too, but he did not let his guard down.

His thoughts narrowed to a knife point as Freya's hands disappeared into the folds of her gown, steel glinting as she withdrew a sword.

"I, Freya Bloom, Queen of the East, bestow upon you, Prince Eliverus Herington, the fabled Sword of Power."

The crowd began to murmur, gasps and excited tones shivering in the air. The Queen rested the blade in her palms and presented it to him. Elijah took a moment to take it in. Every inch was polished to perfection, the high, intricately carved ceiling reflected perfectly in its surface. The metal held an otherworldly glimmer, a luminous glow radiating with a blue, pearlescent sheen. The hilt was wrapped in scaled leather that was a mix between a dragon's scales and underwater shells, the colours changing before his eyes. It was a simple-looking weapon, but what it had been forged from was beyond anything on this mortal plane.

It called to him, tugging at his chest like a siren's call.

Freya smiled widely, the points of her elongated canines showing. "And with this, the full support of the East. We will follow you into war, into chaos, into death if fate deems that it is time."

Elijah stared down at the weapon for a few heartbeats more, his hands lifting with hesitation towards the polished metal. When his skin touched the hilt, the blade flared with light.

When his fingers curled around it, the sword hummed.

"Tomorrow we will prepare to storm north, to the heart of the curse, to the empire forged with the sullied blood of our brothers and sisters. An empire made of bigotry and terror."

The crowd rumbled with vigour, rising cries and the thumping of boots thrumming through his bones.

From the shadows, the Ouroboros smiled, clapping along with the rest. In the silhouette cast against the floor nearby, Elijah swore he saw the curl of a dragon's head, its jaws wide in a soundless roar. The sight brought back the feeling of exhilaration he had felt while sweeping on dragon back through the jewelled cavern.

Determination filled him and he turned to the crowd and lifted the sword into the air above his head.

Cheers erupted, and he heard the steady chant of his name, a mantra of hope elating into the air.

Elijah wasn't one for grand speeches, even now he didn't know how to place into words the promise he had on the tip of his tongue.

He would right the wrongs and leave this place turned upright, no matter the cost. He didn't need to speak though, for Freya called, "Burn this empire of fear and hate to the ground. And from the ashes we will rise again."

CHAPTER TWENTY-THREE

NEMESIS

The realm may have been on the cusp of war, but apparently there was always time for a wedding. Nemesis wasn't very much into weddings, but she had to admit the air of the forest was light, the atmosphere sweet and happy, and she supposed this was an occasion to raise the spirits of the people. There was no telling if they would all return once they moved on Viridya, no telling how the war would end.

The low-hanging branches of the ancient trees were draped with white silk curtains and careful arrangements of white wildflowers, hanging in decorative garlands around a large moss-covered clearing. Two equal groups of chairs faced a wildflower archway, the stage of which was dwarfed by two colossal, ancient pine trees.

Candles glittered on every surface, atop the tables carved of cedar wood and decorated with bunches of wild floral arrangements, lending the place an ethereal, rustic feel.

"Fire hazards…" whispered Nocturne as he passed, carrying a stack of polished wooden plates.

Nem couldn't help the small smile that tugged at her lips.

It was all so beautiful, and utterly romantic. She would have to be truly heartless to be unaffected by the sweet ambience, her gaze lingering on the place where her two friends would soon declare their love.

"You know, this is exactly the kind of wedding I imagined for my brother. He may not let on, but the man's a pure romantic. He chose the flower arrangements, you know. All Luc wanted was for it to be here, amongst the ancient pines, with the whisper of the forest in their ears." Tikkani sighed, placing a crisp white napkin in the centre of a plate laid down by Noct.

Nem blinked, having momentarily forgotten her duty to lay down wooden knives and forks. She cast her eyes on the young elf, wearing a beautiful dusty sage silk dress, her hair plaited down two sides to frame her face. Her uptilted eyes were lined with kohl, a dusting of rose blush accentuated her high cheekbones.

Tikkani continued, laying another napkin down. "My brother would have married Luc anywhere, truth be told. But I think they both hoped for something like this, deep down. A big celebration surrounded by the people they love. Who wouldn't want that?"

"Those who have no one they love." Nem replied, sounding a little sour despite her attempt to hide it.

The girl picked up on it, though. Her smile was soft. "Are you alright, Nem?"

It was strange… no one had asked her that in some time. Was she alright, truly? The turmoil in her chest didn't feel right at all.

Nem sighed, placing another fork and knife down. "Heartless, remember?"

Tikkani grinned, setting down the last napkin, before throwing over her shoulder, "You're not heartless, Nemesis. I can see the twinkle in your eyes. You can feel the love in this place, too. You'd better get dressed, the ceremony will start soon."

She didn't have the heart to tell the elf that that twinkle was just the reflection of the candles, nothing more.

Nem gazed down at her cream tunic and moss-green trousers.

Hm, she supposed she'd better change.

As she made her way back to her rooms, ducking around a few Shifters finishing up the last little details, Nem wondered idly where Krepth had gotten to. Her heart hurt at the thought of him. They hadn't spoken much since the night on the rooftop, the night he had told her that their kinds – Shifter and Goddess-touched – weren't meant to be together. And they'd become even more distant after she'd called him a coward and used him as a punching bag back at the underground castle. Her hurt was a festering thing in her chest, a little monster she wasn't able to scare away. Her behaviour wasn't approachable, and even she had to admit she'd have avoided her, too. But she couldn't help it.

She missed him.

Krepth had distanced himself, though she saw his looks of longing when he thought she wasn't looking. Why was he torturing them both? She knew he was putting space between them for a reason, and she knew he hadn't breathed a word of their discovery to anyone since, especially for fear of what may become of her now that they were back in Shifter homeland.

Nem tugged at the rope linked to the pulleys that lifted her up into the trees. When she came to her level, she secured the rope and headed towards her room amongst the trees. As she approached, her brows rose at the group of people congregating nearby. She spotted Arii on the outer, her friend's arms crossed over her chest, second-hand relief and anger washing over her senses. Freya's striking blonde hair stood out from the crush as Luc's sister, Iniq, stood nearby with a small contingent of warriors.

They were gathered around three people who all looked haggard, as if they'd been through hell. Two females and a male. One of them leaned heavily on the shoulder of one of Iniq's soldiers, her eyes glazed with pain, her legs shaking so badly she would have toppled had it not been for them.

As Nem neared, she saw Krepth, his hands gliding over the face of the other woman, whose hair was as black as his own. Her cheeks were sunken and sallow, bruises below her eyes, her skin leached of colour, as if she hadn't seen the sun in a very long time. The way he handled her… it was tender, yet she could see the subtle shake in his hands. He was relieved, yet there was a hint of anger about to boil over.

Nem paused, because the woman no longer resembled the one she had known for years.

It was Krepth's mother.

Nem paused beside Elijah, who watched on with concern. "They just arrived. Iniq and her warriors patrolling the outskirts of the forest found them. They're all in a bad way, and Krepth's mother, she's well enough but," his profile hardened. "She has been through hell. They all have."

Gods.

Krepth's mother had been snatched away to Bonemire some time ago. It was a miracle that she was still alive, and Nem was as keen as everyone else to hear the story of her escape, but the woman looked beyond exhausted.

Freya helped usher them towards the healing quarters as Krepth looped his mother's arm around his shoulders. Nem itched to help, fingers flexing as they passed by, a feeling which she also knew came from Arii, her companion's purple glare following in their wake. Nem's eyes met Krepth's and held, the charged air between them zinging with pent up energy.

The tale would wait until another day.

"She can hardly speak," growled Arii, joining her. She too still remained in her casual attire, as was Elijah.

"We witnessed Bonemire, we know what horrors are happening behind those stone walls. She will provide valuable updated insight," murmured Elijah. "Which we will need from her quickly."

"She needs to rest," argued Arii, her words clipped, yet her eyes were soft around the edges, a look Nem had noticed was frequent when she gazed at him lately.

Elijah's voice was gentle. "This wedding is only a short reprieve before the war, you know that. Whatever insight we can get before it hits may just turn the tides for us."

Arii's chin lifted. "Well, look at you, Your Highness. All work and no play."

Nem blinked, before her expression hardened. "Spoken like a commanding officer."

Elijah's silver stare lowered, leveling with her own, "You forget, I *was* once a commanding officer."

True.

"I will speak with her when she is ready." Freya said, raising a hand. They halted as Krepth, his mother, and Freya continued on, crossing the wide, wobbly rope bridge towards the hospital tree. Despite his suggestion that they draw information from her, Elijah did not pursue the subject any further, which Nem appreciated.

Nem swallowed, watching Krepth's broad back disappear.

Despite the sombre mood that his words brought, Elijah's eyes softened as Arii rested her hand on his shoulder, before taking Nem's hand in hers, guiding them in the direction of their rooms. "Let's get ready for the ceremony. It could be our last chance to relax before we face the possibility of not returning home."

The harp's song mingled with the murmur of the gathering guests, conversations light and joyful. Nem studied the faces of the people, many of whom were recognisable, but the majority were not. Regardless of their relationship to the pair, all seemed comfortable and cheerful, and in the air of that, Nem felt her rigid spine slacken ever so slightly.

Tikkani stood before the archway, along with Iniq, both dressed in gowns in varied shades of green. Between them, slightly back, stood Freya, the picture of royal elegance in a burgundy gown, adorned with simple strings of silver jewellery, the wedding's officiant. Her smile was subtle, but her midnight eyes were shimmering, as she awaited the couple's arrival.

Nem sat in the front row on Emerson's side, next to Elijah and Arii, who both looked as awkward as she felt. Nem couldn't remember the last time she'd attended a wedding… she was pretty sure she never had, come to think of it. On her other side was Quinn, looking handsome in a white, long-sleeved tunic, wolf-grey vest and light tan pants. He gazed up at Tikkani, his canines finally showing in a grin, as the elf smiled back widely, blowing a kiss in his direction. Quinn made a show of catching the imaginary affection, before pretending to thump it into his heart.

Argh.

Nem tore her gaze away, observing the guests she could see. Across the way was Luc's family, his mother and father, their deep brown skin resplendent against the rustic forest palette of their clothing. Beside them was Krepth, and she sucked in a shaky breath. He wore a deep chestnut jacket over a light brown shirt, the top set of buckles left undone. He had the shadow of a beard, and she suddenly realised she didn't mind it after all. He preferred to be shaven, simply for the fact that she loved seeing the dimples on his cheeks when he smiled, but the rugged look wasn't displeasing. Her gaze took in his profile, the sharpness of his jaw, the sweep of his nose, raven hair falling over his forehead. With her perusal, she found her palms beginning to sweat.

His head turned, as if sensing her attention, and Krepth's eyes met hers momentarily, his lips twitching into the ghost of a smile.

Hers though, did not.

Suddenly, the guests from behind began to stand, a wave of slowly rising bodies as Luc and Emerson entered. The harpist began to strum a gentle tune, and with the crowd's movement, Nem lost sight of Krepth's concerned gaze.

Tikkani and Iniq straightened their backs, and the smile that flashed across their faces were almost as bright as the sun. The crowd turned to catch a glimpse of the couple as they made their way, arm in arm, down the aisle.

When they made it to the front, their hands remained locked, their gazes fixed on one another, radiating nervousness and restless happiness. Nem knew this had been a long time coming.

They were both dressed in off-white tunics and taupe vests, their pants a complementary tan in colour. Pinned to their lapels were matching wildflower boutonniere. Luc's white-toothed smile was resplendent, his cheeks flushed, while Emerson looked a touch more nervous. Luc brought his fiancé's hand to his mouth, planting an encouraging kiss there.

Seeing their exchange of smiles and whispered words of

encouragement to one another made Nem's cool heart flutter, her personal dilemma momentarily forgotten as the ceremony began.

Freya's voice filled the clearing. She spoke of love, triumph over darkness, and how two young boys with a fierce friendship blossomed into an ever-fiercer romance. They were meant for one another, their fates entwined, to which she wished them happiness forevermore.

"These are dark times, to be sure, but in the face of this, love can – and will – prevail. Let this union be a symbol of hope, a light in the darkness."

The crowd cheered, and Nem chanced a peek at Krepth.

He turned his head too, eyes seeking hers, and she suddenly longed to touch him. Perhaps it was the air of the ceremony, or a biproduct of the fact that they weren't meant to be together. No matter the reason, she wasn't sure how long she could stand this torment.

If love was so great, why did it hurt so damned much?

"I, Freya Bloom, Queen of Evergrave, pronounce you wedded. You may seal your union with a kiss."

There was no hesitation as the Shifter and the elf collided, sharing a sweet kiss that had the crowd on their feet, cheers and applause rebounding off the ancient pines.

The celebration was swift to begin.

Luc and Emerson slowly made their way around to each guest, hands tied together, faces split with unflappable grins. Music from a bard bearing a lute, a man playing a pigskin drum and the lady on the harp rose to a rambunctious background noise, making the gathering shake with merriment. Bodies headed to the dance floor, while Shifters mingled with Southerners and Westerners around spits of roast beef and chicken. Plates of roast vegetables and Eastern salads were laid out on long tables, a buffet for the guests to pick and choose at their leisure.

The array of different fashions, of different people, had Nem feeling a little overwhelmed. But the atmosphere was alive with excitement, laughter and discussion, some catching up on old times while others forged new friendships. There hadn't been a gathering such as this in a very long time; the significance of this night was not lost on many here.

Tonight, there were no barriers dividing courts; they were one in celebration and one in cause.

Nem watched the revelry upon the dance floor from a comfortable distance, goblet in hand. The wine was sweet, a lingering taste of cherries on her tongue.

"Will you not dance, young one?"

Nem startled, having not heard the Queen's arrival beside her. She made to bow, but Freya waved a delicate hand. "No formalities tonight, Miss Rion. This is a celebration, a night where all are one in our merriment. Although, your face betrays you. Are you troubled?"

Nem suppressed a wince. Was she that easy to read?

She swallowed her fear and threw caution to the wind as she asked, "My lady… what do you know about the Goddess-touched? We… we came across mention of them in our travels and I was curious to know about them."

If the Queen was perturbed by her question, she didn't show it. "Ah, it has been a long time since I've heard mention of them. The Goddess-touched were a race of demigods, created from a union between a mortal and a God during the night of a full moon. They were made with the purpose of hunting those who stole from the Gods." Freya's dark eyes met hers as she added, "My people."

Nem swallowed, hoping the working of her throat against her suddenly dry mouth wasn't noticeable.

"You know the story of the items stolen from the Gods, and the curse placed upon the Fae responsible. It was a long time ago, a story told to our children, one we tell to scare them from doing things such as stealing." The Queen smiled ruefully. "The last demigod was seen about a millennia ago, and none have been seen since. Perhaps time has softened the Gods, or they have just forgotten about the small items they formerly sought."

Nem had a sudden thought. Never had she seen Freya's animal form, nor had she ever heard what animal the Queen could shift into.

The first which came to mind was an owl – curious and watchful, with snow-white feathers. It seemed fitting. She stored the idea away with a plan to ask Krepth later.

Her chest ached again at the thought of him.

"Demigods were powerful, with the ability to halt a transformation with the touch of a hand, and with that touch they could wrench a shifted Fae back into their humanoid form, snuffing out their connection to their magic. It made dispatching them… easier. Swifter."

Had her touch severed Krepth from his magic? She hadn't noticed any discomfort when they had been on the roof outside her rooms while in Ayrith. If he had felt something, he had hidden it well. Another thing she needed to discuss with him.

"Thank you for entertaining my question, Freya, I appreciate it."

The Queen nodded, smiled, and drifted off to be swept up in the celebration.

Nem turned and cast her eyes across the dancers, surveying the outskirts. She didn't think he'd be amongst them. Despite the running of his mouth, Nem knew Krepth wasn't much of a dancer, preferring to watch and sip a drink on the sideline – much like her. Another thing they had in common. Another little thing she'd retained about him, even though she'd feigned disinterest.

Soon enough she spied his head of thick black hair, standing beside his mother who was seated with a blanket over her lap. She looked far better than she had before, her green eyes alight yet tired, a hint of colour returned to her cheeks. Nem knew the woman well, had known her for years, so the strange sensation in her gut as she neared was a surprise, a sudden urge to whirl and sprint away.

Krepth's mother's gaze found her, and she smiled. "Oh Nem, it is good to see you. You've been keeping my son in line while I was incapacitated, I hope."

Nem let loose a breath. "Of course. I'm so glad to see you're alright, Mrs Hallier. We wanted to rescue you but–"

The woman waved a hand, "Please, don't apologise. There were many in Bonemire, and many were less fortunate than I. I survived, I escaped, and what matters now is what I do with my freedom. I'm not strong enough to be of use in the coming battle, so I'll make sure our home remains ready for when you two return."

Krepth shifted, and Nem met his eyes. His gaze was piercing, vivid green reflecting the light around them, his jaw set. It was the longest he'd held her gaze in days, and she hoped her emotion showed in her own.

I'm so damned angry at you... I'm sorry... I want you... I need you...

Nem kept her eyes on his as she said, "The promise of a home is far stronger than any weapon that we could wield tomorrow."

"I agree!" said Mrs Hallier,

Krepth tilted his head slightly, and she couldn't take her gaze away from the enquiry in his eyes.

"Mind if I take your son for a dance?" Nem finally asked.

Mrs Hallier's eyes lit up, her face following with a grin, "Please, take him. He's being frightfully dreary. This is a celebration of love." She clasped her son's hand before letting it go, picking a piece of fruit from a nearby plate that had been carefully prepared for her.

Krepth made a small sound between a sigh and a grunt but did not resist as Nem grabbed his hand and led him around the dancefloor of people. Nem was about to join them when Krepth's fingers twisted to hold hers and he tugged her away from the crowd and around the side of a nearby hut.

Nem twisted, back to the wooden slats, mouth open on the cusp of a demand for an explanation when Krepth's hands found her face. He was close, staring intently into her eyes, his mouth firm as he said, "We need to talk."

Her anger fizzled, all attention zeroing in on his touch. Her fingers manacled his wrists as she replied, "I know."

Krepth seemed taken aback, as if predicting a totally different reaction. Nem sighed, drawing their linked hands in front of her, all the while keeping an eye on his face, looking for any signs that her touch affected him.

A tick in his jaw, the tiniest flutter of his eyelids and pull of his brows told her what he was hiding.

Her touch was severing his magic.

"Why didn't you tell me? I can see it, even though you are trying your best to hide it. My touch takes away your magic."

Krepth was silent for a time, surveying her face as if he were memorising a puzzle. "I… I didn't want to make you feel… like you were repressing me. Affecting me in a negative way."

She frowned. "Is this why you've been distancing yourself?"

He moved closer. "It was, but the last week has been misery, Nem. Trying to keep away has been absolute bloody torture." His fingers drew her face up to his. "When my mother came back, I realised that no matter what we do, things sometimes have a way of just working out. You may be the first demigod in a thousand years, and may have been created to hunt my kind, but I can't deny how I feel. I can't deny how I've felt for *years*. Nothing will change that."

Nem swallowed, a warmth blooming in her chest. She hadn't realised how much those words would mean to her until he was speaking them.

Krepth continued, his tone low, gentle. "You've been without memory for so long, and you've finally got a lead to grasp. I won't be the one to hold you back from finding out who you are. I want to be there when you make that discovery."

A flicker of determination ignited in her core, a sense of purpose that had alluded her for so long. She sighed, content for now to be in Krepth's company and to return to ideas of self-discovery later. On the same thought, Krepth curved his arms around her, and she rested her hands at the nape of his neck, curling her silver nails into his hair. They moved closer, his nose brushing against the curve of her neck, his gentle breath tickling the sensitive spot below her pointed ear.

They danced away from the crowd, just out of sight, in a little place where their world was their own, under the cover of winking stars and lamplight.

As his arms held her close, a sense of peace found her, and

Nemesis' skin began to glow.

Fire, Fury & Chaos

Nemesis' skin began to glow.

CHAPTER TWENTY-FOUR

ELIJAH

Elijah couldn't help but smile as he watched his friends – and the new faces he'd met throughout the course of the night – dance and mingle on the polished wooden dancefloor. Tiny spheres of light drifted in the air, hovering over the people as they tangled in time with the upbeat music. The lights weren't Shifter magic, he knew that the people of the East were limited in their outward magic, so guessed it was a gift from one of the Western guests. Sure enough, nearby, was Kadec Brolikian, hands raised subtly.

Elijah quietly tapped his foot in time with the beat, not up for dancing in the crush of twirling bodies, content with watching for the moment. He wasn't one for dancing, really, preferring to spectate.

Sounds of a flute began to play, and Elijah glanced up at the stage where the band played. At their forefront was Nocturne, piping on a silver flute, adding a boisterous energy to the melody. A man of many talents, and one he was beginning to tolerate. Noct hadn't shown any signs of pursuing Arii, leading him to believe the words he'd said at the castle of Ayrith were delivered just to ruffle him. He was a shameless flirt, there was no doubt, but seemed harmless enough. His magic though, as well as that of the Ouroboros, were still a huge enigma, no matter how much he tried to understand. Unlike the others, Elijah didn't feel so betrayed by Noct's withholding of information about the Ouroboros. He understood why he'd left the part about the man being a literal dragon, he wouldn't have believed him, and he felt the others wouldn't have either.

Laughter snapped nearby, snagging his attention. When a familiar shock of red hair bobbed towards him, a pirate's hat balancing on her crown, Elijah's brows rose as Valerie hollered "Soon to be King Herington! Long time no see!"

"Valerie," he greeted the pirate, spying the familiar, white-toothed grin of her first mate beside her. He lifted his drink. "Lyda. It is good to see you both."

"As it is to see you! We heard of your predicament earlier and are so glad you are free once again, ready to take back the North. We had a little trouble, for a time there, trying to convince the populace around the South and East that you would be back, that you'd somehow be there to lead the charge in claiming back the land for its people." Elijah winced as the pirate rocked on her heels, grinning. "We've sampled many a drink and spun many a tale, sprinkling hope where there was none. You can thank us with gold later… or perhaps some treasures from your castle vaults? Should there be any left."

Elijah opened his mouth to reply, to thank them, but Lyda cawed a laugh. "She jests, Your Highness. We may be pirates, but we do not always need payment."

Valerie gave her shipmate a look. "Pirates *always* need payment." Her smile, back on him, was wide. "I'm sure there is a future naval fleet he requires a commander for. Or we could just have at the castle wine stores!"

"Thank you, for keeping the spark of hope alive," he replied, laughter in his voice.

Valerie nodded, "Now, let's party like it's our last night, for it very well could be. Come, Lyda, I see a tray of freshly poured elven wine over there, ready to be raided."

Lyda grinned, thrusting a hand to her forehead in salute as they skirted away.

Elijah chuckled to himself, glad to see the two pirates in good spirits since their comrade Gunner's sudden death.

He idly wondered where Arii had gotten to.

As if on the same wavelength, she brushed up beside him, a small grin on her face.

"Not going to join in?" she queried, her purple gaze finding Luc and Emerson locked in a swaying, laughing embrace. Her smile, somehow, became wider, stretching until little dips creased her cheeks.

Elijah side-eyed her, and she tilted her head at his silence.

Gods, he loved when she smiled, especially when it was unchecked and carefree.

Not only was her smile beautiful, so was her entire façade. Dressed in a gown of deep blue, the ends darkened to a vivid purple that looked like an otherworldly sunset, the material inlaid with tiny translucent jewels. The bodice wrapped generously around her, before lightly flaring out in a layer of subtle tulle. It was... breathtaking; her hair curled into soft ringlets with a pinch of the strands pinned back from her face. She wore a small hint of makeup, but it was enough, highlighting her allure in a simple, delicate way.

The way her vivid amethyst eyes coasted over him, with appreciation and something... hungrier... had his insides flaring to life.

Elijah thought about the time they'd first met; when those penetrating eyes had halted him in the gilded stables. She'd been speaking to Lorch, dressed in simple cadet uniform, yet her eyes had held a weight that drew him closer, made him curious as well as cautious. Something had drawn him to her, even then, even when she looked upon him as if he were an enigma – one she'd happily eat for breakfast. The shivers that had coursed his spine then now returned, and unlike before when they'd been together – this feeling was different.

This was the feeling of adrenaline, one that rose in anticipation of battle.

Were there nerves mixed there, too?

His half-hearted scowl didn't quite curve his entire mouth downward as he said, "I'd prefer these people look upon me as someone who can lead them into war on sure feet. If I were to stumble or make myself a fool the night before, I feel they wouldn't take me as seriously."

Arii laughed, taking his hand. "Something tells me that you're better at dancing than you lead me to believe."

He did not protest as they joined the outskirts of the flood of dancers, their hands moving to mirror those around them. Music drifted across the revellers, a harmony of pleasant sound that had them embracing and swaying. Romantic, and perhaps the better beat for them to move to. Elijah moved his hand to splay on her lower back, bringing her close as the fingers of their joined hands twined. He pressed her backwards, and she tipped back, their movements syncing as quickly as if they were sparring in a training ring.

"I think you are better at dancing than you lead on, too." Elijah said.

The music lifted in pitch, sending the swaying forms into a twirl, sweeping them up in a wave of bodies. To avoid collision, Elijah tugged Arii sideways, and his boot tapped her toes, causing them both to stumble. A laugh cracked from Arii, and he chuckled too, as they steadied one another. Warmth from her palms radiated through his sleeves, melting into his skin, and Elijah's eyes lifted from where their feet clashed, up to the face of the woman who simultaneously addled his brain while setting fire to his heart.

The shadow of the thoughts that had been plaguing him for some time hovered on the outer of his mind, thoughts of their future and what he had to do to end the land's blight, and with it came a douse of sadness. Arii smiled, oblivious to the devil on his shoulder who muttered that there would be no future with him. The only thread for him was darkness… or death.

He should be making the most of this night, spending it as close to the one he was falling in love with as possible. He'd kept himself in check, but he couldn't deny what was roiling inside any longer.

Elijah swallowed, hoping his internal war didn't show, but he could see Arii's pupils widen ever so slightly, a subtle tilt of her head and a light pull on her lips that told him what he feared. He couldn't hide anything from her.

Before she could raise a question, he pulled her close once more, touching his hand to her cheek. "It sometimes feels like my heart has known you before, and I believe I've loved you in a thousand lifetimes, not just this one."

Something shuttered across Arii's eyes, a softness he'd only seen a handful of times before. Instead of speaking she stepped closer, resting her cheek to his chest, where his heart beat steadily, sure and true. He curled his arms around her, protective even though he knew she was beyond capable of protecting herself. It was an instinct; one he couldn't ignore. Elijah savoured her scent while resting his chin on the crown of her head, yet his body remained tense. Eyes skittered over them, curious, and assessing, causing him to hold her a little tighter. He felt her surprised breath, her little laugh vibrating against his chest.

He wasn't sure what was wrong with him, but a pricking sensation tingled down his spine.

The beast within him purred, more insistent now, the need to have her close almost impossible to ignore any longer. They may not survive tomorrow, and he couldn't deny what he felt in his heart to be true.

He loved her, and he'd be damned if he didn't show her that before the end.

So, Elijah took Arii's hand in his, and led her from the dancefloor.

ARIIAYA

The skin of her arms pebbled to gooseflesh, causing her to squeeze Elijah's bicep a bit tighter as they drew away from the music and bustle of the wedding celebrations. It warmed her heart that despite the uncertainty of tomorrow, her friends seized the night as if it were their last. And who was to say it wouldn't be the last? While they had the support of all three courts, not to mention an otherworldly being who could shift into a dragon, weeks had passed since their quest began and they had no inkling of the size of the army amassed by Lorch and Valdis.

She cleared her throat. "Where are we going, Your Highness?"

Elijah made a sound beside her, between a chuckle and a grunt, and replied, "You'll see."

"I don't much care for surprises."

"I thought you loved surprises?" Elijah responded, a note of amusement in his deep voice.

She pouted, surveying the darkening path as they left the light of the braziers behind, entering the forest.

"Perhaps once upon a time, but not so much anymore."

There was a layer of meaning to her words that she hoped he wouldn't read into. Thankfully, Elijah seemed oblivious.

"Well, I think you'll set it all aside for this one. And if you don't, then I'm sure Tikkani's offer of a drinking game is still open," he said.

Arii shuddered, "Where does all the alcohol go? She's so small… Where are you taking me?" She squinted, eyes adjusting swiftly to the waning light. The path was becoming narrower, the heels of her shoes sinking into the soft loam. "Should've let me change my shoes first."

"You don't care about the shoes," Elijah said simply, and she shrugged, because he was right. "We are here."

Arii regarded the pocket of trees before them, nestling a moonlit pool in their centre. The sound of running water greeted them like a song, a nearby rise of rocks home to a comely little waterfall – perhaps only big enough for two beneath. The moon towered over them; the cover of stars so clear that she could see hundreds of them twinkling like blinking eyes in the skies above.

It was beautiful and… incredibly romantic.

Elijah turned to her before she could utter something inappropriate, or worse. "Care for a dip?"

She stared at him, at the small smile on his dark, silver-lit features. "A… dip?"

His hands met her arms, gliding over her skin, and warmth rose under his palms. Warmth rose in other places too, places awakened whenever his skin made contact with hers. When her eyes met his, she almost melted into a puddle at the crinkles of laughter forming around his eyes. "But it's cold," she whispered finally, unsure of why she was stalling. Why *was* she stalling? She had wanted this, craved the alone time that felt so fleeting, ever since he had come back. Time was a transient thing, a thief whisking away their moments like loose coins from a back pocket. And soon, there would be none left. Fate would deal its hand in the next few days, and Arii was determined to meet it without regret.

If she were to squander what little time they had left, she knew *that* would be the biggest regret of her life.

The sounds of celebration still hummed, far enough away that the thrum of drums and music mixed together. A star-filled sky winked in the parted trees above and crickets chirped merrily in the thick, dark forest which surrounded them. Shivering moonlight played with a light layer of mist as it skittered along the surface of the pool.

When Elijah's fingers brushed a strand of hair from her face, she found herself leaning into his touch without thought. He remained silent, never pressing, awaiting her lead as he almost always did. He wouldn't press her on it, but closeness was something they both desired – something they had been longing for.

When she finally let her attention move to his eyes – so deep and full of desire – her breath left her in a whisper. "Alright."

His slow smile sent warmth to her core.

Before he could speak, she turned and padded to the pool's edge, glancing over her shoulder. Remaining where he was, he watched her intently, eyes dark and face half shadowed in the moonlight, all the easiness of his body language disintegrating before her eyes. His shoulders curled ever so slightly, head tilting so that his silver eyes were hooded by his lashes. She knew that look, one purely predatory, purely *Fae*, a slowly emerging beast tracking its prey.

A thrill sparked down her spine and she smiled; one she knew was full of temptation. Hitching her shoulder, she drew down the straps of her gown, letting the cool blue material flutter to the forest floor.

Power rippled around them, further driving her eagerness to see how long he could hold himself back. Teasing… tempting a wolf. Warmth flooded through her limbs despite the cool night air, as her skin tingled. What was moving through her now was a compulsion to finish something that they had started long ago.

After everything they had been through, Arii had known for a long time that their fates were tied by a bond, beyond anything the fates could conjure. They were bonded by destiny, by nature. Once their bodies connected… really connected, then she would know this for sure. The look in his eyes told her what words could not, and the dusky scent that touched her nose was one she knew stemmed from his beast, and hers rose in primal response.

Tonight, they would finally confirm what she suspected – if they were true mates.

The prospect had parts of her tightening with anticipation.

The flare of Elijah's nostrils told her that her feelings in that moment were absolutely no secret to him. She could sense his desire on the air and taste his hunger for her upon it, a heavy dose of woodfire smoke, pine and musk twined with starlight.

She removed the last scrap of her underwear before stepping into the pool, tilting her head back to watch the stars. The water lapped at her skin, chilling and refreshing. Elijah murmured something behind her, and when the water reached her collarbones, she turned.

He was still on the shore, but his hands had lifted to his vest, swiftly unbuttoning the silver clips. Without her keen Fae sight, she would have missed the ever so slight tremor to his fingers, and the thought of him feeling the same bubbles of nerves that had begun within her was oddly sweet. Intimacy was not something new to them both, but *this* kind of intimacy was.

Arii took in every bit of his pale skin, every ripple of muscle, every light dusting of hair and every scar that marred his battle-honed body, burned it to her memory as if it could be her last time seeing him. This land was cloaked in uncertainty, and she knew now more than ever that every second should be treated as a possible last. Emotion clogged her throat as Elijah joined her, moving through the water to pause a hand's breadth away. His deep voice skimmed the water like mist.

"Are you alright?"

Gods, she most certainly was an open book to him. "I just…" She closed the distance between them, gliding her hands over the warm, broad expanse of his chest, gaze resting on the light thatch of hair. She toyed at it with her fingers, connecting the pebbles of water beaded on his skin. She felt him shudder and she suppressed a smile.

"This may be our last night together. The old me wouldn't have cared, the old me would have just barged into the next day without care. But now, I kind of wish we could just disappear into this forest and remain here forever and leave the world to its fate."

His arms encased her, his lips pressing to her forehead. "Let's treat tonight as our last, then." She glanced up as he continued. "And treat tomorrow as if it's our last, too, and the day after."

She smiled, unable to hide the note of sadness to her tone as she said, "Until it is indeed our last day."

He pinched her chin and drew her face up. "And until that last day, I'll love you, Arii. I'll love you after the sun sets on that day, and even after the last flower withers on this earth, I will continue to love you. I'll love you until the stars turn to dust in the sky."

She blinked, but her body melded against his, her heart squeezing at his words. "I most certainly can't beat *that*. I'll try until my last breath proving my love for you, though."

"Let's start now…" he breathed, drawing her lips to his until they grazed together with the fragility of butterfly wings. Even now, at this very moment, he was holding himself back, giving her the chance to stop things if she so desired. He pressed her gently closer, until all the soft parts of her met the hard panes of him. The warmth of his breath drifted over her lips, and she found herself holding her own breath.

"Kiss me," she sighed, and as if that were the final shears slicing through his last tether, Elijah drew his lips to hers. It was searing, sending fire through her veins and lighting her blood with sparks. This kiss… it wasn't like the many others before. This was… different. There was a need to the sweep of his tongue and the clash of their teeth, and she met his fervent demand with her own.

He was hers, and she was his, irrevocably.

Arii folded her legs around his hips and he held her, hands squeezing her bottom as water lapped at their exposed skin. The hardness of him pressed eagerly against her, and she groaned against his teeth. His hold was fierce, as if he were afraid that she would float away, anticipation shivered through her as they moved deeper into the water, her body feeling weightless and free. Elijah's teeth grazed her collarbone and she tilted her head back, slick tendrils of wet hair tickling her shoulders and dragging against her neck and back. She clutched his nape, shivering with need as his head dipped to her breasts, taking a peak into his mouth. "Goddess burn me," she shuddered, her voice thick with desire.

Elijah smiled against her, grazing teeth over the sensitive skin. She shuddered again, grinding herself against the hard, slippery panes of his lower stomach, his hardness teasing her.

That earned her a deep, sharp inhale, and she grinned. She drew her mouth to his again, swallowing the sound he made like a bee sipping pollen. She drew his breath into her, allowed the fire to spread from where she wanted him most and up into her chest where her heartbeat in a furious frenzy.

Something shot past her periphery, a little ball of light, then another. Curious and shaking, she broke her lips from his and glanced up. Right before her nose was a bubble of water, a solid sphere of watery magic lit like a firefly. There were many, twirling around their figures in the water, a dazzling display of ethereal magic. Arii's eyes met ones of glowing silver, a ring of blue around his pupils that signalled his use of magic, and she smiled at the humour she saw there, mixed with unabashed emotion. "Are you doing this?"

"Far prettier than earth tremors, hmm?" he replied.

Arii laughed, wholeheartedly and unbound. She'd forgotten that

Elijah's desires had previously translated into earth tremors and thunderstorms, when he'd been unable to control how his emotions influenced his magic. The offset of his magic sparkled around them now, twinkling like the stars above. Beautiful, utterly beautiful. The moment tugged at her heart, filling her with a happiness she hadn't felt in years.

Elijah moved her then, subtly drifting them towards the waterfall. Sprinkles of water feathered over them, beading in their hair and eyelashes as he pressed her to a flat-faced boulder, the cool stone sending a harsh zing through her body.

"Every single sound you make edges me closer to utter madness," Elijah groaned against her now-drenched skin, drawing the tip of his nose along her jaw. He pressed himself against her again, the rigidness of his arousal sending her beast into a frenzy. She tasted his skin, salty from their evening of celebration, and tinged with the sweet bite of his magic. He nipped at her earlobe and she felt the harsh hair of his beard graze her neck, her flesh buzzing at the raw sensation upon her flushed skin.

Feeling bold, she took him in her fist, revelling in the groan that rolled from his clenched teeth.

"Wild little thing," he admonished.

"Stop holding back, Your Highness," she purred, giving him a squeeze. That earned her another very low, very *male* growl and her toes curled. An arm lifted to grasp the stone above her head, his bicep rippling with checked power, as the other grasped her thigh, bringing her leg up and over his hip. She locked it there, shuddering with need as she felt the head of his length brush the apex of her core.

Their eyes locked, lips parted on shivering, panting breaths. The forest silenced then, as if they were the only two beings left in the world.

There was a question in his dark, storm cloud eyes and she answered it with a whisper. "I'm yours, and always have been."

Always will be.

Elijah brought his lips to hers at the same moment that he drove himself home.

And in that instant of startling, expected, and welcomed intrusion, Arii closed her eyes, stars bursting behind her lids.

Shockwaves rippled through them both and they stilled, absorbing the moment, absorbing the feeling of being wholly *combined*. Something rested in the apex of Arii's sternum and her eyes snapped open. Her hand shot to her chest and pressed there, and shock rippled through her when she saw Elijah do the same.

They stared at one another, transfixed, as if seeing each other for the first time. They whispered their names, voices heavy with awe, their hands clutching at one another like lifelines in a storm. The joining of their bodies, the solidification of the bond forging into place within their souls felt utterly and ineffably *right*.

Fire radiated from their joined bodies, sizzles of tension hummed through their bones. Arii relaxed, her body growing used to the perfect intrusion of him.

He began to move, and their panted breaths mingled in another searing kiss as her hands caged his back, touching his jagged scars in an absentminded caress, nails lightly digging in.

The water spheres whirred around them, and mist rose from the pool in twisting tendrils. Her mind began to haze with a fog of heavy desire and if she was not slowly losing her sense of self to the cacophony of sensations wrung from the growing friction of their grinding bodies, she would have noticed that the water had become almost tepid. Perhaps it was just the heat generating from their out-of-control heartbeats, or perhaps it was the fervour of Elijah's residual magic.

Arii angled herself, allowing him deeper, and locked both legs around his hips, meeting him stroke for stroke. Elijah murmured a prayer that could also have been a curse against her shoulder as the quickening pace of their frenzy reached a fever pitch. The sound of splashing water was drowned out by the song of the waterfall as lights spiralled around them like a tornado of rainbows.

Delicious tension coiled low in her stomach, tightening everything from there. The stone was absolute at her back, pinning her with no place to go. She moaned, head pressing back to the stone, mist clinging to her breath. Water ran in rivulets from her hair, tracking tingling lines down her feverish skin as his movements became stronger, desperate, almost possessive. Elijah's hand fisted against the rock as he closed his mouth over the sensitive skin of her neck, sharp canines almost piercing as they came together again and again, his hips pounding against hers. Then he bit down, the compulsion overtaking him, fangs sinking deep. Jolts of pleasure and pain ricocheted to every nerve ending in her body and Arii cried out, so utterly swept up in the moment that she made no effort to stifle herself.

This was beauty. This was madness. This was *everything*.

When his fingers snaked between them to circle the nerves at the apex of her thighs, it took but a moment for Arii's world to rupture. She cried out again, the crash of her freefall into pleasure so fierce that she saw stars burst behind her eyes once again.

Elijah shuddered to a halt, his low gasp muffled against the crook of her neck. Quakes shot through him, sending ripples of nearly intolerable pleasure pulsating through her in the aftermath of her climax. In that instant, the little spheres of light dropped like marbles, pattering against their skin like rain, causing them both to laugh.

He reared back, smoothing the hair stuck against her forehead as she remained clinging to him. They stayed that way for a time, kissing, investigating each other's faces, running fingers through their hair. Committing all to memory while burning inside one another. They stared at each other for a time, sharing breaths, wholly absorbed, magic a sizzling sensation from his chest to hers, their tangible connection now glaringly clear.

For a few moments they remained silent. Elijah was deep in thought, the tiny ridge between his brows the only tell on his features. This was new to both of them, but she knew the truth behind the feeling they shared.

Arii finally whispered. "You can feel that too, can't you."

The tip of his chin was subtle, but she saw it. Her gaze roved his face, the beads of water in his beard, the shine of curiosity in his eyes. "There has always been something between us… volatile yet strong, as hot and as violent as a forest fire, as familiar as my own heartbeat. A link, a chain, a *thread* between our chests. Now it feels…"

"Solid. Final." Arii supplied tentatively, allowing him a moment to process. "We are mates, Elijah."

"Mates?" he breathed, as her palms pressed to his chest, feeling the pulse of his thundering heart, *needing* to feel it.

She swallowed and traced his strong jaw. "Fated, to be exact. This is a fate neither of us could have ever escaped. Our souls are meant to be together."

"I've still so much to learn about being Fae," Elijah sighed, before kissing the tip of her nose.

Arii grinned, but the time for talk was quick to flee. The beast within her rose, unsated, eager to use every moment of their isolation together. Arii kissed the bow of Elijah's lips and ran her fangs along his rough jawline.

She had him twice more before the moon peeked over the tops of the trees, and the cool dead of night draped upon their naked bodies as they lay together on the mossy bank.

Elijah's callused fingers tracked the curve of her hip. "You're so beautiful," he murmured, "My mate." He paused, brow rising. "Still sounds strange to me, but I guess I'll get used to it."

It would take them both some getting used to.

What she could most definitely get used to was this. Her body felt like melted butter, warm and content and deliciously sore in all the places that mattered. Sated, finally sated. Her beast purred in sleep, and the bite on her neck tingled. Fae were beasts, ones with the natural urge to bite the one fated to them, and she treasured the mark as if it were a gift. The compulsion to do so would have been impossible to ignore. With it he would have seen her memories, felt her emotions, drank upon her infatuation with him. Nothing was sacred now, as it would be with the bond between them. Complete, irreversible, fated.

Unbidden, thoughts of tomorrow, of what they were going to face, had Arii drawing her attention back to his face. A dark coil of hair hung over his forehead, his cheek pressed casually against his palm as his quicksilver eyes drank her in. He looked so at ease that she felt a sudden, fierce burn spark in her throat. He had been through so much, and thoughts of all they had learned of his destiny began to creep upon this moment like tainted fingers, pinching like biting ants.

She cleared her throat, "Well, you'd best be getting used to it. You thought I was a thorn before, I'll most certainly be a jagged spearhead now."

He laughed, the sound low and throaty, sending another pound of heat between her legs. Insatiable.

A throat cleared nearby and they both craned their heads to see Roarke standing with arms straight at his sides, head tilted so that his eyes roamed the moonlit trees, and not their naked bodies. "Apologies for the intrusion to your... moment, but urgent correspondence from our spies in the North has arrived."

Elijah reached to drape his heavy cloak across her, his voice laced with not-so-subtle agitation at the universe.

"Roarke... we were heading back shortly, anyway."

It made Arii grin.

She was sure that wasn't true. They would remain here all night, making love until the sun rose, if the world wasn't at threat of ending tomorrow.

"Can the message wait?" tested Arii, but she already knew that answer to that. She stood as Elijah pulled on his pants.

"My lady," Roarke paused, and had his tone not been laced with urgency, she would have laughed at the blush upon his cheeks at their lack of dress. He squared his gaze instead on Elijah, who had much more skin covered than she. "Your Highness, I have news from Viridya. It's... it's urgent." He inhaled sharply then straightened. "It's about Lorch Kruel."

Elijah became deadly still, long fingers pausing in buttoning his tunic. "Lorch?"

A jolt of trepidation zinged up Arii's spine, and she tasted sweetness. It settled from above, from the air around them, like a cold mist. The last of the butterflies faded, but Elijah's magic was still a tangible thing, something warm within her chest that settled with their bond.

"Lorch Kruel has been found guilty of treason, discovered fraternising with a resistance of Fae," Roarke's tone was quick and practical, but that slowly changed as he continued. Trepidation slowly turned to acidic dread, and Arii and Elijah's eyes met hers with the captain's words.

"He has been sentenced to execution, as ordered by his father, the Hand of the King."

CHAPTER TWENTY-FIVE

GHILA

Ghila hadn't felt like she'd ever had a purpose. Life for her had been almost nothing but pain and torment. Her life from before the death of her family was a distant memory, one she had trouble recalling from the recesses of her mind, the part of the labyrinth where she kept such things safe… protected. So safe that even she could not quite bring them back with the clarity of before. For so long, the promise of revenge was the only thing stoking the fire in Ghila's chest. With the brunt of that flame now merely glowing ashes, she was no longer sure what her purpose was.

It had been a week since her separation from the amulet, and a week since she'd begun to feel strangely detached from those around her. Despite the group's attempts to welcome her into their fold by including her in conversations and trying to learn more about her powers, she still felt like an outsider. Ariiaya hadn't given her any more grief since their spat in the tunnels, and her silence suited Ghila far better than any alternatives.

She ran her palms down the front of her gown, the sleek black satin reminding her of a panther's glistening hide. Most at the wedding were dressed in tones inspired by the forest around them – greens and browns and whites – but when given the choice of an array of gowns in the town tailor's shop, her eyes had instantly slunk to the darkest colour on display. Ghila had never attended a wedding before, she knew nothing of wedding etiquette, but the tailor had smiled and said that if she felt most comfortable in the obsidian piece, then she should choose it.

So, she had.

The old Ghila, the one who was young and sweet, would have chosen something far brighter, one that would draw the eyes of every single patron at the party. Perhaps a mixture of hues, like taking a rainbow from the sky.

Now she wanted to remain a shadow off to the side, an afterthought in the sidelines.

Her foot tapped to the music, acting of its own accord, almost like the old Ghila wanted out. And perhaps part of her was still there inside – *deep* inside, somewhere she was yet to discover. Perhaps someday she'd like to dance again, wear brighter colours. But for now, she was content with what she had chosen.

"I thought I'd find you here," came a voice, and she tilted her head to meet the bicoloured eyes of the realm-travelling stranger, Nocturne, as he paused beside her. "You're not joining in?"

She blinked, surprised that he'd sought her out after her glimpse into his mind. Ghila pressed her lips together, the steel manacles clinking as she pressed her hands together. "It's been a very long time. I… I don't remember how to dance."

Noct was silent for a beat, before he said, "I would offer to show you, but we are in need of you in the infirmary. The healers have tried everything to save one of the Shifters who returned from Bonemire, but their magic isn't succeeding." He worked the words around his mouth, adding, "I thought you could attempt to use your gifts, perhaps see what is stopping the healers' magic."

They needed her? *Her*?

Ghila eyed him suspiciously. "They requested me? Really?"

"Well, I may have suggested you as an option. There aren't any others, and they've become desperate."

Ghila didn't believe they'd have accepted the suggestion if they weren't truly out of options. So, she nodded.

"Alright, lead the way."

The infirmary smelled strongly of bitter herbs and alcohol, and the sounds of low, frantic voices and groans met her ears as Ghila and Noct entered. The room was carved into the oversized knot of a tree and lit by flickering candles, with two rows of beds running either side, each separated by white sheets on wooden frames. Ghila looked around the chamber, noting the ceiling curved in a craggy arch, still rough with the honeycombs of the termites that formerly lived there.

A woman motioned them over, her grey hair cinched in a tight bun. "Is that her? Come in, please."

Ghila fingered the cool metal of her manacles nervously, unable to look away from the form laying on the cot a step away from the apothecary. The woman's deep red hair was stuck to her forehead with sweat, her eyes squeezed shut and her lips parted as pained breaths puffed through her teeth. The navy-blue blanket draped over her could not hide the horribly thin body underneath, her skin a sickly shade that told Ghila that she had suffered and continued to suffer still. There were two more healers either side of her, both wearing cloth face coverings, staring wide-eyed at her approach.

They knew of her, and her history, then.

The voices in her head whispered from behind their bars, anxious and perhaps slightly afraid.

"Is this truly a good idea?" came the muffled voice of one of the healers, her green eyes shiny with disapproval. The first apothecary nodded.

"We haven't any other options," she returned, eyeing Nocturne with raised brows. "You think she can help her?"

Ghila didn't like how they spoke as if she weren't present, but she kept her displeasure to herself.

The woman on the bed groaned, her body jerking. The healers snapped into action as her limbs began to flail, the covering slipping from the ruin that remained of her chest. The wound was ragged, raw and circular, dark red fissures gouged deep into her skin. Her left breast was in bloody tatters, peeks of white hinting at bones. Bandages were strewn across the floor, and Ghila spied leather bands on the female's wrists. They'd attempted to restrain her at some point, but judging by the way she fought them now, the healers hadn't attempted to try again.

Ghila wondered why there weren't more people here, trying to help. The infirmary was significantly smaller than the one she remembered from the castle of her childhood, when she'd been sent to have her clumsy cuts and scrapes healed. What she knew of Evergrave was that it was a peaceful place, one perhaps without real need for a large medical wing, or many healers. But she had expected more than three.

The woman on the bed began to howl as one of the apothecaries pressed glowing hands to her chest, the attempt at healing only seeming to distress her more.

A sweep of moonlight hair moved from a cot a few feet down, where a male lay sleeping. Freya swept towards them, still dressed in her gown from the wedding. Her large dark eyes met Ghila and Noct in turn, their starlight depths shadowed with woe. "You came, child. Thank you."

Ghila nodded, her voice fleeing under the Queen's heavy gaze. With pinched brows and a glance at the struggling woman, Freya said, "Whatever ministrations conducted upon Kiley in Bonemire seem to be hindering our healing magic. She is living, but it looks to me that they began the process of making her a monster. They stopped, and why, I cannot work out. But whatever they did to her is killing her, slowly and painfully, and I fear there isn't much we can do." Her eyes roved back to Ghila. "I need you to delve below her flesh, into her mind if you must, to find what they did to her."

She could do that, surely.

Freya touched her fingers to Ghila's manacles, and with a flash of light, they snapped from her wrists and clanged to the floor. She rubbed at the exposed skin, feeling the tingle of her magic move through her limbs as a limp cloud rose from the forefront of her mind, like a sheer curtain being tugged aside. The voices rose timidly, but Ghila pressed them back, gritting her teeth. She was too busy keeping the voices in check to see that the people around her had tensed, all except for Noct, who shoved his hands into his pockets and smiled encouragingly.

Yes, she could do this.

Purpose flooded her, and with a sharp inhale, Ghila turned and approached the bed. Kiley continued to struggle, her back arching like a bow, mouth gaping wide in a silent scream. One of the healers edged aside as Ghila leaned over the patient, reaching for her face. She'd always had the best success when touching the one she wished to seize, particularly the face and temples. It created a seamless doorway, one where she did not need to fight or break through. Breaking through the barriers set in a mind unwilling to be crossed would bring pain, something this female didn't need any more of, so Ghila needed her to allow her to enter willingly.

She touched her hands to the female's cheeks, storm grey eyes meeting bloodshot blue. The female halted her struggle, breaths hissing through her teeth like snakes.

"I'm going to try to help you, but you need to allow me to enter your mind. Should you fight it, it will only cause you more pain – and I can see that you do not wish for any more of that."

The female whimpered, but nodded, the dip of her chin ever so slight.

Ghila didn't hesitate. She dove through the fragile barriers of the female's mind, brushing them aside like curtains of gossamer.

When she entered Kiley's mind, Ghila was greeted by roiling clouds of chaotic darkness. Lightning flashed beyond them, figures pacing like reapers in the dark.

The woman hunched in the middle of a grey field, her hands over her head, her bony shoulders shaking violently as she cried. She was naked, the mist drifting around her curled toes.

"K-Kiley?" Ghila whispered, lifting a hand to her.

Her head lifted, her arms falling away. "The pain, make it stop." She stood, turning, tears tracking down her pallid face. "Please," she wailed. Just like in reality, Kiley's chest was a ruin, all sinew, gore and bone. Blood ran down her stomach and legs, red rivers of crimson pain.

Thunder rolled, the explosion of sound rumbling the ground beneath them as Ghila's gaze snapped up, passing the woman's shoulder to the black smoke beyond, the bowels of which expanded in anger. Kiley glanced over her shoulder, her body beginning to shake, her arms tightening around herself. "Please. Please, I don't want to be here anymore!"

A deep, long, keening wail met their ears, and Ghila clenched her jaw as the smoke rolled closer, the wall so high and so dense in the endless sky that Ghila could not see where it began, nor if it ended. Tendrils reached for them, like hands, threatening to drag them into the darkness.

Ghila knew what this was…

What they faced was death, dark and eternal. Within that blanket of thick smoke was not a chance to pass on to a place of peaceful rest. No, what lay within was immutable pain for Kiley's soul. Within that place of dark smoke was hell.

"Kiley, you must tell me what they did to you in Bonemire."

The smoke pulsed, moving closer, curls of the stuff reaching like bony fingers.

Panic rose within Ghila, but she schooled her features, grasping the female's shoulders. "Quickly!"

Kiley's throat worked in a harsh swallow, "T-They tried to make m-my heart stronger… T-Tried to keep my humanity while also trying to… to… make me like *them*. Iron. They put it inside me. I-Iron. When it didn't work, they t-tried to take my heart. But I escaped before they could ruin me further." She groaned, shoulders curling inward. "P-Please… I want to die. But not in *there*."

Iron.

Ghila's heart sank to her toes.

There was no way to save her if iron caged her heart. It was an absolute miracle that Kiley lived at all. Perhaps the Gods had taken pity, perhaps they'd weaved Kiley's fate in order for them to meet.

Not for Ghila to save her, but for her to assist her in her passing.

Sometimes wounds could not be healed – a life couldn't be saved.

The mind was a powerful thing, Ghila knew that better than anyone. With a strong will and trained thought, one could deflect pain, so they could no longer feel it.

"Do you have family, Kiley?" Ghila's eyes shifted, watching death's advance. If she couldn't save her, she could prevent her death from being one that would cause her soul to never rest. "Think about them. The ones you love."

Kiley cried, fresh tears spilling down the grime on her cheeks. "They are all… gone. Dead. Gone."

Sympathy curled within Ghila, but so too did determination.

The smoke curled around their feet, loving as a killer's embrace. Ghila sucked in a breath, turning Kiley gently, so that it was Ghila's back that shielded her from the coming wall of darkness.

"Kiley, I need you to think of a happy memory, the best one that you can recall. Can you do that?"

"I don't know if… if I can."

She gripped Kiley's shoulders a little tighter, and the female recoiled, wincing. Ghila suppressed her own shudder at the cool touch of skin beneath her palms. She could see Kiley's eyes passing her, widening at the horror converging upon them. Ghila chanced giving her a little shake. "We can slow the darkness, but you need to try. Think of those who make you happy. You can do this."

Dark curls of smoke whispered over Ghila's shoulders, deathly cold fingers caressing the skin of her cheeks and neck with pins and needles, a reaper's kiss. It was upon them now, slowly swallowing them. The storm grew impossibly louder, the resounding boom rattling her bones.

Death was here to take a life, violently and painfully, but Ghila would not let the darkness win.

She was *done* allowing it to win.

The woman's eyes squeezed shut just as Ghila twisted, facing the darkness as the thunder reached a deafening pitch. Ghila used herself as a shield, unable to think of anything else. She thrust out her hands as if to halt death's advance, spearing them deep into the thick, acrid smog. Ghila gritted her teeth against the cold, so fierce and biting that she feared her skin would melt, the sensation so acute that her eyes squeezed closed. Pain lanced up her arms, seizing her body in a vice, and she cried out just as the world around them warped and snapped.

The pain dissipated, and Ghila's eyes fluttered open to skies of astonishing blue.

She fell forward, winded, breath rattling through her clenched teeth. Her palms grazed soft grass, so vivid and green that it took her a few more breaths to realise that they were no longer within the smoke, but in the middle of a sprawling field of wildflowers. Hills rolled into the distance, and from their place on a rise, she could see the peaks of snow-capped mountains towering in the far distance. Beyond that, dark smoke roiled like angry clouds, batting against an invisible barrier that kept it from tainting this peaceful retreat. Whether this was a memory, or something conjured up in a panic by Kiley, Ghila was not quite sure. But it was working, keeping her consciousness separated from the death shrouding her body.

Laughter found Ghila's ears, and as she righted herself and continued to gape, Kiley passed her side, her body no longer naked and wounded. A simple white dress covered her willowy form, a thin leather belt cinching her narrow waist, her hair dancing around her shoulders, free from blood and grime.

It took a few moments for the scene to register. The colour, the vibrance, the warmth, the sounds, and the two figures – one large, one small – together in the field. A child's laughter echoed in the air, and Ghila hadn't heard anything like that in as long as she could remember. It was… foreign, yet it made her chest constrict with an emotion that hardly visited her anymore.

Was it… happiness? Hope? Relief?

Kiley paused a few steps from her, hesitating. Then she turned back, meeting her stare with clear eyes.

They stood in silence, conveying through their eyes what words could not express.

Thank you.

Ghila's lips curled in a hesitant smile, watching as Kiley turned and descended the hill, heading for the man and child. They greeted her with smiles and embraces, including her in their games as if she had only been gone for a few minutes, while Ghila's intuition told her they had been apart for a long time.

That image, of a happy family, of one reunited and whole, remained behind her eyes as Ghila inhaled.

And let the female's consciousness go.

Her eyes opened to the infirmary once more.

Kiley's lips curled into a gentle smile as her last breath whispered through her lightly parted lips, her death as peaceful as a gentle tide escaping to the sea from a sun-kissed shore.

It took a few moments for Ghila's hold on the female's lifeless hand to loosen its vice-like grip, and for her breath to escape where it sat in her throat.

The silence in the room was deafening, but it did not bear weight upon her shoulders like she thought it would.

Murmured voices met her ears, and Ghila glanced up to see Freya, Noct, and the healers watching her with a mixture of expressions, but all were softer than before. The apothecaries no longer exuded an air of distrust, instead what she could see of their eyes looked soft, shining with grief... and relief.

"Kiley, she... she calmed. She stopped fighting." One of them said, moving to the side of the bed to check her pulse. "You helped her pass to the afterlife with peace in her damaged heart."

Unable to move, fingers still clasping ones which were quickly turning cold, Ghila cleared her throat but was still unable to speak. Freya's hands folded over her own, and Ghila's grey eyes tracked up to the Queen's face, to the depthless black eyes filled with stars.

She unsure of how to feel. Was she supposed to be sad?

She wasn't.

What she'd seen – Kiley being embraced by her family, enveloped by their love in her last moments, was something she wouldn't soon forget. She couldn't be sad after witnessing that. Ghila had been a shield, using her powers to stave off her pain, allowing Kiley a chance to pass on to her next life – one which Ghila knew contained her lost loved ones.

She hadn't saved her, no one could have done that, thanks to the iron in her chest. But she'd granted her a kindness that no one else could have, either.

A peaceful death. A compassionate death.

She could do this for many others, too.

This would be her purpose.

Sometime later, when Ghila returned to the party, Nocturne in tow, her eyes skirted across the floor in search of her brother. It felt as if something were awakening within her, a sleepy beast rising with a long yawn, a part of her that felt softer, gentler, protective, more *alive*. A guardian lying dormant until now.

She needed to tell him about what she'd seen, and what she'd *done*.

Ghila found Elijah exiting a walkway from the forest, fingers linked with Ariiaya, their voices low. Trailing in their wake was a man in polished rose armour – a guard from the western Prince's entourage, she assumed. Music hummed in the air, an upbeat tune that warred with the look on her brother's face. Upon seeing her, he headed her way.

"What… what's happened?" said Ghila.

"It's Lorch. He's been sentenced to death," he explained.

The guard spoke as he passed them, armour clinking. "Treason. He will meet with the noose tomorrow."

"Can the King even be sentenced to death without a trial?" asked Quinn, emerging from the party with Tikkani. The newlyweds pushed out from the crush of revellers to join them too. Ghila had a feeling, after observing the group, that there was a level of intuition between them. The fact that they gathered now, when there was alarming news, only endorsed that thought. The only ones missing were Nem and Krepth, she'd seen them together a little while ago, and Ghila guessed they wouldn't be far behind.

Despite being part of the circle as discussion quickly picked up, Ghila still felt like an outsider looking in. She remained silent, eyes skipping from Elijah to Ariiaya as the Fae spoke.

"Valdis has proven that he thinks he is exempt from all rules. He's going to kickstart this war by killing his own son." There was a note of pain carefully concealed within the growl of Arii's voice, one that Ghila analysed. Their gazes met, and Ghila didn't flinch. Had this come a few days before, she would have glanced away under the Fae's penetrating stare, but now she remained still. Arii seemed to care fervently for the young king, punctuated when she added, "I can't let that happen."

"You're going to Viridya?" Nocturne guessed, crossing his arms.

Arii's reply was a subtle narrow of her eyes as they moved to him. "I'll come with you."

Every set of eyes shifted to Ghila once the words were in the air, and rather than balk, she lifted her chin, the uneven bob of her hair wavering around her cheeks. She rubbed at her wrists, free of shackles, the absence of which she knew they'd all noticed. She swallowed and continued, keeping her voice even. "I've learned much about my gifts. I can use them to distract, I can use them to hinder, and I can use them to help aid those passing into death, if I cannot be of any further help than that. I may be weak of body, and have no outward magic, but I want to help. I *need* to help. If I am to make amends for what I have done, this is where I can start."

She didn't need to look at her brother to know he disapproved of the talk of returning to Viridya. It had been twenty years since she'd been there last, and she kept her thoughts from branching off into questions of how her home looked now. The voices in her head murmured, tugging at her concentration, but she ignored them.

Arii's eyes remained on her, as heavy as before, but there was a spark there. It gave her the confidence to continue.

"If I am to have a purpose, I want it to be to help those who are unable to help themselves. I want them to have the chance that I did not."

"Ghila aided one of the people returned from Bonemire using her gifts," Noct supplied. "The woman was beyond saving, in severe pain. Had it not been for Ghila, she would have passed while in a world of agony."

Arii's eyes assessed her with a new light.

Ghila held her gaze, placing every ounce of determination into her face, every ounce that sizzled inside of her. She needed this, this purpose.

"We will need you behind the front lines, helping those who need it." Arii nodded in confirmation of Ghila's words, but it was also as if she were accepting something unsaid, perhaps putting her bitterness behind.

Ghila took comfort in the Fae's acquiescence, placing it in the part of her mind where the happier memories of her life had begun to accumulate, like a special box of trinkets.

Finally, she met her brother's eyes, and in them she saw herself, saw the smile that had tugged at her lips without her knowledge. She hadn't known how much the Fury's approval had meant to her until that moment.

Elijah smiled at her, without hesitation, prompted by relief at Arii's words. The siblings shared a moment, before Elijah's eyes roved back to Arii, expression a mixture of worry and pride. Her brother really cared for her, she'd seen this in his mind, and in his expression when he thought no one was looking. Ghila hadn't seen her brother wear such an open look before, he'd always been the guarded, quiet brother, one who kept his emotions close to his chest. Brohem had been far louder, and far more open with his emotions.

Ghila struggled to recall what she'd been like herself, had she been open with her emotions, too? Or had she been a little more hesitant to show her cards, keeping them close?

She decided that how she'd once been no longer mattered. She'd spent too using them only to inflict pain on those who had wronged her, or to those directed under the orders of the Fates.

Ghila's small smile widened to a grin, and it felt… good.

She had purpose after all.

CHAPTER TWENTY-SIX

CELADINE

Images flashed behind her closed eyes as Celadine curled around the sleeping form of her daughter, her face twisting in sleep.

Lorch's deep blue eyes, gazing down at her as he took a breath through their fervent kisses, his lips lightly swollen, his cheeks flushed pink.

A noose, swinging on a deathly cold breeze.

Flashes of light, fingers tipped in talons as they curved around the rim of a crackling void of light in the sky.

An eye, red as blood, and glowing with ancient malice.

A serpent curved in a figure eight.

Golden walls, rivulets of red cascading down them like miniature waterfalls.

Blood.

Blood.

Blood.

A scream cut from her throat, startling her awake as the world snapped so swiftly into focus that she felt nauseous.

Mia's little arms were around her, the curls of her hair pressing against Cela's face. She trembled, yet her hold was firm, her embrace bringing Celadine quickly back to her centre, drawing her from the terror of her prophetic nightmares. She kissed her daughter's hair, shaking, carefully peeling the girl back.

"I'm alright," she whispered, cupping her cheeks, meeting her large round eyes. "I'm alright," she repeated, before signing the words, as if she needed to hear them in a loop until they were true.

It had taken her so long to find sleep after Lorch had been taken away, her fear for him keeping her from finding rest. She'd wanted to burst from the closet and rip him from the clutches of the guards, but there had been more of them than she'd thought as she'd peered through the slither of space between the doors. Lorch went willingly, his hands in the air, bare back lit from the fireplace. His father had thrown a cloak at him with a look of disgust, and as he was towed away by men in red, Lorch had thrown one glance over his shoulder, a glance that had somehow found hers through the crack.

'Don't you dare move.'

So, she'd waited, fingers curling to fists, heart thundering in her chest, as the copper-haired king disappeared, the thump of boots soon giving way to startling silence. Only when she was sure they were gone did she emerge from the closet, her throat bone-dry and nose twitching at the lingering taint in the air.

Lorch.

He'd been discovered, despite the care in which he had taken to get to them every night. Gods… she'd been so stupid. Of course, the absence of the King would be noticed, even during the dead of night. Of course, he would have been followed, a presence watching his every move day and night. She'd let her guard down, so had he, and now he was going to pay for it… with his life.

Cela knew then that the noose she'd seen in her vision was one tied for him. His discovery was about to set in motion the events she'd witnessed in her nightmares, she knew this down in the marrow of her bones.

Mia stared at her for a time, her face changing to one of resolve, her little jaw jutting forward in a look very like her late father. She twirled her fingers and thumped her fist against her chest, and Cela swallowed back a lump of pure, proud emotion.

'We have to save him, mother.'

Never before had Celadine tried to alter fate, and because of that, she'd lost so much. Friends… family… Mia's father. She'd seen things before they'd happened yet had never done anything to prevent them. She was tired of waiting for things to get better, tired of moving in the shadows, preparing for things to change, fearing what was to come.

"Stay here, tell your grandfather that I'm going to the castle. Tell him to prepare for war." Cela clutched her daughter's shoulders, "Tell him that time has run out. We cannot wait any longer."

Mia shook her head, her curls whipping around her face. "No!" she said, blinking back fierce tears. She didn't know what her mother had seen, but she knew this look on Cela's face from countless times before. Bad things happened when she looked like that, like a deadly storm were coming, and they needed to seek shelter. They lived in a world of danger, and Cela hadn't seen any point in veiling anything from her daughter, especially not her visions. Everything she'd seen in the past had come true, and she had no doubt about these ones too.

"I come with you," her daughter said, making her heart clench. She then signed, hand movements bold, brokering no argument.

Who was she to deny her daughter the same attempt at weaving fate? Perhaps they could present themselves as they would any other day, arriving at the castle to carry out another normal day of healing duties. Then, once they had Lorch, Mia could unhook the latches that kept the gates locked, allowing their resistance to finally strike, while the majority of Valdis' forces were gathered elsewhere in preparation for the war southwards. She'd heard whispers that they were mobilising, masses of forces traveling to the East by night.

She had to at least try to change Lorch's fate, not only for him, but for herself and her daughter too.

Cela was sure that, given more time, she could love him. Perhaps she already did.

And there was no way she would allow him to take the fall for them.

ARIIAYA

Arii made quick work of saddling a tawny brown mare, rubbing its snout as the beast's flanks shuddered with anticipation. She had considered riding bareback to save time, but the thing about her newly acquired bond meant that her anxiety and her intentions were no longer something she could keep masked. Elijah had sensed the moment well before their group had dispersed, bypassing the thick of the party and heading straight to the vine-covered stables. He'd sensed her panic at the news Roarke had brought about Lorch.

Now Elijah stood like a weighted shadow over her shoulder, arms folded over his broad chest, dark hair still faintly damp from their time in the pool. It was swept back in that way she liked, so damned distracting.

So, to keep herself on track, she busied herself with readying her horse, while trying to ignore the thrum of his disapproval through the bond. When she could take no more, she turned to him, chin lifting in challenge. "I can get there quickly, and I'll get him out. I'm the only one who can, and you know it."

His mouth parted to speak, and she felt a spark of something down their bond. It was… so strange, yet it felt right. A piece that had been missing until now.

She held up a hand. "And no, you can't come with me. You're needed here, to prepare to move against Viridya."

Elijah pinched the bridge of his nose. "I know, but… I can't just let you…" He seemed to struggle with his words, with a weight that she too felt upon her back. Smoothing a hand over the flank of her horse, Arii drew breath, hating his torn look.

She moved to him and took his face in her hands, leaning up on the tips of her toes to stare into his eyes. But before she could speak, he said, "I can't let my mate go into the heart of the enemy stronghold without me. The thought of you in danger, even though I know you are more than capable of holding your own..." His eyes closed, hands encircling her waist. "It *kills* me inside, Arii. It's like telling my instincts to turn off, it's like..."

"Like letting a piece of your heart go into the unknown..." she finished, smiling sadly as his grey eyes flicked open. "I know. That's what happens when you find your fated mate. I feel it too. I don't want to go, Elijah, not really. But I *must*."

"How can I let you go, when I just truly found you?" he whispered, dredging up a feeling of sorrow in her chest. Instead of telling him with words that Fate had drawn them together, and that Fate wouldn't allow them to part, not truly, Arii kissed him, placing her feelings into it and allowing their bond to send the message that words couldn't quite explain.

"I love you," she murmured against him, as he held her close. There was nothing but them in that moment, the world around them muting to shadows.

She wouldn't allow herself to think of this as a final goodbye. She was too stubborn for that, far too possessive. The feelings thundering down the bond at her words told her that Elijah was perhaps far more dominating than even her.

"You're my desire, my passion, my fire, my home. No matter what happens tomorrow, I'll find you, Ariiaya."

She shivered, sweet memories of their joining causing her limbs to turn languid with heat, the growl in his voice filling her with hot desire. Gods, she would never get enough of this, his whispers, the strength in the way he held her, the way he said her name, the way he professed his love in words – something she knew she was not very good at.

"I love you too, my fated mate."

"Fated mate?" came a voice from behind them.

Both turned to see Nem and Krepth in a halo of moonlight at the stable door. Her best friend's eyes were bright as Nem approached. "I'm glad to see that our theories were correct."

Arii peeked up at Elijah, as his eyebrows quirked. "Theories?" He repeated, a note of amusement in his voice.

Arii pursed her lips but didn't respond.

Nem continued. "I knew you two were up to something –" Arii was about to complain about invasive bonds when Nem raised a hand and added swiftly "–when our life bond suddenly disappeared."

Wait, what?

Arii blinked, realising that all she felt now was the mating bond with Elijah. There was nothing else beyond that, no subtle presence of her best friend, no lingering of the feeling that she'd shared with Nem.

Arii stared down at her hands, unsure why her gaze went there, perhaps thinking of the moment she grasped hold of the thread sprouting from Nem's dying body. The moment she'd saved her. "Our bond is gone? Just like that?"

Nem shrugged, but Arii could tell that she was uncomfortable. Perhaps adjusting to the silence. "I suppose so. I guess that's another way to sever a life bond, if one of us finds our mate."

The four of them stood for a moment, coming to terms with the change. Krepth rocked on his heels, turning to the horse, who huffed and swished its tail in agitation.

Nem was first to speak. "I wish you could feel how happy I am for you both." Her lips curled in a rare smile, one Arii sadly returned. As annoying as the bond was at times, Arii had grown used to the solid presence of her best friend. Knowing she was there, no matter where they went. Nem pulled her into an embrace, one that left Arii lost for words. Then, the silver-haired Fae brought her mate in for a hug too, her slight form reaching up to fold her arms around his neck. He hesitantly hugged her back, the embrace spanning only a breath, before Nem stepped away.

"We are *both* happy for you," she added, casting a look at the dark-haired Shifter.

Krepth passed judgement over the horse's saddling, making sure the beast was ready for a swift ride. Then he straightened to face Elijah, his expression unreadable. Arii felt an odd sort of panic stir at his look, even though she was anything but ashamed of her discovery, perhaps only a little unsure of how it all truly worked. She'd heard of males acting… aggressively around other males after the first time bedding their mate.

So far, Elijah looked to be in control, if not a little unsure himself.

Krepth paused before him to scan the future king's face up and down with an expression that screamed of a brother's protectiveness. "So, you're fated mates, hmm? Don't suppose you'll pop the question at some point, should we survive the coming war?"

Arii stared at the Shifter in shock.

Nem dramatically rolled her eyes.

Elijah's stare did not falter. "After I'm crowned, I won't merely propose… I'll make her my Queen."

My Queen.

The words sent a mixture of surprise and satisfaction zinging down Arii's spine.

Krepth laughed, deep and gentle, slapping a hand on Elijah's shoulder. "Fantastic answer!" His canines glinted as he grinned widely. Arii could see Elijah was fighting back a smile, the skin around his eyes creasing.

During their little man-to-man speech, Nem had quietly retrieved two more horses from the stalls. Arii didn't need a bond to know that Nem intended to come with her, Krepth too. She wanted to be difficult, to tell them to remain here, but her plan of traipsing into Viridya in the hopes of rescuing Lorch from death by noose was already loaded with uncertainty. They would provide ideal backup.

Arii, Nem and Krepth mounted their horses, Elijah placed a hand on Arii's leg, his warmth seeping through to her skin.

"I won't say be careful, because we all know that there is no care where you're going. So, instead, I'm going to ask you to come back to me, no matter what." Their gazes held, and Elijah whispered, low and fierce, "Get him, then get yourselves out."

Lorch.

Arii leaned down, tangling her fingers at the nape of his neck, pulling his lips to hers. She placed all of her unsaid words, her love, her fear, all that was within her, all that he had awakened in her, into the kiss, whispering against his mouth, "Look for me on the battlefield, I'll be the one cloaked in blue."

LORCH

The rope of the noose chafed his neck, leaving it red and raw, as if a thorny crown had slipped down to cut off his breath. Lorch's hands moved behind his back, bound so tight that his fingers had begun to turn numb, but that didn't dissuade him from trying to wriggle them loose.

He knew he wouldn't be able to set himself free, but he had to do something under the small sea of eyes that had gathered in the town square to watch his execution, called here by the bell chiming from the upmost towers, and the town crier who usually stood here to spout the end of days or upcoming performances at the local theatre.

He should have known he'd be discovered. He should have taken more care moving through the shadows at night, but it wasn't himself that he feared for. This was far beyond himself now. He just hoped they'd left Cela and Mia alone, as well as the other Fae hiding in the tavern.

He was alone on the elevated stage, leading him to believe they hadn't bothered to apprehend anyone else. He shot a small prayer of thanks to the Gods, because surely it had been divine intervention.

Time was running out, not just for him, but for the entire resistance. For the entire land.

Lorch hadn't spilled any information, even when his father's face hovered inches from his own, eyeing the blooming purple bruise he'd inflicted on his son's jaw. Lorch could see the anger, the revulsion, rolling from his shoulders in waves while his face remained impassive save for the twitch in his left eye.

He wouldn't give them away, no matter the pain inflicted upon his body or his mind. He'd spent years fixing a mask to cover what others saw, one that remained even under immense pressure. Lucky for him, his father, despite the acidity of his disposition towards the Fae, did not press as hard as he might have. Perhaps he was holding back because somewhere in his cruel heart, he still loved his son.

Lorch's eyes coasted the outer of the square, his throat working against the rope. Guards were lacking, only a few handfuls of men in red and gold, not enough to stave off a potential rescue attempt.

He hoped Cela wouldn't be reckless enough to come for him. He hoped she'd remain with her father, planning their next course of action from the information he'd given them.

Valdis leaned in, his wickedly cruel smile half in shadow. "They're here, your new little Fae slut and her daughter. They presented themselves at the castle doors under the guise of performing their usual apothecary duties, but I know better. I know the healer is the one you have been meeting, the one you'd throw away your crown for. The one you'd betray *me* for."

Dread whirled in Lorch's stomach, making him feel sick.

"I allowed them entry, to resume under the false pretence that I do not know who they are, and that they are here for you. It's no matter though, because I'm sure word of this little spectacle has reached the pointed ears of the one I truly wish to draw out of hiding."

Lorch jerked forward, and his father let out a laugh. "Once the false Prince hears that your neck is headed for the noose, he will come. You have far too much history for him not to. You considered yourself brothers once."

"I killed his nursemaid, the woman he considered as his mother. He hates me." Lorch spat, the words coating his tongue in venom. Had his father forgotten what he had done? The order he had given, the one Lorch had been regretting ever since?

Part of his siding with the resistance was because of his actions that day, the violence of his decision. In a small way he hoped, in aiding others of Elijah's kind, some of the blackness on his soul would perhaps one day ease, or perhaps, if they lived to see the end of this war, Elijah may forgive him. Perhaps they'd *all* forgive him.

If not, at least he knew in his heart he'd tried.

His father's head tilted slightly, revealing the side of his neck. Something glittered on his skin, barely visible in the dull light, but Lorch saw it. At first, he believed it to be the chain holding the amulet of cursed magic, the thing Valdis used to control his beasts. But as his father continued to speak, Lorch found his gaze fixated on the odd glitter. He blinked twice before finally realising what it was.

Tiny crystal smatterings covered areas of Valdis' skin, like microscopic structures forming between rocks underground. The skin around them appeared raw and furious, odd sores festering like a newly-emerging rash around miniature clusters of amethyst breaking through his skin.

Amethyst just like the stone housed in the amulet, the one his father never parted with.

The magic was affecting his body like a poison. Was that even possible?

"You'd really kill your own son in the hopes that you may spark the beginning of the war you know is already coming?" Lorch growled, dismay coating his words. Was he really so expendable?

Then, Lorch stopped, his father's earlier words popping back into his mind as the man stepped back, the curl of his lips never easing.

Spectacle…

Lorch's eyes darted over the crowd again, to the undulating sea of risen hands and thunderous words. To the town crier who began the chanting, and to the people who parroted him. To the amassing force of red capes and golden armour of the guards as they began to multiply, rimming the town square in red. To the shiver racing down the middle of the crowd, like a disturbance churning through water, heading towards the stage.

Traitor, traitor, traitor.

The noose never tightened further, nor did the creaking door at his feet fold in. He kept expecting it to, staring down again at the weathered, blood-stained wood beneath him.

Then he realised that the door wasn't going to open. He wasn't going to die, not now and not yet. For behind his father's stone façade – he loved his son, perhaps more than anything else.

Lorch was his weakness, a vulnerability that his father wasn't willing to admit.

Valdis sent him one last look, before exiting the stage with a flutter of his cape, the overcast sky rolling with angry dark clouds in his wake.

Cloaks of red continued to rim the outskirts of the crowd, preceded with the stench of decay.

Someone swore, bodies toppled, and a woman broke from the crowd. The face he saw, twisted in fury, was not the one he was expecting.

No no *no*.

His father had set a trap.

As Celadine raced for the stage, knife in hand, so too did the guards.

"It's a trap!" he cried, but it was too late. Cloaks of red converged upon her from all sides. Panicked, Lorch thrust forward, forgetting the noose. The binds slammed against his windpipe and he choked, flailing backward on unsteady feet, righting himself just in time.

Below Cela clashed with five guards, shockingly all human, as the crowd fled in a mad rush of fear. He thanked the Gods that she was Fae, which meant she was faster than them, giving her a small chance at surviving.

One guard dropped his sword as her blade sliced through his bicep. Celadine set herself upon another, savagely driving her blade into the space between the soldier's helmet and his pauldron, until his blood gushed onto the cobblestones.

Lorch called her name again, but his bellow was lost in the battle. Cela was swift, but she was outnumbered.

She rolled, springing to her feet, continuing her dash towards him, soldiers diving in her wake. Their gazes met, just as two soldiers grabbed her arms and jerked her backwards.

A sound of rage escaped her, the sound mirroring his panic and frustration. As Cela struggled, Lorch chanced a look over the scattering crowd, hoping desperately she hadn't been foolish enough to come without backup. Thankfully, Mia was nowhere in sight, but he couldn't see anyone else in the chaos, no one but the woman struggling under the hands of four soldiers as she was forced to her knees before the hangman's stage.

No, no, how could she be so foolish?

How had *he* been so foolish, to let his guard down, allow her to grow close, knowing that the possibility of being caught in some sort of crossfire was inevitable? He was a king, one who had done a shocking job, one on the brink of war with three other courts, and he'd allowed his heart to open to her none the less. He should have been more careful, more detached, easing pawns into place while keeping his hands behind his back. Now she would suffer for a cause he didn't think was worth it.

His life wasn't worth *hers*.

"No, Cela!" he cried, his heart a ferocious thing thundering as their eyes met again. Her hair was unbound, a wild tangle of brown curls plastering her red cheeks, her fangs bared in a wild grimace. She wasn't a fighter. She was a healer – someone who eased hurts, not created them.

A fifth soldier plus a small army of undead joined the scene until Celadine, in her moss green and white apothecary garb, was a speck in a sea of red, a green thorn in an angry red wound.

A soldier lifted a sword above his head.

Then from the skies above, a tawny and white hawk arrowed down, claws colliding with the sword wielder's eyes, tearing them to jelly and ribbons, as either side of him the undead collapsed, heads lolling, hanging upon fleshy threads from their shoulders with a slash of thrown steel.

There was a moment of silent, shocked panic, and through the flap of the hawk's wings Lorch spied three hooded figures standing in the centre of the square.

The one in the middle had their hands poised in the air – the one to throw the blades, purple stones in their silver hilts.

Their hands rose to pull back their hood, and he wasn't sure if it was elation or fear that hit his heart first, as Ariiaya's wide smirk revealed the full glory of her fangs, purple eyes alight with the promise of violence.

"Looks like I'm just in time for the show. Too bad it's about to be cancelled."

CHAPTER TWENTY-SEVEN

ARIIAYA

Ariiaya's fingertips tingled at the promise of conflict, her tongue darting across her teeth as her eyes took in the small sea of red cloaks before her. The clop of boots – many of them – echoed from beyond the square, and she knew they had barely a moment before the enemy's backup arrived. With the thunder of boots came the moans and manic scraping of inhuman movement. Their cries had her heart kicking up a notch. Undead were coming, and *a lot* of them.

"Get him, then get out," said Krepth, repeating Elijah's words as if she needed reminding. He was beside her, eyes glowing with building magic. Nem took up her other flank, drawing her blades, face fixed in concentration.

Get Lorch, then get out. She didn't need to be told a third time. She didn't wish to be here in the heart of enemy territory for any longer than needed– nor did she wish to be separated from Elijah for any longer than necessary.

The shock of the trio's sudden appearance faded, and soldiers sprang towards them, drawing their swords, leaving the struggling female healer on the ground.

Whipping a second pair of daggers from her boots, Arii sprang forward to meet them. The one to her right swung first, and she deflected his strike with a swift skid of steel and a dip of her shoulder, coasting around his manic attack to slam the hilt of her weapon into his uncovered face. The soldier's haste to meet her in combat left him woefully unprotected, at mercy to her weapons and Fae strength.

There was a crunch of bone as she ruined his nose, before flipping her dagger back to the pointy end, jabbing it savagely into his throat. The man gurgled as she jerked the blade free, blood spurting like a fountain over another soldier as he blindly slashed at her head with a wild yell.

She ducked, sidestepped, grasped the man's sword arm and wrenched upwards. A sickening pop heralded the breaking of his limb, his strangled cry like a bell to her ears, before she drew her blade across the slit in his helmet. He collapsed in a heap, the clang of his weapon and armour as loud as a gong. As Arii watched, he writhed, clawing at his face with his undamaged hand. She could have pitied him, a throwaway piece in a power game, but sympathy was a waste of time in battle.

A sense of peace and detachment took hold, her emotions withdrawing to a familiar place formed from years of training. With Krepth and Nem covering her flanks, they dispatched the soldiers quickly as fearful townspeople fled or hid, watching from behind carts and stalls.

Arii scrambled up onto the hangman's deck, ignoring Lorch's manic protests as she sheared her blade through his noose.

"What are you *doing* here?" He yanked the rope from his neck and tossed it as he continued his tirade in disbelief. "After everything I've done, you came to save *me*? Is Elijah here too?"

Arii scoffed, manacling his wrist with one hand, tugging him towards the stairs. "You'd know if he was here. We can talk about what you've done later. We need to leave!"

The woman in healer's robes followed beside him, Lorch reaching out his free hand to her face, as if checking for wounds. The healer scanned him in return, intelligent eyes the colour of jade. Arii witnessed the exchange with an odd sense of detachment. She expected her emotions to crackle and ignite, but instead she felt calm wash over her. The feelings she once had for Lorch were still there, but they had morphed into something muted, different. Perhaps before she would have felt something akin to jealousy, but now – as Lorch's face moved to a look of pure relief – she knew she wasn't the only one who had changed.

"Mia is in the castle," said the woman, and Lorch swore.

"We're going to have a whole lot more company in a matter of minutes, I suggest we go now." Krepth shot over his shoulder, as he and Nem joined them on the platform as they finished off the last guard, his red cape fanning across the stones to join the blood.

Above their heads, angry grey clouds began to spin. It was subtle at first, the sound of whirring and snapping drawing their attention up. A feeling of anticipation and dread filled Arii, for the sound was familiar – yet far louder and *larger* than before.

A wind picked up, dragging at her hair as she turned to Lorch once more. His expression was pained, fixed on the healer. "Cela, I–"

"I'm going back for her," the woman said, and Arii could see her hands shake. Whoever this Mia was, she meant a great deal to the apothecary. From the look on Lorch's face, she meant a great deal to him, too.

The hawk circled overhead, cawing madly. Arii shot Quinn a quick look. She didn't need to be reminded of the mounting danger heading their way. He squawked in protest, but with an impatient signal from Arii, he darted into the cloudy skies and out of sight. He needed to warn the others of the strange movement in the air above them, and fast.

An animal scream ripped through the air as the first of the undead soldiers entered the town square.

"Arii," cautioned Nem, readying her blood-flecked blades.

Lorch took the woman's face in his hands, drawing her in for a fierce kiss. The wind swept her hair back, revealing pointed ears. The Fae woman grasped Lorch with equal intensity as he said, "Go get her. You'll be faster on your own. Sneak out, I'll find you again."

The Fae female, Cela, nodded. Her jade eyes were wide with worry, and they finally met Arii's curious, cautious stare.

"Protect him, Fury," she said, her words calm but wobbly.

Arii nodded silently, hearing the emotion there.

With one last long look at Lorch, Cela spun, leapt from the platform and sprinted towards the stone arches that led to the main gates of the castle.

Arii handed one of her daggers to Lorch, who hesitantly took it. "Stay behind us. We'll fight our way east, take the back streets to the canal stairs and take a boat out of here. Let's hope these bastards can't swim."

"But the depths are frozen," said Lorch, and Arii cursed. Of course, how had she forgotten? She'd seen the desolate icefield on her way to the castle, but she'd been so focused on making it to Lorch on time that she hadn't paid it much mind.

"Guess we leg it across the ice, then. Elijah is amassing the army nearby, once we reach him, you'll be safe."

Lorch nodded, but Arii could see his mind was elsewhere, his blue eyes glazed with worry. It clawed deep that she hadn't seen him smile in so long. He did look better than when she'd last seen him, though. Astride his warhorse, his eyes devoid of light, skin sallow, hair limp as he curled his lip at the man who had once been his bodyguard and the woman who had been his lover. Now, some of his spark was back, possibly due to Cela.

The remainder of the townsfolk fled the square as it was swamped with undead pouring in like a crimson dam breaking. They scrambled over one another, teeth snapping, eyes like streaking blue lights of violence. A few townspeople too slow to flee were set upon with such violence that she heard Krepth gasp a curse.

Arii knew they'd been let loose with no other order than to annihilate. There was no rhyme or reason to their movements, no practiced formations, no planning. They charged like bloodthirsty rats, some on all fours, some with nothing to fight with but their bony, clawed hands. The sight reminded Arii of their clash in the graveyard weeks ago, except these soldiers were armoured for combat, a strange thing. Why clothe the undead in armour? Was it to keep the conflict going for as long as possible?

There was a sound behind them, like little explosions coming from the castle.

Had the war begun already? She hoped not, at least not before she could charge head on beside Elijah.

She could hear the sharp inhale by Lorch behind her, and the thunder of his heart that matched her own, as her senses were overcome by *them*. Death, decay, and horrible, inhuman wails. Arii, Nem and Krepth formed a triangle flank around Lorch, leaving the hangman's platform at their backs, charging towards the wave of oncoming threat.

The front of the line met them with wild, slashing claws, steel and teeth. Nem took out the first, crossing her knives and lopping off the creature's head as it reached for her face with flailing, cracked nailed hands. Her palm snapped forward, blasting a punch of magic into the mass, blowing bodies back as their enraged shrieks tore the air. Krepth fought with a growl akin to his animal side, kicking, punching and lopping limbs with his short sword as some flooded around behind them, charging for their flanks.

The undead continued to come.

They were fast being overwhelmed, even with three Fae fighting as quickly and as savagely as they could. Panic made Arii's arms swifter, but her movements were no longer pre-empted. She slashed and stabbed with as much mindlessness as the madness around them, as did her friends.

The narrow street, their destination, loomed ahead, but it felt like they were no longer drawing near. The mass of bodies began to pile around them, and Arii realised suddenly that she may have gravely overestimated herself. She'd overestimated everything. She'd doomed them, doomed herself, her friends, Lorch… She'd failed them.

She'd failed *him*.

Elijah's rugged face shuddered before her eyes, silver eyes narrowed. A look she'd seen when she began to lose hope or felt the darkness of her past rear its ugly head.

But he wasn't here. They were apart, something she'd sworn that when they re-united, they never would be again. When they'd made love and sealed their bond under the moonlight, magic swirling, she'd never felt so empowered, so *whole*. So wildly full of *hope*.

She'd been a fool to think she could do this.

Fingers yanked at her hair and clothing, threatening to tear her apart. She heard Lorch's frightened cry, Krepth's smattering of curses and Nem's yell of anger as they were pressed together, the lack of space growing dire.

Her beast yowled too, overwhelmed, her vision seeing nothing but red, red, *red*.

She screamed with rage and frustration, and longing.

Suddenly, like a dormant volcano, fire ignited in her chest, heating her bones from the marrow out.

Magic; pure, fiery magic.

His magic.

She saw an image of Elijah's lips in a smile that promised she could do this, blue magic ringing his irises. She felt the ghost touch of his hands passing over her skin, the strength, the *love*, filling her with power. Though he wasn't nearby, they were connected, forever and always. He believed in her enough to send her on this assignment because he knew she could do it, and her friends believed in her enough to follow her into the heart of the mayhem.

Their mating link seemed to have additional benefits. His borrowed power filled her with crackling energy, almost too much, and her frustrated scream changed into one of furious joy.

Krepth and Nem sensed the change, grabbing at Lorch's tunic, shielding him with their bodies as time seemed to slow.

Arii threw her arms out, fingers splayed, palms out, and the bodies between them and their escape were swallowed by a torrent of raging fire. Her boots skidded back an inch as she braced against the sheer power of the magic. Her arms shook, the heat lashing from her palms like wildfire warped with electricity, a combination of chaos she'd never witnessed before. Twines of golden thread spun up and around her arms, as if the Gods themselves aided her. The undead just out of the firing line had enough sense to scramble out of the way, and when the inferno fizzled and the charred remains of their colleagues littered the cobblestones, they hesitated enough for Arii and her friends to charge ahead.

They raced down the street, undead snapping at their heels, clawing at their clothing. Nem threw a punch of magic at a nearby cart, sending it and its contents of barrels into the path of their pursuers.

Glass shattered suddenly from the nearby buildings, falling over them like violent rain as shadows descended from above.

"The resistance!" bellowed Krepth as they ran.

Magic doused the air as five cloaked figures lifted their arms to throw up a barricade against the wailing hordes, temporarily barring their way into the street.

It would not last long, Arii knew that, but relief hit her like a punch to the stomach. Her legs wobbled and she sucked in air as if starved of it. How Elijah walked around with such power, she'd never truly know. It must be maddening.

A man approached from a nearby home, ash and dust speckling his dark beard and close-cropped brown hair.

"Yarn!" Lorch cried, his voice heavy with relief and perhaps a speck of dread.

"That won't hold them long," Yarn said, casting a stern gaze over them as if looking for someone. "Where is she?"

Lorch stepped forward, chin raised. "Cela went back into the castle for Mia."

Yarn swore. "Little lass is as stubborn as her father, plus a good helping from her mother."

"I'll find them both," swore Lorch with a sincerity that Arii believed.

Yarn thumped a hand on Lorch's shoulder, and Lorch managed not to wobble, though Arii saw him wince.

"My daughter and granddaughter know this place like the backs of their hands, but so do you, I'll wager. You're needed with the resistance outside the gates." The Fae male laughed gruffly. "Thanks to your information, we were able to bar the majority of exits from the castle grounds to the city, keeping most of Valdis' army at bay. It won't keep them long, but they seem to have their attention set upon the castle, like they're awaiting an order."

Arii's blood cooled. They were awaiting the order to unleash themselves upon the forces amassing from the east. The force with Elijah at its head.

"Go, we'll begin evacuating the city. Something is awakening in the skies above," Yarn called, throwing Lorch a meaningful look as they dispersed and continued their retreat towards the far east wall.

They approached a junction, and suddenly Lorch threw himself to the left.

"Wait! That's the wrong way!" Arii yelled, grabbing at his shirt, her limbs still shaking from expending magic. Lorch spun to face her, his face ashen and speckled with blood. His expression held such seriousness that Arii drew up short.

"I have to find Cela. I can't leave her here to be found by those things. I've been a fool for so long, I allowed things to manifest beyond control, and it's only a matter of time before my father loses his grip on all this," he threw his arms out, "all of the chaos he's created. He's delved too deep into magic not of this world, tainted and evil."

Ari opened her mouth to reply, to tell him to shut up and follow them, but his eyes held a flare of something she hadn't seen before – and it made her halt.

"I've been a terrible king, a dreadful human being, an abhorrent friend and an even more awful brother. I have to atone for my mistakes. Helping the resistance was the start. Now I have a Fae healer and her daughter who returned to save me and put themselves in grave danger. They're my priority. Nothing else matters to me."

Arii swallowed and nodded. She would do the same if the roles were reversed, and Elijah – or any of her friends – were in Cela's position.

She steeled her spine. "I'll come with you."

"No, you have to help them evacuate–" Lorch began.

Nem rested her hand on Lorch's arm. Even though they were no longer connected, Arii could see the emotion in her friend's aqua eyes. "We will help evacuate the town. You have a better chance finding the healer with Arii by your side."

Lorch nodded, relief softening his features.

Arii glanced at Nem and Krepth and saw their hands were linked. Her heart squeezed.

There wasn't time for goodbyes.

She would see them again, because to die here was not their fate. She was sure of that.

She twisted to Lorch and said, "Let's go save your healer."

CHAPTER TWENTY-EIGHT

ELIJAH

The earth beneath his feet was solid yet he could not shake the feeling of unsteadiness. Mere months ago, the very place where Elijah now stood had been the centre of the Sapphire Depths which surrounded the castle of Viridya. The corrupt magic had spread from the golden castle, coating the adjoining city and lake in a strange substance, like crystal, so black that it reflected the darkening afternoon sky above. A shudder beneath his feet drew his attention downwards, and he saw whirling dark torrents of water beneath the cracked, obsidian ice. The lake was still active and thoughts of the dark depths below them, alive and raging, caused Elijah to shiver.

As they marched upon his family home, Elijah noticed the foliage closest to the shoreline was also coated in the stuff, frozen in time. He shivered with reckless anticipation, the thrum of his heartbeat a steady tempo within his chest. Part of it was a shadow from his bond with Arii, whose emotions nestled in a corner of his mind. He could feel her now, ahead in the city somewhere. He'd given her his magic when those emotions had become overwhelmed with dread. If he could feel her, sense her life force, he knew she was alive.

Lending his magic to her was as easy as handing over a shimmering parcel, one which throbbed like a ticking time bomb. He knew she could handle it, though. She'd been made his fated mate for a reason – she was an extension of him, and he of her.

A cooler than average breeze pushed hair into his eyes, his expression remaining impassive. He looked to the sky, where a speck was approaching fast. A hawk landed on the ice, and with a flash of light, Quinn shifted mid-landing, continuing to cover the space at a swift jog, his hasty breaths puffing mist before his red-cheeked face.

"Arii has Lorch, they're making their way to the eastern wall where they'll escape down to the canals; and the resistance has emerged. They're evacuating the city."

The news was welcome, but Elijah knew they were far from resting yet. "Thank you, Quinn."

When they had arrived at the black frozen lake, he had made the decision to continue across, instead of storming the castle via its two bridged entries. He knew there were innocent people still in the city, and he wanted to give them the chance to flee. He wanted Arii to have as few as possible obstacles escaping the castle, too. In truth, Elijah had no desire to storm the city. He hoped that if Valdis saw the army massing against him, perhaps the man would find a tiny semblance of sanity within the dark shroud of his mind to pause and have a conversation – before any bloodshed could begin.

That was his hope, but he did not hold onto it as fiercely as he had once.

Try as he might, he could not shake the want… no, the *need*, to avenge all who had been scarred by Valdis' tyrannical reign. His family, Ghila, Colleen, the countless others living without loved ones, existing under prejudice and fear. The torture of Arii.

For Lorch, who had been deprived of the life he truly deserved.

Fae and human alike had suffered for years, and Elijah couldn't allow it to go on any longer.

Boots, claws and paws crunched over the cracked ice in his wake as Elijah glanced back at the disappearing shoreline, then to the sky beyond. Clouds were scattered thinly over a tangerine and navy sky, but as his eyes tracked towards Viridya, those clouds began to darken and twist into a colossal tornado of grey and red above the city.

As he watched in horror, the ominous swirl cracked open to reveal a sizzling, cracking void, a yawning portal so large that it began to take up the entire sky over Viridya. The ring of ancient magic was growing rapidly, the tips of the clouds sucking into the hole like a huge drain.

"It's happening, just like he said," Roarke voiced from his left, eyeing the growing void with apprehension. Shortly after Arii, Nem and Krepth had left for Viridya, Elijah and the rulers of the courts all met to decide their next move. Elijah had introduced Ouroboros, watching the widening, awe filled eyes of the usually very composed rulers. All except for Kadec, who'd greeted the tall man as if they were friends reunited after years apart. It made sense, Elijah had learned, shortly before his trial at the Western Court, that Kadec and his family line were Gatekeepers, people who had helped the dragons move through the portals to another realm for their own safety. They'd also discovered that Ouro possessed not only the ability to shift into a dragon, but also the gift of prophetic foresight. He'd seen the voids opening above the city in a dream only a few days past.

"This land will tremble under the might of a terror far greater than Valdis and his undead puppets if we don't get that portal closed fast," said Kadec, flanking Elijah's opposite side. "What lies within that void is something ancient, something *primal*."

"Brilliant," whispered Luc, voice dripping with sarcasm, Emerson close by his side. "I hope Arii is alright."

Through their mating bond, Elijah could feel the comforting presence of Arii's consciousness – flickering like a gentle flame. She was no longer manic but he wanted her out of the city before whatever further madness brewing there was unleashed. Her *and* Lorch.

Elijah still held anger towards Lorch, but it was dampening with each day. He understood the acidic influence of the man forcing him. It didn't dampen the heartbreak of losing Colleen, but he knew she would want him to forgive and move on.

Freya's voice was a gentle caress, yet her eyes were as hard as speckled flint. Her moonlight hair was woven into intricate braids that kept her regal face free from obscurity. "Nocturne, Ouro, and the Sisters of Fate are positioning themselves on the highest ridge that they can find. They will wait, and when the battle begins, Nocturne will use his power to close the portal above the city. My hope is that with the chaos below, Valdis will have too much occupying his attention to find them and stop them." Her heavy gaze slid to Elijah, and he nodded in reply. The sisters and a dragon were assets that could turn the tide of the war, and he knew it was best to keep them from the thick of the fray for as long as possible.

As their army passed the centre of the lake, Elijah lifted a hand to halt them. From his viewpoint, he could make out the sparkling shards of the frozen waterfall, a glimmer of the fish imprisoned within. A thrum and crack resonated in the air, suggesting that the waterfall could still be moving underneath its suspended crystal surface. An eerie sense emanated from the castle above, not a flicker of light in the high windows, as if it had been long abandoned. From his angle, Elijah could glimpse the high cathedral windows of the throne room, with the long terrace of the Dragon Landing just below them.

From the southwest appeared another mass of dark bodies, the drumming of their heavy boots like distant thunder. At their head rode Jero and Thogan, upon war bears made of blue ice. Magic salted the air as the Princes joined them, the armies melding as one.

Elijah made to dip into a bow, but Jero slid from his mount, his boots rattling the ice beneath their feet. His palm shot out, thumping against Elijah's chest. The rugged man's face lit up in a smile under his thick beard, "Don't you dare, boy."

Elijah's lips quirked in a small smile.

"This is it, the calm before the storm," growled the twin, Thogan, staring at the golden castle above. "Gods be good, I have never seen the castle so lifeless."

"Are there still people there? Townsfolk, I mean," asked Luc, pointing to the few flickering torches high upon the battlements. His wedding band shone on his hand as his green eyes narrowed in concern. The wedding, although it had only been yesterday, felt like so long ago to Elijah. The happiness of the occasion had cooled like morning dew, the people around them, filled with merriment a matter of hours ago, now stood sombrely, fearful yet determined.

"Look." Emerson pointed towards the castle, where there was suddenly movement. Some soldiers above had noticed their approach, the little flickering flames sporadically dotted along the walls as their light bounding off gold and stone. Save for those few specks of light, the city was dark… eerily silent. If there were any residents left inside, he prayed they were taking shelter.

The enemy they were to face did not need light, not like regular human soldiers. Valdis' undead army needed naught but the stench of fear in the air, leading them like breadcrumbs through the night.

Voices rose up from the army behind him, from the mix of races who believed in him enough to follow him into battle. Believed in the possibility of change. Humans, elves, Fae alike checked over armour and prepared weapons, sharpening steel and claw. Shifters warped into their animal forms as others donned their helmets. All manner of beast that could fight had been enlisted, even those small enough not to be considered a threat. Birds, critters, and spiders peppered their ranks as well, and Elijah was certain that they would come as a complete surprise to the human warriors who remained amongst the enemy.

Ghila approached, dressed in lightweight black armour, rose crescent moon blades at her hips. There was confidence in her stride, chin higher, shoulders back, her eyes upon him. His sister stopped before him, cleared her throat, before placing her hand upon her heart.

He mirrored the action, before touching her shoulder hesitantly.

She did not flinch, but instead offered a small smile.

Elijah squeezed, putting his feelings into the soft gesture, grateful she was here.

Against his will, a shiver of foreboding cascaded down his spine, and the feeling of eyes upon him drew his attention back to the castle. One lone figure was moving to the forefront of group of Red Guards.

Upon the Dragon Landing stood Valdis, only just visible from their position, yet his presence absorbed attention like a black hole. His copper hair stood out like a beacon, his pure black robes a speck of grime against the golden backdrop. Flecks of blue pulsed around him, seemingly encrusted on his clothing and perhaps his blanched skin – Elijah could not be sure. More obviously, something glittered on Valdis' brow. The golden crown of Viridya.

Lorch's crown.

Elijah's crown by right.

Realisation hit hard, snatching the breath from his lungs.

"Valdis has taken the throne," Kadec called, confirming Elijah's fears. The execution had been a stage for Valdis to usurp the crown. Questions swirled in his mind, soon overtaken by thundering anger. He'd been using Lorch as a pawn since the beginning, and that fact had always been clear.

All of this was because of Valdis and his fear and hatred of the very magic he now wielded. Magic twisted and stolen, magic ancient and tainted.

That *bastard.*

Valdis' voice flew through the air, amplified by his stolen magic. "Eliverus Herington, you waste the time and breath of all who have followed you here." The man snickered as more guards in red uniform flanked his sides. "The North is mine, the power is mine, and soon, all of Fythnar will be *mine.*"

Murmurs skittered behind Elijah's back, whispers of shock and anger mingling in the rapidly chilling air.

"Are you prepared for the blood of your people to forever stain your hands? Because if we should proceed, and you continue in your pathetic attempt to oppose me – I promise you, *boy*, I will not hold back."

Elijah shook, fists clenched by his sides.

Valdis continued, "You attempt to delay the inevitable, and all you have done until now will be for naught when the ancient one arrives."

Ancient one?

Elijah stepped forward, magic rising to project his own voice. He knew his words now were crucial. He had countless lives at his back, people who were looking to him now with warring emotions. Even the court monarchs watched, awaiting his response. Elijah took a deep breath and spoke.

"Why do you continue to uphold this ideal of hate and fear? History isn't perfect, I am not naive enough to think that magic has never brought about destruction or caused division amongst our races."

Valdis sneered at this, but Elijah continued. "The world is not black and white. There have been dark chapters written with magic, yes, but also tales of healing, unity, and triumph against insurmountable odds. Magic is a force that transcends mere spells and incantations; it is the essence of our shared existence, the very fabric that binds us together. Let us speak. Let us work together to build a better future, for both humans and Fae. For *all* races. You need not continue to inflict pain and death. You need not continue this monstrous reign."

Valdis' brows pulled, his sneer ever present, "You speak as if I am the only monster here, when I know of your family's history." Across the distance, Elijah could see the dip of the man's chin as his gaze skirted to Elijah's boots, and back up to the tip of his tapered ears. "Power such as yours will result in madness. Such is the history of your *kind*, and the cycle that will repeat, even if you manage to defeat my forces today."

There was silence as Elijah's fists clenched, knuckles white. He felt the weight of the usurper monarch's eyes on him. He was struggling to find the words to break through to him, to the man he hoped was beneath the hateful armour. Thoughts of Elijah's uncle, the one said to have gone mad, sprang to mind, as well as his own lapses towards a lingering darkness. His magic hummed beneath his skin, eager, bordering on impatient, rising with the emotions he was trying so hard to keep in check.

Valdis grinned. "You've tasted it, haven't you? The madness?"

Something must have shown on Elijah's face, because Valdis began to laugh, the sound carrying the distance and snapping around them.

Beside him, Ghila stared at the castle, at the space that Valdis tainted, her hands clenched by her sides.

"He speaks from his own personal experience, obviously..."

whispered Emerson angrily, and Elijah felt a rush of gratitude for the break in tension brought by that one line. "Don't listen, Elijah. History is history. We need to focus on the future, together."

Elijah looked back at his friends, the court rulers, and an endless sea of anxious faces. Emerson was right. Unlike Valdis, they were fighting for a cohesive future, where everyone could live in peace. Perhaps Valdis was also fighting for his own twisted version of this, too, but all Elijah foresaw with Valdis' plan was division and death. So much death.

"This is your last chance to prevent a war, Valdis. Let us settle this in a peaceful manner, let there be no more death." Elijah couldn't prevent an almost pleading note. "Please."

Valdis laughed again, his face twisting into a look of sadistic delight. "You are weak in the spine, boy, and that will spell your downfall. I will rid this land of your scourge, and your magic, and bring forth a new world where all will hail to one ruler, one king, one *god*."

He was beyond saving, if he thought he was above even the Gods. Divine beings hadn't graced the mortal realm with their presence in a long time, and Elijah wondered if this would be the prompt to finally make them return. He wasn't sure what would be worse, though.

A world ruled by a madman with tainted magic, or the return of the Gods, rumoured to be far worse.

He'd wanted to allow Valdis some grace, a chance to change his mind, be redeemed. But it was obvious that he'd gone too far down his dark path to turn back to the light.

If it was war Valdis wanted, then it was war he'd get.

As if they felt a change in the air, the masses behind Elijah began to churn.

It was then that Elijah noticed his sister was gone.

Trusting she was preparing herself for what was to come, he turned his back on the castle to cast his eye over the sea of faces. Elijah wasn't one for speaking in public, let alone delivering speeches that stoked hope before a battle, but he kept his voice even despite sweaty palms and thudding heart.

"Brothers, sisters, my friends, my people. We stand on the precipice of war, and while you may have fear in your hearts, know that we are united as one. I will reconcile our severed courts and we will rise from the ashes of this hateful empire to forge the land anew." Elijah's voice rose, magic ringing the iris of his steel grey eyes. "We will stamp out the embers of bigotry and embrace all who wish for peace, no matter their race, no matter their history."

Valdis continued to laugh in the distance, almost wheezing. The army shifted, as restless as the churning clouds above them. Elijah's words lingered in the air as Valdis' laughter snapped short, his face stern again.

"This can all be avoided if you come to me willingly, Eliverus Herington. Come to meet your death readily and all will be spared. You served us faithfully for twenty years, and for that I will allow you this mercy."

Elijah didn't believe the man for a single second.

"I know that all this death won't end with mine, Valdis. I'll fight until there is nothing left of me, because all of us have everything to lose should you continue. Your fate has been woven, and it is to end under my sword."

Valdis had the gall to look disappointed.

"You choose chaos, then? Fine, I'll grant you death with devastation." His voice became monotone as he glared, hand moving to the folds of his cloak.

"I cannot allow you to play God any longer. This ends now," Elijah called, hand on the ancient sword at his hip.

A whirr and hum sounded in the skies above as more portals sprang into existence, smaller than the swirling void that had taken up residence above the city. Valdis' face was maniacal as he threw his arms wide, head tipping back as a barking laugh erupted. More evidence of the immense magic he wielded contributing to his insanity. Elijah was determined that would not be his own fate.

Lightning snapped from the widening voids, pulling the clouds around them into twirling whirlpools in the darkening sky. Magic sizzled and cracked, and from within the growing portals, winged nightmares emerged. Like ants escaping an overcrowded nest, dark shapes poured out, spindly arms and serrated teeth flashing as the creatures dropped into the city below.

Then the city began to scream.

Valdis' laughter faded behind sudden, rising screeches of the undead. His forces scurried from either side of him, cascading down the frozen waterfall like liquid tar. Hungry, rapid, feral, terrifying.

Heading their way.

"Gods be good!" gasped Jero, drawing his axe just as Elijah raised his sword.

There was no stopping the chaos now.

No turning back.

The army at Elijah's back shivered with anticipation and horror, and he blanketed his nerves in steely resolve. What they were about to face was unlike anything seen in their lifetimes. They needed him to remain strong, even when he felt as brittle inside as spun glass.

Lifting his sword into the air, he let his magic flow up into the blade, igniting the dormant magic slumbering within. The weapon erupted in blue flames, a torch to guide them all.

Elijah called to his army. "I was told that once measured, there is no escaping your final fate. I've since learned that is not true. We each hold a thread, one that can be changed if we try hard enough."

For his home, for Fythnar and every single soul in it.

"Let's change fate. For Fythnar!" he bellowed, thrusting the sword high.

The air erupted with war cries and the thrashing of weapons against shields and ice. Roars, snarls and howls of beasts mingled with the snapping chorus of portals opening above.

Elijah twisted, his feet moving before his mind had fully caught up. His own battle cry was lost in thunder and chaos as the army charged towards the rolling wave of Valdis' undead forces.

Elijah sprinted, breaths slashing his throat, body humming with anticipation and the rumble of the masses at his back reverberating to his toes.

Until the rumbling intensified under his feet, from deep below the ice and water.

And the ground beneath them moved.

Suddenly the black ice surged up, bowing like a barrier rammed from beneath. It cracked and splintered open like a toxic flower as something emerged from the lake, directly in their path – water and ice showering over a form of obsidian scales and bleached bone. Enormous wings of frozen, decaying skin and bone unfolded, followed by glowing orbs within a long, tapered skull. With a thundering roar, framed by pure pandemonium, a thing of nightmares emerged to the sky.

From the bowels of the Sapphire Depths rose an undead dragon.

CHAPTER TWENTY-NINE

NEMESIS

They fell from the sky like rain. Creatures of horror, things created to bring torment and deliver death. Their cries were unlike anything Nem had ever heard, deep like a feral dog's warning growl, then rising with keening screech like steel-tipped nails raking down a chalkboard. They landed upon the roofs of houses and in the streets, quickly setting on the fleeing townspeople.

Nem flew up the street, boots thumping on the cobblestones. Krepth was close behind, his breaths acute in her ears as sounds of mayhem mingled with the whirring void holes in the sky above. Several Fae followed, members of the resistance, darting into homes and shops to tell their people to flee.

Nem took a quick mental analysis of the creatures as they ran, spying one perched on the roof of a ransacked bakery. It was on all fours like a wolf, hide as black as burned bone. Long forelegs were tipped with blade-like claws; moth-eaten membranes flapping like bat wings. Short hindlegs also claw-tipped and moulded with muscle to easily propel its body of skin and bone, jagged spines along a crudely-arched back, ending in a long whip tail.

The creature lifted its horned head, serrated teeth dribbling, the nostrils of its snout flexing as it took in a deep, rattling breath.

Nem noticed last that the creature was eyeless.

"The fuck are those things?" rasped Krepth.

"Not something made by the Gods of our realm," she replied, grabbing his hand.

The golden city was on fire and painted with blood. Every storefront, every home they passed was under siege by a force of otherworldly beasts and undead.

Nem and Krepth pressed on with five of the Fae resistance, checking for any straggling townspeople.

Horseshoes thundered on stone as a rider tore through the street in a fearful dash to escape. As a frightened scream rang out, Nem glimpsed a woman crouched over a young child, directly ahead of the horse.

"Move!" she called, waving her arms.

Then she saw the woman's leg, bent at a strange angle under her tattered cloak crimson with blood.

Nem didn't have to think, she was already moving.

A screech split the air, an eyeless head rising from the shingles of houses behind them. The creature's attention flew to the fleeing horse, and it let loose a wicked sound of excitement as it flared its wings and rocketed from the rooftop. In its wake were two more, jittering with glee at the prospect of flesh and violence.

The rider glanced back, blind with panic as the creatures' shadows fell upon him. He didn't seem to see nor care about the woman and child in his path, wailing with alarm.

Nem's legs pumped, her blades singing free of their sheaths. She could hear the loping gait of Krepth beside her in wolf-form. He streaked ahead like a shadow to the woman and child, shifting mid-leap in an impressive transition to land beside them.

The horse skidded and reared back as Nem dodged its flailing hooves, twisting around to its rear where the jaws of one of the creatures was seconds away from latching onto the animal. Nem slammed her blade into the space where the creature's eyes should have been, sinking deep into its skull of leathery skin as easily as carving butter. The monstrous thing screamed, limbs scrabbling as it slumped to the stone.

Nem stared, knives lifted, preparing for it to recover and attack again.

When it landed on its side to die, shivering and bleating, she blew out a breath and checked the sky. The others seemed to be occupied with attacking the resistance fighters nearby, who took notes from her to aim their attacks at the creature's skulls.

The man on the horse tried to control his startled mount as it reared again. Krepth moved through the flailing hooves like water to grasp the reins and calm it, murmuring gently. Nem joined them, wiping black blood from her blades on her pants as she bent to check the sobbing woman and child.

"I'm so sorry, I didn't see them, I just needed to escape," the hapless rider cried, beard and hair slicked to his fevered skin with grime.

Krepth huffed as he ran a hand down the horse's shuddering muzzle. "Allow this woman to use your horse. She's injured." He gestured to the equally haggard-looking Fae around them. "They will help you all to escape."

Without argument, the man slid from his horse, eyes roving the sky in terror.

Nem was sure they had moments before another attack. She helped the woman into the saddle as gently as possible. The man jerked back, noticing the woman's tapered ears. Then he glanced around, barking fearfully, "Fae. You're all Fae!"

"And the problem with that is?" Krepth growled. "This place is about to be overrun by beasts conjured of pure nightmare and you're offended by those who help you?" His green eyes pinned the man.

"My son!" The woman wailed from the horse, clutching her daughter close. "He's within the castle grounds. They all are! So many children! Please find him, I beg of you."

Nem stared up at the castle, its reflective surface strobing the cosmic light from the portal above.

He's within the castle grounds, they all are.

Children... Valdis had abducted... *Fae* children.

The thought had her stomach roiling. Nem turned in the opposite direction as a resistance fighter took the reins to calm the horse.

"Nem, no, we can't go in there."

She ignored Krepth's protest, casting her aqua eyes upon the haggard Fae soldiers who awaited instruction. At some point, they'd wordlessly promoted her to leader of their little group, it seemed.

"Take them to the gates, I'll meet you there shortly with the children, and whoever else is caged in the castle grounds."

They nodded, not delaying or questioning her directions.

"Nem, wh–"

Nem shot Krepth a glare, "I *will not* leave children here to die."

Krepth's colourful curse rang out in her wake, but he'd follow, she knew he would. She was beginning to learn that he'd follow her into the heart of a volcano, despite it being a stupid idea. He'd burn right next to her.

They slipped through the unmonitored gates and sprinted across churned lawn, mud caking their boots as a small sea of carts mounted with barred boxes came into view.

Nem could hear the cries of frightened children upon the wailing wind.

When they approached, little hands reached through the bars, tens of them. Krepth cursed again as Nem scouted for the latches to set them free. Krepth leaned into the bars, murmuring gentle words of encouragement, as the children clutched at his robes as if he were an anchor. "We'll get you out, hold tight."

Finding the locks, Nem enchanted her blades so they could slice through them. As she broke open the doors, Krepth ushered the children from the carts, until a sea of grimy, tear-streaked faces looked up at them in fear.

Above them, creatures streaked by, and the portal whirred in a roar.

They had to hurry.

"Follow me!" Nem cried.

The children, though frightened, did not hesitate. They clutched hands and helped the smaller ones along as a handful of winged beasts descended from the sky. Nem aimed a burst of magic towards them, weaving a temporary shield for the creatures to slam against. She winced, the energy sapping from her quickly with each jolt.

Hurry.

Krepth scooped up two toddlers, clutching them to his chest as they barrelled through the gates and streamed into the city streets. The children moved as quickly as they could as Nem fought off the swooping creatures from the sky, their cries and the clacking swoop of their talons reminding her of birds defending their nests in spring. She grabbed two more straggling children, willing the magical shield to remain for just a little while longer.

She'd help the children and the last of the townspeople escape, and then she'd go back to find Arii. Even though their life bond had been overtaken by the one between Arii and Elijah, Nem still felt a relentless need to find her best friend. It would take more than a war full of undead and festering winged creatures to take down Arii, but that didn't mean she'd leave her to fight alone.

The towering main gates came into view, still firmly shut. Fae resistance soldiers fought alongside townspeople, the latter using brooms, pitchforks, whatever they could find to fend off the enemy.

Yarn was barking orders, his burly face streaked with blood. "Get that gate open, now!"

Four Fae worked frantically, using their magic and hastily-made bombs to blast open the castle gates.

Nem's breath hitched at what she saw beyond.

As they poured through the smouldering doors, the way ahead was obstructed by a fast-growing blockade. Creatures fell from the portals littering the sky, their cries twisting with the sounds of battle, as undead scrambled up the sides of the bridge like ants, their way forward quickly becoming unpassable.

Nem turned to the cries of the children behind her, meeting a small sea of frightened eyes. Even the resistance soldiers looked fearful. They would be quickly overwhelmed. She couldn't protect them all, and the small force of resistance fighters were strong, but it wouldn't be enough. She'd been a fool to think they'd be able to escape easily.

She'd saved these people only to lead them into perhaps a far more violent end.

A hand took hers, warm skin enveloping her clammy, blood-stained fingers. Nem stared up into the intense jade eyes of Krepth's handsome face, his look of determination. He could read the rising terror inside her, could see that every soul around them was looking to her to guide their way.

"You've always been better than you credit yourself, Nem. You may not remember your past, and you may think you've been put on this earth to cause strife to my kind, but none of that matters. Weave your own fate, Silver Moon. Be the beacon these people need - that we *all* need."

He lifted their linked hands between them. Her skin had begun to glow.

"But… how can light ward off those things?" she whispered. How could she use whatever this power was? She wasn't even sure *what* it truly was.

"Sometimes, when all seems dark, all we need is a little light to find our way." Krepth pressed her palm to his lips and as she shivered, the light grew brighter.

So too did the small spark that ignited within her chest. It was something she hadn't truly felt in a long time.

A spark of determination, and hope.

It flickered where her bond used to be, searching for purpose.

Perhaps she could be the beacon these people needed.

She had to at least try.

In the light of her growing glow, the small mass of Fae and humans watched her in awe. One woman wept, another man lifted his arm high, praising the Gods. On his wrist glittered a bracelet of starlight to ward off the Dragon's Breath Fever curse. Elijah's magic was spreading, and even here it now reached. He had been so heavily against magic at first, had wanted nothing to do with his destiny.

Now he was the biggest beacon of hope against the dark horizon.

She could do this, and if not, then at least she had tried, with a flicker of purpose in the end.

Krepth saw the moment she had decided, his roguish smile appearing. "Why settle to be a moon, when you can also be a *sun*?"

Her beast rumbled, her magic spread through her veins. The sun… she felt warmth through her limbs, saw sparkles and the reflection of her ethereal face in Krepth's eyes as he smiled. Then he pulled her close, heart to heart. His lips crashed against hers in a searing kiss, as if it were their last.

It wouldn't be their last, she'd make sure of that.

It was the beginning of many more.

Her blood roared in her ears as they broke apart, and she saw that despite the significant side effect of their shared touch, his moss green eyes were filled with intense emotion.

Their hands fell apart, whispers of promise unsaid between them.

She stepped forward, her skin rising in glow like an oil lamp igniting. She tipped her face up to the sky where a shivering mass of creatures streaked their way, like a storm cloud made of bats.

Fear flickered in her bones but was quickly doused by her magic as it rose to shimmer over her skin like fallen stars.

And she grew brighter.

Her true purpose was *this*. A golden shield of protection, one that would be there for those who needed it most. Perhaps she had been made to find stolen artefacts, but the threads of her fate had spun a different course the day she washed up on the western shore below the School of Fate, with no memory, only a burning anger.

She knew now that she was thankful for all she'd been through to come to this point, whether by her own design or that of a higher power.

Perhaps the Gods were not done with her yet.

Nem stepped forward to face the almost endless length of the bridge connecting Viridya to the rest of the continent. Crowds of undead scurried mindlessly up the side, drawn to her light, tearing over one another to get to her, to the children, humans and Fae sheltering behind her.

The hairs on her arms rose as her magic began to sing.

She grew brighter again.

Like the breaking of dawn upon a stark horizon.

"Be a sun, Nem," Krepth whispered, shielding his eyes as did the others.

Nem splayed her arms wide, her light rising to a fever pitch, her heart humming, skin coursing with fire.

The hordes of darkness drew near, and only once they were almost completely upon her did Nemesis let her light explode.

CELADINE

Cela grasped her daughter's fingers tightly as they forged through the golden halls. She'd found her quickly, held between two soldiers as she called for her mother, fighting them with her budding Fae strength. The soldiers' curses were cut short abruptly when Cela flew upon them like an enraged mother bear, ending their lives quicker than she could ever heal wounds. The fright in her daughter's eyes remained as they ran, dodging the last dregs of palace staff as blackening skies followed them from window to window.

Ominous whirring sounded outside, humming through the halls. Mia pulled away suddenly to peer out a window, Cela clawing her sleeve in desperation. "Mia!"

"Look, mama, there are holes in the sky!" Mia signed wildly.

Celadine took one look at the terror unfolding across the city, her stomach knotting with dread, and she knew.

Her premonition of chaos was unfolding.

And they had run out of time.

They needed to take cover fast. She couldn't protect her daughter from what was coming, and even though it killed her to admit, they could only wait out the storm and hope to be found once the turmoil ceased.

Cela pulled Mia by the arm towards a nearby doorway and into the kitchens. She slammed and locked the door behind them. Her Fae hearing picked up the otherworldly sounds of the creatures, and panic made her heart gallop. Mia whimpered beside her.

Crashing sounded beyond the door, of glass shattering and expensive vases toppling. The creatures had entered the castle, their screeching bouncing off the metal walls like a nightmare choir. Cela could smell them already through the closed door, like sewerage seeping from the gutters, overpowering everything else.

Shadows moved on the floor, cast through the cracks under the door.

A tug at her skirts drew her attention. Mia's little hands twisted in the moss-coloured fabric, her eyes wide and uncertain.

Cela stood frozen, sweat beading at the base of her spine, her mind wading through fear in search of a way out. She'd made the wrong choice locking them in here. Her fingers twined in her daughter's hair, massaging her nape in a bid to sooth her.

Think, Cela, think!

A male voice, muffled through the door. "Get back! Come no closer. Gods have mercy, what are they?" It was one of the castle soldiers. Steel rang, leaving a scabbard, and Cela felt a momentary glimmer of hope. The guards! They could help them escape.

"Stop, no, NO!"

A screech then a heavy thump behind the door caused them both to jump. The man screamed, and as his body thudded against the wood, Cela's hope fled through her toes.

Silence.

Cela snapped into action, pulling Mia towards the rear of the kitchen. Heat radiated from the stove where a pot of lamb stew bubbled as they dashed towards the secondary exit. Cela threw herself against the wood, fumbling with the latch as an ear-splitting screech ripped the air, the door they had been standing near moments ago shuddering, splintering.

They weren't safe here. If anything, they were as easy as sitting ducks.

Another heavy thump and a cry – one so high pitched that Mia wailed in fear.

The creatures knew they were in the kitchens.

"Mama!" Mia cried, clutching her leg.

Come on, unlock! Why won't you unlock?

Cela shoved her shoulder under the latch, grunting with effort. Then she saw the metal padlock far above them, and her breath hissed from her clenched teeth.

Locked.

Before a curse could form, the kitchen door blew open. She grabbed Mia, dropping to the floor and scrambling behind the island bench. Every single instinct she had screamed *don't look*, but she couldn't help tilting to peer out.

The creature stood in the doorway, its lean body taking up the entire space. Long, spindly arms tipped with claws clutched the doorframe as a reptilian head snaked into the room, jaws hanging wide in a saw-toothed smile. It seemed to be a mix of scales and skin, black as night and beaded in vermilion droplets, like rubies encrusted on leather. A strange whining sound rolled from the creature's throat as it stepped across the threshold, its earlier prey falling into the room with a thud.

The creature smelled… different. Celadine expected the stench of carrion and death to proceed their terrible presence, yet what assaulted her senses was age-old earth mixed with ancient ash, touched with something unexpectedly sweet, like rotten apples. She scoured her memory of beast lore from her time in herbal school, but drew up short. She was an apothecary – her mind stored lists of herbs for healing and poultices for the opposite. Creatures were not her strong point, but even she knew these things were not of this world.

Cela's gaze locked on the body sprawled at the creature's taloned feet. The man's armour and red uniform had been torn away, his chest a tattered mess of flesh and bone. But it was not that that kept her horrified stare.

The man's head was tilted back, mouth agape, ruined sockets where eyes once were.

The creature had eaten his eyes.

Her hand flew to her mouth, stifling her muffled gasp.

The creature's nostrils flared wide as its head snapped in their direction. Cela saw that the monster, like its victim, lacked eyes. Where they should have been was smooth, leathery skin. Near the taper of its skull, where two horns began, two tiny holes nestled within triangles of skin, most likely ears.

Cela jerked back against the cool frame of the kitchen island, the thunder of her own heart like a drum in her ears. Mia shivered like a leaf against her side, panting. Cela cupped her daughter's cheeks and drew her terrified gaze to her own. She needed to be strong, remain calm, or they would not leave this room alive. She did not possess offensive magic like many of her kind, but she did have something this creature lacked.

Knowledge and a will to survive. Not for herself, but for her daughter.

A soft clicking and shifting of hide drew closer, but Cela refused to break her determined stare as she put a finger to her mouth. Mia nodded, pressing her own lips together to form a bloodless line. If the creature lacked sight, then it would most probably be using scent and sound to track its prey. Cela turned to the shelves behind them, scouring the array of terracotta pots and glass jars, turning them as silently as she could to read their labels.

When she found what she was looking for, she wrapped the lid in her skirts and popped the sealed top without a sound. The smell was instant, biting and potently fragrant. Beside her, Mia hovered her hand in front of her mouth, wiggling her fingers, signing a word.

"Garlic," whispered Cela in answer, dipping her hand in the jar to take a fistful of the moist crushed vegetable. Mia's eyes widened as she began heaping the stuff on her cheeks, neck, and chest.

Mia's hands moved swiftly, signing, *"What are you doing?!"* as the creature clacked its teeth and made a barking sound deep in its throat. Cela paused for the briefest moment, blinking the tears springing to her eyes. They had to hurry.

Mia squeezed her eyes shut as Cela smeared the garlic over her face, covering her exposed skin as if it were a beauty ointment. They could smell like garlic for weeks if they survived, but Cela hoped that it would help confuse the beasts as to their movements, rather than make them taste more exotic should they be consumed.

They moved, silently crawling to the opposite side of the bench as the creature clacked towards the back door, inhaling along the floor like some sort of deranged bloodhound, its snorts and grunts seeming so loud in the quiet room. The tip of the creature's tail whipped at the pots and pans, the loud clang splitting the quiet, stealing a startled yelp from Mia.

The beast whipped its head in their direction with a screech of excitement.

"Go!" called Cela, pushing to her feet as they made a break for the main door.

Only to find the way blocked by a second creature.

"Curse it!" spat Cela, clutching her daughter and veering towards the stove as jaws snapped in their wake. Cela whirled, putting herself between the beasts and her daughter as the girl clung to her back. Her eyes darted, seeking possible escape.

The second creature roared, claws scraping as it sprang at them.

Cela swiped a nearby kitchen knife, her bellow mixing with those of the monsters as she brandished the steel like a weapon, slashing the muzzle of the creature. It screeched, lips quivering as it tried again, snapping between the whizzing of steel as Cela slashed wildly, almost blindly. She may not be a warrior, but she still had a Fae's strength and speed, and she used it. Her fist gripped the hilt as she thrust the knife into the side of the animal's neck just as its fangs tore at her upper arm, her well-timed strike preventing it shutting its jaws entirely. The beast's head jerked to the side, colliding with the other.

The second monster, unconcerned, catapulted over its sibling, launching over the island bench with jaws open. Cela spun, pushing

Mia out of the creature's path as its skull crashed into the cast iron stove. The boiling pot above rattled dangerously.

Cela fell back, avoiding flailing claws as she scrambled backward only to hit the cupboards, toppling pots and pans piled above. She covered her head as they crashed down over her. The monster shook its head, tongue lolling, nostrils flaring wide as it began to turn.

Towards Mia.

The girl cowered on the floor, eyes wild, breath heaving in long, audible gasps. She was far too terrified to remain quiet, and Cela knew what she had to do.

"Hey!" she barked, earning the swift attention of the creature. Its long neck slithered her way like a snake, teeth clacking together in some sort of deranged animal speech.

"There is much more of me than there is of her!" she cried.

Mia wailed a protest and as the creature faltered, Cela grabbed a pot and slammed it against the stone floor, drawing the beast's interest again. Celadine gestured wildly as she called, "Mia, listen to me! Go, run and find someone to help you."

"No, mother!" Mia signed frantically.

"You're small," Cela signed as swiftly and clearly as possible while speaking. "You can escape; the beasts won't smell you. Travel silently."

The creature's back legs bunched flexed as its lips quivered into the semblance of a menacing smile. The light of the stove fire danced across its jet scales, and despite it being a thing born of nightmares, Cela noted as if mesmerised the smooth elegance of the pattern across its body.

This was it.

This was how she was to die.

An image wavered before her eyes, a man with copper hair, his face lit with a smile as he sat with Mia on their floor, attempting to learn the language that aided her in life. Unlike her mother, Mia was patient, showing the young king slowly, a shine of appreciation and happiness in her eyes.

Lorch.

She hadn't told him how she felt. Not truly. And now, because of her stubbornness and desire to shield her heart, she wouldn't get the chance to. She'd let some of her defences drop when she kissed him in the Inn, but had that been enough to show him how she felt?

She saw movement, a flurry of cloth, and her heart squeezed, thanking the Gods that her daughter had the chance to escape.

"Go. Tell Lorch that… tell him I…" Her words were lost to a keening cry as the beast's jaws flew wide, so close that she could see down its gullet.

Her eyes snapped shut, awaiting the end.

"HEY!"

Both Cela and the creature stopped and looked up to the voice above the stove.

Mia stood feet either side of the large bubbling pot, the ends of her skirts blackening upon the coals of the stovetop as she leaned against the tiled splashback. She lifted her hands, hooked her fingers and motioned a simple sign.

Run.

Then she pressed her back to the wall and kicked over the pot of boiling stew. It hit the lip of the stove with a clang, its contents spilling over the creature in a sizzling wave. The thing may have been covered in scales, but it was also made of flesh which burned immediately as the liquid made contact. It screamed, the sound jarring and full of pain.

Mia leaped from the stove, smoke trailing in her wake as she ducked the whip of the creature's flailing tail.

Cela clambered to her feet, pride a thunder of adrenaline in her chest as she grabbed her daughter's tunic and practically threw her towards the door, stealing a fleeting glance at the thrashing creature. They broke into a run, shoes slipping in remnants of stew and blood as they headed for the hall.

And slammed into two bodies.

Chapter Thirty

ARIIAYA

Arii wasn't sure what she had been expecting to emerge from the portals opening in the sky, but sightless, bloodthirsty creatures from another realm? Hell no.

Windows blew in around them as Arii and Lorch sprinted down deserted golden halls, only pausing for a second at each room to look for Celadine and her daughter. She was sure the castle staff had either fled or died already.

Then two bodies fled from the kitchens, beastly screeching in their wake.

A sound of alarm erupted from Lorch, and he flew forward to pull the woman into a fierce hug. Celadine yelped. "Are you mad? Why didn't you flee the city?!"

The sound of a crash and roar made them all jump.

Arii tugged forcefully on their arms. "Explanations later, now we run!"

They sped down the halls, their reflections a golden blur. When they found an enclave, they paused for breath. Lorch cupped Celadine's face in his hands. "Are you both alright?"

As he spoke, he grasped the little girl's shoulder as she buried her face in his tunic, clutching him as if he might disappear. He blinked, nose wrinkling. "Is that… garlic?"

Arii's nose wrinkled too.

Celadine lifted her chin, managing to look regal despite hair in tangles around her face and flecks of garlic dotting her skin. "Those things rely on scent and sound. We were trying to get past one when we became trapped in the kitchens. What are those things? And where did they come from?"

"The magic that my father possesses is far more complicated than we first thought," replied Lorch, spearing a hand through his mussed copper hair. "This isn't normal magic, is it?" As he spoke, he looked to Cela, who shook her head.

"Thank Fate you're both alright." Lorch breathed, shaky with relief.

It did not take Arii long to place the pieces of the puzzle together. This was the Fae he had been discovered with – the one Lorch had been sentenced to death over. And she was part of the resistance.

"Ariiaya, this is Celadine – my… the crown healer. And her daughter, Mia." The girl waved tentatively from behind her mother's skirts.

Arii returned the wave awkwardly. "One of the resistance?" She voiced her thoughts aloud, intrigued. Cela nodded.

"And the reason that he was almost executed." The woman's gaze was unflinching, but her eyes betrayed the emotion crackling behind her mask. "Thank you, for saving him."

Arii was taken aback but recovered quickly. "When he was apprehended, why were you not arrested too?"

"Fortunately, I was undiscovered thanks to His Highness."

She threw Lorch a pointed look which he deflected with a slightly embarrassed grin. "We can all agree that under moments of pressure, I may not always keep a level head."

"You shoved me into a closet!" Cela exclaimed.

Lorch winced.

Cela sighed then said, "Others would argue that you did what any of us would." Again, she held her gaze and Arii was briefly reminded of her best friend's unshakable façade. "But you should have allowed me to take the fall alongside you."

"You're needed by the resistance," he lifted Mia into his arms and she nuzzled into his neck. "Mia needs you."

Sounds echoed up the hallways, reminding them that they were in the throes of escape. From their enclave, Arii could sense a strange tension in the air, mingling with the tang of garlic. Things felt unsure yet resolute, shivering with the uncertainty that came with war.

She knew they shouldn't dally, especially with the creatures now within the castle.

Lorch's voice drew her thoughts back. He stared intently, blue eyes bright.

"My way of thinking has changed. Cela… she opened my eyes to what is truly happening, right beneath my nose." Arii blinked, mouth opening to speak, but Lorch wasn't done. "My father… his magic has surpassed this world. What he has access to now is beyond anything this reality can offer. At first he was 'given' the magic, borrowed and transported in Nexus Crystal. Then, my father found a way to syphon magic from wielders – particularly older people and… children."

Cela took over the story then, a tiny waver hinting at the grip she had upon her emotions. "Then Bonemire was becoming crowded. Children could not make soldiers, and their magic was pure and powerful but it recovered too slowly. Valdis began to experiment in something that has only even been a whisper of myth. Soul magic."

Soul magic. A concept of wizardry so ancient, so unchartered, that it had almost vanished from living memory. Arii knew very little of it, but what she did know was that it was forbidden. Texts on the subject were hard to come by, and only smatterings of it were mentioned during her time at the School of Fate.

Disgust coated every syllable of his words as Lorch spoke, his teeth a flash of white in the dim light. "He has found a way to gain more power by harvesting the magic within souls, and in doing so, opened up a tear between our world and someplace else."

The void above the city, this was caused by soul magic? She wondered if Nocturne or Ouro could tell them more. Her father's Library Inbetween would be useful right now but time was of the essence.

As they spoke in whispers, the echoes of chaos in and outside the castle mingling, Arii realised with a jolt that they were in dangerous proximity to the throne room. She flushed with anger – and then another thought hit her.

She could find Valdis and end this right now. Surprise could be on her side, if his attention was fully taken by the battle which had begun on the frozen wasteland below.

"There is another kind of power at work here that we… where are you going?" Lorch said with a start.

Arii growled. "To end this."

Lorch did a double take in shock. "Face my father alone, without Elijah? Are you insane?"

"You know I am," Arii threw over her shoulder, tearing the daggers from her belt. Footfalls behind told her that they were following. As the throne room doors came into view, Arii twisted, almost colliding with her pursuers. "Take them somewhere safe, Lorch."

"You cannot go in there alone! He is far too powerful; he will tear you apart."

"Not before I leave a few tears upon him, too."

Suddenly other voices came from inside the throne room. They all fell silent, moving towards the golden doors, left slightly ajar.

"I have given all that you asked for, if not more. Power, much power, and the purest on offer in this land." It was Valdis, his voice low and tinged with irritation, "Now it is time for you to fulfil your part of the bargain."

"It is not yet complete," came a new voice. It was wavering and distorted, as if its maker were speaking through a hollow cylinder of tin. "The void is not yet large enough for my beast to fit through."

Arii inched one eye into the crack. She was not expecting to see the once grand, golden room covered in layers of glittering black crystal, coating the furnishings, walls, and floors in formations of jagged dark quartz that looked as if they'd been growing there for centuries. Stalactites of stark obsidian crystal dripped like teeth from the ceiling, framing the scene as if they were within the maw of a colossal beast.

All around the room stood the undead, swaying like mourners at a funeral. They watched their master blankly, mouths gaping, some without much of their faces at all.

And then her eyes moved to Valdis.

He wore a long black cloak stitched with gold filigree, a plain yet regal piece that draped his broad shoulders and set the copper of his hair aflame. Where he stood, near the centre of the room, was a colossal piece of crude amethyst, coated in the same black, glittering grime that plagued the rest of the hall, swallowing up most of the oaken table it sat upon. It stood like the peak of a mountain with a jagged tear through its centre, revealing a face of crystal that almost resembled the polished surface of a mirror. Within that surface, an eye blinked, the iris as red as blood. That was all she could see, hardly enough to determine if the person behind the glass were human at all.

Valdis slammed his fist on the table, chalices and old plates clattering. "I have done all that you asked, and more. You promised me you would bring him back. You gave me your oath!"

Arii tilted her head to look at Lorch, who was staring at his father in contemplation. Before she could ask, he placed a subtle finger to his lips.

"Oath…" the voice mused. "I will, mortal. All in good time."

"That time is *now*."

The voice tsked an invisible tongue. The tone was deep, arrogant, inhuman. Male, Arii believed. "Humans – your kind has always proven impatient and hungry for power in all realities that I have visited. Driven by desires of the heart and longing for those no longer living."

"You obviously do not understand. Have you never lost someone so dear that you'd risk everything by turning into the very thing you hate most, reaching across realms and razing cities with just the tiniest hope you could get them back?" Valdis' voice wavered, ever so slightly, but Arii heard it. So the heartless tyrant had a motive, to bring back someone he'd lost. But who?

"I do not fall victim to petty emotional qualms like that of a mortal.

It makes you weak… and easily moulded.”

“What?” Valdis screeched.

The voice laughed. “Calm yourself, human. I will make good on my promise, once my beast breaches your portal completely. When your world is consumed by fire, and his hunger is sated with the blood of your enemies, then I will bring back the person you desire most. For the spell to work though, I will need a vessel. A sacrifice.”

Valdis nodded, far too eager. “You'll do it, you'll bring back Micah?”

Lorch stiffened, and Arii felt it. Did he know this person?

Valdis was a cruel, slimy parasite with a black heart. Arii didn't believe he possessed a single caring bone in his body. She doubted that bringing back someone had been his motivator all along.

“When the beast is sated, and you have a worthy sacrifice.” The voice repeated, and Valdis leaned forward, shoulders trembling as the voice continued. “I am nothing if not true to my oath, mortal. Tell me, are you true to your oath too, Valdis Gerard Kruel? You said your son, the traitor, had been taken care of, but it seems he has slipped the noose and now eavesdrops where he has no business.” The eye focused over Valdis' shoulder, iris shrinking as it glared.

Directly at the throne room doors.

“Shit,” whispered Lorch.

His father whipped around, extended a hand and with a flash of dark magic, ripped the doors wide open.

There went their element of surprise.

Seeing no point in holding back, Arii stormed into the throne room, Lorch, Cela and Mia in tow.

“Ah, Miss Trillia, welcome back.” Valdis' smile was cruel, skipping from her to his son, not bothering to peruse the apothecary and little girl. Then his attention fixed solely on his son.

Lorch stepped forward.

“And my son, still alive I see. That is… good.”

“No thanks to you, *father*.”

“The execution spectacle served its purpose. The war has begun, and soon Fythnar shall tremble under the might of an ancient creature who will raze this sorry realm to the ground, brushing away the filth so that humans may begin again." As he spoke, he stepped forward. "In a world free of magic."

Even as Arii's keen eyes noticed he limped, possibly injured, his words brought bile to her throat, fists clenching. Celadine held the same look of disgust.

Valdis continued, his voice a snarl. "After all I've done for you, you throw it all away for these... Fae. You disappoint me, Lorch. You were meant to inherit my legacy, not betray it for these wretched creatures."

"Wretched creatures?" Lorch's voice rose incredulously, hand up to stop him. "Father, do you not see what you've *done*? You use the magic that you once feared so vehemently. You use it to do what you claim the Fae have done to humans for years. Suppress them, hunt them, make them fearful, make them feel *insignificant*."

Valdis remained silent as the eye in the stone whirled behind him, and if Arii didn't know any better, she could have sworn the eye was shaking with eager amusement.

"And what legacy?! The creatures you've let loose outside care not who is friend or foe, neither do the undead once you let them loose. They've set themselves upon our own townspeople! They don't care whose flesh they dine on, as long as it's flesh. That thing–" he pointed towards the eye, which blinked slowly, "will not spare the humans when the realm falls. There will be no legacy left. And it doesn't matter. I'd rather be sleeping in rags in a back alley than be a king for an empire forged in blood. I'd rather *die*."

Valdis' impassive expression faltered, eyes turning to slits. "I suppose it matters not if you're alive or dead, either way, you'll continue on my legacy, willingly or not." He lifted a hand, and for a moment Arii thought he was about to offer it to his son, a gesture that didn't match his acidic words.

Then his fingers flicked up, sending Lorch soaring across the room, straight onto the golden throne, its shine dulled by a slick black coating of obsidian ice. He hit the backing with a thud, and with another flick of Valdis' fingers, the ice curled around his wrists, fixing him to the seat. Flashes of blue light strobed through the cathedral windows as Lorch yelled, "He won't bring back Micah! The thing inside that crystal is using you!"

Valdis turned from his son, throat working on a swallow, the only indication that Lorch's words fazed him. "Consider my sacrifice obtained, ancient one."

The eye in the crystal flashed.

Then Valdis smiled, slow and sardonic as the room erupted into chaos. The undead ringing the area converged on Arii, Celadine and Mia, the latter squealing in fright. Cela moved her daughter behind her as Arii tore her daggers free, lips curling.

"My pets are hungry," said Valdis, and from behind, the glass windows blew inward, shards raining down upon them as Valdis let out a laugh. Winged creatures clambered through the frames, slithering down the walls like lizards. He held up his hands as magic snapped and cracked around him, the red eye of evil blinking its approval. Arii schooled her features, but she could feel terror radiating from her companions at her back. Her eyes met Lorch's upon the throne, and she could see the pleading in them.

Valdis called, "Now it is time for them to feast!"

Arii knew when best to stay and fight, and when best to flee. Now, the time was to retreat.

Her heart screamed for her to stay, to save Lorch, but her instinct to save Cela, Mia and herself told her to *run*. There was something in his eyes, a softening that told her that's what he wanted her to do. She could only put as much emotion into her own features to return a message.

I'll come back for you. We all will.

"Run!" Arii snapped, tearing her gaze away, spinning on her heel and bolting. Cela and Mia were already streaking across the marble floor as fast as they could.

As soon as they passed the threshold, Arii whipped her arms back and threw a punch of magic at the doors, slamming what remained of them into the path of their pursuers. She turned and threw her magic along the front, creating a temporary barricade. Cries and shrieks sounded as the crazed beasts assaulted the doors.

Arii winced, the drain on her magic almost instantaneous.

"Go, I'll distract them!" she called.

"We can't leave him!" Cela cried, looking just as angry as Arii felt. Her daughter was crying, tears streaking her grimy cheeks.

"I know we can't! But we will die if we stay!" Arii barked. With her power quickly depleting, she did not have time to argue. A strange aura followed Celadine, one Arii couldn't quite decipher. A Fae with a different sort of magic, contained and not wielded physically. A seer?

Finally, Cela nodded, anguish in her eyes.

Arii said, "I'll do everything in my power to bring him back to you. I promise. Sneak out, head to Evergrave. They'll protect you there."

The doors thumped and crashed again and the hold Arii had on the barricade buckled. Sweat bloomed on her forehead and pooled on her lower back. She couldn't hold it.

"Go, please," she whispered between clenched teeth.

Cela nodded again, her green eyes now heavy with sadness, as if she knew something Arii did not. Then she took Mia and ran.

As soon as they were out of sight, Arii let loose her grip upon the door.

They flew open and undead and beasts alike crashed out, tearing and clawing over one another like spiders in their lust to flay her.

"Shit," she rasped, allowing just a split second for the creatures to see her before she turned tail and ran.

Valdis' laughter echoed behind her, mingling with the excited cries of his pets. She swore she could feel claws sand fingers catching on her cloak, mere inches from grasping it.

Gold streaked her vision, the once-pristine halls littered with shards of glass and blood and bodies. Terracotta pots lay shattered, long red carpets torn to ruins, paintings shredded. Creatures fought their way through the windows, keening and frenzied, but she continued to run, legs pumping like pistons, heart breaking the further she got from the throne room.

Arii slammed through the doors, hurling herself towards the flat straight of the Dragon Landing. Memories assaulted her, flashing behind her eyes as the wails of the undead echoed in her wake.

Lorch's fingers drawing her face up, a golden crown on his brow, his expression inquisitive.

It was the moment they met, when her heart had flipped strangely after being dormant for so long.

The moment she'd changed forever.

Her threads of fate had twisted that day, branching off into a whole new direction. Perhaps she'd felt it, this shifting of her destiny, in amongst the awakening of her emotions. She'd thought fate could not be changed; she'd believed vehemently back then. She'd ushered others into the endings given by the golden threads of the Gods, but never had she thought she could guide her own.

Space yawned before her as she pelted across the Dragon Landing, quickly nearing its end. Hands and claws and teeth ripped at her cloak, but it didn't tear, moving from their grasps like water.

Ariiaya's boots hit the lip of the landing, the battlefield spread out below her. Determination – and acceptance – steeled her heart.

She leaped.

†

Arii had a strange sense of déjà vu as her body plummeted towards the darkness of the frozen lake below. The sight was familiar, yet completely different from the last time that she had flung herself from this exact spot. No crash of a raging waterfall sounded in her descent; no muscular arm clutched to her side as wind whistled past her ears.

A boom thundered in the distance, and her eyes tracked the chaos of war below.

The undead littered the black ice field like ants, thousands clashing against what she could only guess were Elijah's amassed forces. Flashes of light sprinkled the battlefield, blips of magic in amongst the madness of death and destruction as human, elf, shifter and Fae took on the hectic might of a seemingly impossible foe. There were darker forms too, the winged creatures and Kryvern.

She did not have long to take it in, hyperaware of the ground rushing to meet her.

Then there was another sound amongst the rage of wind.

Whistling.

At first it was subtle, a hiss as she fell towards her doom. Then it rose, becoming louder, *closer*. She had only heard it once before, in the caves under the Dragon Teeth Mountains. It was the sound of air slicing around scales in a slipstream, the sound of something large falling at a dizzying speed.

She saw the black streak dropping from above, and her pounding heart almost thudded to a stop.

Ouroboros.

Her final warning was a boom of wings springing open before she slammed into the solid, scaled mass of his back, breath tearing from her lungs as the black dragon rescued her from freefall, seconds from becoming a splatter on the ice.

Arii couldn't help an unladylike screech as she scrabbled to clasp two large spikes between Ouro's shoulder blades.

"That was an incredibly reckless thing to do, little Fae," rumbled Ouro, his voice dripping with disapproval at the forefront of her mind. As if to punctuate his thoughts, he angled up, massive wings beating the air as they ascended, the golden castle towering like a cursed monolith in their wake.

"I knew you'd catch me," she panted, eyes squinting against the wind. "Well, I *hoped* you would. You have a promise to keep, after all."

Ouro huffed, smoke slithering from his open jaws, a draconic version of a laugh. *"Cannot risk you coming to an untimely end and having to live with your father's animosity for eternity. You make it a difficult promise to keep, though. Are all your kind inclined to take leaps of faith from cliff edges, child?"*

Had she not been so preoccupied with holding on, and the sheer chaos below, Arii would have laughed. Hysteria bubbled up from her heaving lungs to claw her throat. But any notion of amusement was ripped away as she saw what their forces faced in the middle of the lake.

Was that a dragon?

"The length of Valdis' abominations has no bounds, it seems. That is Keledrel, lost to the depths during The Battle at Twilight over one hundred and seventy years ago. He is ancient."

"You know about our history?" Arii gasped.

"I know yours, as well as countless other realms," was his simple reply.

Fear gripped Arii's insides as she spotted a speck at the dragon's feet, flurries of light shooting from the figure's hands as they battled the unimaginable. She knew it was Elijah. She did not need to see his face to know it was him. No one else could face an undead dragon and still be standing. He wasn't alone, either. As they neared, she spied Jero and Thogan, mowing down undead soldiers with steel and magic, keeping Elijah's back clear. Bears made of ice tore and mauled their foes.

Arii's thighs burned, boots wedged into Ouro's scales as she pushed up to get a better look. Her hair whipped around her face, cheeks stinging from the biting wind.

"We have to help them!" she called.

"Hold on."

Arii didn't need to be asked twice.

Ouro dipped into a dive, wings snapping close to his sides as they plummeted. It felt like gravity punched a hand through her chest and wrenched her spine against her ribcage as they rocketed towards the heart of the battlefield.

Ouro's voice held a snarl as he cried, *"Let's even the odds of this war, shall we?"*

Then he let loose a thundering roar.

Ouro angled his body, wings gathering air as he levelled out, mere feet above hundreds of warring soldiers. Her own roar exploded, face twisted in her war cry as Arii dropped from her perch, sliding down the dragon's forearm to hit the ground rolling.

She skidded to a stop, tearing her daggers through the heels of two enemy soldiers, felling them swiftly before her body could feel the jarring impact of her fall.

Lightning crackled in ribbons from the sky as Ouroboros collided with Keledrel, their colossal forms shaking the battlefield with a thunderous boom.

CHAPTER THIRTY-ONE

ELIJAH

He breathed sparks and exhaled ash, every gasp scorching his lungs as he pushed to his feet and saw scattered flames dotting the battlefield. Utter chaos surrounded him, bloody and brutal in the dimming light. The waning sun bathed the icefield in orange, mixing with blood and the bodies of the fallen.

Undead swarmed over their forces in waves, fighting as if demon-possessed. With no fear, no sense of self-preservation, some fought with weapons, others simply flung themselves unarmed at their prey, biting and tearing at fur and flesh. Rattling roars cracked through the air as several Kryvern cut their way through the masses, setting iron jaws upon their victims with furious vigour.

The titanic dragon that had emerged from the lake let loose a thundering roar, a bellow neither alive nor dead. It pulled the remainder of its skeletal form out of the ice, its footfalls quaking the frozen river beneath Elijah's feet. It belched blue-green fire, torrents tearing through the masses and leaving nothing but charred husks behind.

"Elijah!" called Jero over his shoulder. "The Void Stone!"

Elijah tore the oval stone from his pocket. He still hadn't figured out how to use it. With an undead dragon added to the Kryvern and winged creatures, calling the dragons home was more imperative than ever. But he had nothing, no clues or riddles or prophecies to unravel. Simply a stone that appeared to have a galaxy within – a pretty paperweight. A cry of frustration tore from Elijah's throat, seconds from flinging the useless thing away.

Something stopped him though, a feeling deep within his gut.

He shoved the stone back into his pocket.

"Look out!"

Someone shoved him to the ground, just as fire erupted around him. A firm hand grasped his armour, hauling him back to his feet. Jero's face was speckled with black blood, the depths of his eyes lit with residual magic. Elijah gasped, blinking frantically as a swathe of crystal bears formed a protective circle around them. Thogan appeared, boots caked with dark ice, thick arms bare to the chill, his cheeks pink under the smattering of his beard.

He swung up his axe to lop off the head of a nearby soldier in red just as Jero bared his teeth. "You must lead our forces towards the castle. Go!"

As the flames cleared, Elijah sprang forward, flinging himself through a break in the bodies clashing around them. Screams of the living and dead chorused around him as he ran. He saw the rose-gold pauldrons of Kadec's bright armour as soldiers fell to their knees around him. Their faces ranged between slack, blissful and outright horrified as his illusionary magic overtook the minds of living soldiers. As he streaked by, Elijah's eyes met those of the dark-skinned prince, magic lighting his irises like flaming orbs as Kadec cleared him a path. White teeth flashed in a ghost of the man's roguish smile, strain cracking across his face as he tossed out his hands to fell more forces.

Thank the Gods the court leaders were on his side, because the might they displayed was unmatched.

Heat burned suddenly nearby and he turned to see a huge draconic smile lined with serrated, moss-covered teeth, flames licking up the corners of its parted jaws as the undead dragon hunted him. The flames burnt a strange blue-green, like a candle burning too hot; claw-tipped wings scrabbled the ice as it bowled over friend and foe alike in its pursuit of him.

Elijah snapped out his hand, calling forth his magic. It answered, swiftly and without mercy, fiery plumes of blue magic and electricity scorching the dragon's decaying form. The thing hardly flinched, and released another gout of green fire.

He rolled, narrowly avoiding the attack, cursing in a ferocious way he knew his fated mate would appreciate.

Arii. Gods how he wished she was here, fighting by his side now. He hadn't known he needed her strength until now.

The dragon threw its tail, obliterating a contingent of soldiers to his right, driving up a gust of air that almost blew him off his feet. In the distance, above the city, more flickering portals opened to rain down otherworldly creatures.

The ancient dragon's roar shook the air as one of its massive claws came down on the heads of battling Fae and elves only a few feet away, the sickening crack of bones pulverising against ice rolling Elijah's stomach as he ran.

This was impossible. All of it.

A sickening weight of hopelessness pressed down on him, so sudden that he gasped.

He couldn't do this. Despite being surrounded by forces that included friends and family; in that moment, he felt sickeningly alone. Perhaps if he were facing Valdis head on, just them, he might possibly prevail. But now, with thousands of undead soldiers (some of whom he may once have known), ferocious winged creatures and an undead dragon, Elijah was struck with the overwhelming thought that they would not outlive this chaos.

He ran, sprinting past people he had no chance to help. One Fae man dragged himself across the ice, crying for his mother, his legs useless weights painting the snow with red.

Another woman screamed, set upon by three undead, their claws and teeth tearing her apart.

Elijah, bile rising, kept running, blocking out the thunderous noise behind him.

The sound of wings punching air and a new dragon's battle cry stopped him in his tracks.

Elijah spun to face the eclipsing sky.

Fire coursed through his veins, and it was not from the battle raging around him.

It was her, his fated mate.

Arii's entrance upon the battlefield was something Elijah was sure he would never forget. She rode upon Ouroboro's back, hair whipping behind her, midnight blue cloak fanned out like smaller dragon's wings. She slid from the dragon's back to roll across the ice in a dismount that seemed so practiced, so elegant that he would have sworn she was a born dragon rider had he not known it to be wildly untrue.

She sliced through bodies, her attack more akin to a dance than anything else, until she joined him, cheeks blushed with windburn below wild purple eyes. When she spoke, her voice was cool and collected, as if she had just been astride a tame pony and not a titan made of scales, but he could see the adrenaline shaking her limbs.

"Hello, Master Wolfe."

Gods, she was irrevocably alluring, and were it not a life and death situation, he'd kiss her until he shook, too.

"Took you long enough," he murmured, watching as the massive black shadow of Ouro in dragon form collided with their largest adversary. Arii watched the clash, too, plumes of mist clinging to the heat of her breath.

Despite his words, a smile tugged at Elijah's mouth. "That was quite the entrance."

"And it won't be repeated ever again," Arii quipped. She jerked her head up, motioning towards the skeletal dragon. "Ouro tells me that is Keledrel. How Valdis found his remains when they have been lost for decades is a bloody mystery, but no point questioning that now."

Uncertainty glimmered in her eyes as she twirled her daggers, and Elijah knew she was anxious for their shapeshifting ally. Ouro was large, but he was half the size of Keledrel.

Then she turned to him. "We have to get to the castle. Valdis is in the throne room. Our best chance at ending this is to end *him*, and hope that will be enough to save us all."

Elijah nodded, narrowly dodging a careening enemy body. There was hardly a break between friend and foe as he and Arii scouted for the quickest path to Viridya. Some of their army were astride horses, but none were close enough to help. Elijah once again thought about the stone in his pocket, mind picking at everything he knew about it.

Open the stone, call the dragons home.

They could really use more dragons right now, he thought, just as a draconic screech tore the air. In the chaos of fighting, he couldn't tell who made it.

"Open it, and they will return home." Elijah repeated Ouro's words, hoping that with repetition, the answer would magically present itself.

"Shit. Still haven't figured it out?" Arii said unhelpfully as she ducked the swipe of a bone-clawed hand. She removed the undead soldier's hands before efficiently taking off its head.

"Open it..." He said once more, perhaps more to himself than his mate.

"We will figure it out. We *have* to," Arii said.

So, they danced, falling into a practiced flurry of sword and daggers to a background symphony of roars and shuddering thunder as they fought in the shadow of two warring titans.

⸸

Open the stone, call the dragons home.

That one statement played over and over in Elijah's head as he sliced through fetid flesh and bone to battle impossibly slowly towards the towering golden castle alongside his mate.

Jero, Thogan, Kadec, Luc and Emerson fought nearby, but even with that support they only moved inch by inch. Not even the unsullied formation of Iniq's trained woodland warriors could make a dent in their path, the female's dark skin shiny with blood.

Too slow.

Arii craned her head, searching, their bond alight with her worry. Elijah hadn't seen Nem or Krepth yet. He hoped they had gotten out of the city.

He also hadn't seen his sister, but he knew her abilities and knew she'd be fighting somewhere.

The two dragons fought at their backs, crashing like thunder as they came together again and again, jaws latching, claws tearing. Thanks to his smaller size, Ouro seemed to be narrowly avoiding the brunt of Keledrel's unhinged jaws.

With a roar, the titan spewed green fire, tossing its head wildly as the torrent slammed against the ice then tore towards them.

Elijah whipped around. "Arii!"

She cursed, her hand found his and he grasped it as if it were a lifeline. Surrounded by the crush of the battle, they were caught directly in the path of the wild green fire.

He flung an arm over Arii by instinct but before he could throw up his own shield to protect them, a dark mass plunged them into shadow as Ouro curled his body around them, wings acting as a shield.

Keledrel's flames engulfed them, the heat overwhelming. A dragon's hide was its best defence against dragon fire, but the intensity of the titan's power couldn't be resisted for long. Ouro's scales sizzled, the ice steaming and bubbling around them as Elijah locked eyes with Arii. Her eyes were wide, faces barely an inch apart.

The blood, dirt and grime marring her beautiful skin, the shine in her eyes, all called to his inner beast like a siren, shaking him. Her violet eyes were shadowed with fear, her lungs heaved. Unflappable as she was, even she was showing signs of overwhelm. In all his own years of battle, he had never seen such sights as these.

Elijah kissed her then, with all his pent-up emotion. She kissed him back just as vigorously, hands gripping the chain metal on his chest.

"Now is the time to open the portal, young King," said Ouro, his pain-filled voice filling Elijah's mind. *"One dragon is not enough to take down this foe. Open the stone, call the dragons home."*

"How?!" Elijah cried, the stone in his pocket like a heated, dead weight.

He pulled it free and held it in his palm. He and Arii stared down at the swirling galaxy within its polished surface.

"Open it," Ouro said, repeating the phrase as he had many times before. Still, he did not offer up any more than those two words, but now, under fire, his words were heavy with meaning.

Elijah stared, transfixed, into the glittering stars of another world. Constellations moved in unfamiliar ways, wisps of colours within, illuminating their faces.

Something began to hum inside him, raising the hairs on his arms, sizzling from his gut into his chest.

His very breaths felt heated, as if fire was rising from his throat.

"Open it," Ouro said again, his tone biting with a snarl.

His magic suddenly sprang forth, crackling like threads of light around his fingers. The stone began to glow.

Finally, Ouro roared, his bellow full of anguish, *"Open it!"*

Open it. *Open* it.

"Do something stupid, Elijah," Arii growled.

He had no other thoughts and acted on the sudden feeling blowing like a gale through his body.

As if sensing the moment, Ouro's wings snapped open, breaking his shield, just as Elijah threw up his hand and punched a blast of magic at Keledrel's open maw, stopping the torrent of flames. The beast's head jerked back, allowing them a split-second opening. Elijah clasped the stone high above his head, light from his magic and the orb itself washing over the warring battalions around them.

The second was all Elijah needed, as he threw all caution to the ashen wind and pelted the stone at the frozen surface beneath his feet.

The Void Stone shattered like glass, galactic shards bursting across the ice.

Keledrel's head slowly turned, eyes dropping to the mess of glitter around Elijah's boots.

When nothing happened, Arii muttered, "Oh fuck…"

Then something *did* happen.

A sudden gust of wind pelted their backs, causing Keledrel to blink its undead eyes. The battle around them paused, animals, Fae, undead and humans all tossing their heads towards the sky.

Elijah wasn't sure what possessed him in that moment, but recalling it after, he would describe it as instinct.

He threw out his arms as if to welcome home an old friend, magic igniting his palms as he said, "Time to come home."

In the sky, a golden portal snapped open, followed by many more.

Dragons of all colours poured from the openings, their cries filling the atmosphere.

"Yes!" Arii squealed, punching the air, as Ouro reared back and roared.

Elijah watched as three dragons, a touch smaller than Ouro, flew straight into Keledrel, jaws snapping and claws renting its decayed flesh. Ouro, hide still sizzling, propelled himself at the fray to join his brethren. The dragons from the portal clung to Keledrel as the beast snapped at their hides, spewing green fire in a frenzy over their heads. As one of the dragons curled itself around Keledrel's neck, jaws sinking into the beast's heavily decomposed brow, Ouro took the opening presented and reared up before the ancient beast. He sunk his winged claws into the thing's chest, cracking apart its rotted ribs before ripping out Keledrel's pulsating stone heart with his teeth.

Keledrel's glowing eyes winked out, and it fell, the thunderous boom of bones striking the ice-covered soil like an earthquake.

All around them, dragons rained fire upon the undead.

Hope ignited Elijah's bones, the beasts' cries of war mingling with the cheering of his army.

Golden fire disintegrated a hoard nearby, and a blue-scaled beast landed upon the charring remains, the ground shuddering from the impact.

"King Eliverus," called the scarred dragon, her gentle yet strong voice lilting in his mind. *"Come, I'll take you to face your foe."*

Elijah and Arii made their way across melting ice to the sky-coloured dragon. Something flashed, moving below the surface and he halted suddenly.

Cracks emerged in the ice, opening wide as undead soldiers were sucked into the icy waters below by arms as white as snow. Just as Elijah tensed in preparation for another beast to emerge from the depths, a face he knew appeared from the nearest crevasse.

Queen Vexia Silverfin emerged from the water, silver hair flat against her face, jagged teeth flashing in a shark-like smile.

"A life for a life, promised king. The kingdom of Sapphine is here to aid you. Go, unthaw my home, and consider my oath fulfilled."

With that, she ducked back under the water, heading off to help her sisters drag more enemy forces to watery graves.

"Thank the Gods she is on our side, for now," said Arii as they continued towards the blue dragon. Something about the ancient beast sparked Elijah's memory. This dragon seemed familiar, but how could that be?

As they halted before her, she said, *"I am Lysander. I knew your grandfather."*

This was his grandfather's dragon?

Queen Freya emerged astride a large elk with horns twisting into the sky. Her army, Shifters in mortal form as well as predatory beasts – wolves, tigers, cougars and bears, protected their flanks as Lysander nodded her colossal head in thanks.

"Quickly now, climb aboard and hold on tightly," her tone was chiding, grandmotherly, as Elijah and Arii clambered upon the dragon's back. He tensed his legs, arms folding around Arii to grasp the prominent spike between Lysander's shoulder blades. Without much warning, Lysander's powerful legs propelled them into the air, and Elijah felt Arii's thighs tense against his own as they held on.

Lysander whipped above the battle still raging below, plumes of fire and charred remains littering the ice. In the distance, the golden castle of Viridya loomed before the backdrop of a rising moon.

Anticipation, as well as anxiety, stabbed Elijah's stomach.

Once they got there, he knew what he had to do.

SYBELL

Sybell couldn't quite believe her eyes as she watched the battle from a raised hill overlooking the city's eastern face. The lake that was once Fythnar's greatest inland body of water had frozen solid in black ice, and the waterfall under the castle had frozen into a cascading fall of jagged shards. The undead clambered over the golden castle walls like ants escaping their nest, spilling onto the battlefield in endless waves.

The sheer number of the undead had Sybell feeling sick. How had Valdis gathered so many in such a small amount of time? The thought crossed her mind that perhaps he hadn't limited himself to abducting people from nearby towns, but also drawn bodies just lain to rest. Sybell did not question the theory since she now knew the actual level of his madness and craving for power. When portals opened in the sky above the city, and dark beasts began to emerge, it also dawned on Sybell that Valdis may not have limited himself to their world alone to fatten up his forces.

The largest opening in the sky continued to grow, yawning wider than the astral warps around it, directly above the castle. So far nothing had emerged from it, but Sybell had a terrible feeling that was going to change very soon. Gooseflesh peppered her skin, and she shivered violently.

"I do not like this. Not one bit," groused Tora. The warrior crossed her arms and frowned at the strange man with silver in his hair.

"No one truly likes war, well, unless you're on the side that is winning, I suppose," Nocturne said in his unusual lilting voice.

Noct had been on this hill with Ariiaya's friends, Tikkani and Quinn, when Sybell and Tora had arrived.

Sybell eyed him, wondering why they had been marched here by the Fates, instead of into the fray below, now teeming with dragons in all colours of the rainbow. He had done it. Elijah had figured out how to open the stone and call the dragons home. Perhaps all hope was not yet lost.

"So, you think you can close that void?" said Klotho, her raven black hair whipping about her seemingly permanently scowling face.

Noct ran a hand through his hair, blowing out a whistled breath. "I believe that I can, but it will not be easy. A void of that size is only possible with ancient magic – and a lot of it. I'll need to be uninterrupted while I close it," he fished a small, leatherbound book from his pocket and added, "I mean, not even the brush of a butterfly's wing can touch me, or the ritual will cease." He flipped through the book, touching a finger to a page and studying it with mismatched eyes. "Did you bring what I asked?"

Ritual?

Tikkani hefted a bag down from her shoulder and squatted to pull items from it. Candles, salt, chalk… and some jagged offcuts of Nexus Crystal.

"He some sort of witch?" said Tora, surprise smoothing her face.

Sybell felt a flutter in her stomach at the momentary drop of the woman's stone defences.

Nocturne's expression could have been taken as jovial, had his eyes not been as hard as chiselled stones. "Of a sort, yes," he replied.

"Oh," breathed Tora.

Noct's movements were swift and practiced as he began laying out a small foundation, pressing candles into the dirt and dropping salt in a circle around him. The group stood there, hyperaware of the ticking time bomb in the foggy, darkening terrain below.

Slapping his hands together to dust away the salt, Noct said, "Where I come from, magic is a touch more difficult to master. I can open portals for short trips with nothing but a clear thought and some well-practiced runes, but for such a large opening, I'll need the help of this grimoire." Flipping the pages, he planted a finger on one, clicking his tongue. "As I said, I cannot be interrupted once I've begun," he eyed them each in turn, pausing upon the three Sisters of Fate. "And our position here will not remain a secret much longer. When I connect with the mother void, our little patch of heaven here on the hill will light up like a flare for all to see, and I suspect we will be set upon within seconds of that happening." He shifted his feet, turning towards the castle.

Lakhesis tipped her chin up, the faces of her sisters equally determined as she motioned to the small battalion of cloaked women converging around them. "You have the might of the Furies of Fate at your back, young magician. We will do what we do best and *fight*."

Roars shuddered in the distance, flashes of dragon fire lighting up the battlefield.

Noct grinned, hair swept back, eyes alight, "Let's slam the door on the faces of those fuckers, shall we?"

Sybell glanced at Tora who stood like a fixture beside her and was surprised to see the woman staring back at her. Sybell swallowed, seeing something spark within her deep brown eyes. Was that… worry? Fascination? Anticipation? Fear?

Whatever it was, Sybell hadn't the time to think on it.

They all watched warily as Noct muttered a passage under his breath and flicked one hand in a flourish.

Suddenly he dropped the pocketbook and threw up both hands as a thread of power burst from his outstretched palms like a striking snake, crossing the distance between them and the city like a sizzling thunderbolt. The magic twisted with that of the mother void, a loud groan tearing through the air.

The group began to step back, giving space to the perimeter of Noct's ritual circle.

"Oh my Gods," gasped Tikkani, palming her bow and arrows, her hair whipping around her face in the wake of Noct's pulsing magic.

On the field below, like tiny moths drawn to flame, battalions of undead broke away from the fray, scrabbling wildly in their direction. From the walls of the city, dark shapes flung themselves into the sky, winged clouds also heading their way.

"Ready yourselves, they're coming," called Etropos, a smile in her voice as she drew her daggers. Her bright crimson hair spilled like blood over her dark leathers.

Well, she was the mad one, after all.

It did not take long for the sounds of wailing to reach them, followed by a wave of quickly moving bodies.

"Defend Nocturne at all costs. Use every drop of magic, every bit of your skill, use your life if you must. Do not let them lay a bony finger anywhere near him," ordered Klotho.

Sybell had but a split second to suck in a breath before glowing blue eyes and gaping mouths were suddenly upon them, ravenous like mindless, bloodthirsty dogs. The stench of blood and death rode the wind in their wake, their feet ripping their grassy hill into muddy slush. She threw herself at them, replacing fear with hardened steel, drawing upon the countless hours of relentless training with Tora to toughen her against the macabre screams. Their motley faces blurred as she tore through one, then two, then three, her weapons seeking tainted flesh. Beside her, Tora did the same, cleaving one man down the middle with her heavy sword.

"Good! Again, princess," the warrior called.

Sybell threw her braid over her shoulder, a grin rising unbidden to her bloodless lips. A hand grasped her shoulder and Sybell turned to be greeted with a gaping, jawless scream. Sybell gagged at the smell of the dead woman's breath, the thing's grip harsher than she'd ever anticipated.

An arrow whistled over her shoulder, thudding between the eyes of the undead woman, the force of it sending her flying backwards. Sybell glanced back, catching Tikkani amid a swift reload, knocking another arrow to her bow and firing, while her partner Quinn watched her back with a blade-tipped polearm.

Sybell spun to see Noct's face, twisted under the strain of the warring magic spurting from his palms.

"Come on," she heard him mutter.

Suddenly a pulse of power pushed them backwards a few steps.

Whatever was beyond the portal was fighting back.

"Finally," hissed Nocturne, teeth bared as he slammed his palms together, fingers making a cage around an invisible force between his hands. "Give me a good story to take home, you bastard."

From within the mother void, something called, a roar so deep, so ancient, it shuddered the land like an earthquake.

Sybell and the others clapped their hands involuntarily over their ears as the being beyond the veil continued to call, colossal fingers breaching the swirling portal sides, curling around its edges as if to hold open a closing door.

"Don't you fucking dare!" snarled Noct, squeezing his hands, causing the thing to cry out. The void pulsed, and Sybell wasn't sure if it was the intensity of the roaring, or the waves of pulsing magic hitting them, but she swore the opening shrunk just a tiny bit.

Shadows dropped from the sky, fire and moonlight glinting off their black scales as bat-like creatures attacked them. Sybell's eyes locked with Tora's, just as something streaked past, collecting the warrior with a screeching cry.

"Tora!" Sybell screamed, thumping back an undead man, who could have been the same age as her brother. Sybell couldn't deny she had been scouring every face that flew her way, hoping with every slither of her being it would not be her brother's face, frozen in death, to meet her blades.

The young undead's skin suddenly lit up from within. Gold light poured out of his eyes, mouth, partially cut belly, and just as he leaped towards her, he exploded in a shower of violent magic. Behind the golden dust cloud stood Klotho, strings of magic writhing around her bare arms like snakes. "Go!" she called.

Sybell threw herself at a sky creature, its leathery wings beating around a struggling Tora. Back to the dirt, she held its jaws open with her bare hands, the thing's eyeless head bearing down on her. Blood smeared one side of her neck, and Sybell realised Tora was injured, her sword a few feet away. With no time to retrieve the heavy weapon, Sybell threw herself at the creature, cleaving her daggers through its tail. It screeched, head whipping back, just as Tora punched a burst of magic against its chest. The beast flared out its wings, halting mid-air as Tora lunged for her weapon. It landed with a thud to stalk its prey.

Sybell's weapons clanged against the scales of its hide as she attempted another strike, her arms straining with exertion. It paid her no mind, sights set upon the woman who had taught her so much, even begun to let down her icy stone walls, even as Sybell did. She'd come to respect Tora's calm firmness and loyalty.

Perhaps she was even falling for her…

This could not happen again. She wouldn't allow her heart to lose again.

"You fucking leathery arsehole!" she screeched, stabbing at the creature's hide like a mad woman. She had no magic, no immortal strength to leap upon its back and stab it through the head.

All she had was her fury.

Clenching her dagger in a death grip, Sybell ducked under one of the beast's wings to plunge the weapon up and into the soft area where the arm met its body. The blade met no resistance as it slid through skin and lean muscle. The creature screamed, jerked back and flung its head, catching Sybell in the stomach and sending her flying.

She could have sworn she heard Tora call out, just as she hit the dirt, rolling through the dust. She coughed, winded, staggering to her feet. Just as she looked up, the creature was there. Its jaws were so wide and so close that she could see straight down the thing's gullet. It screeched, barrelling into her, her back thumping the ground. Her breath left her in a violent whoosh as her fingers scrabbled on its slick scales. Wrestling with open jaws full of teeth, Sybell groaned, her arms quaking.

If only she had Fae strength and magic. Perhaps then she might survive this. Make a difference rather than just be a hinderance.

But no… she was human. Weak and mortal.

Sybell tasted sourness. She sounded like Valdis.

She was human…

Stubborn, with a pulsing desire to fight and a will to *live*.

A human… one with a fiercer desire than any other to prove herself.

The thought brought fire to her muscles, and a fierce cry wrenched from her throat as Sybell let go and rolled aside. The beast rocketed forward, snout slamming into the dirt, and as its head yanked up to bite, Sybell brought her spare dagger up through the creature's bottom jaw, shoving the blade so deep that its jaws clapped shut. Blood rained down on her, the creature warbled and wrenched away, flailing madly.

Sybell tore her gaze from the black blood staining her hand up to the creature whose life she'd just taken. Shock and adrenaline caused her to shake, paralysed, watching as it died. A hand came to rest on her shoulder, the weight snapping her from her stupor.

"Princess."

Sybell blinked up at Tora's silhouette. The Fae's grey eyes shone with pride and relief. They locked hands and Tora helped Sybell to her feet. They stood for a moment, fingers linked, eyes locked, in a slither of time where there was no war around them, no winged beasts or blood or gore.

It was just them, for a single moment, and Tora, a dour, stoic Fury, smiled.

A small tilt of her pale lips that set Sybell's heart afire.

Somewhere nearby, a loud groan snatched them from their moment.

They stumbled back towards the others.

Noct groaned again, and Sybell glanced at Lakhesis, the Fate's face tight with concern.

"I can't close it." Noct said. "The creature beyond the veil is a Titan, a being of incredible power. It's holding the portal open."

"Draw upon our collective power, use it to close the void," offered Klotho, wiping her half-moon slither of a blade against her thigh.

"I fear we can only stop the hole from widening, not close it completely. We must sever the connection between it and its host," groaned the man, sweat beading his forehead.

"More are coming," called Quinn, pointing as a sea of strobing blue lights washed up the hill towards them.

"What do we do?" cried Tikkani, sweat and grime pasting her hair across her face. She looked exhausted; they all did. And there was no end in sight.

The Fates took up a triangle formation around Noct's circle, their magic flaring to life as he said, "All we can do is hold it back and hope to the Gods you worship that Eliverus can stop Valdis in time."

CHAPTER THIRTY-TWO

GHILA

In the dimly lit throne room, the air was heavy with the stench of malevolence, the walls echoing with the distant sounds of war.

Ghila strode into the heart of darkness, stagnant red light emanating from a large, jagged piece of crude crystal, warring with the blue strobes from the overhead cathedral windows. She gripped the handle of her crescent moon blade, her steps silent, her eyes burning with an unquenchable thirst for revenge.

It hadn't abated after all.

The main doors had been blown open, and so far she had hit no resistance in her trek from the battlefield, up through the ruined back streets and into the castle. Despite the passage of time from when she'd last been here, she could recall the least-observable route. When the life of a royal child had became too much for her, she'd utilised this way to sneak in and out of town with her brothers.

Ghila's guard did not fall, even as she moved further into the seemingly abandoned throne room, a grotesque and dark version of the light, golden place she remembered from her childhood.

A sound caught her attention as she sidestepped the strange crystal. Her eyes shot to the golden throne, where a copper-haired man struggled, pinned there by dark magical ice.

"No! Get out of here!" cried the man, his struggles increasing.

A deep rumble of laughter had Ghila spinning, blade raised defensively, as Valdis stepped from behind the crystal column. At the same time an eye of malevolent red opened within the crystal. But she stared at the man, the one she'd dreamed of meeting again.

Valdis wasn't as she remembered him… this man was the shade cast in a reflection, all shadows and harsh lines. His beard was unkempt, his dark garb tattered and caked with a strange glittering substance. Spindly spider webs of dark magic curling over what exposed skin Ghila could see. As he limped towards her, the point of his blade grazed the marble, the scrape of steel like nails on a chalkboard.

"Little baby crow, how far from the nest you have flown." Valdis said, lips curling into a sardonic smile, magic shuddering in his eyes. He knew exactly who she was, had expected her return, if the satisfaction in his voice and twisted smile were any indication.

With that one line, the entirety of Ghila's wretched past came thundering back. The voices whispered anew from deep inside, telling her to make him pay, slowly and without mercy. He was the reason her family was dead, why she had been tortured, why her mind held scars that would never, ever heal.

After all the years she'd been preparing, her revenge was now so near that the taste of her magic was both bittersweet and acidic.

She would be his poison.

The bane to end the monster of *all* monsters.

Ghila didn't hesitate, she flew at him, years of repressed pain and anger spitting forth as a scream. She threw all her weight behind her blade, aiming for his throat. Valdis threw up his sword, deflected her as his cackling laughter echoed.

"So much *anger*, little baby crow. So much fury towards the one who set you down the path that made you strong. You were destined to be a meek little flower married to a lord, gracing his elbow as nothing more than a broodmare of stupid little heirs. But look at you now. Your power is exceptional, and without the trials *I* put you through, you would not know your true potential."

Her mind speared out, delving for his, only to meet with an inky black void.

Ghila visibly flinched as she returned to her body.

Valdis hooted. "Come now, did you really think I'd allow you access? Besides, I don't think you'd like what you'd find buried within."

She clenched her teeth and whirled on her heel, using the movement of her attack to drown out his words, to drown out *all* voices. Her demons remained to an extent, their cries, jeers and screams muted behind a wall in her mind, but always there.

The man on the throne continued to struggle and plead for his father to see reason, that the 'eye' in the crystal would not give him what he wanted, only destroy them all.

Magic pulsed from across the room, just enough to pinch a slither of her concentration. In that split second, Valdis brought his sword down, eyes flashing with the intent to kill. Ghila didn't have the elevated strength of her Fury sisters, but she did have speed. She brought her weapon up to block the stroke, his blade but a hair's breadth from the tip of her nose.

Ghila shook under the pressure of holding him back. He was stronger than she'd given him credit for.

"Micah!" called the hostage, and Ghila saw Valdis' eye twitch. "He was your love when you were a boy. I remember the story now."

"Shut up, son!"

So, the man on the throne was Lorch, Valdis Kruel's son.

"All this for a promise that you'd be reunited with someone long dead. Whatever that thing in the crystal has promised you is a lie. You *know* that kind of magic is impossible."

Despite the predicament she was in, Ghila couldn't help but watch with terrible curiosity as Valdis' eyes took on a glazed quality, his mind no longer enthralled in their fight. "I have brought back those who are dead. Who is to say someone far more powerful could not do the same – for someone long beyond my reach."

Lorch scoffed, his voice pained. "The wretched things you brought back are mindless corpses, nothing more. Not even the Gods could do what you want, it's against the very fabric of the universe. The creature beyond that stone has been using you and your undying love to breach this world. It won't spare you, nor will it bring Micah back.

You are smart, father, please stop and think. This madness has to end."

Valdis made a sound of despair as his son whispered, "Micah would not want this."

There, an opening, a tear in the warped black gates of his consciousness. Ghila saw a chance and took it, casting her magic like a spectral spear to slam into the very centre of Valdis' mind. When her boots fell upon a floor made of slate, as dull and flat as a lifeless desert, she lifted her head to stare into the blue eyes of Valdis Kruel.

What she saw next had her stepping back in pure shock.

The man was strung in manacles of iron, the circlets stretching up into the dark mist and nothingness that surrounded him. Crystal and rock curled around his legs, his body seemingly moulded into the earth, as if a millennium had passed and he had not moved, allowing the stuff to form around him. She stepped closer, tilting her head to better look at him. His skin was smoother, less lines of time around his eyes. His hair was shorter, chin shaved clean.

He even lacked his gruesome scar.

A small sound drew her attention to the base of the pyre, where another version of Valdis sat, back against the stone, head back and mouth agape, eyes rolling, as if just waking from sleep.

Ghila's throat tightened as she swallowed, the sensation reminiscent of the fear she endured during her captivity under the merciless grip of the Red Guard. A terror surged through her that rivalled those harrowing memories, coursing down her spine with chilling intensity.

She'd traversed many minds, but *never* had she seen one quite like this.

Behind Valdis, on a wall of blood and stone, were more copies of him, their faces frozen in a variety of emotions that reminded her of the voices. Angry, sad, bitter, happy, manic… so many emotions, so many sides to the same twisted coin.

"Fascinating sight isn't it?" came a voice, and she spun to stare at another Valdis, free of constraints. This one was dressed in royal garb, skin glowing but crawling with spider webs of taint. He was much like the man Ghila fought in the throne room, yet here he seemed less encumbered by the build-up of terrible magic. "He speaks every now and then, they all do, but they have learned after all these years that their words are nothing but dust upon the non-existent winds here, and I will not listen."

Ghila lifted her hands, and Valdis watched the movement with an impassive look. "What did you hope to find here, little crow? Memories to manipulate? Humanity to appeal to?"

"I don't think you had any humanity to begin with," she quipped, her voice coming out far stronger than she felt inside. Pain blossomed in her forehead; the beginnings of an ache that meant this mental link would not last long.

Valdis was trying to push her out, despite the picture of calm crossing his arms before her.

She had to hold on, she had to…

"You feel it, do you not?" Valdis cocked his head, watching as the pain began to project to her face. She may have broken into his mind, but this was his space. She was the intruder, not welcome here. For a moment Ghila forgot why she'd pushed her way inside.

Then she remembered.

As much as she had craved retribution for so long, she'd learned something about the world since being separated from the Locket of Dreaming: revenge would not heal the scars of her past. Helping bring about a better world was what mattered now; using her skills as a balm, not a poison. To heal, not to ruin.

Her thoughts went back to the Fae female she'd helped in Evergrave, when she'd witnessed a little family united in a field of wildflowers. She'd kept Kiley distracted, peaceful, as death gently whisked her away. Ghila had shielded her from a terrible, painful passing.

A distraction for a gentler fate.

The pain flamed anew, and Ghila felt the last of her claws wrench from the folds of Valdis' tainted mind. The last thing she saw was his uncertain eyes as she was yanked from the room of slate and faces to crash against the marble floor of Viridya's throne room. Her sword, as well as Valdis', clattered to the floor. Her head hit the solid ground so harshly that stars burst before her eyes, and terrible pain lanced down her spine to instantly numb her limbs.

"Blasted Fae scum, you'll pay for that intrusion," snarled Valdis, limping towards her, hands swirling with grotesque magic, fingertips blackening as his face twisted with anger.

But the distraction had worked, redirected just enough of his cruel magic to allow the man on the throne to escape.

From her place on the floor, cheek pressed against marble and grit, Ghila smiled with blood-stained teeth as Lorch Kruel picked up Valdis' fallen sword and drove it into his father's stomach.

ARIIAYA

Wind whistled past her ears, a symphony of dragon cries thundering in the air as they sped across the black ice field, the crush of warring bodies a blur underneath them. Dragon fire rained upon the swarms of scurrying wretches below, annihilating scores of them in one swoop, the sounds of celebratory roars bringing a feeling of triumph to her chest.

Perhaps they could win this war after all.

Elijah's fingers squeezed her hips, mirroring her feeling. Arii looked back over her shoulder, but when she saw his wide eyes and mouth a sharp line, dread smacked away the sensation of accomplishment.

Her head whipped back ahead to see what caused such an expression.

A black cloud billowed towards them, expanding so rapidly that Arii knew instantly they couldn't avoid it. The mass wavered like schools of fish dashing to and fro, the sound of screeching and flapping wings building to a crescendo.

"Hold on, little ones," Lysander said, aiming towards the core of

the swarm.

Arii clutched the thick spikes tighter, bracing herself for the blow.

They smacked into the mass, plunging into darkness.

It was as if they'd leaped into a dense thornberry bush. Wings, scales and claws hit them from all sides, like overgrown tree limbs assaulting a rider on horseback. Arii ducked her head, vaguely aware of Elijah's body bending over her, protecting her head and back from the claws and teeth. They tore at her armour, pulled at her cloak in frenzied madness, their blows causing Elijah to thump against her back. Panic laboured in her chest and she tilted her head but could only glimpse the angle of his chin.

Lysander roared, belching a torrent of fire and the screeches turned to high pitched animal screams, as sparks and ash stung Arii's eyes. She squeezed them shut again, heat searing her face.

The aerial beasts were relentless, scratching, clawing, biting. Arii felt warmth flare into fire in her chest as Lysander's roar twisted into an agonised wail and they began to tip sideways. She glanced up, catching the scramble of claws on blue scales.

Creatures clung to Lysander's hide, talons digging in deep as some began climbing the dragon, sightless skulls fixed on the riders on her back. Even the mighty movements of Lysander's wings didn't shake all of them.

The dragons surrounding them cried out too, consumed by the mass of winged creatures.

They had to do something.

Elijah had the same thought, the weight of him easing as he straightened, the call of his magic snapping like lightning around them. Arii leaped to her feet to balance precariously on the small space of the dragon's back, staring down Lysander's quivering spine. She ripped her blades from her hips as she growled, "Cover me!"

Two creatures came at her, jaws impossibly wide. She struck out, keeping her feet firm. One tried again as Arii dodged, barely holding on as she twisted to shove it off balance. The thing cried out, teeth snapping at her face, carrion breath burning against her skin. Her blade clanged off its scales before she followed through with her elbow, her bones rattling as its maw snapped to the side.

Her boots slipped and she gasped, heart lurching up her throat. She concentrated her weight into her hips and legs, to swipe at the creature's throat. She sensed Elijah's amassing power behind her, and knowing he was there kept her from falling.

The creature snapped again, spittle spraying her armour. Teeth scraped against her pauldron, far too close, but momentarily within range, the thin skin over its eye-sockets flexing. Arii yelled, twisted her arm to send her blade deep into the creature's skull. The winged beast screamed, and Arii yanked her blade free before it flailed and fell from Lysander's back, determined not to lose her weapons yet.

Before she could take a breath, another was upon her. They kept coming, and she continued to battle them, balancing on the rippling scales beneath her feet. Nothing could have prepared her for this, miles in the air above a fire and ice drenched battlefield. No amount of training at the School of Fate, nor her adventures thus far.

She could feel the steady build of Elijah's power as it coalesced into a sphere around them, pressing the mass of creatures back, unable to annihilate them for fear of harming the dragons nearby. The bat-like creatures clawed and slammed against the barrier, the shield springing them back like a bubble as Lysander sighed a smoke cloud of relief. The darkness began to dissipate as they broke through the ranks, the remainder of the creatures diving to avoid the dragon fire and drawn to the violence of the battle below.

Charred flesh and scales burned the inside of Arii's nose as she tore her blade from the last remaining creature, watching it spin and fall out of sight. She twisted, the thick mass of her hair billowing around her face as she stared wide-eyed at Elijah, who mirrored her awe.

"Where in Fythnar did you learn to do *that*?" she cried, falling back into the space before him.

"I didn't think it'd hold them off long," Elijah's voice was tinged with astonishment and pride, as if he too were surprised by his own weaving of magic. "I just… acted on instinct."

Arii couldn't help but grin wide. She shouldn't be surprised that Elijah was still amazing her, or himself. She'd felt his power, had dipped her fingers in the endless pool. He was incredible, and she was sure that if they survived this war, he'd be surprising her until the end of their days.

She dipped forward and placed a hand on Lysander's shivering scales. "Are you alright?"

"I have endured worse, little one. But thank you for your concern."

Endured worse? This dragon was not just something from the pages of books; Arii had little doubt she was full of infinite stories.

The darkening, golden castle expanded below them, painted in eerie, strobing blue light. Lysander's wings sprang out as she descended into a dip, membranes billowing like the sails of a ship, gliding around the castle's biggest tower, her shadow rippling across the throne room's stained-glass windows.

They were *so* close.

Elijah's hands squeezed her hips, his thoughts on the same wavelength. She hadn't had the chance to tell him about the crude crystal yet, nor the blood red eye inside.

Lysander landed upon the flat expanse of the Dragon Landing with a rumbling thud, crouching to allow them to dismount, before shaking her hide like a dog. Her serpentine head dipped, eyes unblinking as she hovered for a moment, running her ancient gaze over them both. *"Be careful,"* she rumbled, taking another look into each of their eyes before flaring her wings wide, blasting a tremendous rush of air to the floor, twisting to fly over the lip from which Arii had hurled herself only a short time ago.

For a moment they simply watched the blue dragon dive back into the battle as an ash-specked breeze toyed with their hair, mist clinging to their steady, panted breaths. Arii swallowed, glancing at her mate, catching his silver gaze. His jaw slid forward, the expression on his dust-smeared face one she'd seen him don before; the mask of a soldier. Separating himself from his emotions. To take on the skin of a bodyguard.

The exact mask she'd seen fall when they were alone, when he looked upon her in the moonlight, when he'd touched her and made her come undone.

He was preparing himself for what was to come.

She laced her fingers with his, and he squeezed, a light entering his eyes as she reached up and kissed him.

They didn't need words for the moment, she knew he could feel her love as it poured through the bond, as hot as a thousand suns, as ferocious as a wildfire.

Where you go, I follow, always.

Elijah exhaled against her lips, the sounds of war ringing from above and below.

"Let's end this, together," he said.

Together.

With hands still linked, they headed towards the throne room, prepared to meet their fate.

†

Glass crunched under their boots as they moved through the golden halls, the sconces on the walls long since extinguished, the only light that of the portal crackling in the sky beyond the windows. The unnatural combination of blue, purple and green prisms cast ripples over the reflective walls and devastation which littered the once pristine palace.

Arii and Elijah moved cautiously, weapons ready as they stepped over broken vases and sprawled bodies. Arii's gaze swept over her mate, his broad, armoured shoulders and scowling profile. This was but a shadow of the place where he'd grown up – where they had *both* grown up. She hardly recognised it anymore.

The world raged outside, yet in here it was eerily silent.

A number of the castle staff hadn't been fast enough to flee, some sprawled and torn apart, some slumped against walls with their eyes torn out. Her fists squeezed around the leather hilt of her blades, drawing comfort from their solidarity, the feel of them in her palms, their simplicity in a world where magic had become wild and untamed.

The very air they breathed was thick with it, worse as they neared the crooked open doors of the throne room. Where were Valdis' guards? She'd expected the place to be teeming with scurrying undead and perhaps a few living guards, but the place was deserted.

As they neared the threshold, Elijah lifted a hand, halting their progress. Going straight through to face Valdis felt like marching into a lion's den, but entry from any other point felt futile.

Valdis knew they were coming.

His garbled laugh startled them both, and as they passed the threshold and beheld the scene before them, Arii couldn't hold back a loud gasp.

Valdis was slumped, his shoulders shaking around his maniacal laughter as Lorch stepped back from him, his eyes wide and staring at his blood-specked hands. Valdis straightened, the glint of metal drawing Arii's eye.

A sword was firmly lodged in his guts.

"Ah, just in time," the man wheezed, grasping the hilt.

Lorch looked like he was about to be sick. Arii wished she could protect him from the beast that had taken over his father. She wished she could take him back to the Fae healer who had made him so happy. Far from the violence of this place.

Valdis grunted as he wrenched the blade from his body and tossed it aside. It clattered on the floor, and that was when Arii saw Ghila's crumpled form. Elijah too; and she knew the exact second when anger ignited his magic. It snapped across his iridescent sword in shocks of electricity as his face twisted into a snarl that rendered it unrecognisable.

Valdis turned to face them with a hacking laugh, back to his son, no longer seeing him as a threat. Arii could almost agree, Lorch's face awash in disbelief, his hands frozen in shock.

"Now I can end what I started so long ago. Funny, isn't it? That you were in this room, standing like a guard dog, taking orders from the very people who murdered your family." Valdis laughed again, the sound grating on Arii's nerves.

"You failed, and you were none the wiser…" Elijah snarled in response, taking a step forward. "Only fitting that your short reign finishes here, in this room, beside the throne that you desired so badly. This ends now, Valdis. I won't let you continue to tear our land apart."

Thanks to Lorch, Valdis was wounded, giving them an advantage. Elijah's magic picked up, scattering the loose shards of broken amethyst around his feet. Now was the time to strike.

Arii moved towards Ghila to brush her hair aside and place fingers against her pulse point.

Alive, but barely.

Lorch skidded to his knees at her other side, "Is she?"

"Alive," Arii whispered, "but she needs a healer. Here." She unclasped her cloak, throwing it over his shoulders. "This cloak is imbued with magic; it'll help shield you. Get her out of here. The Fae resistance is at the gates, evacuating the city. Find a healer for her. Get yourselves *out*."

"But what about you? And Elijah?" His watery blue eyes slid over her shoulder.

"I stay with him, no matter what happens."

His eyes met hers again and held, the weight of her words hovering between them, and she saw understanding in their depths. She also saw something else, perhaps. Resignation? Acceptance?

"Ha, HA!" Valdis cackled, and Arii felt her brows rise, failing to see what was so funny about the predicament he was in. Valdis shifted towards the jagged monolith of amethyst in the centre of the room, black blood trailing in his wake. The thing came to life, humming with ancient energy as a blood red iris opened, eying them. Valdis' grey skin shimmered, webs of red magic pulsing through the ripped folds of his heavy black attire.

He straightened, rolled his shoulders and sighed, healed of the wound that should have ended him.

"Fuck," Arii growled, a pulse of panic rattling her chest.

Valdis' head tilted to the side, his face cracking with a wicked smile. "It will end, but not for me."

The eye narrowed within the crystal, and then the floor began to shake.

Valdis lifted his arm, an amulet clutched in his fist. Magic, as black as the blood that had run from the veins of the cursed creatures, twisted around Valdis' feet, as if seeking to consume him. It quickly built, turning into a tornado, wild magic rising to his twisted command. She could hear the screams of tortured souls, the keening of children, the wails of heartbroken people. The sound brought angry tears to her eyes. So much pain, so much chaos, all in the pursuit of power.

Just as quickly as it had risen, the dark magic curled and warped, taking the form of a mighty serpent, its teeth as sharp as daggers, jaws wide, ready to strike.

Elijah threw up his free hand, his own wild magic rising to his command, blue and silver electricity enveloping him. Threads twined his clothing, caressed his armour, silver and gold snakes of magic, melding into the bones of a mighty dragon, wings fanning out behind him in a dazzling display of power. Its jaws widened, a roar shaking the ruined chandeliers above as the two titans of raw magic faced each other down.

Arii didn't have time to call out, to tell Lorch once more to take Ghila and retreat.

The two sides, light and dark, collided with a resounding *boom*.

They twisted around one another, biting and tearing, until they melded into one whirlwind.

Just as a tornado of crackling energy twisted to life around Elijah and Valdis, Arii saw movement at the corner of her eye as Lorch sprang to his feet to sprint straight to where his father and best friend stood.

He leaped, headfirst into the maelstrom.

"Lorch!" she cried, rising, boots slipping over crystal and polished marble, hair whipping in a frenzy from the violently coalescing war of darkness and light.

But she couldn't enter, as if the people inside were shielded by a forcefield of static magic.

Arii slammed her fists against the barrier, rage and helplessness taking hold as she began to scream.

CHAPTER THIRTY-THREE

ELIJAH

Magic warped around him, tearing around his clothing with such force that Elijah had to hold his feet firm, widen them slightly to bear against the brunt of their battling powers. His beast bayed and roared with fervour, as the eye in the crystal swivelled his way, blinking and shaking with greed.

Valdis' form wavered ahead, his heavy cloak whipping around him.

Elijah's arm began to shake, his limb taking on the ache of an invisible weight. He gritted his teeth, tossing his sword aside so that he could hold the burden of their warring magic with two hands.

Valdis looked to be struggling as much as he was. The man's face was twisted, his scar a slash across haggard features. His jaw was clenched so hard that his neck pulled taught, veins popping from his ashen skin. Any residual colour of life was gone, his face almost skeletal, overtaken by a force that his human body wasn't designed to bear.

The eye moved back and forth between them, shaking with excitement over the battle.

Specks of glittering stone began to peel from Valdis' exposed skin, like paint peeling from old wood.

The throne room became a blur around them, raw panic churning inside Elijah for his mate and sister, unable to stop the turbulence around them. Things had gone too far now. He hoped desperately that Arii would retreat, take his sister and go. But his heart knew she wouldn't go without him.

He could only hope that fate would spare them.

Massive chunks of debris rained down like a deadly hailstorm, each impact sending shockwaves through the very foundation of the castle. The room was being torn apart, wood, plaster and dented gold entering the tornado around them. The castle and its once-lively city seemed doomed, even soon to be erased from the maps of history.

He thought of all the people he'd loved and lost, their faces flashing before his eyes, but one stopped and held itself there.

Lorch.

His best friend, his brother, his sworn enemy. He hadn't had the chance to speak with him; to make him pay for what he'd done; nor had he had the chance to forgive him.

As if Elijah's thoughts drew him forth, there was a ripple in the chaotic shield around them, and suddenly Lorch broke through, hitting the ground arms first. He sprang to his feet, Arii's shielding cloak wrapped around him, copper hair a wild tangle of strands.

"Elijah!" he bellowed, shielding his eyes against the howling wind.

No, he shouldn't be here!

But Elijah couldn't help him, it took all his strength to keep Valdis' magical chaos dancing with his own. Above them, serpent and dragon continued to war, snapping and striking at each other, looking for breaks in each other's defences – a magical, theatrical display of their belligerent power.

His mortal friend would be torn apart in here.

"Lorch, no!" Elijah growled between gritted teeth, as another piece of the ceiling smashed just a few feet away.

But Lorch's face held a look of pure determination as he picked up Elijah's discarded sword. He braced to shout against the wind that whipped around them. "I never had the chance to tell you how sorry I am, brother. For all that I let happen, for all that I did, for all that I didn't do."

Elijah's heart fractured, eyes filling with tears, the vision of his best friend wavering as Lorch lifted the heavy sword.

Behind him, Valdis screamed towards the red eye. "It is time you fulfilled your side of the bargain, you have your sacrifice – two in fact! Bring him back. Bring my love Micah back *now*."

The eye within the stone squinted at him, then boomed, "You know what must be done now. I have enough power and my beast is almost through. Sacrifice the soul to me so that I may have a vessel."

Sacrifice. Vessel.

Valdis conjured a blade of darkness, eyes bulging against the colossal force of the chaos around him.

Lorch pointed towards his father. "That's what all this was for, all the death and destruction – to bring back his love killed by a Fae long ago. His entire vendetta against magic, against your kind; all because of his loss. I can't let this go on. I've sat back long enough."

He pivoted on his heel, raising his sword towards the figure before him. Though his son's defiance was nothing new, Valdis' red rimmed eyes glimmered with an unsettling blend of disbelief and simmering fury.

"No!" Elijah bellowed, helpless as Lorch and Valdis collided, magical steel against pure darkness.

His beast roared, revelling in the destruction, feeding on the chaos of his shared connection with the ancient alchemy that resided in the room. Memories broke through the maelstrom. He heard the words Kadec had spoken, while his mind was in the illusion where he had seen the land's destruction and faced a conjured dragon.

"The magic you possess is beyond powerful, it is catastrophic. One day it will consume you, unless you do something about it."

Since then, his magic had only gotten stronger, so strong there had been times when he felt that if his grip lacked, even just for a second, he would lose control and destroy far more than those he aimed for.

"There is no kingdom without sacrifice."

He'd known for a time that he wouldn't make it out of this alive. Everything had been pointing towards this, towards his death. All he could do was to make sure it was worth it.

"The only way to stop this, to stop all of it, is for you to die, Eliverus."

An idea began to bloom like a flower in his mind. A way to end it all. He watched as Lorch swept the sword towards his father in a perfect arch reminiscent of the many times he'd insisted they train together. His friend had been taking their sessions seriously after all.

"The only one who can stop the coming apocalypse is you. But not without sacrifice."

Sacrifice.

"Magic such as yours should not exist and cannot exist without eventually causing calamity. Tell me, Prince who was lost... Will you do what is wrong, to make things right?"

Arii. He'd never known someone to care so violently or readily sacrifice herself, like Ariiaya did. She'd forged the life bond between herself and Nem without a thought for the consequences.

Magic worked in strange ways. There always seemed be a balance to keep, rules that couldn't be broken yet could be bent, and it achieved the impossible while still failing to solve all problems.

Elijah had marvelled at his miraculous life bond with Arii, which had then broken hers and Nem's. A loophole in the spell of life magic.

What would happen now if he were to forge a new bond? Would Arii feel theirs snap? Would she live if he were to die?

He hoped beyond hope that she would survive, that a new bond would simply sever theirs – like Arii's and Nem's. His mate was too strong for death. He knew if it came knocking, she'd expose her teeth and growl, sending it scurrying away, only to foolishly try again another day.

He hadn't told her of what Kadec had prophesised, for he knew she would have torn the castle down with her bare hands, through golden metal and stone until her fingers were bloody bones, rather than see him die. Yet he knew she would build a new world from the ashes, to protect the land and people she loved.

He loved her so much that it hurt.

The only problem with Elijah's hasty plan was that Valdis wasn't on the brink of death, so he wasn't sure that a life bond was possible without death's near-embrace.

Lorch wielded the sword as if it were his own, bringing the weapon down to clash with his father's dark blade. "You foolish boy. Reckless, dim-witted *child*. I'll kill you. I'll kill all of you!" Valdis roared, eyes rolling with madness and grief. Lorch grimaced against the whipping tendrils of darkness that emanated from the blade, his arms shaking. He stepped back, twisted to duck under Valdis' wretched weapon.

Then he threw himself forward, blade tip aimed straight at his father's chest.

But Valdis was faster.

Darkness slammed into Lorch's stomach; the blade lodging so deep that it split from his back just as his own blade jammed into Valdis' chest.

Everything else– the tornado of darkness and light, the warring sceptres above them, the crumbling throne room outside the ripples of their battle – faded as Elijah's heart stopped.

Valdis choked, Lorch gasped in shock, their bodies teetering. Valdis stumbled, staring in wild disbelief at the sword protruding from his chest.

Lorch's hands folded around the hilt of the blade made of darkness. His knees smacked to the marble floor, his fingers passing through the thing like water. He stared at his hands, then up at his father.

No. No. NO.

Valdis yanked the sword from his own chest, blood fountaining even as he attempted to stanch the flow with one hand.

"You… fool," he rasped, teeth black with blood in a grim smile.

Rumbling quaked beneath their feet, and Elijah wasn't sure if he was making the earth tremble with his grief, or if it was something far beyond the shard of light that housed a son and his father during their final moments before death.

Nothing else mattered in that moment. Nothing else but the copper-haired boy who had just given Elijah the opening he needed. He had to move fast, the red magic already healing the damage to

Valdis' chest.

A voice rumbled from the jagged shard housing the eye, its deep resonance shuddering. *"Finish it. Prepare the vessel!"* The eye glowed crimson as its magic worked on Valdis' wound.

Elijah was running out of time.

He set his sights upon Valdis' back as the man stepped towards his son, another blade of darkness already coalescing into existence, his other hand swinging his amulet like a pendulum.

With the distraction, Elijah felt a tiny lapse in the chaos around them. With one hand he made a pulling motion. A tendril of darkness exploded from Valdis' hunched back, and the man cried out, spine arching under an invisible force. Elijah's other hand motioned to his own chest, and a golden thread emerged, dancing from him like a snake awoken from slumber.

Numbness spread across his heart as he aimed the thread while also tugging the one from Valdis, willing for them to connect. But Valdis was healing, aided by the being in the crystal, and the threads began to slow.

Elijah was losing his chance, the moment quickly slipping away as Lorch coughed blood, face angled up under the shadow of the one to give him life, soon to take it away.

Hopelessness doused Elijah's body, making him cry out in anguish, while the might of his magic raged around them, destroying the home he'd fought so hard to save.

He couldn't do it. He wasn't in control of his magic any longer.

The dragon above keened, its song one of massacre and remorse.

Elijah was going to be the one to bring about the destruction he'd fought so hard to prevent. He shook, tears cascading down his cheeks as Valdis lifted the blade with a cry of triumph.

He'd failed.

Darkness slithered like snakes up his arms.

Everything slowed, as if time itself wished for rest. A hand settled on his shoulder, and a voice split the madness whirling around his mind. It was gentle, like soft silk against his cheek.

"Eliverus, you've never been one to give up before, and I do not see you giving up now."

Through watery eyes he saw his mother, her beautiful face set in a smile.

How, how could this be?

"You bear the burden of the land on your shoulders, impossibly heavy, but it is a weight I know you can bear," came another voice, low and strong, like forged steel. He twisted his head to see a spectre of his father, eyes bright against wrinkled skin and salt-flecked beard.

Elijah sucked in his breath, and had he not been staring at the faces of his dead parents, he might have registered that he was hyperventilating.

Another hand touched his arm, one slightly wrinkled and kissed with sunspots. Colleen's gentle face tilted towards him, nothing but peace in her eyes. Her body was whole.

"You can do this, my son. Breathe."

Elijah willed his breaths to steady, focusing on the faces around him. They all looked upon him with such pride.

How could they not see the darkness inching up his fingers and hands? How could they not see the spots of madness in his eyes? The destruction his magic was causing as it swelled to tear their home apart from within?

That was when Lorch stood, as if oblivious to the blade in his stomach. He threw himself at his father, and the man yelped in surprise as they collided. Lorch wrapped his arms around Valdis to lock him in a precarious grip.

His brother was trying to give him more time… another opening.

Elijah felt himself eroding, pieces chipping away like weathered rock. His arms shook as he pulled upon the connection with renewed vigour, the black tendril jerking and lengthening from Valdis' back as his body fought against Lorch's hold.

Then a new voice sounded, almost a mirror of his own. A man perhaps a few years older than Elijah, not the age when his life had been so mercilessly taken. "Use the weight you bear and make it a shield and sword against those who bring darkness. I've seen you take stars from the sky and make talismans of hope and protection against curses. You're still needed here, little brother." Brohem smiled from beside their father, silver eyes bright in his clean-shaven, handsome face.

A sob wracked Elijah's throat. His family, all here, in a space between life and death as the strings of the bond he tried to forge crept closer together, across a seemingly impossible distance.

A new hand rested on his outstretched arm, small and petite.

"You're stronger than you know, brother, but it isn't your time to go yet."

It was his sister, wide storm-grey eyes fixed on his, dark, choppy hair wind-blown. Then he felt like the madness was truly taking over, as another wavering spectre stood by his side, his hand coming to rest beside Ghila's.

His eyes locked with depths so blue, they resembled a bright, cloudless sky on a clear summer day. Skies that once graced the north almost every day.

Lorch stared back, his face set with a knowing smile.

"Lorch?" Elijah breathed, his whole heart in that utterance. He was here, but not truly. Elijah's mind was reeling as he glanced at each spectre's face in turn, heart stuttering.

None of them should be here.

Was Elijah dying? He couldn't be sure, yet he could feel his soul fraying, unravelling like a ball of golden yarn. His oldest friend, his brother in all but blood, looked wiser somehow – the playful glint that the young copper-haired boy had always possessed now absent, lending him to look older… resigned.

"I'm so sorry for all that I've done, and all that I didn't do for you, Elijah. Please forgive me."

Elijah blinked, perplexed at seeing Lorch beside him when he could also see the same man battling with Valdis. It was as if he stood on another layer of existence, watching the scene play out on a stage.

"You're needed here, to pick up the pieces and build a better world from the ashes, Elijah.”

Elijah's eyes widened, moving from the image of his best friend down to where Lorch's body warred in its last moments with his father.

“I know you won't allow my sacrifice to be in vain, nor will you allow any of the sacrifices up until now be in vain.” Lorch's voice was firm, a smile wrinkling his eyes.

“I am so sorry for everything, Lorch.” Elijah managed to gasp, pain in his heart. Lorch's eyes softened as Elijah rasped, “I forgive you, if you'll forgive me too.”

For the bond I'm about to make, for the sacrifice thereafter.

Lorch nodded, giving Elijah his answer.

He angled his head to his sister, sure she was using telepathy as she had before. “And I'm sorry, little sister, for not saving you from the monsters, for not finding you before.”

Ghila's smile was sad. “There is nothing to forgive,” she said, giving his arm a squeeze.

Elijah's legs began to buckle. And yet, he still stood, held in place by the hands of his loved ones.

Focusing on the bond, he attempted to guide the threads together once more, warring against the Gods in forging Fates. The strings grew longer, and his own golden thread reached out, so close that they were only moments from connecting.

“NO!” the thing within the crystal cried, sensing the shift.

Elijah shook uncontrollably as he gazed at the people holding him upright, the people he loved so dearly that he'd face death just to see their faces again.

“You can let go now, Eli.” Ghila said, as the ghosts of their family dissipated, leaving only his little sister and his best friend, side by side.

He had to hold on, complete the life bond with Valdis, and then upon his own death, Valdis would die too.

It had been his plan all along, even before he had even known it himself.

It was his fate. To die for all he loved was his fate.

Ghila turned to where the cords stretched, inches away from one another. She paused, staring down at the two threads with a look of gentle resolution. She glanced back at him once more, lips curling, eyes crinkling.

Kadec's earlier words flowed around him. *"The only one who can stop the coming apocalypse is you. But not without sacrifice."*

Sacrifice…

A cost.

The cost was not his own life, but the life of someone dear to him.

"Ghila… Ghila, don't!" Elijah moaned with realisation.

She lifted a hand and pulled a thread from her own chest, feeding it to the darkness, intercepting Valdis' thread before it could connect with her brother's.

No.

No.

He couldn't. He couldn't let go of them. This sacrifice wasn't fair to ask this of him. It wasn't fair to *take* this much.

Ghila sighed deeply, taking the darkness of the thread into herself. The bond snapped into place.

Elijah bellowed her name as the raging inferno of his magic sputtered and stilled, emptying until there was nothing but a shallow puddle where his power once remained. Above them the jaws of his dragon gripped the serpent to wrench out its throat in a violent shower of sparks.

Valdis' back bowed, mouth wide, eyes rolling back as he slumped to the floor, taking his son with him. Lorch held his father tightly, energy spent, face resting against Valdis' shoulder, eyes fluttering as his lips moved without sound.

Elijah watched heartbroken as Lorch embraced his father, a man who had held on to love so dearly that he'd burn the whole world down for just one chance to see that love again.

Beside Elijah, the spectre of Lorch squeezed his arm, moving to meet Ghila in the middle as a bright light yawned in the darkness ahead, spilling over them like a new dawn. They watched him, their eyes bright.

"I love you, brother," whispered Ghila, her smile wide. The smile she'd worn when she'd mounted the dais in her dress made of all the colours of the rainbow.

"Look after them for me, Eli," said Lorch, and Elijah knew that he spoke of his family, and those he was leaving behind.

Elijah's body shook, his magic almost completely spent, naught but a flicker left from the inferno of before.

"I promise," he replied.

Ghila and Lorch turned to the light, two complete strangers, never having met, yet they linked hands as if dear friends. The light flared brighter, swallowing them whole, taking them somewhere Elijah could not follow.

Something pulled taut the further they went into the light, tugging at the centre of his chest until close to breaking.

Elijah felt his world collapse. The incessant tug was replaced with nothingness, a sadness beyond anything he had felt before.

Elijah knelt in the slowly fading light, watching the golden passage to the beyond slowly begin to fade.

All he could hear was his breath, ragged and laboured. All he could feel was the raging thunder of his heart, like waves crashing against a broken shore.

The world returned with a dizzying slowness as the remnants of their magical inferno blew away like dust, and he was left with nothing but flickers of his magic, and his own heartbroken scream.

LORCH

Lorch held on to his father, even after the light left his eyes, and his form slumped, held aloft by the sheer mass of black ice coating his body. He held him, even as the half-closed wound in his chest trickled the life from his body, thickening in a pool around them. As his life ebbed away, he swore he heard his father utter his name.

Lorch wasn't angry. He was far from that. Feeling was something foreign, all sensations in the mortal realm drifting away like a boat leaving a harbour as his soul rose, greeted by the golden light.

He stared down at the shell of his body, at the man embraced in his arms.

All of this had been for the promise of lost love. Lorch knew, if he were to feel anything in this moment, it would have been sorrow, but the maelstrom was fading, and he knew that the war was almost over. Warmth glowed over his back, and he turned to see a golden portal opening wide.

He gazed at the rift, knowing where it led.

He was joined by another. A girl with raven hair, one side chopped a little too short. She was the one who fought his father, who had taken him on alone in the throne room, giving Lorch a chance to escape. He'd been so determined, so angry with his father, but now, those feelings were so far away, as if harboured by someone else completely.

The girl's grey eyes were so familiar that their depths brought him a feeling of peace. She lifted her hand, as if reaching to touch him.

Was she easing his pain, pushing aside all feeling?

She nodded, and her gaze swept past him, to the distant sounds of rumbling. He followed, seeing dark clouds just beyond where the golden light reached, as if held back from spilling over.

Lorch looked down.

The wound where the blade had entered his abdomen felt like a distant memory, as if it had never happened. The weapon of shadow was gone. He looked to the girl, questions bleeding across his quietening mind.

"We have both served our purpose," whispered the girl.

Yes, yes she was right. He'd helped save the land he'd helped to ruin, and he knew Elijah would be the king that the people truly needed.

Lorch swallowed, looking at the light once more.

He felt nothing, but at the same time, saw *everything*.

Images flashed before his eyes, faces, their features morphing together, cycling through the people he loved, as a boy and an adult. He saw his mother, her gold-spun hair, the smile she only ever wore for him, and his sister, her dark eyes missing nothing, yet affection for her big brother showing in the way her face softened when he spoke.

He saw Elijah as he had first met him, his timid little smile, his guard up even though he very much wanted a friend. And he had gained that friend, the guardedness in his eyes warming to affection. Brotherly love.

He saw Ariiaya, her unguarded smile as he spun her through a kaleidoscope of dancing courtiers on the night of the Winter Solstice. He felt her firm hand holding his as she pulled him to safety after fighting waves and waves of undead nightmares.

Shockingly, he saw his father, leaning over his crib, his face younger and smooth with surprise. His eyes – the same as Lorch's own, as bright as an ocean under full sun – were wide in a display of rare awe as Lorch's own little newborn fingers curled around a hand that would one day cause so much death.

Those hands morphed to his own, moving in tandem with much smaller ones, Mia's laughter of surprise and excitement, helping heal a few of the cracked pieces of his heart.

Finally, he saw Cela, her bright jade eyes staring intently at his arm as her magic mended his hurts, and then flaring with emotion after he kissed her in the Inn. They had just begun to know each other, had finally broken the fragile barrier between Fae and human, with a whole world of possibility to explore.

Lorch knew though, that his time was at an end.

They'd mourn him, his mother, his sister, Arii, Elijah. As would Celadine and her daughter, their time together but a drip in the fountain that was their immortal lives. He felt sorrow at this, unable to tell them a proper goodbye. But Lorch had an overwhelming sense that whatever lay beyond the light was meant for him, a path he *had* to follow.

Some fates could not be woven.

Some fates just *were*.

The Fae held out her hand, her face open and resolute, making him feel like whatever lay beyond the shimmering veil would not be a challenge, but a step towards an existence of peace.

Lorch's fingers twined with hers.

As one they stepped through the golden void, hearts free of sorrow, souls lightened of burden, on to whatever came next.

CHAPTER THIRTY-FOUR

ARIIAYA

This was where it had all begun, and so too would it end here. The threads of fate had begun to spin, in this very room, and so too would they be cut. Arii had thought she would be the one to do it, as she had been charged by the Gods to do so. But she realised that it mattered not who cut the strings of fate, only whose threads of life those strings had belonged to.

"We see a crown, and a royal seat covered in blood…"

Arii had thought the threads had been destined for Lorch, then later for Elijah.

"Your next target sits upon the royal throne…"

He had been the last to wear the crown, had been the last to be King. Now, she knew without a shadow of uncertainty, the thread that had started it all had been meant for Valdis Kruel.

And he was dead.

All souls, magically entuned and not, knew the exact moment his thread of life had been cut. The portals above the city roared as if in fury, warping closed with a thunderous clap that sent shockwaves across the land. The magic holding the corpses upright winked out and their bodies fell in heaps, bones clapping in a jarring chorus. The red eye in the stone screeched, wretched, furious, making the entire chamber shudder. Then, in a chilling instant, it winked out, leaving an ominous silence in its wake.

The battle was won. Elijah had done it.

But why couldn't she cross the barrier keeping them apart?

All Arii felt was fear, so gut wrenching that it reverberated in the marrow of her bones. The wall of magic around Elijah, Valdis and Lorch was impenetrable, like a shivering wall of gold and blue ice. She could barely see within, slamming her fists against it and calling until her skin split and her voice ran hoarse.

Three figures wavered. One, slightly apart from the other two, was on his knees, hands braced against the floor. The other two appeared to be embracing each other. She could make out the copper of their hair, their pale skin, two that were like reflections in an aging mirror.

Valdis was dead, she had felt it, like a thick smog lifting from the realm.

Yet the barrier remained.

Elijah, he had to be alive, *had* to be. Lorch too.

She screamed, the connection between her and her mate flickering like a dying candle, the overwhelming regret of allowing Lorch to dive into danger she was supposed to protect him from, all becoming too much.

With a keening sound, the barrier, like a shimmering sheet of water, began to fall.

Arii remained on her knees as it faded slowly, revealing a glimmering, fallen object.

A crown lay cracked, blood dotting its scuffed golden surface like rubies.

The Fate's visions hadn't been totally inaccurate after all.

Recovering, Arii threw herself at Elijah's slumped form. His lashes fluttered before his eyes opened slowly, his grey irises bright with fading residual magic.

Relief had her almost losing hold of his broad shoulders, eyes swimming, liquifying her sight of his beautiful, tired face. Tears tracked her cheeks to patter against Elijah's armour. Relief, sorrow, anguish mixed into one force, one thread that ran from her chest to his. What they felt in that moment was shared. The heartbreak they felt as one.

Elijah's glassy grey eyes skimmed from her face across to where one of the bodies fell, as if finally released from an invisible hold.

"Lorch," Elijah rasped, throat sounding parched, as they moved. A tinny whine filled Arii's ears, making her feel as if her head were under water. Her movements felt sluggish, too, as her eyes took in the prone form of the fallen king.

He couldn't be… he wasn't…

Nem knelt beside Lorch, placing a hand on his chest. Arii hadn't even seen her best friend enter the room, so focused was she on the lack of movement in Lorch's chest, the bloom of red darkening his cream tunic. She slung Elijah's arm over her shoulder, shuffling under his weight as they drew near, his rugged breathing growing louder.

Numbness overtook her as she absorbed the terrible wound in the ruin of Lorch's clothing, but what truly had her tears streaming was the look of peace upon his beautiful face.

It was as if he were sleeping.

"I'm… so sorry," whispered Nem. "He's… gone."

No.

No, he wasn't.

Denial made her ears ring.

Elijah was the first to break, his yell of anguish echoing around the room. He held Lorch to his chest. Their bond thickened with the trembles of his sorrow, a sorrow she felt so acutely that the salt in her tears did not register. They spilled down her cheeks as she bowed her head, watching the uncontrollable droplets spill on the bloody marble floor. For a time they all remained silent, Elijah's shoulder shaking under the press of Arii's cheek, their friends watching on, heartsick. Arii lifted her gaze to Nem, unable to find any words to fill the silence.

Nem's eyes, wet with her own tears, lifted to something over Arii's shoulder, and she followed her gaze. Krepth knelt nearby, beside Ghila, who was on her side, seemingly resting. Her face, like Lorch's, was peaceful, her lips in a small smile. She was far too still, though, her skin far paler than it had been before.

Arii swallowed, and when her eyes met Krepth's, a tiny shake of his head confirmed her thoughts.

She too, was gone.

CHAPTER THIRTY-FIVE

ELIJAH
(ONE WEEK LATER)

Elijah knew there would always be casualties in war. It was inevitable, but that didn't make it hurt any less. The loss of his best friend had broken him, but the loss of his sister had truly threatened to shatter him beyond repair.

If it hadn't been for his mate, for the golden thread that wove through their bond and around his form, hugging him in sympathetic warmth, he didn't know how he would have survived. He tried to relay what he'd seen as the chaos of his magic, about how he'd seen Lorch and Ghila walk hand in hand through the gates to the beyond, but it just felt like madness coming from his lips.

He was also left with but a fraction of the magic that he possessed before. That fact was to remain silent, his advisors recommended, lest he be challenged as soon as he was crowned. It was strange, not to feel the thrum of power constantly moving beneath his skin. His beast was silent too, docile. There was a chance the power needed time to regenerate, but Elijah couldn't be sure.

As far as he was concerned, he hadn't felt this light in… years.

The week that followed was a whirlwind of court meetings, clean-up of the castle and a hastily planned coronation. The damage to the city was extensive, and many of its residents were displaced until their homes and businesses were repaired. In amongst the carnage, little shrines of remembrance began to blossom, carved with the names of the fallen, and decorated with the summer flowers that had begun returning to the land.

The war had aptly been named *The War of the Realms*, and those who had survived would forever live with the horrors they witnessed, along with the pure astonishment of live dragons. The beasts soared above, watching over them, their cries filling Elijah with hope.

Slowly, the skies above the North returned to their blue glory, adrift with lazy white clouds. The cool bite of the unnatural winter eased, replaced with welcome warmth. The black ice crystal melted under the sunlight, and the spread of the Sapphire Depths thawed, returning to the tranquil blue waters of its former self.

The rebuild would take time and patience and persistence. Valdis' support network ran deep – deeper than Elijah had originally anticipated. Contingents of Red Guard soldiers rebelled, still in support of Valdis' ideals even after his demise, adding another layer of complexity over the fragile state of the land.

Elijah often found himself thinking about the eye in the stone, and what kind of creature it belonged to, and what kind of land it inhabited if it was so eager to extend its claws into this one. Those thoughts returned as he oversaw the deconstruction of the now-lifeless shard of amethyst, its depths devoid of the eerie glow and thrum of power. The rough stone cracked beneath the pickaxes of guards who had hastily promised fealty to the lost Prince, the horrors they'd experienced during the conflict making them all too ready to alter their ways.

Most of the corroded ice had been cleaned away, and the throne room was slowly beginning to look like itself again. Work had begun on replastering the walls and replacing the tall windows with new glass of patterned crystal, allowing evening light to douse the hall in a warm glow. The surplus gold from the devastation was scraped and melted down to help pay for the city's reconstruction and the people's food. The taint was almost completely gone, the castle employees who had survived eager to rid the place of the darkness that had taken over.

Tomorrow, he would be coronated here, officially made King by the members of the council who had survived. They'd be joined by the other court monarchs, and unlike the last time that such an event was held here, Elijah hoped it would be a happy occasion, a union of the land under a new reign… a new hope. Whatever doubts that had plagued him in the months leading up to this day were now far from his mind. Left with but a fraction of the power he'd possessed before, he felt lighter, less burdened, less *unstable*.

His eyes slid to the throne, perched alone on the dais, freshly upholstered with red velvet, the intricate gold carvings around it buffed until he could see multiples of his own face in the metal. He placed his fingers against the tip of the arm, letting the cool substance ground him.

Lorch had sat upon it last, and despite not him not belonging there, Elijah had a moment where he wished his best friend were perched upon it once more.

"Your Highness," came a voice from behind, and Elijah turned. The woman stood with her chin held high, her golden hair drawn into a meticulous crown braid, watched him with dark eyes and a regal air of authority, well beyond her twenty years of age.

"Commander," he replied with a slow smile, watching the colour spread over Sybell's pale cheeks. The title had once belonged to her father, but Hawke had decided to retire to a small farm on the border, just where the rolling pastures began to thicken with forest to the east. At first Elijah had been disappointed that Hawke hadn't wanted to return as Commander of the Red Guard, but he understood that the man wished for a simpler life, one filled with farm utensils rather than steel weapons. And one where he could live happily with Sybell's mother Lynnera, finally his fiancée after so many years of secrets and longing.

So, Elijah had offered the job to his daughter, who had accepted with a twinkle in her eyes and a determination he could see in every facet of her demeanour.

At Sybell's back, a few paces away, was Tora, the tall, stoic Fury whom he'd appointed as his second in command. He'd heard of the way they'd fought during the war, the way they'd not only defended Noct and the Fates, but each other, too. Shortly after the portal had closed, another one had opened, a pair of foreign, female arms pulling Nocturne through. It had been so swift that even the Fates had been left perplexed, and despite a rocky start with the stranger, Elijah was disappointed to have not been able to say goodbye.

Something told him the man would be back, though.

Now, his attention skipped between the two women, watching their subtle interactions. It also wasn't a secret that the two had feelings for one another, even though they tried to keep things quiet.

As a man in love, he could spy the telltale signs.

Sybell had proven herself for the role. He could see the healthy glow of her mortal skin. Like many living in the North, she had been without purpose, and now that purpose had been found. She emanated confidence, had a way of speaking to the council and the courtiers, thanks to her royal upbringing.

"Preparations for your coronation are almost complete… well, as complete as they can be given the state of the castle." Sybell's eyes dropped to the throne, watching the space where Elijah's fingers had paused. Her eyes darkened, her confidence slipping ever so slightly. He knew that she, like him, thought of Lorch often, missed him so much it hurt, regretted not doing more to save him.

"Thank you, Sybell." He tipped his head to the stone-faced Fury a few steps away. "Tora."

The two bowed low, placing their hands over their hearts.

A man in long, deep blue robes entered the hall hastily. In his wake strode Krepth, black cloak swishing against the heels of his boots, wearing an expression of easy nonchalance as he whistled. He was clean-shaven and looking far better than the last time Elijah had seen him.

Close behind him was Nemesis, her silver hair swept back into a tight plait against her head, accentuating her angled face and high cheekbones, her aqua eyes fixed upon him. She too looked better. Lighter, somehow. Her skin reminded him of a polished pearl. Had she always had a subtle radiance to her skin, a glow even?

Quinn and Tikkani appeared, their clothes covered in dust and grime. The young Shifter blew deep brown curls from his eyes as Tikkani pulled down her shirtsleeves to cover her arms. Emerson and Luc followed, a little tidier if not still dirty from helping clean up the city.

When Elijah had seen his friends for the first time since the end of the war, he had felt immense relief, and he had seen the same shine in their eyes. They'd all survived.

Almost all.

His mind drifted back to the ones he'd lost, the pain in his heart returning like a vengeful shadow. It never quite went away, remaining like a fissure through his soul, waiting for his attention to slip. Elijah knew grief, had felt its icy fingers caress his heart before, when his memories had begun to return, revealing the loss of his family.

But this… this was a break in the dam compared to the slow trickle of a life he barely remembered.

"Your Highness, I must once again insist against your wishes for the coronation to include an open invitation to the townspeople," said the man in blue robes, after a practiced and impressive bow.

Nem's brow rose in question, and Elijah shook his head.

"Councilman Spokes," he greeted him, keeping his expression schooled. "The Sisters of Fate and their Fury contingent have offered to be a secondary layer of protection around the castle during the ceremony. They will be our eyes in the shadows."

"But they are cutthroats… assassins…"

Elijah held up a hand, gently. "I trust them. They helped to slow the opening of the portals, and they aided us in the war as much as every other. They lost sisters on the field, lost friends, as we all did."

The man was silent, his expression resigned.

"The people deserve a moment to celebrate, a moment to feel welcome," added Elijah.

"It is a large risk. Valdis' taint still remains, not enough time has passed for us to weed out those who may wish to seek revenge." Councilman Spokes wrung his hands in his cloak nervously, adding, "I say this with the utmost respect, sire."

Elijah felt sorry for the man, who had been on the council under Valdis. He talked with fear, and Elijah knew it was because he was afraid of the implications of being honest or expressing something the king did not wish to hear. He feared being punished just for lending his opinion – which was ridiculous. It was what councilmen were employed for. He remembered Councilman Spokes from his childhood. A gently spoken man, an honest man, a lot greyer now. He had been welcoming, as had the other surviving councilmen, albeit they all seemed… skittish. Unsure.

"I understand your hesitation, Councilman Spokes, I truly do." Elijah reasoned gently, "And I also respect what you are saying. It is a risk, I know, but a risk worth taking. The people suffered; they need to know that the place that once was a symbol of division is no longer that, but a place where all are welcome."

"Now is the time for unity. In unity, there is strength," came a voice from the freshly repaired doors.

Her voice was like a siren's song to his ears, drawing his gaze to the door. Ariiaya entered, chin high, honey-tipped hair up in a messy bun, her neck and cheeks smeared with work grime. Her sleeves were pulled up, and even in dirty clothing, Elijah's blood heated at how beautiful she was. She'd been out in the city, helping with the clean-up, in the dirt with everyone else.

Even under the evidence of hard work, she still looked like she could be royalty.

His heart squeezed with pride as their eyes met. The edges of those violet eyes crinkled with her grin.

Councilman Spokes's mouth shut, nodding quickly. "Yes… Yes, I suppose you are right. We are gathering more willing cadets into the army, people who wish to be trained to defend our court so that history never repeats. That and the uptake in Fae soldiers wanting to join your army, we should have more than enough to watch during the celebration." He sighed, waving a hand before folding into a bow.

"It'll take time for the people to trust that what they witnessed is truly over, and also it will take time for them to trust me." Elijah's gaze lingered on the man, and in that moment, he saw a shift in the councilman's stance. He began to relax, the wrinkled skin around his eyes smoothing just a fraction at Elijah's words as he continued.

"My time serving under the Kruel family won't be so quickly forgotten, but I do not wish to begin this period of proposed peace with division. Every soul living in the North is to be treated as equals. That's why I want to invite everyone. The courtyard will be open to all once the formalities have been done."

Spokes nodded, while the others followed suit. Elijah glanced down at his hand, still pressed against the arm of the throne, and suddenly a thought came to mind. Or perhaps it was a memory.

Two thrones, his father on one, his mother on the other, their hands linked in the middle.

"And I'd like another throne, next to this one, if possible…"

Spokes' brows shot up.

Elijah swallowed, straightening his spine, aware of the silence in the room. He added, "Like my parents used to have."

This councilman's eyes softened further. "Very good. Your wishes will be seen to, Your Highness." Spokes offered a timid smile, before sweeping from the room.

"A big-arse party. Now that sounds like a grand idea!" Quinn chuckled, grinning at the petite elf by his side. Tikkani smiled, shaking her head, but Eljah knew her partner had taken the words from her mouth.

"The people already see you as their savour, Elijah." Emerson said, before halting with a hand to his mouth. His wedding band sparkled as he whispered, "Oh, sorry, do we call you Eliverus now?"

Elijah chuckled as Luc said, "Tomorrow, we call him our King." The Shifter swept into a low bow, to which Elijah's cheeks began to flame.

"As my friends… as my *court*, you can all still call me Elijah. Let's keep the formalities to formal occasions, shall we?"

The group laughed, falling into a comfortable conversation.

Elijah smiled, one that was genuine, one that felt natural, free of worry, as he gazed at his friends.

He couldn't do the future alone. And thankfully, he had never been alone, not truly. Though he'd lost Ghila, the last living connection to his family, and Lorch, his brother in all but blood, and his heart would take time to truly heal, he knew the journey there would be easier with the family he'd found along the way. The love, the friendship, the trust. He trusted each and every one of them impeccably.

Together, with his fated mate, and with his friends, they would bring forth a new age from the ashes, for they were his court.

His court of hope.

There was one last thing to do, though.

He was going to ask Ariiaya to marry him.

ARIIAYA

Her hair was still lightly damp, the golden ends curling in the warm breeze. Ariiaya had washed the sweat and grime from her body, scrubbing away the remnants of the day while soaking in a tub far too large for one person alone.

It had been pure bliss.

Her quarters, like those of her friends, were grand and accented with gold. Unlike the rooms she'd lived in during her time training here, this was a space worthy of a royal. Velvet red curtains draped over wide glass doors, which were open now to a generous balcony. The walls were white with gold leaf detailing in the crown moulding that was so intricate, even Arii's Fae sight had trouble taking it in. Her bed was a four poster, sheer white curtains veiling the plush, perfectly made bed beneath, piled high with beautifully detailed pillows.

There was a reading corner with two comfortable couches, a clawed foot table with a glass top and an empty teacup on the surface. She'd requested a herbal tea earlier, but it hadn't quite hit the spot. Arii found herself pining for a cup of rich coffee and missing her father even more so. Once things settled here, she promised herself she'd go and visit him, as often as she could.

A large bathroom adjoined the room, curls of steam still filtering from the open door. Arii sighed as she stood on the balcony, sweeping her gaze over the city below.

Her mind skipped back to the last few hours. After briefly discussing the coronation to be held tomorrow, Elijah had shucked his royal cloak and headed for the city, pulling up his sleeves to help the people with the cleanup. It was strange, seeing him soil his white tunic and deep blue pants while knee deep in debris, hauling away the remains of damaged homes.

The fact that Elijah was willing to get his hands dirty wasn't a surprise to her – she would have been surprised if he hadn't – it was the way the people accepted his presence so quickly.

Then he'd retired to get cleaned up, placing a chaste kiss on her brow before a hasty exit.

"I'll come and find you tonight."

She guessed that he was tired, but the bond between them, normally so attuned to his emotions, seemed closed off a little, as if he were holding something back.

Either that, or he was still grieving his lost friend and sister.

They were all definitely still grieving their losses and would be for a long time.

When Arii closed her eyes, the final moments of their confrontation with Valdis were still as clear as day. She could still taste the tainted magic, see the leering red eye within the jagged crystal and hear Elijah's heartbroken scream as Lorch's lifeless form slumped to the floor. Arii felt a dark weight in her heart, a clinging, fetid feeling of regret that she hadn't done more to prevent the needless deaths in the room. That she hadn't tried *harder* to save Lorch, and Ghila too. That regret would forever remain and strengthen her to prevent losing anyone else in her future. Fate wasn't truly set in stone… but no matter how hard one tried, fate was not always malleable, either.

She had learned this the hard way, resulting in the loss of two lives.

Arii's fingers caressed the smooth marble of the balcony railing, thinking back on the few intimate moments she'd had with her fated mate since Valdis' fall, which had primarily been at night, once they'd retired to Elijah's chambers. Those chambers were decadent, far more than anything she'd seen before. High ceilings trimmed with gold and walls pressed with subtly patterned red wallpaper that shimmered in the sunlight.

Arii hadn't been able to hide an awed gasp as she spun around the room while Elijah leaned against the doorframe. Royal blue drapes framed the windows, letting warm light span across the huge bed.

Everything was trimmed with gold, deep blue and crimson, a palette of royal decadence.

This had been his father's chambers.

Chambers made for a King.

There had been changes to the suite since his father's time, Elijah had told her as she'd fallen back onto the bed, grinning at the elaborate chandelier on the ceiling. This room had been Lorch's last, which had confused Arii at first, for she swore that these were not the chambers she'd accompanied Lorch to when they'd been together.

When the thoughts shivered down their bond, she'd winced, hoping not to let on to Elijah, but she was a fool to think such a spike in her emotions wouldn't travel to him. He'd gently explained that Lorch was known to take courtiers to his other room, the one adjacent. The one that once held his mother's ladies in waiting.

Lorch preferred this room to be his place of solace, one for him and him alone. A headache bloomed when Arii tried to envision the castle floorplan, and how many rooms there could possibly be on this one side of the palace. This had sobered her, but when she'd turned her head to look at Elijah, his expression wasn't sad. It was gentle, his eyes hinting at unshed tears.

Lorch's things had been removed, as had the Kruel family crests woven into practically every soft item of furniture – previously a palette of red and gold – but not before Elijah had taken in the intimate space where his best friend had once resided. Elijah told her that Lorch's possessions that were right where he'd left them; his deep blue coat with gold filigree, that he'd used for court meetings, draped haphazardly over his reading chair. A crudely whittled horse accompanied a quill and pot of ink, a notebook left open on two blank pages, as if Lorch had been moments away from scribbling a note. Unlike almost every other room in the castle, this one had been mostly untouched by the carnage of war, frozen in a moment of time.

Those belongings would go to Lorch's mother, all except for the little whittled horse – a gift Elijah had made with his own hands for his first friend, when they'd first met. The thing was flawed, not a perfect carving, and perhaps that was why Elijah loved it, a reminder of their friendship.

It would take time for the quarters to feel like his own, and Arii promised to help him by simply spending time here with him, creating new memories.

They talked, between fervent kisses that infused their fatigued bodies with new adrenaline, making love when words became secondary to their lust. Lying together, Elijah divulged everything he'd seen and felt in the lead up to his confrontation with Valdis, and his state of mind heading into the battle. He told her of his anxiety, of how the promise of madness influenced his decision to attempt a life bond, to end Valdis' life when he ended his own. He told her of Valdis' motives, of the love he had almost destroyed the land to bring back.

So much destruction, all in pursuit of lost love.

Love made people do terrible, unspeakable things.

Valdis had brought about so much destruction, just to heal his own broken heart, and to stoke the fire of his hate.

That knowledge, along with that her mate was seconds away from sacrificing himself, made her blood boil anew.

Arii had been so angry, unable to speak for a time. They'd lain in silence, the gentle caress of his fingers over the exposed skin of her arm and their steady, mingled breathing the only sound. Elijah's silence was not out of shame or regret, but out of patience, allowing her time to process what had almost transpired.

She'd almost lost him.

He'd been willing to die to save them all.

And Ghila had taken that decision from him.

Elijah's little sister had sacrificed herself – used her mind-wielding power – to take over the bond, and when she died, she'd taken Valdis with her. Regret was a harsh emotion, one which Arii was feeling far too often.

The bitter taste remained now, as a gentle knock at her door caused her to turn, reveries whisked away on the warm breeze. She did not need to speak, nor answer the courtesy, she knew exactly who entered. Elijah joined her on the balcony, the late afternoon breeze teasing his hair.

"How did your meeting with Freya go?" she asked him, running her gaze over his face, as if searching for answers there.

Elijah stared out over the darkening city, over rooftops dotted with canvas, halfway through their repairs. The faint sound of music drifted to them upon the wind from the city, and the corner of his mouth tipped up. The people seemed to be celebrating, a hopeful sign and a welcome one after the screams and devastation that had filled the air almost a week ago.

"The Court leaders are convinced that the threat posed by Valdis' followers has been contained for the time being, but they have made every effort to prepare for anything to occur before and during the coronation tomorrow." He turned to her and she watched the way the depths of his silver pupils expanded when he looked at her. "We all agree, though, that to let our guard down would be unwise."

Arii nodded wholeheartedly in agreeance. It felt as if the immediate threat was past, but she was sure it was far from over. Realm travel was a thing now, who knew what would happen in the future?

Elijah moved a hand to the pocket of his pants as he added, "Another thing I suggested was the possibility of dual monarchs… something that hasn't been in effect since my parents. They too agreed that two rulers, a united front, would be the best thing for the court right now."

Was he suggesting?...

Elijah shifted, and her heart gave a violent leap as he lowered to one knee before her.

Wait…

Her sluggish mind homed in on the moment, making the simple motion of his hand leaving his pocket run twice as slow before her eyes.

"Arii," he began, and she swallowed past a lump forming in her throat. "From the first moment we met, I knew there was something about you that sang to me, even before you spoke your first word in my direction. You test me, you challenge me, and perhaps sometimes frustrate me to the end of my tether, but gods, I wouldn't know myself without you, I wouldn't *be* who I am now without you."

Arii swallowed again; shuddery legs glued to surprisingly steady feet as he pulled back the lid of the box. A silver band was twined like a braid, encrusted with diamonds that sparkled in the afternoon light. Residing in the middle sat a sizable oval diamond, its clarity so sharp that she could see her own wide-eyed reflection within. The entire stunning piece was nestled in a little purple velvet pillow.

It was the most exquisite thing she'd ever seen.

"You are already my fated mate, my soul's other half, and the bringer of fire to my veins. You're already the anchor keeping me in harbour, while also being the storm that pushes me beyond the bay. It feels like we have met in a hundred lifetimes, our souls continuing to find each other across the ether of space and time, and now we are here, and I know that all I want is to remain by your side, until we are nothing but dust – our souls ready to meet in the next life. Ariiaya Trillia, will you be my wife?"

A sound escaped Arii. Her stoic warrior, with his heavy, serious silver eyes and drawn brows, was on his knees before her, lips tipped down in a look that he'd worn during the countless times they'd trained and argued. It was an assessing look, one that made a shiver course down her spine.

She'd always thought he'd worn that expression to keep his inner frustrations in check – a mask over his inner emotions.

Now she realised… this was the look he wore when he was about to speak directly from his heart. Pure, unfiltered truth.

At her silence, her uncharacteristic, dumfounded look caused Elijah's face to change, the entirety of his rugged, beautiful face transforming with the simple pull of his lips as he finally asked, "Will you be my Queen?"

She fell to her knees, hands reaching for his face as she touched him with shaking fingers. The pure, potent glow of his emotions poured down the bond, washing her with weeks of withheld sensation that she knew he'd been masking as to not overwhelm her, or hint of what he'd been planning. Her heart opened like a flower, petals spreading to absorb every speck of his warmth, every speck of his love into her, her shock reverberating back to him.

He knew the answer before she spoke, a bubble of a laugh making its way through his lips as she drew him close, breathing him in, pressing her forehead to his.

She whispered, her voice breathless with emotion, "A thousand lifetimes, *yes*."

Then, she kissed him.

EPILOGUE

ARIIAYA

Arii had expected the weight of the crown upon her brow to be more of a burden, but as time went by, she found a strange comfort in the feel of it on her head. A week had passed since their war, a whole week in which she should have been letting herself recover from the chaos.

But instead, she stood on a grassy hill, accompanied by her court, a mere hour after the history-making coronation ceremony. Nem, Krepth, Tikkani, Quinn, Emerson and Luc stood a few feet away, and a few beats to the other side were Celadine and Mia, accompanied by Ouroboros, watching as Arii's fingers intertwined with her husband's.

Her husband.

Their King.

The crown shifted on her brow, and she placed a finger against it. It was an elegant piece, one which was once worn by Elijah's mother, passed down for generations, polished beautifully, looking almost newly made. The piece had been protected deep in the castle vaults by those who still mourned the last Queen's passing, keeping it safe from greedy, unworthy hands. Two dragons met in the middle of the crest, their wings forming a resemblance to proud mountain peaks. Between them nestled two diamonds, pure white in clarity, capturing the sun's shine.

The crown was a weight Arii hadn't thought she'd grow accustomed to, but when she'd seen the look in Elijah's eyes as it was placed upon her head – *hers* – his Queen, she felt she'd get used to it, if he were to look at her like *that* every time she wore it.

Queen Ariiaya Herington.

Gods, the title was going to take some getting used to, just like the jewellery on her temple.

They stood beside graves which resided on a small rise on the southern outskirts of The Sapphire Depths, a tranquil little space with a stunning view of the golden castle, backgrounded by the monolith peaks of the Dragon Teeth Mountains in the hazy distance. Specks of colour dipped and dove in the skies above, the wingbeats of dragons reaching her ears even here. Some were perched on the battlements of the golden castle, flat areas that appeared to have been created just for resting dragons, a feature she'd never noticed before. The presence of the beasts had quickly become a natural sensation, their absence almost totally forgotten, their presence providing the citizens with a sense of protection.

Before seeing it for herself, she had wondered why Elijah had chosen this particular spot to lay his family to rest, and not the castle vaults where royal families of the past lay. But as they stood together on the green hill, arms brushing, surrounded by their friends, it did not take long for her to realise that this was the perfect place for them.

Arii's eyes danced over the five golden plaques, each laid upon marble slabs.

The first was for King and Queen Herington, mother and father to the realm. The next was for Prince Brohem, son of light and laughter. The third, she lingered on a little longer, studying the delicate sweep of the name. Princess Ghila, daughter of strength and resilience.

Arii paused, tilting her head towards the solid presence beside her. The threads of their bond twined invisibly between them, and she felt his sadness.

King Eliverus Herington, her fated mate… her *husband*, stood like a statue beside her. Their wedding had been a swift affair, one held in a quickly erected, purple wisteria-draped gazebo overlooking the lake. Willows swayed, thawed and returned to green glory, framing the backdrop of their intimate ceremony. It had been… simple.

Perfect. A moment in time where Ariiaya felt truly peaceful, while also feeling like her heart may just be too full for her chest. They had been surrounded by their closest friends then too, the wedding officiated by a wisp of a man who had conducted the ceremonies of many royals before them.

Shortly after that had been the coronation ceremony, where not only was Elijah crowned as the new King of Fythnar, but his wife made Queen. Half the realm seemed to be in attendance, a melding of different faces, skins, ear shapes and clothing, voices intertwining in a rumble of cheers, draconic roars and celebratory shouts. The air was filled with magic and wingbeats, dragons, Shifters, Fae, elves, humans, all coming together as one, for the first time in over twenty years.

Now, Elijah remained in his royal finery, although opting to leave the red royal cloak behind, remaining in a cream-coloured tunic embroidered with fine gold details and red velvet pants, tied at the waist with a bronze sash. His presence at her side kept her grounded, kept her from shattering as her gaze skipped from his soft grey eyes, and down to the space before them. She lingered on the last stone, a knot forming in her chest.

Lorch Kruel; protector of the realm, saviour of Fythnar.

Despite the sadness that welled at seeing his name, the words chiselled into the stone brought pride to her heart.

"The realm goes on, knowing that they used their last moments to save us," said Tikkani, her gentle voice sweet and solemn. Quinn squeezed her hand, and the two shared a look, all playfulness gone, replaced with embers of love and support. They both looked older – all of the recruits did. Weathered by events, matured by war, scarred, but stronger than ever before.

"We wouldn't be standing here if not for them," whispered Celadine, her wild curls wavering around her face. Her eyes held unshed tears, perhaps held back because of the little girl by her side.

Arii's fingers bunched in her crimson skirts, an emotion she wasn't familiar with tugging at her heart. The Fae woman had just begun to love the copper-haired king, as had he begun to love her. But he was gone, and their love now would never have a chance to fully bloom. The thought brought ice to her fingertips, a numbness that bled from her own broken heart.

Elijah's fingers squeezed hers.

She squeezed back.

"If Lorch could be drawn from the toxicity and hate that consumed his father then those who still follow in Valdis' steps may just be worth saving, too," said Emerson.

"Their sacrifices will never be forgotten," said Elijah, voice deep with suppressed pain.

Because of Lorch and Ghila, the land was on its way to healing, and despite the time it would take to find and purge the hate, their home was now better because of their sacrifice.

Nem's voice drifted over them, and when Arii looked at her, she could see a soft glow beneath her skin as her best friend's eyes met hers. "Whatever comes next, we will be ready, and we will face it," Krepth's hand laced hers and they shared a look, before she whispered, "Together."

Together.

This wasn't the end. Arii could feel it in the very marrow of her bones. She soaked in the peacefulness of the moment, sure that it wouldn't last.

She turned to look back at the golden castle, to where it all began for her, allowing a long breath to slip, releasing pressure from her rapidly beating, emotionally charged heart. A heart which she'd once held locked away, one she'd never again hold back.

Silently Ariiaya Trillia vowed never to be the person she once had been, a merciless assassin with a heart of stone, a shadow of a person whose only purpose had been to deal in death and take orders from silent gods. No, she promised to grow into this new shell, this new purpose, a Queen who would be a guardian to her people, protect them with the brutality she'd learned from the Fates, because this world and its people were worth the fight.

She owed much to each person who flanked her. She looked at each of her friends in turn, her chest tight, her heart full. The feeling of golden threads twined around her, holding her in a warm, sure embrace, and she knew those who were no longer here in body accompanied them in spirit.

She could easily remain like this, feet planted upon land bathed in golden light, hair drifting in a summer breeze, her fingers enveloped within a strong, warm hand, the solid presence of her mate and friends by her side.

Forever could she remain here, in this perfect reality… a perfect twist of fate. This was hers, one weaved by her own hands, the beginning of a new string of fate. No longer was she alone.

"Find your home, Ariiaya."

Never had she felt so sure of anything in her life.

Finally.

Finally, she was home.

$\mathcal{A}$CKNOWLEDGEMENTS

Writing a series, let alone finishing one, is truly daunting. But thinking up the words to thank all whom supported me from its inception through to its conclusion? I think that's perhaps harder than writing the trilogy itself! Most of you know how hard this last book was to write – with my son hitting the terrible twos, work picking up, and months of writer's block casting its shadow, each step forward felt like an uphill battle… but I got there! We made it! And I couldn't have gotten here on my own.

I'll start by thanking my husband, Greg. You're my rock, and my quietest yet most avid supporter, and though you may not say it outright – I know you're my number one fan. I couldn't have made this journey without you, from the times you gave me reprieve from being a mum, allowing me days to write in peace, to helping with my timelines to make sure everything was done on time. I love you and appreciate you beyond words.

To my son, Elijah. Watching you grow into a cheeky, happy, and headstrong little boy has been the highlight of the last three years. Though you've made writing time challenging, I am so proud of the strong, beautiful little boy you're growing up to be. One day, if you want to, you can read mummy's books, and when you do, I hope they make you proud.

To my parents, Lynne, Allan and Carolyn. I'll always be grateful to you all for your love and support, and for nurturing my love of reading. It's because of you that I love books, and because of you I have the creativity to write stories. I wouldn't have had the confidence to tell this story without you. I love you all so much.

To my friends, family and colleagues at work. Your enthusiasm, whether in cheering me on or eagerly obtaining copies of my books upon each release, has meant the world to me. Thank you for being there through every twist and turn, for lending a sympathetic ear to my frustrations, for rejoicing in my triumphs, and for continuously urging me to persevere. I appreciate you all so much!

To Alisha, thank you for pushing me to write the scenes that scared me most. You've always been so supportive, and I appreciate every idea you've thrown my way. Your love of these characters is obvious, and your enthusiasm towards anything and everything bookish just makes me adore you endlessly. We were cut from the same cloth, honestly. I'm so thankful to have such an incredible sister-in-law.

To Kate, thank you for being the first to read book three, and the one to give me some really fantastic brainstorming moments. Many of the ideas you've given me made it into the books, and I hope you enjoyed your little easter egg in the form of 'Mrs Mulvany'! I cannot put into words how much I appreciate you, and all you've done for this series. It's been made all the better because of you. Thank you for being so supportive!

To my amazing editor, Carolyn, I can't truly express my gratitude for all that you've done for me throughout this journey. From the first page of the series to the very last, you've been there, infusing each word with your expertise and passion. Your willingness to offer constructive feedback, delivered with kindness and honesty, has been invaluable to me. I've grown so much as a writer thanks to your guidance and mentorship. Thank you so much.

To Kalynne (Kalynne_art on Instagram), I am continually awestruck by the sheer talent and dedication you pour into every piece of artwork. Your ability to capture the essence of each character, to convey their emotions and personalities in your art, is nothing short of extraordinary. I still feel my heart squeeze when I look at each and every piece you've created for me. Your artwork has added an extra layer of magic to this series, enriching the reading experience for my audience in ways I could never have imagined. Their response to your art has been overwhelmingly positive, and I am so grateful for all you've done for the series. You know I'll be back for more very soon!

To James and the team at Dymocks Knox, who have lovingly accommodated all of my books and supported me for over two years now, I can't thank you enough for your endless excitement and enthusiasm for my story. By having my books on your shelves, you've given my series a platform to reach new audiences, to touch the hearts of readers who may never have stumbled upon them otherwise. I've also had so much fun and learned so much at some of my first signing events with you. I am endlessly grateful and look forward to many more years and books to come.

To Caitlyn at A Thousand Lives Book Haven and Naomi at Novel Nook, I cannot thank you enough for your support for my adventure, and for giving my series a place on the shelf in your beautiful little stores. You've created havens for book lovers, spaces where imagination can flourish and connections can be forged. Thank you for taking a chance on my series, and for your passion and dedication to local small businesses!

To my BETA readers, Nikki, Kei, Amber, Rachel, James, Jazlyn, Sandra and Jessica. I am so grateful to you all for taking the time to read the unpolished story and for braving the barbs of my messy draft. Every single one of you provided valuable feedback, and also some very hilarious notes that made me laugh out loud. I must say that the feedback given about the ending had me close to tears, because I could see how much you cared for this story and characters. Knowing you love them as much as I do truly warms my heart. I am so appreciative of you all. I hope you enjoy the polished story!

To my ARC readers and all who have given my series a go. I am truly awed by the amount of love, excitement and support that has been shown for this series and its characters. Every single post, mention, video and personal message means the absolute world to me, and fuels me to keep going. I've also met so many authors, traditional and indie who have been so supportive, offering words of wisdom, advice and genuinely wishing to see me succeed. The support for indie authors, especially Aussie ones, is absolutely incredible. I've met so many likeminded readers, people who love books endlessly, people with massive TBRs and stars in their eyes, hungering for the next story to get lost in. I've found my people in this community, and I'm SO thankful.

I truly hope you enjoy the fiery conclusion. Though Arii, Elijah and Lorch's story has concluded, they will never be too far from my mind, and who knows… maybe one day we will be back in Fythnar once again.

I promise I'll be back with more stories in the near future, but for now, thank you for sticking with me, for bringing my stories into your home and into your hearts.

I'm off to weave more fates, devour more stories… and create more chaos!

Return to Fythnar...
One Year Later!

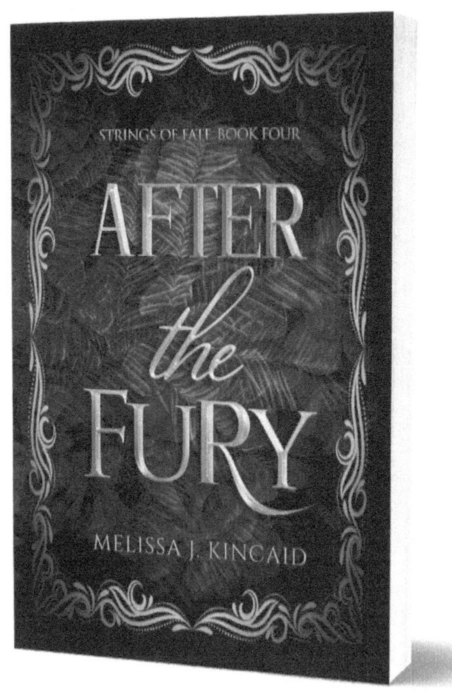

A Light
in the Darkness

This spin-off follows Nemesis and Krepth through a world slowly rebuilding in the wake of the war that shook Fythnar to its core.

The shadows hold secrets, destinies entwine, and the pulse-pounding adventure continues, so expect the unexpected as we dive back into the world of Fythnar, one year on from the events of Melissa J Kincaid's bestselling *Strings of Fate* trilogy.

Melissa J. L. Kincaid is a fantasy author from Melbourne, Australia, who has a passion for creating worlds filled with magic, adventure, and heart. Known for her rich world-building and strong female leads, her stories often weave together forbidden love, powerful magic, and epic battles, a blend that draws in fans of both fantasy and romance.

Melissa took the plunge into self-publishing in 2021 with her debut novel, *Love, Blood & Fury*. She went on to release *Magic, Midnight & Starlight*, before bringing the trilogy to a breathtaking close in 2024 with *Fire, Fury & Chaos*. Not yet ready to leave the world behind, she returned in 2025 with *After the Fury*, a spin-off that invites readers back into the realm they had come to love.

With a background in graphic design, Melissa brings her creativity full circle by designing her own covers and book interiors, ensuring every detail matches the vision of her stories.

When she isn't writing, illustrating or curled up with a fantasy book, Melissa enjoys exploring the outdoors with her husband, Greg, and their son, Elijah Gregory, often camping under the stars.

www.**lotsoflovecreations**.com.au

 /melissa.j.kincaid

 #melissa.j.kincaid.author

 @melissa.j.kincaid.author

THE
Strings of Fate
SERIES

STRINGS OF FATE BOOK ONE
LOVE, BLOOD & FURY
MELISSA J. KINCAID

STRINGS OF FATE BOOK TWO
MAGIC, MIDNIGHT & STARLIGHT
MELISSA J. KINCAID

STRINGS OF FATE BOOK THREE
FIRE, FURY & CHAOS
MELISSA J. KINCAID

Spin-off
STRINGS OF FATE BOOK FOUR
AFTER the FURY
MELISSA J. KINCAID

Melissa Kincaid

ROMANTIC FANTASY AUTHOR
WWW.LOTSOFLOVECREATIONS.COM.AU
Available in Paperback, Hardback and eBook.

Did you enjoy the story?

PLEASE LEAVE
a Review!

KALYNN

goodreads

fable

THE STORYGRAP

Reviews help independent authors like me reach more
readers. Every review means a lot!

Scan the code to go to Goodreads.